Enduring Love
A Historical Novel of Key West 1846

SUSAN BLACKMON

With the exception of historical figures, all characters in this novel are fictitious. Any resemblance to living persons, present or past, is coincidental.

This book contains an excerpt from the forthcoming book *Once Upon an Island Christmas* by Susan Blackmon. The excerpt has been set for this edition only and may not reflect the final content of the forthcoming edition.

Dream Publishing

Dream Publishing
Lawrenceville, GA

ISBN-13: 978-1-7358287-0-1

www.susanblackmonauthor.com

Cover illustration: Susan Blackmon

Edited by Linda Alston

Proofread by Samantha Mullaney

Printed in the United States of America

DEDICATION

I owe thanks to many who gave me their first-hand accounts of hurricane experiences. Most especially to Kathy Smith who unintentionally endured Hurricane Michael. I won't ever forget watching it on TV while giving her text updates after the local news station lost its signal. She was very helpful in writing the post storm experiences. I want to thank Yevette Veliz for reviewing the book for accuracy based on her experiences surviving George, Wilma, and Irma in Key West. Thank you Linda Alston and Samantha Mullaney for edits and proofreading. I also need to thank Key West Historian, Tom Hambright, for taking time to share his knowledge and insights one sunny afternoon in the Key West Library.

Thank you to my family for all your love and support. Without you, these books would not be possible. I am blessed.

Love in Key West series

Salvaged Love

Love in Key West – a novella

Love Again

Enduring Love

Once Upon an Island Christmas – a novella
Fall 2020

Divided Love
2021

Chapter 1

Moisture gathers above the dry grass catching a Sahara wind.

Key West, Florida, September 2nd, 1846

The prodigal son returns. At least that was how he felt. Apprehension made Henry James Whitmore nervously check his cravat and smooth the lapel of his new suit with his free hand. In his other, he carried a carpet bag with all his worldly possessions; a shave kit, trousers, two shirts, small clothes, a bundle of oft read letters from home, a well-used Bible, a ragged sketch pad nearly full of drawings, a small bundle of charcoal pencils wrapped in a piece of burlap, and his prized Paterson Colt revolver. The island breeze ruffled the fullness of his dark blond hair and long sideburns, cut in the latest style according to the New Orleans barber he visited before leaving the mainland. His tanned, normally clean shaven, face was scruffy with three days growth. Most of the sail from the mainland to Key West was accompanied by stormy weather. Henry may not have been seasick like many of the other passengers, but even so, his sea legs were not worthy of taking a blade to his face. The first thing he planned to do when he got home was shave.

Home?

He wondered if his parents' house would still feel like home. Five years had passed since he left the island. Five years had wrought a lot of changes in his body and soul, but in this moment, he felt younger than his twenty years. He remembered the day he fled the island leaving only a letter behind to say goodbye to his family. He recalled the foolishly confident feeling he had of being ready to take on the world. Standing here now on the busy wharf of Key West bight surrounded by the pungent smell of fish and the dry goods being loaded and unloaded from the merchant ships, he felt anxiety not unlike that of a disobedient child about to be disciplined. Their letters assured him of their acceptance. Still, he felt he had failed his parents and would have to atone for his sins before he could feel at home again.

Until two months ago, he thought he was satisfied with his life and content to be a soldier on the Texas frontier. But then he received a strong premonition God wanted him to return to his family. He didn't understand why, but the feeling persisted and nagged. He finally requested his resignation from the Texas Rangers and headed towards the coast to find a ship sailing east. His solitary, dangerous trek across lower Texas to reach New Orleans with a constant threat of an Indian attack was easy compared to the courage he needed now to step onto the Key West dock.

Multitudes of seabirds flew about the wharf looking for an easy meal. Their familiar sounds and antics momentarily brought a half smile to his grim countenance. He stood at the end of the wharf looking at the town of Key West unsure why he was there or how long he would stay. He took in all the ways it had grown since he left. More buildings clustered between the soaring palm trees and blocking the view to the verdant green depths of the island. More people moved about the busy streets. More ships filled the harbor, their tall wooden masts too numerous to count. Stevedores and sailors passed up and down the aged and worn wooden planks not paying him any attention. There was a time when he knew the names of every man who worked the docks. Today, he recognized none of them. At least the huge warehouses towering over the bight still bore the painted names of Tift, O'Hara, Browne, and Green, giving him a small measure of familiar comfort.

As he neared the end of the dock, a putrid odor drew his attention upward to the sponges drying in the sun on the roof of a small work shack. It brought to mind long summer afternoons spent cleaning the sponges before climbing up on a scorching hot roof to lay them out to dry. He would come home smelling every bit as awful as the air around him did now. He smiled as he recalled his mother never complained, other than reminding him to wash up before supper.

He shifted the carpetbag to his other hand and walked towards shore, noting again the new buildings added over the past few years. Where once there were wide spaces between structures there was now in some cases only alley ways. It made him feel even more like an intruding stranger.

With a deep breath, Henry stepped off the dock onto the crushed white limestone that was the island's foundation. He made his way between Asa Tift's salvage warehouse on his left and, judging by the rich earthy smell, a cigar factory on his right. From inside, he could hear the low murmur of a man reading to the workers as they went about their repetitive task of rolling dried leaves. Henry passed from the shade between the buildings onto Front Street. As he left the bight, the citizens' attire changed from that of the sailors and stevedores in their loose shirts and pantaloons to the shop keepers in aprons and businessman in their suits and top hats.

Across from him were familiar weathered gray buildings mixed with many new ones of fresh cut, butter-hued lumber. All around him were signs of the town's prosperity. It was evident in the number of new buildings and thriving businesses with their neatly kept store fronts. It was evident in the people as well judging by the suited businessmen and well-dressed ladies in wide skirts under cover of their parasols going about their day.

Coming from the open frontier, it made him feel hemmed in. Something he hadn't felt since the last time he returned to New York when he was a child. Then he hated the close feeling of the city streets after leaving the carefree summer days of roaming the undeveloped hammocks of this island. For a moment, he wished again to be on the wide open range of Texas. But a few steps further, and he was once again caressed by a zephyr. It filled him with recollections of his youthful summers. A glimpse of the open tidal pond behind Front Street and the uncleared woods beyond the town also brought him comfort. At least some things hadn't changed.

One might consider his roots to be in New York. It was where he was born, where his father and grandfather grew up, and where the family's ancestral estates and trust were still located. But for Henry, home was Key West. He was four when his father first brought him to the island and seven when they permanently moved there. The salty air and ocean breezes were not to be compared with icy winter winds or shiftless summer air that held all the rank odors of city life. Young Henry reveled in the warm tropic sun and frolicked in the turquoise waters surrounding the island. It was paradise, and thinking back on those sunny days of his youth, it was hard to remember why he felt so desperate to leave.

He turned to his right and worked his way down Front Street away from the wharfs and warehouses heading towards the residential side of the small waterfront town. Few paid him any attention, and as of yet, no one recognized him. His progress was arrested when he saw the willowy profile of Mrs. Eatonton exiting the mercantile across the street with her daughter behind her. At least for a moment, he thought it was Emily, but then he realized it couldn't be. Emily was sixteen now and this girl was several years younger. It must be her cousin, Laura, visiting from Montgomery. *My how they favored each other.* Catching up to the cousin on the steps was another girl nearly the same age. He knew without doubt the blue eyes and raven hair belonged to his half-sister, Brianna. The two girls had their heads together whispering and giggling as girls often do.

Next to appear was his mother, Betsy. Truthfully, she was his step-mother, but he could only recall vague images of his true mother having lost her at the tender age of four. Betsy's raven hair now had strands of gray – a sad reminder of the passage of time – but her blue eyes were as round and as bright as ever.

All of the homesickness he had not allowed himself to feel since he left the island suddenly engulfed him. He could only stand there staring at the ladies who were as yet oblivious to him.

In the next moment, his mother's eyes met his. She searched his face. He could tell she had not yet placed him. He missed the moment of her recognition for his eyes were drawn above her to the enchanting young lady appearing last in the doorway. His heart lurched.

Emily.

It had to be her; his childhood friend now all grown up and unexpectedly beautiful.

Heartstoppingly beautiful.

Sunlight glinted off her red-gold hair loosely gathered in a braided coil at her nape. A few tendrils, moved by the ever present sea breeze, caressed her cheek. One was long enough to touch her shoulder drawing his gaze downward to the pull of gingham across her ample bosom. Those were a surprise. She was still flat-chested the last time he saw her. His gaze traveled further past her narrow waist to her gently flaring hips. Guiltily, his gaze shot upwards in search of her light gray eyes that always reminded him

3

of a summer squall over the Keys.

She must have felt his regard, for she looked his way. Her recognition was immediate. He could flatter himself that she would have known him anywhere, even after the changes of five years, but in all fairness she had the advantage of a miniature drawing done by a fellow soldier he sent to her on a whim.

Emily felt the heavy regard of the hatless, young man. She turned to give him a withering glance to convey her displeasure and reproach, but the moment her eyes met his, annoyance turned to startled surprise.

Henry!

A wide grin spread across her face. She could not have withheld it if she tried. The moment she had dreamed of for five long years was finally upon her. Unlike the other boys, his look of appreciation sent a thrill through her, and for the first time, she was proud instead of ashamed of her curves.

She cast her eyes down his figure. His overall physique was now that of a man, and it intimidated her. All traces of her childhood playmate were gone, except in his eyes. His piercing blue gaze skipped back to hers, and she noticed they still held a glimmer of youthful insecurity. His voice was deeper, and the pleasing sound of it as he greeted his family sent shivers down her spine. Slowly, she descended the steps, never taking her eyes from him for fear he was a figment of her imagination. She trailed behind the others as they rushed to greet him.

Henry finally forced his gaze from Emily. Both his mother and Brianna were leading the ladies coming towards him as fast as they could walk. He moved to intercept them in the street catching his mother about the waist. He twirled her as she held his neck in a tight hug. Tears of joy streamed down her face while Henry was still overcoming the shock that he now towered over her. When he left, he was nearly her height. Aware they were creating a scene, he put her down. She stepped back but kept both hands on his cheeks, obviously looking for signs of her boy in the man before her. He was first to break eye-contact. He looked to Emily but could do no more than glance in her direction before Brianna launched herself into his arms. He twirled her too before moving them all out of the middle of the road to give way to a milk cart pulled by a donkey.

Henry's gaze was drawn back to Emily. Up close, her beauty stunned him. The skinned-knee tomboy who bravely followed him on his escapades around the island was gone. She had grown into a lovely lady who probably had no interest in the returning proverbial, prodigal son. More than likely, she had a beau. The thought of her affection being given to another hurt. He was having trouble breathing normally and didn't hear his mother's question. He was aware she was speaking but failed to pull his attention away from Emily until she forcefully called his name.

"Henry!"

Reluctantly, he turned his gaze away from Emily's luminesce eyes, radiant complexion, and auburn hair catching fire from the sun. His mother's lips were pursed in displeasure. He hoped it was due to his inattention and not because she knew his thoughts, although he suspected it was the latter. If so, was it the object of his desire she objected to or the thoughts in general? Surely, she didn't object to the daughter of her best friend. Whatever was bothering his mother, she pushed it aside to smile broadly.

"Are you home for good?" He heard the excitement in her voice drop. "Or is this a visit?"

He hated the disappointment he would see in her eyes, but he could not be less than honest with her. "I am not sure." She accepted his words as if they were expected. Eager to redirect the conversation, he asked, "Where are Agatha, Emmaline, and the boys?" He was surprised his two little sisters and baby brother, James, were not with his mother, nor were Emily's four younger brothers with Mrs. Eatonton.

"The older boys are playing with their friends. Agatha is helping Mrs. Baxley watch the younger ones at Mrs. Eatonton's house. Are you anxious to see them or would you rather go home first and freshen up from your journey?"

"I suppose a wash cloth and a change of clothes would not be remiss."

Betsy grinned as she nodded in agreement.

Emily stepped forward to greet Henry. With unaccustomed shyness, she said, "Hello."

"Hello, Emily."

Unexpected, his deep voice resonated in her heart causing it to skip a beat. Suddenly she couldn't breathe. Her reply was stuck in her throat.

Henry was kept from saying anything more as his mother took his arm and turned him away, anxious to get him home. He cast a glance over his shoulder and noticed Emily was disappointed as well. Surely there would be a chance later to speak with her. His gaze drifted past her to the other end of the street with its grog shops, ships chandlers, and a shingle in the distance hanging over his father's printing shop. Part of him wanted to turn and head there now, but he knew he would feel better facing him after he had a chance to freshen up from his journey.

As a group, they headed down Front Street gaining attention as they passed the open doorways of the shops. All who knew Henry greeted him warmly and welcomed him home. Some joined in their walk turning it into somewhat of a parade. Henry's heart was warmed by all the fond greetings of remembered names and faces. Fortunately, he was often able to put one with the other only stumbling over a few names.

They came to the bend in the road with Mrs. Mallory's Cocoanut Grove boarding house on the right at the foot of Duval Street. If it could be called a street. A hundred feet further inland Duval Street intersected with the tidal pond spanning out behind the town. He smiled to see the well-remembered rock piles and plank boards still in use for crossing to the other side. They were a strong fixture in his childhood memories from the first time he nervously inched his way across the expanse to later racing other boys to see who could do it the fastest. The view beyond the pond was so altered, his mind was jolted back to the present. When he left, Judge Marvin's house was the sole structure on the other side of the footbridge and there were only a few houses in total beyond the pond. Now, there were many, several rows deep, reminding him once again of his absence.

Next to the boarding house was City Hall, a two story building in which the first floor was used as a meat and fish market. Continuing on, they soon passed Fitzpatrick Street on the left. A few more paces brought them to the corner of Whitehead Street where stood Mr. Patterson's dry goods store beneath the cooling shade of a large cocoanut tree. They turned left onto Whitehead, or Main Street as it was often referred, passing the triangle plot of Clinton Place on their right. In the past, it was the unofficial gathering place of the town. Henry wondered if it still was. On the opposite side of Clinton Place, hovering over Front Street, the Custom House still proudly stood and next to it was the custom collector's abode commanding a clear view of the comings and goings of the harbor. On the left, they passed Captain Geiger's modest home gracing the corner of Green Street with its famous tree dominating the front yard. Famous because John Audubon declared the arching branches with clusters of orange blossoms to be forever known as the Geiger Tree in honor of the captain's hospitality during his visit fourteen years earlier. Henry vividly remembered the famous woodsman who seemed larger than life to his young mind.

A few yards more brought them to the well-remembered front porch of his youth. He paused in front of the house he considered home. Being here was almost surreal. He had woken up from many a dream at the moment of opening the front door. Now, here he was, walking up the steps. He could easily believe this moment wasn't real, and he would wake up any minute to feel alone and bereft, if not for all the friends and family gathered behind him.

He turned to face the crowd. Over their heads, he noticed there were many more houses built between Whitehead Street and the beach fanning out to the left. A new house was even behind his mother's old seamstress shop across the street. It now blocked his once clear view to Mr. Fielding Browne's house and the coast. Henry's attention was pulled back to the expectant faces before him. Hating the attention but feeling the need to speak, he said, "Thank you for welcoming me home. It's good to be back." He hesitated a moment before turning his back on them, anxious to retreat from their questioning gazes.

He paused as he touched the wrought iron handle. As if she understood, his mother placed her hand against his back for support. Taking a deep breath, Henry opened the door. He stepped into the foyer and as his gaze took in all he could see, he was assaulted by memories. He could almost hear the echo of his sisters' laughter as they played hide-and-seek on a rainy afternoon; Brianna's triumphant smile as she won her first game of chess against him with their father's help; Agatha and Emmaline begging him to play tea party or swing them around in the backyard; his father's chair where he gathered the girls on his lap and would make up a story to entertain them. Henry turned to the stairs and remembered all the times his sisters raced down them to greet him in the morning. Just behind the staircase, he and Emily had a pretend wedding the day his father wed Betsy. He remembered panicking for a moment when her father caught them, but Captain Max simply picked Emily up and tickled her as he admonished that 'weddings of any kind could wait'. The sweet memories gave way to the more bitter moments of when he disappointed his mother. He would escape the hurt look on Betsy's face by turning his back on her and climbing the stairs to his room. And the worst memories of all were the times he watched his father walk out the door leaving them for months on end as he reported on the Indian wars, especially when they were left to handle the deaths of Aunt Agatha and his sister, Madalyn, without his support.

His reverie was broken as his mother slipped her arm around his waist.

"Welcome home, Henry. We left your room much as it was other than making room for James to share it. I don't believe he has bothered any of your things. Why don't you go on up and get settled in. I'll find you something to eat."

Henry glanced down into the beloved face of his step-mother and teased, "I don't suppose you have any cinnamon bread."

She gently admonished him. "If I had known you were coming, I would have had a whole loaf waiting for you, as it is you'll just have to wait until I can have some ready to bake tomorrow."

It shouldn't surprise him, but it did. "You would do that for me?"

"Of course."

He then realized none of the others had followed them into the house. He really wanted to see Emily again.

Betsy noticed his bewildered look. "I sent them on to the Eatonton's. We'll join them as soon as you're ready."

Henry bit back his temporary disappointment, "Of course. I'll be but a moment. Unless... do you think I could take the time to shave?" He ran a hand over his scruffy chin anxious to be rid of the growing beard.

She gave him an understanding smile. "I don't see why not."

He left her standing in the foyer to take the stairs two at a time. He entered the first room on the left and saw his neatly made bed and nightstand looking just as he left it, but the wash stand was gone. The chest of drawers was moved to a corner by the door to allow room for the small child's bed. He knew he had a little brother from his mother's letters, but this was the first time he was faced with the reality of it. The knowledge was only superficial while he was living out west. He was curious as to how he would feel when they actually met. Would he feel the same sibling bond he felt for his sisters?

He placed his satchel on his bed and removed his clean shirt. He was in the process of unbuttoning his cuffs when Betsy appeared in the doorway with a pitcher and bowl.

"Pardon me. I remembered you didn't have water so I brought you these." She turned and placed them on the chest of drawers with a washcloth and towel. "I have some water heating for your shave."

"It isn't necessary. For the sake of time, I will make do with the cold water. I have many times before."

"Very well. I will wait for you downstairs."

As soon as the door closed behind her, Henry pulled the suspenders from his shoulders and unbuttoned his travel stained shirt letting it slip off and fall to the floor. The breeze whispering past the curtains of the open window brushed across his bare back drying the heat drawn moisture gathered there. It was as refreshing as the cool water he now splashed across his face. The heat didn't bother him so much as the humidity, and he was grateful for the momentary respite from it. He washed his face, neck, and armpits and then stood a moment at the open window overlooking the pond behind the house. When he left there was only one handful of houses on the other side. Now there appeared to be two streets of houses, four rows deep. In his mind, the island had remained unchanged. It was disconcerting to see how much really had progressed since last he walked these streets. The town had changed in subtle and obvious ways just as he had.

With a sigh, he turned back to the room and retrieved his shave kit from the satchel. He made quick work of it with the advantage of a mirror. He had grown used to trail shaving without one. Once finished, he wiped his face and then ran his hand appreciatively over his smooth cheeks and chin, happy to finally be rid of the annoyance. He slipped into his clean shirt, brushed the dust from his trousers, and picked up his dirty shirt to wipe the dust from his boots, leaving it hanging on a peg to deal with later. He then combed his hair. He was now as presentable as he could be without a bath and pressed clothes. Last, he tossed the dirty water out the window to land in the flower bed below.

He walked down the stairs and found Betsy waiting for him on the front porch.

She smiled broadly. "Much better."

He smiled in return and offered her his arm. As they walked down the steps together, Henry asked, "Should we go by the shop to let Poppa know I am home?"

Betsy patted his arm. "Your father is in Tallahassee. He should be home in a day or two."

Henry was unexpectedly disappointed. He didn't realize how very much he yearned to see his father until now, when he was forced to wait longer to do so. And yet, it was the way it always seemed to be with his father. Once again, he was absent and Henry was waiting for his return.

They walked the short distance further down Main Street to Emily's house in silence. It was a distance he had walked almost daily in his youth. Now, in the quiet of just the two of them, Henry noticed the road improvements. The dirt was smooth and the edges were straight and well defined, keeping the vines and plants at bay. The houses on this stretch of road were still the same with only one or two additions, but behind them on either side were many added dwellings. Just past the corner of their porch, they crossed the wooden planks spanning a ditch where the water at full tide flowed from the pond behind the town out to a swampy lagoon on the southwest beach and retreated back again at low tide. This in between flow of water was not a pleasant place. It was full of cacti, scrubby bushes, vines, and teeming with a heavy concentration of mosquitoes. Thankfully, a few steps took them past it while waving away the black swarm of hungry insects. A more substantial bridge covered the pond's northern ingress at Simonton Street.

As they approached the Eatonton house, they found Mrs. Baxley rocking on the front porch. She called out over her shoulder and soon Henry's eight year old sister, Agatha, came running out. Her laughing azure eyes sparkled in greeting while her chestnut hair defied being contained in a braid. She squealed in delight and launched herself into his open arms. She was followed by six year old Emmaline looking elfin with her angelic hazel eyes and neatly braided red hair. She too ran to Henry, but he was sure Emmaline likely was mimicking her sister more than she actually remembered him. He lifted them to his chest and swung them around much to their delight before placing them back on the ground.

Over their heads, he could see Brianna and Emily descend the porch steps and behind them were Emily's four brothers. The girls stepped aside for the eldest to approach with hand outstretched. Henry warmly grasped the proffered hand of fifteen year old Christoff who once tagged along after him and his friends as they trolled the island. It suddenly occurred to Henry, Christoff was now the age he was when he left the island. Christoff seemed so young. No wonder Henry's mother had been desperate to keep him from leaving.

Henry greeted the other brothers in turn. He did some quick math to come up with Hawthorn, better known as 'Thorn', was now eleven and Nathanial, or Nate, was nine. Emily's youngest brother, Jacob, was only two when Henry left and would soon turn six. He was the same age as his sister, Emmaline. Jacob held back from the others, having no recollection of him. Henry was surprised Nate recognized him being so young when he left. Christoff and Thorn often trailed after Henry in the old days, and now they were quick to offer good natured teasing of his former efforts to dislodge them, acknowledging how burdensome they must have been to a teenage boy.

The parade of boys ushered Henry up the steps of the porch where Mrs. Eatonton waited in the doorway holding the hand of a golden-haired toddler with features similar to his own. When their eyes met, the little boy timidly moved behind her skirt. Henry felt an instant kinship to the youngster despite his expectations otherwise.

Betsy stepped forward to pick up her youngest child and straddle him on her right hip. When he buried his face in her neck, she grasped his right hand to gain his attention. "Jamie, this is your brother, Henry. Remember? We told you about him and how he lived far away. He has come home, and he wants to meet you. Be a good boy and shake his hand."

Henry watched in fascination as the toddler overcame his apprehension to dutifully hold his little hand out to him. Henry grasped the small hand with what he hoped was a friendly smile. "Hello, little brother."

James pulled his hand away and once again hid his face in Betsy's neck.

Betsy patted the little back indulgently as she smiled at Henry. "Give him time. He's shy at first with strangers."

Stranger. The word hurt, but it was the truth. He was a stranger in his own family. He had only himself to blame. He knew he had a little brother, but James was too young to be aware of him until now. The look on his mother's face told him she felt his pain and regretted her choice of words. He let the moment pass with a self-deprecating smile before turning his attention back to the face peeping out from Betsy's shoulder. As they moved into the house, he said to James, "Do you know we share the same name? My middle name is James, same as yours."

Jamie belligerently raised his head and in all seriousness said, "My name James Lawrence, not yours." He then stuck his thumb in his mouth and turned his face away.

Henry wasn't sure how to respond, so he remained silent. He was rescued from the awkwardness by Christoff. "Come Henry. Race you up to the Captain's Walk."

Christoff and Thorn raced past him. He was quick to follow with Nate on his heels. Jacob, Henry's sisters, and Emily followed too. Climbing out of the hatch onto the rooftop deck of the Eatonton's two-story house never ceased to give Henry a thrill. As far as he was concerned, the only better vantage point offered on the island was from the lighthouse. The hatch opened beneath a large cupola and an open walkway extended from opposite sides following the ridge of the roof. It was pleasant under the shade of the cupola with the unhindered ocean breeze. The mosquitoes were practically nil at this height. He turned to assist the younger children and the girls over the hatch threshold. Emily was last. Her engaging smile as she looked up into his face stopped his heart. The touch of their hands as he gave his assistance jolted it back into a rapid beat. Just as he was going to speak to her, Christoff called for his attention.

"Henry, have you seen the fort yet?" Christoff wildly motioned for Henry to join him. "They are building it offshore. Have you ever heard of such a thing?"

With Emily safely on the deck, Henry reluctantly broke their contact with a rueful smile. He turned to join Christoff, pleased when Emily followed. Side by side at the railing Henry and Emily dutifully looked to the southwest, away from town. Looking towards the water's edge, there were a few houses and numerous tree tops before opening up to a large two story building that wasn't there before. The pristine gleam of white paint told Henry it hadn't been there long. Over its roof, bustling activity could be seen in the harbor. Down the coast to the left was a lagoon. Next to it was an encampment, massive stacks of brick and lumber, and other building materials. Men scurried back and forth across a wharf stretching from the land to what would eventually be the fort. Henry guessed it to be about a thousand feet offshore, but there wasn't anything to be seen at this distance. If walls were being built, they were not yet above water level. The logistics of such an unusual build peaked Henry's curiosity. He had never known a structure other than bridges to be built in the water. He hoped to get a closer look in the coming days.

Henry nodded to the large white building. "What is that?"

Emily was quick to answer. "It is the Marine Hospital. It was finished last year. I suppose many things have changed since last you were here."

He gazed down into her soft gray eyes and quietly said, "Indeed, they have." A soft blush stained her cheeks following his words. Least her brothers notice his growing interest in Emily, he turned away from her to walk to the southward edge of the roof walk to view the rest of Main Street. He could make out the Courthouse and Jail at Jackson Square. More houses filled the space in between than before. Over the tree tops, the lighthouse stood tall and familiar, perched on its rise of sand at the southernmost point of the island facing the Straits of Florida and the Atlantic Ocean. The northern side of the island faced the Gulf of Mexico. Positioned as it was, Key West had a strategic advantage. Hence, the reason for building the fort.

He crossed the cupola to the opposite side of the walk to view the town. It was the same as before in that Front Street followed the western coast of the harbor and continued along the northern bight to the east coast. Simonton Street ran inland from its eastern end and Main Street on the western side. Duval and the pond bisected the middle, but now more lanes and cross streets ran in between. From his bedroom window, he had already noted the additional streets and houses running behind the pond. He guessed the island boasted twice as many streets as before and at least two hundred more buildings had been added while he was away.

His attention was drawn to a man walking up to the front of the house. Henry soon identified him as Emily's father, Captain Max Eatonton, returning home. When Emily's brothers noticed him, they went running downstairs to greet him. Henry helped Emily cross the hatch threshold to descend the stairs. He was last so he closed the hatch behind him.

Henry was enthusiastically greeted by Emily's father as he entered the drawing room. Captain Max's sun bleached blond hair had changed little, but the passing years had added more lines to his face. He stood straight and proud in his domain but perhaps a little softer around the middle. Henry supposed being a captain of a merchant ship was easier work than a being the captain of a wrecker.

Captain Max firmly shook Henry's hand and clapped him on the back. "Welcome home. I heard you've been soldiering out west. Did you like it?"

"Yes sir."

"Were you fighting the Indians or the Mexicans?"

"Both, sir."

Henry made small talk with their parents for a few moments before Christoff pulled him away. He and the three Eatonton boys made their way outside. At the bottom of the steps, Henry turned. He was surprised to see the empty doorway, having expected Emily to trail after them as she had always done. Recalling the drastic change in her appearance from tomboy to young lady, he was saddened to realize she was too grown up to tag along with the boys.

Chapter 2

*Puffy cumulus rising high, ominous thunderheads to become
Shifting winds, a westward spin
Over sun drenched waters below*

Emily stared at the closed front door wishing she dared to follow Henry as in days of old. She wanted him to notice she was all grown up, and he had, judging by the way he looked at her in town and for a moment in the cupola. But being grown up also meant she could no longer run freely about the island. She hated that she was forced to return to the parlor and sit quietly, pretending she had the patience to stitch flowers on a handkerchief, while quietly visiting with his mother and sisters. She would rather have fun traipsing after the boisterous boys. How odd that she hadn't missed such things while Henry was gone.

In recent years, many boys had expressed interest in her though few had made it past her over-protective younger brother. Christoff was her self-proclaimed guardian much to her chagrin. Those few suitors brave enough to face off against him usually wavered under her father's scrutiny. Only one or two had made it as far as daring to walk her home from school. They only did so once for in the end she found the poor lads, although brave, a poor substitute for her former companion. None of them could make her laugh the way Henry did or challenged her mentally. At any rate, their appeal was not enough to encourage their pursuit.

She thought back to the moment this afternoon when she stepped from the dry goods store into the bright sunshine to see Henry across the street, standing still, as if a figment of her imagination. She knew it would happen unexpectedly. One day he would return without warning. She imagined the moment hundreds of times, but always, they were alone and could speak freely of their feelings for one another. Of course, reality was far from her dreamed reunion. Today, at the moment of their meeting, four other females stood between them. His mother and sister had first rights to his attention. Social proprieties gave her none of the freedom to express her true emotions. She supposed it was just as well considering she had no idea how he might really feel about her after all this time. His letters were few and far between and mentioned only matter of fact details of his life in the west. Sending the miniature likeness of himself was the closest he had come to anything personal. She would be foolish to construe its meaning as anything more than friendship.

At least while everyone else was distracted by the familial greetings she had been free to study the changes in him. The tiny portrait hardly did justice to the breadth of his shoulders. The harshness of life and the Texas sun added planes and lines to his face removing the last vestiges of boyhood.

The sparse blond growth on his cheeks and chin enhanced rather than distracted from his pleasing appearance. It was with some trepidation that she recognized her attraction to him was different now. It felt more physical. Not just her heart but her whole being was drawn to him. It was most evident in the fact that she not only longed to be in his presence, but she also had a strong desire to know what it would be like to be kissed by him.

Unfortunately, they barely exchanged greetings before his mother pulled him away. Nor had they a chance since then to speak, which explained her frustration of the moment. She spent the last four years secretly pinning for him. She was impatient to have her chance to get reacquainted. She smiled inwardly sure of one thing. Henry's return was certain to end the monotony her life had become of late.

Her attention was brought back to the room when she overheard her mother inviting Mrs. Whitmore for supper. It brought a secret, hopeful smile to Emily's lips.

* * *

Henry had forgotten how spirited meals could be at the Eatonton's. Soldiers ate swift and quiet, and his meals growing up were sedate affairs with his well-behaved younger sisters. In this house, with Emily's four brothers, conversation was lively and hands were always reaching for something. It was a good thing the Eatonton's had a large table as there were fourteen of them dining together with their two families combined, minus his father, but with the addition of Emily's cousin, Laura.

He watched the proceedings in fascination from his position next to Emily's father at the head of the table. Every once in a while, he caught Emily's speculative look from across the table despite trying to keep his attention from her for fear he would be caught staring. He couldn't get over the changes in her. She was the most beautiful creature he had ever seen. Unlike his sisters, she didn't have dimples in her cheeks but rather indentions bracketing her mouth. Her plump lower lip seemed to be always on the verge of a smile, enticing him to lure her lips to further curve upward.

He forced his gaze back to his plate.

Earlier, Christoff mentioned in an offhand manner how the local boys started buzzing around her at fourteen, and how he had his hands full discouraging them. Henry could well imagine his difficulties. It was a brave lad who dared to discourage much older boys. Henry asked him how often it had come to fisticuffs. Christoff replied with a proud smile, "only a few," which Henry took to mean he had prevailed, and in doing so, discouraged others from trying to best him. Christoff was not a strapping lad by any means, but he was bellicose when the need arose, and in a fight that often mattered more. Henry certainly wasn't about to challenge him or get into trouble with Captain Max, so he kept his gaze adverted from Emily as much as possible.

Captain Max pulled Henry from his musings. "I suppose you've noticed all the changes?"

For a panicked moment, Henry thought he had read his thoughts. Captain Max's calm demeanor and common sense reassured Henry he was referring to the town and not his daughter. "Yes, sir. A lot of new buildings. Judging by the citizens I passed on the street and the number of specialty stores, I gather business has been prosperous."

"It certainly has. My wrecking ships have brought in three times the money of the merchant line."

"You have more than one wrecker now?"

"I own two and have shared interests in four more. I would be out on the reefs now, if I hadn't made a promise."

Henry noticed the indulgent smile he bestowed towards Mrs. Eatonton sitting at the foot of the table. He supposed it was to take the sting out of the complaint. Captain Max's desire to be out wrecking was easy to see. Henry supposed he could understand the draw of challenging a storm versus the necessity of avoiding one on a merchant ship. It was something similar to his need to join the Texas Rangers versus doing odd jobs around a fort as an errand boy.

Captain Max smiled broadly. "Indeed, the wrecking business is so lucrative, I hear it has made us the richest city in the state."

Henry returned his smile. "Impressive."

Max raised his glass of wine. "Yes, indeed."

Looking around the Eatonton home, one would have to be blind not to realize Captain Max was doing well. The furnishings, while of a practical nature, were of high quality. Nothing was too ostentatious, but the house lacked for nothing. It reflected Mrs. Eatonton's excellent taste and Captain Max's humble beginnings. The dining room, for instance, was richly appointed with silk covered chairs, silver candelabras, fine oil paintings, and on the table, crystal stemware, delicate bone china, and fine linens, but one felt comfortable enough to lean back in the chair and enjoy each other's company.

The Eatonton's lived their life in much the same way. They employed only the minimum number of servants and treated them more like family than employees. It was also not unusual for the family members to help with the chores. Captain Max treated his crew the same way and Abby treated all her patients, rich or poor, the same as she would her friends and family. It was why the Eatonton's were so widely accepted and liked among all the classes in Key West society.

The conversation was soon turned towards Henry. Christoff asked, "What have you done the last five years?"

Henry was reticent to share too many details. He kept his answer simple, likely reiterating facts they already knew. "I left Key West with the vague idea of joining the army."

Mrs. Eatonton said, "But you were too young. Surely you knew that."

"Yes ma'am, I did, but I naively thought I could convince them otherwise. By luck, or divine providence, I ended up at Fort Gibson in Arkansas Territory. The same fort Poppa once visited with the Seminoles. The commander was no fool. He called me out for trying to enlist underage, but then he kindly took me under his wing. He gave me room and board in exchange for menial labor."

Christoff said, "How did you end up with the rangers?"

Henry smiled at his impatient eagerness. "About a year later, I left the fort headed for Texas. I figured since they were fighting Mexicans I would have a better chance of getting into the army. Fortunately, I met Captain Hays, and he recruited me to join the Texas Rangers."

Henry left out the struggles and trials to get to that point, and the horrors he had seen since then. For his mother's benefit, he assured them he had spent most of his time in the rear, well away from the heat of battle.

Mrs. Eatonton said, "You have had quite the adventure but I doubt it was easy."

"No ma'am. There is nothing easy about being a soldier or living out west. I wouldn't recommend it."

Abby cast a pointed look at her sons. She lightened her expression when she turned back to Henry. "I trust you have noticed the changes since you left."

"It is hard not to, especially the Marine Hospital. I recall before I left you were helping Mrs. Eatonton advocate for the new building."

Her smile was tinged with pride. "It has been a true blessing for many a sailor."

The others joined in eager to mention all the changes to the buildings and residents, and the events he had missed. The Eatonton boys turned it into a contest trying to best each other's stories.

Nate's eyes grew bright and excitement nearly made him stand up. "Poppa, tell him about the fire engine." The other boys eagerly agreed.

Henry waited for what must surely be a good story.

Captain Max ran the napkin over his mouth and grinned. "Do you remember the hand engine purchased by the town after one of Judge Webb's outbuildings caught fire?"

Henry nodded. "Yes. I got to ride on it in the next parade."

"Parades proved to be all it was good for after Mr. Thouron moved to Charleston, and it was left to fall into disrepair. About three years ago, Mr. Browne's warehouse caught fire."

Henry noticed upon his arrival that the warehouse seemed larger and the lumber fresh compared to his memory. A fire would explain it, but where was the humor in a fire severe enough to destroy a warehouse?

"The blaze grew rapidly. The fire company was called out, and the engine hauled down to the wharf, but it proved useless to battle the blaze. Mr. Browne not only lost the building but a fortune in goods from ship salvages. As you can imagine feelings were enraged, not just Mr. Browne's, but all those who worked so hard to battle the blaze. They needed a release. I don't remember who first suggested it, but those nearby were quick to take up action. Before a protest could be made, some strong men began pushing the engine down Mr. Browne's wharf..."

Impatiently Nate rose from his seat. "They pushed it right off the dock. It made a huge splash." His hands rose high in the air.

Captain Max indulgently smiled at his son. "And the crowd cheered."

Lighthearted laughter circled the table. Henry could almost see the scene played out in his vivid imagination. It felt good to laugh. Watching those surrounding him, Henry thought, not for the first time today, how nice it was to be home.

When the meal was over, they adjourned to the parlor where the ladies gathered at one end to discuss feminine interests. On the other side, the men enjoyed their cigars and brandy while the older boys listened to their conversation. The younger children played their own games in between the two groups. Christoff and Max were soon deep in discussion of their upcoming sailing. It was to be the first time Max was taking his son on a merchant run from Mobile to New Orleans, Savannah, and Charleston before returning home. They expected to be gone two to three weeks. Christoff was rightfully excited by the prospect. Thorn was sick of hearing about it. He pulled Henry into a game of chess.

Emily soon came over to watch, standing at Thorn's shoulder. "I want to play the winner."

Henry glanced at her eager smile while he waited for Thorn to make his move. It was soon obvious Henry would win the game. He hoped her smile was as much for the prospect of her opponent as for the game itself. A few moves later, Henry declared check mate. Thorn relinquished his seat to his grinning sister. Henry started resetting the pieces while trying to ignore his rapid pulse. Emily settled the full skirt of her blue, stripped taffeta dress and then began helping him. When their hands brushed, he felt a jolt of visceral reaction. His eyes flew to her wide-eyed gaze. The corner of her lip quirked upward before her eyes demurely returned to the task at hand. She felt it too. Excitement made normal breathing difficult.

When the pieces were all in place, Emily raised her eyes to his in question. He gestured to the white pieces on her side of the board. "Ladies first."

Emily moved her e-pawn. Henry answered with his d-pawn. She moved her knight to block him. He smiled. Her strategy had improved while he was away. The moves continued closely matched, and he was forced to admit she was now a worthy opponent. They soon garnered more attention. Christoff and Thorn supported Henry. Brianna and Laura were in support of Emily. The spectators participated in good natured ribbing, but Henry and

Emily remained focused and silent. When he realized the game was a draw, he lifted his gaze to find Emily watching him with twinkling eyes and a very self-satisfied grin as if she had done something better than winning the game. Perhaps she had in proving his equal without embarrassing him with a loss. And in that moment, he knew without a doubt, he was smitten with her.

He rose from his seat and held his hand out to her. "Your skills have greatly improved." She placed her warm hand in his, and the connection sparked as before, surprising them both.

Emily smiled demurely. "Thank you."

They moved off to the side allowing Christoff and Brianna to take their places at the board. Henry and Emily stood close enough to spectate, but a pace away, giving them a chance to converse without disrupting the players. Emily's first question was true to her direct nature.

"How long do you plan to visit?"

"I'm not sure." Curiosity made him ask, "What if I planned to stay?"

"Then you would need a job."

He laughed. Of course, she would give him a practical answer instead of a hint of her feelings which he had been fishing for. "True. But what kind of job?"

She waited for him to answer his own question.

"I suppose I could go back to cleaning sponges."

Her pert nose wrinkled in distaste. "Oh please, no. You smelled horrible."

"Ah, true, cleaning them is an odorous task, but I was thinking of fishing for them."

"Well then, I suppose that will do if someone else is doing the cleaning."

He laughed again. "What do you have in mind for me then?"

"The fort is always hiring construction help. They would probably take you on without hesitation."

He frowned. "Why is that?"

"Your military background, of course." She paused a moment before very softly adding, "And your broad shoulders."

She blushed becomingly, and his gut tightened. His gaze dropped to her mouth as her tongue swept across her bottom lip leaving it shiny with moisture. Suddenly, the only thought in his head was how much he wanted to kiss her, to find out how her lips felt pressed beneath his. It was a surprising revelation, and a first for him. He had never wanted to kiss anyone, and he had only kissed one girl outside his family before now. The experience had been anything but pleasant.

He had just turned eighteen and had been with the Texas Rangers long enough to establish friendships with the older men. Upon learning how innocent he truly was in the ways of women and men, they made it their mission to initiate him. The next town they passed had a bordello, so they convinced Captain Hays a rest was required. That night, they snuck Henry into town and straight into a seedy room and the arms of a barmaid wearing only her underclothes, with rolls of exposed flesh, rouged lips, powdered face, and reeking of heavy perfume. When he hesitated on the threshold, they pushed him into the room and pulled the door closed.

The woman - he couldn't bring himself to call her a lady - pulled him forward. She said, "You don't have to worry about a thing, Carmelita is going to take care of you." She stepped close to him, entirely too close to him, pushing her bosom to his chest. She ran a hand over his head before bringing his mouth to hers. She licked his lips while her other hand brushed much lower. The revulsion he felt was full and immediate. That certainly was not the way his father kissed his mother. Wanting nothing further of the experience, he spun away and rushed to the door, jerking it open. He was dismayed to find it barricaded by his so-called friends. They pushed him back and pulled the door closed. Desperate to get out of the cloying room, he peered out the window and was relieved to find a balcony beneath it. Without a backward glance, he raised the sash and slipped from the room. His friends gave chase as he climbed down to the ground, but he beat them to his mount. He rode hard for camp without any concern for his companions and what they might think of him. He was simply relieved they weren't following.

It was Captain Walker who calmed his anger and assuaged his shame. He explained that while some men only needed a warm body, others preferred meaning in their relationships with women, and there was nothing wrong with that. In his opinion, it made Henry more of a man, not less, and Henry would know when the time was right for him.

Staring into the dove-gray eyes before him, Henry finally understood what Captain Walker was trying to explain.

Chapter 3

Fits and starts it falls apart
But try it will again

Henry awoke to the sound of James whimpering in the throes of a nightmare. He crossed the room and laid a hand on his small forehead, smoothing it in the way he had seen his mother care for his sisters. With a catch of breath, cerulean blue eyes opened to peer into his lighter ones. For moments James silently stared at him as if deciding if Henry was a friend or foe. In the hopes of swaying the decision, Henry gave him a friendly smile. "Good morning, little brother."

James suddenly scooted out from under the covers and padded out of the room. Henry stood from the bed and walked to the door in time to see James disappear into their parents' room, closing the door behind him. Henry's eyes flared in surprise. He would have never gone into their room uninvited, not even at Henry's age. He didn't recall his sisters ever doing so either. Henry waited but nothing happened. He guessed James didn't go in there for help, so what was he doing? With an unconscious shrug of his shoulders, Henry turned back into his room to dress. He then quietly walked down the hall and stood listening outside his parents' door. He heard nothing from their room, but as he passed by his sisters' door on the way downstairs, he heard rustling. He stopped to listen just as Brianna opened the door, surprising them both.

Brianna's hand flew to her chest. "My, you gave me a fright." Her face relaxed into a grin. "Good morning, brother. It's good to have you home."

Henry thought she seemed tall. He leaned in and brushed a kiss on her cheek. "Good morning to you, sister. Did you sleep well?"

"Yes. Thank you for asking." She turned and started for the stairs. "I need to start the cook fire and the coffee." She tossed back over her shoulder. "Care to join me?"

Henry followed her to the outdoor kitchen awash in the pale light of early morning as the sun was just beginning to show above the horizon. Brianna donned a full apron over her slender ten year old frame. Henry watched as she confidently moved about the room appearing older than her years. She was certainly more responsible than he had been at her age.

While she stoked the banked fire in the cast iron cook stove, he took the bucket and drew water from the cistern residing between the kitchen and the house. He returned to the already over warm kitchen and filled the coffee kettle. Brianna shut the stove door and deftly stood up, taking the kettle from him and placing it on the back burner to heat. She retrieved a glass jar from one of the shelves built into the wall on the other side of the kitchen. Placing the jar on the heavy wood plank work table, Brianna unlatched the lid to pour coffee beans in the metal grinder attached to the table's edge. She placed a bowl on a stool beneath the grinder and began turning the handle. Henry noticed she inherited her mother's same graceful efficiency.

He stepped forward. "Allow me." He was no stranger to grinding coffee. It had been his job while riding with the Texas Rangers.

Brianna relinquished the handle with a surprised smile. Not many men would offer to help with woman's work. "Thank you."

While Henry ground the coffee, Brianna left the kitchen with a wire basket to tend the chickens. When he finished, he followed her intending to take over the egg retrieval and save her from the hen pecking. Instead, she shushed him and handed over the basket now holding several eggs, thus freeing both hands to retrieve the rest. He watched, fascinated, as she soothed and lifted the hens before reaching underneath to retrieve the eggs. When this was his task, it was not unusual for him to return with at least one bleeding mark and a coop full of riled hens. When Brianna was done, all was as peaceful as the start.

They returned to the kitchen. Henry pulled the boiling pot off the heat. He would give it a moment to cool before adding the grounds to steep. He turned to find Brianna holding out a dry sponge. "Would you mind cleaning the eggs, so I can start on the bread?"

Henry smiled. "I suppose not since you see it as a foregone conclusion... And I'm starving."

Brianna laughed lightly. "As I recall, you were always hungry." She briefly left the room to clean her hands at the outside wash basin. She returned and wiped them dry on a clean towel before gathering two bowls, a large fork and wooden spoon, flour, and a linen covered crock containing the sourdough starter. She placed them all on the work table.

Henry watched as she poured a careful amount of water from the bucket into the large wooden bowl. Judging it to be too much, she returned some to the bucket. She just as carefully measured the flour into a glass bowl set on a scale. She then removed some starter from the crock and put it to float in the bowl of water. Brianna nestled the wooden bowl in her arm and began whisking the starter into the water.

Henry put the cleaned eggs in the egg bowl and took them to the counter against the back wall. He leaned down underneath to lift a small trap door in the kitchen floor. He placed the eggs in the recess carved out of the limestone next to the covered milk. It was the coolest place in the kitchen. He replaced the trap door and returned to his stool to watch his sister work while his thoughts turned to the day ahead.

First he must find a job. No matter how short his stay, his father would not approve of idle hands. He supposed he would start down at the docks. There was always work on the water for a strong back.

Brianna broke the silence. "Penny for your thoughts."

Henry smiled. "They are not very interesting, I'm afraid. I was thinking of where I should start looking for work. I must earn my keep."

"Is that why you are helping me this morning?"

"No." He grinned. "But now that you mention it, I suppose it counts."

She laughed softly. "I suppose it does." She began working the flour into the starter mixture. "They are always hiring over at the fort." Her head nodded in the direction of the construction taking place just off shore between the end of town and the lighthouse.

"Emily mentioned it as well, but for now I've had my fill of army life. Even if I hire on as a civilian, I would be working under the Corp of Engineers and for certain commanded by a West Pointer." He shook his head in disgust just thinking of the restriction such an enterprise would put on him. "I think I'll start my search at the docks."

"Have you returned to stay?"

Henry's mouth thinned. "I don't think so."

"Then how long do you plan to visit, other than long enough to need a job?"

"I haven't any plans."

She eyed him speculatively. "What brought you home?"

He smiled at her use of the word home and was reminded of yesterday's worry. He wouldn't say he felt completely at home in this house, but he did feel welcome. He was somewhat comfortable with returning to his family although he still felt a bit out of place. It was nice to know his sisters and his mother still considered this his home. Little James would eventually accept him. As for Brianna's question, he wasn't sure how to answer. "A feeling."

Brianna dipped her hands in the bucket to moisten them and began working the sticky mixture into a ball. Softly, she said, "What kind of feeling?"

Their eyes met. The warm sincerity he found in hers brought forth his confession. "It was as though God was commanding me to come home." He expected her to laugh, or at least smile, but she didn't. Her expression remained solemn.

"Why do you suppose? Perhaps to keep you out of the war with Mexico?"

Henry considered her suggestion. "I don't think so. It felt more like I was needed here."

"Needed? In what way?"

Henry shook his head. "I honestly don't know."

They fell silent for a few moments. Brianna wiped her hands on a towel and then covered the bread bowl with a clean cloth and put it aside to rest. Later she would add salt and stretch the dough and then let it rest again. The process would be repeated several times throughout the morning before letting it rise and preparing it to bake this afternoon. She was glad bread making was not a daily chore. The amount of attention it required limited her freedom.

With the full light of morning, Agatha appeared in the doorway, tucking a stray chestnut lock behind her ear. She stopped suddenly at the sight of Henry and put her hands on her hips. "I didn't expect to find you here."

Henry tried to hide his grin behind his greeting. "Good morning, Agatha." It was so much like something Aunt Aggie would say, he was having a hard time holding his laughter.

"Good morning, Henry."

Agatha grinned as if she knew why he was smiling, but how could she? Aunt Agatha died before she was born. Perhaps his sister gleaned something of her namesake's nature from all the stories told of her.

It was Agatha's chore to help Brianna make breakfast while Emmaline set the table. Afterwards, Emmaline would help Agatha clean the dishes. Henry watched as the two sisters worked together to heat the oatmeal that had soaked overnight and cook the bacon and eggs. While the girls worked, the three of them reminisced of childhood. Henry's mouth was watering by the time the food was ready. He gladly helped carry the serving dishes into the house and placed them on the dining table.

James was seated on a stack of books with his hair slicked back by a wet comb in order to smooth the riotous gold curls. Emmaline was next to him in a freshly pressed cotton sprigged dress. Agatha took her seat next to Emmaline, slightly flushed from the heat of the kitchen. Betsy assumed her seat at the foot of the table next to James. Brianna took her usual seat on the other side of Betsy, across from James, leaving Henry the chair he had always occupied on his father's left at the head of the table. Although, today, Theodore's chair was still conspicuously empty. Much as it had been throughout Henry's childhood.

Betsy bowed her head and prayed over their meal. When she was done, everyone filled their plates and the food was quickly consumed.

Betsy asked Henry, "Do you have plans for the day?"

Henry swallowed his bite of light and fluffy eggs before answering. "Yes, ma'am. I intend to look for work unless you need me for something?"

"No. I was just curious. I pray you find gainful employment. Will we see you for the midday meal?"

"I expect so."

She smiled deeply, even her eyes glowed. "I am so very glad to have you home, Henry. You can't know how much I've missed you. Your father is going to be thrilled to see you too. I am hoping he returns this afternoon."

Her words gave him a jolt of anxiety and excitement. He both dreaded and looked forward to reuniting with his father. Putting the emotions aside for now, Henry finished his food, thanked his sisters for the delicious meal, and excused himself.

The sky was clear and bright, dotted with a few puffy white clouds, as he made his way through town to the wharves. The closer he got to the bight, the closer the wooden structures became, and the more he felt the same claustrophobic feeling of yesterday. But today, he also noticed the lush green of all the tropical plants and trees set between the buildings. The emerald green verdure softened the straight lines of the buildings.

Reaching the wharves, he soon realized his mistake. Most of the fishermen set sail just after dawn. He would have to wait until late this afternoon or try again tomorrow to speak with them. Same with the sponge fishers. Henry was headed back home when he noticed an old man sitting on a small barrel in the shade of Tift's warehouse studying him. A fishing net lay stretched across his lap which he appeared to be repairing. Henry slowed his pace trying to determine if he knew the deeply tanned, wrinkled sailor with thin white hair staring at him with brown eyes under slanted lids.

The sailor spoke from the side of his mouth. "You's the eldest Whitmore boy, used to work the sponges."

Henry nodded, only half surprised the man knew him. "Yes, sir. I'm afraid you have me at a disadvantage. I can't recall your name."

"Don't rightly recall ever givin' it to ya. We've always been more like ships passing than ship mates."

Henry stepped up to the man and offered his hand. "Then we shall change that. Henry Whitmore, sir."

The man untangled his hand from the netting and leaned forward to shake Henry's but didn't rise. "Tom Bly." He leaned back against the building and returned his hand to the knot he was working. "Who you lookin' for, son?"

"No one in particular. Just trying to find some work."

"There's work to be had at the fort."

Henry grimaced. "So I've heard. Not really interested in army work, if you know what I mean."

He gave a grunt of understanding. "Looking for work on water or land?"

"Either, though I was really hoping to sponge fish."

"Are ya now? Got any experience?"

"A little. Went out a time or two before I left."

"Might know a man interested in help. Come back tomorrow - at dawn, if you 'spect to find work. Meet me at the north end and I'll introduce ya. Now get on with ya. You're blockin' my breeze, boy."

Henry gave a nod. "Much obliged, Mr. Bly." He started walking off when the sailor called after him.

"Be sure ya wear a hat tomorrow, you fool boy."

Henry smiled and waved, not taking any offense at the sound advice. He had left his ragged sombrero behind in New Orleans. Maybe he could find his old sailor hat, otherwise he would be forced to buy a new one which would hardly set the right impression with an old fisherman. He would have to do something about his footwear as well. The heeled riding boots he was wearing were not suited to keeping balance on a small boat. He made a quick stop at the cobbler to buy a pair of flat sole, lace-up, leather shoes.

On his return walk to the house, he crossed paths with an old friend on his way to town for supplies. Miguel Mabrity was the youngest son of the lighthouse keepers. His father died from yellow fever when Miguel was a toddler. His mother took over as keeper of the Key West lighthouse. Growing up, Miguel had little time to play between chores. It was typical for him to seek out Henry's company on the days he fished for the family meal.

The two young men greeted each other warmly.

Miguel looked at him with admiration. "I bet you've got some grand stories to tell."

Henry smiled. "That I do. Do you still have time for fishing?"

Miguel frowned. "It's harder these days. Just me and Mama working the light now. All my siblings have married off."

"Don't you ever have a hankering to get out of here, to go explore?"

Miguel snorted. "Of course I do."

"Why do you stay?"

Miguel's lips compressed. "I couldn't leave Mama. She needs me more than she'll ever admit. And I owe it to Papa to take care of her. I couldn't just leave."

He didn't say it, but Henry heard it as if he had. *I couldn't just leave like you did.*

Miguel's face brightened. "I better get going. Good to see you, Henry."

Absently, Henry replied. "You too, Miguel."

The bright, beautiful day was now tainted with Henry's guilt. Slowly, he trudged home thinking that most of the island community probably saw his leaving in the same light as Miguel - as abandonment of his mother when she needed him. He knew he had to earn his parents' forgiveness. He hadn't considered that he would also have to earn the town's pardon as well. It was a daunting expectation.

Feeling the need to draw to settle his troubled mind, Henry returned to the house for his sketch book and pencils. A brief search of his dresser revealed his old, straw sailor hat and clothes. He was too tall for the breeches, but he would still be able to wear the loose fitting shirts. He left again by the front door, relieved not to have to explain his destination to anyone.

Henry placed the hat on his head as he considered which direction to take. Behind the pond towards the undeveloped side of the island, or maybe something of interest along the coast. To his left, the clean lines of the lighthouse looked appealing. He decided the lighthouse would have a good vantage point from which to draw. He walked across the street and behind the house that used to be his mother's seamstress shop, crossing the new extension of Front Street – at least new to him – and onward until he reached the water. He followed the shore eventually crossing the landings of the two attached docks behind the Marine Hospital and passing the old cemetery. It reminded him of Aunt Aggie and his baby sister, Madalyn, buried in the new cemetery on the southern coast. His heart tightened as it always did when thoughts of them crossed his mind. He continued onward, passing the lagoon, bringing him to the edge of the army construction camp.

The sun was a couple of hours from its zenith. It beat down unmercifully upon the backs of those toiling to move brick and mortar across the dock to build the offshore fort. The lighthouse was still roughly a half mile away around a bend in the coastline. He could barely make out the top of it from above the trees. He stopped for a moment to observe the fort progress, at least what he could see of it from shore.

Henry was disturbed from his musings by the approach of an army officer. He noted the two bars on his shoulder strap. Out of habit, Henry saluted, generating a smile on the face of the middle-aged officer as he returned the salute.

"A military man, I see." He held out his hand. "Captain George Dutton, Corp of Engineers."

Henry shook the proffered hand. "Henry Whitmore, former private, First Regiment, Texas Mounted Riflemen."

"Former, you say. Discharged?"

"Yes, sir. Honorably, sir."

"No doubt. You're a long way from Texas. Is Key West home for you?"

"Yes, sir."

"Any chance you're looking for work? I can always use another strong back, and I could find right good use of someone with your military training."

"I am sure you could, sir, but I'm looking at sponge fishing. I've had my fill of army life, if you don't mind my saying so."

"It's not for everyone. Shame, though. If you change your mind, come see me. Most of these laborers make a dollar a week. I'd be willing to pay you two."

Henry's eyes widened.

"Thought that might get your attention. I think you could do well to help supervise the men and jump in and help as needed. As I said, your youth and experience would be mighty handy to me."

"Can I think about it?"

Captain Dutton chuckled. "If you need to. Take all the time you want. This project's a few years from completion. Meanwhile, you want a tour?"

Henry grinned broadly and snappily replied, "Yes, sir."

As they passed through the camp on the way to the dock, Henry found a place to leave his drawing materials. Tents were lined up on the outskirts of the camp. In the center, building supplies were piled high, including large stacks of cypress timbers, granite blocks, mountains of bricks, and covered piles of mix for mortar. The grounds included a stable and tool shed, both of which were open and empty, their contents being employed. The two men strolled down the dock side by side except when they had to stand aside to let a laborer pass by usually with a full or empty wheelbarrow depending on their direction of travel. As they walked, the captain explained the dimensions and planned building of the structure along with a history to date of its construction.

When they reached the fort, Captain Dutton stepped from the dock to the breakwater wall built around the site. It held back the sea water while the foundation was being completed. Henry followed him, carefully keeping his balance on the uneven rock surface. On one side of the wall, salt water gently lapped a foot or so below his feet, on the other side was a twelve foot drop to the limestone bed where a few feet inward the beginnings of the fort rose up. From his new vantage point, Henry could see the trapezoid outline of granite blocks, and within them, the maze of cypress grillage constructed to support the future massive structure.

Henry called out to the captain standing a few yards from him. "Why are you building out here in the water? Wouldn't it be easier to build on land?"

Captain Dutton walked back to him. "Aye, it would be easier and cheaper, but it was decided that this location would best allow for the defense of the four shipping channels leading into the harbor." He pointed outward indicating the location of each of the four channels. Henry could easily see how the fort would command a view of all the nearby vessels. He was fascinated by all he had seen, but he still felt no compunction to work for the army.

Noting the high sun, Henry thanked Captain Dutton for his time and hurried back to shore. Picking up his sketch book, he raced back to the house not wanting to be late for the noon meal.

* * *

Henry entered the front door and came to a sudden halt at the sound of his father's voice. Emotions swamped him; happiness and guilt, excitement and trepidation, hope and fear. He took a deep breath and quietly walked to the parlor door to see his father handing out gifts to his sisters. He waited to enter the room not wanting to spoil the joyful reunion. It gave Henry a moment to study the changes in his father. Easily noticed, his temples were feathered with gray and the creases at his mouth and eyes were deeper. Beneath the surface, Henry noticed more significant differences. Gone was the heavy burden he carried during the war years. It showed in the lightness of his demeanor. He was still a quiet, somber man, but there was also a jovial spirit that Henry's younger siblings brought out in him.

It only took a moment for his parents to discover his presence. Betsy looked to him first, and Theodore's gaze followed. His father's face

27

broke into a grin as he stepped forward to embrace Henry.

"Welcome home, son."

Henry choked back the sudden and unexpected tears overwhelming him as his father's arms tightened around his shoulders. In the space of a heartbeat, five years of separation felt like a lifetime. When they broke apart, he still couldn't speak for fear his voice would wobble. His eyes clung to his father's face, gradually realizing he now stood eye to eye with him. It was a novel experience.

Betsy eased them from the emotional moment. "Come to the table. Dinner is ready."

A familiar scent drifted in the air. His face split into a grin. "Is that cinnamon bread, I smell?"

Betsy rubbed a hand down his arm as she led the way to the table. "Made especially for you."

Henry was grateful to his mother for keeping the conversation light during the meal. He could see in his father's eyes he had much to say. Henry was sure most of it would be uncomfortable to hear, and though the delay in speaking increased his anxiety, he was still grateful to put it off a while longer. Most of the conversation centered on his father's recent travels. Florida's attainment of statehood last year naturally created an increase in political activity in the capital city of Tallahassee. His father's visit was to get an update on legislative activity to include in the publication of his newspaper, the *Key West Weekly*, and to check on the status of relations with the Seminoles still living in Florida.

After their meal, Henry followed Theodore to his study. He was surprised when his father paused before the bookshelf and carefully picked up the revolver lying next to his flintlock on a high shelf.

Theodore turned to his son. "Is it loaded?"

"No, sir."

He turned it over in his hand, studying the workings. "A Colt?"

"Yes, sir."

"It's a nice gun. It must have cost you a pretty penny."

"It was well worth every bit of its price. I hope you don't mind me putting it in here. It didn't feel right keeping it in my room with James."

"A wise decision."

His praise made Henry fight not to smile. "Although I must admit, I feel as if I am missing a part of myself not having it within easy reach."

Theodore nodded. "It's only natural. I felt the same way every time I returned home from the Indian War. It will pass with time."

Their conversation was neutral, but the undercurrents were far from it, and Henry's next words were spoken defensively in response to his growing tension. "I know you don't approve of what I did."

Theodore's gaze cut to his son's. "To what are you referring?"

Henry swallowed hard. "Joining the Texas Rangers."

Theodore lifted his chin. "I was more disappointed that I had to find out from your uncles than I was in your decision to flee to Texas. Why didn't you write?"

"I didn't want you to talk me out of it."

"I didn't talk you out of leaving here even when it was a rotten time to leave your mother hurting as she was with the loss of Madalyn. I left the decision up to you."

As usual, the mention of her name brought flashes of the horrid days following the death of Emmaline's twin from asphyxia; reminders of his mother's deep sorrow, Emmaline's constant crying, his inadequacy to deal with the situation, and his anger towards his father for not being there. "And you believe I made the wrong one." He said it as a matter of fact. He knew how his father felt about that decision from his letters.

"Hmm." Theodore placed the gun back on the shelf taking a moment to hold his tongue before turning back to Henry. "Son, I only wished you had waited as I asked."

Henry's jaw clenched. "It wouldn't have changed anything for me." His father's piercing gaze intensified his guilt.

"Likely not, but that wasn't the point. The wait was for your mother's benefit, but you didn't see fit to consider anyone but yourself and your feelings." Theodore's voice remained steady, but his tone intensified. "That's what disappointed me."

Defensive anger exploded in Henry's chest. "Watching over mother is your responsibility, but you were always gone giving those Indians more attention than your own family. We were left to wait and hurt alone." His father's wince confirmed he hit his mark.

Theodore took several deep breaths while forming his response. "You are right. I spent too many years away, but they were not selfishly spent. I made those decisions, and I have to live with the consequences. But, I also had faith in you as man of the house. It struck deep when you let the family down."

Remorse hit Henry in the chest. His father was right. Unlike his father, he left for selfish reasons, acting on his own feelings without any regard to his family. Henry cast his eyes to the floor. "I see your point." He slowly lifted his gaze again to his father. "And you think I did it again, only thinking of myself, in going to Texas."

"Yes, in as far as not telling us yourself."

"I knew you would not approve of killing Indians, so I couldn't bring myself to tell you that was my intention."

"Why?"

Henry shook his head, confused as to what answer his father was seeking. "Why?"

"Why did you want to kill Indians? I would have thought you had learned something of them at the fort."

"The Apache and Comanche are not like the Creeks and Seminole."

Theodore fought to keep his voice steady not wanting to turn this topic into another argument. He wanted to understand his son's reasons. "And that makes it right to hunt them?"

Henry frowned. "Father, we weren't hunting them. The Rangers protect the Texas citizens from their raiding and vicious attacks. From the Mexicans too."

Theodore clapped Henry on the back. "Good to know your intentions were noble even if your actions leave something to be desired." He looked at the revolver again, and his voice sobered as his own past rose up to haunt him. "Did you kill anyone?"

Henry sighed in remembered frustration. "Major Hays and Lieutenant Colonel Walker kept me out of most of the battles or far behind the action. Still, that gun came in handy more than once."

Theodore gave a single nod. "Then I'm glad for it, and glad you made it home safe. Why are you home now? Isn't General Zack Taylor in the heat of war with Mexico?" Forgetting his earlier resolve, his eyes narrowed on his son. "You didn't desert your post?"

Henry's chin dropped in shock, and then clenched in anger. "No, I did not. I properly resigned. I can't believe you think so little of me."

Theodore sighed heavily. "Son, I haven't heard directly from you in over two years, and I haven't laid eyes on you in five. If not for your uncles and General Taylor, I would likely believe you were dead. As for your character, you've shown little to me of which to be proud."

The truth of his accusations cut deeply, and in response Henry lashed out. "You had my uncles spying on me. Is that why I was left behind in battle?"

"I admit I had your uncles reassigned to Fort Gibson to watch over you as much for your mother's peace of mind as for your safety, but I had nothing to do with your ranger or army duties. General Taylor happened to mention you to me in his letter."

"What did he say?"

"That you must be a good soldier. Lieutenant Colonel Walker insisted on having you assigned to his detail."

Henry heard the telltale note of pride in his father's voice. It helped to ease the sting of his rebuke. "Sam Walker's been good to me. He took me under his wing when he joined the rangers." Henry paused to gather his courage and push aside his pride. "Father, I am sorry for disappointing you and for not thinking of mother."

Theodore placed his arm across Henry's shoulder. "I know, son. I forgive you. It will not be mentioned again."

The fullness of his words rendered Henry speechless and fighting to hold back the moisture welling in his eyes.

Theodore was first to pull away, turning to the sideboard and pouring them each a measure of brandy. He handed a glass to Henry. "Now, back to my earlier question. What brings you home?"

Henry felt the amber liquid burn down his throat. It was by no means his first taste of alcohol, but it was his first drink with his father. It was also the first time his father treated him like a man. His emotions since entering the room were taking wild swings from fractious to contrite to swelling pride, leaving him feeling a little faint. He took a second swallow to help settle his nerves. As for the question, he hoped his father might understand his reason better than he did. "I felt called by God."

Theodore's rounded eyes lifted from his glass. He held Henry's gaze for several silent moments before saying, "How so?"

Henry looked down shaking his head. "It was more a feeling, but not my own; a feeling that I was needed here. The more I resisted it, the stronger it grew, until one morning I found myself approaching Lieutenant Walker with hat in hand asking for my release. It took us both by surprise. The urgent need to return persisted as I rode across Texas and into New Orleans. It didn't fade until I was finally aboard ship headed this way, but the notion I needed to return didn't leave me altogether, only the urgency was gone."

"And do you still feel it?"

Henry paused to consider. "No."

"Then perhaps the true purpose was to remove you from harm's way."

Brianna had suggested the same thing. Henry considered their conclusion. He was sure the calling had been for his family's safety, not his. But maybe they were right. The feeling was gone. He was here on the island with no immediate plans to leave, and his own safety would not have been enough inducement to make him leave. Another thought occurred to him sending a chill down his spine. He sent a silent prayer heavenward asking God not to take his parents from this earth so soon.

Theodore leaned against his desk. "And now that you are here, what do you plan to do?"

Henry relaxed with the change in subjects. "I'm meeting with a sponge fisher tomorrow."

"I can't say I understand your fascination with sponges."

Henry smiled. "Key West has the best, and one day the world will know it. It's a growing industry, and I want to be a part of it."

Theodore raised his glass. "Cheers to having aspirations."

Henry clinked his glass and grinned. "Cheers."

Theodore took a sip. "And if sponging fails, there's always the fort."

Henry rolled his eyes.

Theodore frowned.

"You are the fourth person to mention it to me."

"Hmm"

"I did meet Captain Dutton on my walk earlier. He took me out to see their progress. It is amazing what they are trying to build."

"Yes, it is, and the nice part is, it will help the economy for years to come just in the building of it, not to mention, it will likely mean the army's permanent occupation."

Henry smiled. "You are always thinking of the community. Have you ever considered running for mayor?"

Theodore grunted. "I did. Once."

Henry's smile turned serious. His comment was meant as a joke, but he sensed a story in his father's reply. He tilted his head in curiosity and waited.

"Do you remember when Will Whitehead left the island?"

Henry nodded.

"Do you remember why?"

"Not really other than it happened the same time the barkeep, Mr. Saccheti, was elected to replace him."

"The council passed a tax that some of the citizens opposed. Mr. Whitehead did his job enforcing it, but things got heated when the council didn't support him, and he resigned. Mr. Saccheti was the only candidate running. I happened to return the day before the election, and for a moment considered opposing him, until I realized there really wasn't time to mount a campaign. It was just as well. Your mother was right when she said I needed to see the Seminole War to its end, such as it was."

Here was an opening to ask the question Henry had been harboring for years. He opened his mouth to speak, but his courage failed him. He took another sip of brandy instead.

Theodore noticed his hesitation. "What is it, son?"

His father's concern broke the barrier to at least ask the surface question. "Did you ever regret getting involved in the war?" He held his father's probing gaze. He knew his father was trying to figure out why he was asking the question.

Theodore took a seat in one of the two captain chairs facing his desk and waited while Henry took the other. "That question has so many answers. In terms of what it did to our relationship and the sacrifices our family had to make without me - yes. I very much regret it. If I had any inkling how long it would have lasted going in, I don't believe I would have gotten involved. No one expected the war to go beyond the first skirmish, or if they did, it wasn't to be more than a few months. Personally, I knew it would be more than a battle or even a few months, but I could not have imagined it would take me away from home, away from you, for seven years. I suppose in that regard, I should ask for your forgiveness. I put impossible pressures on you at a young age."

Henry's lips compressed. "I'm not the first boy to face those expectations and certainly more fortunate than most of them as you did, eventually, come home."

Theodore's chest filled with pride. "That kind of attitude will take you far in life. I am proud of you Henry."

It was the second time his father said it since entering this room, and it affected him just as powerfully as the first time. If nothing else came of his return home, this conversation with his father was well worth the trip. The rift between them was healing. "I'm proud of you too. The last two years have opened my eyes to some of the sacrifices you made for the Indians."

"If you are referring to creature-comforts, they were of no concern to me. It was the loss of time with you and the girls that hurt the most, and not being here when Betsy needed me. I wasn't around to help you become a man. I wasn't here to see the girls take their first steps or to help all of you cope with the loss and grief of Aunt Agatha and Madalyn. Time is so precious, and so often we take it for granted. You never know when it's going to end."

"I was thinking of the loss of comforts, but I was also proud of how well you were spoken of by everyone who knew you. Soldier and Indian alike were impressed by you and how you always handled yourself with honor and dignity." It was his turn to watch his father swallow hard holding back his emotions.

Theodore cleared his throat. "Well, thank you. I'm glad to hear it."

"How was your trip to Tallahassee? Anything new with the Seminoles?"

"The legislature is still pressing for removal of all Indians from Florida."

"Are the Indians causing trouble?"

"No. They are limiting their contact with whites as much as possible, knowing it will only end badly for them."

"Then why not leave them be? Didn't we all suffer enough with the Florida War?"

"There are those who don't care if it takes another war. Their reason is the same as always; fear and greed. Did you ever meet Captain John Sprague?"

"No, but I have heard of him by reputation and from you."

He has been placed in charge of Indian affairs. I am hopeful his sympathy for the Seminoles will keep things from escalating. I met with him while in Tallahassee. Actually, he sought out my council. He can't get the chiefs to agree to a meeting."

"What did you tell him?"

"They are understandably distrustful. Too often their chiefs were seized under a flag of truce. The only suggestion I could make was to somehow gain their trust, though I doubt it is possible."

Long into the afternoon, father and son continued talking of the town, the country, and the escalating land war with Mexico. They were both surprised when Betsy called them to supper.

Henry went to bed that night feeling more at peace than he could ever recall.

Chapter 4

Fed by warm salty water
Nurtured by cooling winds
Ocean's devilish child is born

Henry rose before dawn, before anyone else in the house. He dressed in the dark hoping not to awaken James. His little brother was growing fond of him. If he awoke, not only would he pepper Henry with questions, but Henry would be forced to wake one of his sisters to keep an eye on the youngster which would detain his leaving. Henry slipped into his trousers and a loose fitting, long sleeved shirt. He donned his socks and slipped his feet into his new shoes. He picked up his old straw sailor hat and silently slipped out of the bedroom leaving James peacefully slumbering.

Excitement coursed through Henry as he left the house and entered the kitchen where he grabbed a slice of bread, a bite of cheese, and downed a glass of water. Today could be the start of something big for him. Today, he would hopefully start learning all he needed to know about being a sponge fisher. He filled one of the canteens his mother kept hanging by the door in anticipation of being out on the water for hours. Finally ready, he left to meet Mr. Bly.

The withered old fisherman was waiting for him as promised along with his friend who appeared to be even older judging by his weathered face. As soon as Henry was within hearing distance, Mr. Bly said, "Charlie, this here's the young man I was tellin' ya about. Henry Whitmore, this here's Charlie Tate."

Henry couldn't help feeling a little self-conscious as Mr. Tate gave him an appraising look from the old straw hat on his head to the brand new shoes on his feet.

Though Mr. Tate's face gave the appearance of being older than Mr. Bly, his sprightly physique said otherwise. He stood arrow straight and tall at nearly six feet. His ragged hat covered a full head of short gray hair above an elongated countenance with wiry, gray sideburns. He was serious in nature although not unfriendly. His shirt and trousers, while clean, were well-worn and covered in stains. However, it was the object in his left hand which increased Henry's excitement for the day. It was a pole over twice Mr. Tate's height. On its end were four metal tines, something like a small pitchfork but curved like a rake. Henry recognized it as a sponge hook, and he was anxious to learn how to use it. The few times his former employer, Mr. McHugh, took him out sponge fishing, he did so diving with a knife. To Henry's way of thinking, hooking would take less energy than all that swimming. He hoped it was a quicker method so more sponges could be harvested.

Henry held his hand out. "Pleased to meet you, Mr. Tate. Do you remember me?"

"Aye. You used to clean sponges for McHugh."

"Aye."

"I'm not bringing in so many sponges as to need help cleaning."

"Well, Mr. Tate, to tell you the truth, I was hoping you might teach me to be a hooker."

"That so."

"I was thinking I could do most of the hard labor in exchange for your teaching, and if I can help you bring in larger harvests perhaps we could split the profits."

The old man rubbed his grizzled chin in thought. At his continued silence, Henry impatiently shuffled.

Finally the old man nodded. "You get twenty five percent of the take 'till you prove you can earn your keep. Get more when I say you get more. Can you live with that?"

Henry held his excitement in check. "Yes, sir."

Mr. Tate's mouth curved upward to reveal several missing teeth. "We have an accord. Now grab this here hook and follow me to the boat. Good day for sponging. Fair weather makes 'em easier to see."

Henry grinned. He had done it. He was going to learn to be a sponge fisher and better yet, a hooker. He turned to thank Mr. Bly only to find he had disappeared. Eagerly, Henry skipped after Mr. Tate wondering if he should call him captain. Henry placed the hook in the simple eight foot long row boat. The handle extended more than a yard over the stern. When the old man was seated, he pushed the boat into the water and climbed in as well. Mr. Tate had Henry row them a ways off shore out over a shallow reef only about two fathoms deep. The old man had been peering over the side as they cut through the chatoyant water, but he suddenly sat upright and told Henry to stop.

Mr. Tate rose to his feet and then stepped onto his seat easily balancing his weight from a lifetime of experience. "Hand me the hook."

"Yes, sir." Henry placed the oars in the boat and lifted the handle of the hook for Mr. Tate to grasp.

He dropped the fork end in the water. "Now you watch how it's done."

Henry peered over the side of the boat.

"Not from there, you lubber. On your feet. Can't see nothing that close to the water."

Henry carefully rose and climbed up on his seat doing his best not to excessively rock the boat while he found his balance.

Mr. Tate maneuvered the tines of the fork under a black blob Henry hadn't noticed at first amidst all the different corals wavering beneath the undulating surface of the water.

"You hook it and give it a little twist as you pull up." He brought the fork to the surface and dumped the blob into the hull.

Henry recognized the black skinned sponge as a sheepswool, having cleaned so many in his youth.

Mr. Tate sent the hook down again but didn't hook the next sponge. "You see how this one's smaller than the hook. We'll leave it to grow. Only want to take the ones bigger than the fork." He moved on to another sponge and showed Henry again how to work the tines under and give the handle a twist and a pull to tear off the sponge.

"Think you got it?"

"Yes, sir."

"Good. Your'n turn."

Henry took the hook from Mr. Tate and scanned the water. He tried to guess at locating the sponges, but identifying them was harder than it looked. Mr. Tate ended up having to guide him most of the morning. By the afternoon, he was doing better. Henry was baffled by how easily the old man seemed to find them. Fortunately, he mastered the technique of pulling the sponge rather quickly, pleasing Mr. Tate.

As the sun rose higher, Henry was feeling the strain of heat and hunger. He kept waiting for Mr. Tate to take a break, but he seemed determined to keep going. They had a pretty large heap of dark oily sponges piled in the space between them. Surely he would call a halt soon.

Somehow, Mr. Tate must have perceived his discomfort. The old man squinted up at him. "You've heard make hay while the sun shines? Well, we sponge while the water's calm. You never know what the next hour may bring. Winds and clouds mask the depths making it harder to find them, and you can well imagine what a storm would do to us in this small craft. So we work as long as we can while conditions favor."

Henry nodded in understanding and resumed his task. A few hours later, the sponge pile was well above the rim of the boat and gray clouds were gathering. Henry had never been so excited to see a storm. Mr. Tate finally called a halt to the hooking. Henry took up the oars having barely enough room to sit on the bench. The boat was stuffed with smelly sponge blobs, but it didn't bother him. This, he was familiar with, and to him it was the smell of success.

They reached the shore in good time. Henry pulled the boat above the water line. Mr. Tate got out, and together they carried the boat to a small shack Mr. Tate used as a warehouse. The boat, along with its valuable cargo, was secured inside. Much to Henry's relief, Mr. Tate suggested they get some food and drink at his favorite pub before tackling the next project.

The storm let loose while they were eating.

A short while later, they returned to the shack under clearing skies. Muggy heat surrounded them as moisture evaporated from the limestone. Mr. Tate pulled two half barrel tubs, each with a bucket inside, from his warehouse. They dragged them down to the shore. Mr. Tate then picked up a rope Henry had failed to notice staked a few feet above the shore. He followed it into the water up to his knees where he began pulling on it. Henry sloshed into the water and took over the task wanting to be sure he put in the full labor he promised in their partnership. The weight on the line was more than he expected. It gave him a new appreciation for Mr. Tate's hidden strength.

Henry cast a glance over his shoulder as he hauled on the line. "What's on the end of this?"

"Sponges ready for cleaning."

Henry took that to mean it was his previous catch of sponges left to soak in the water after having been dried in the sun for several days to rot the outer skin. He finally pulled in a sponge filled fishing net turning his face away as he was assailed by the putrid odor. He forgot how potent it was the first time it hit the nostrils.

Mr. Tate grinned. "Get used to it boy. That's the smell of money."

Together, they carried the reeking bundle to shore, placing it on the ground near the tubs. Mr. Tate deftly untied the string holding the sides and ends of the net together. He then removed a short paddle from one of the tubs and started beating the sponges to further loosen everything clinging to the skeleton of the plant or animal, depending on one's opinion. Spongers had been known to get into heated debates over sponge classification. Henry leaned towards believing it to be a plant but could see validity in calling it an animal too. After demonstrating his technique, Mr. Tate passed the paddle to Henry to let him finish the task while he began filling one of the tubs with saltwater using the buckets. The sponges were then given a good shake before repeatedly soaking and squeezing them one by one in the tub of water. When a sponge was deemed clean, it was squeezed as dry as possible and tossed into the dry tub.

Mr. Tate held up a particularly nice specimen. "One day the world will discover we have the finest sponges around."

Henry felt a touch of destiny in the old man's words.

When the net was empty, it was rinsed in ocean water. The wash barrel was emptied and they carried everything back to the warehouse. The empty net was then spread out alongside the boat and the newly harvested sponges were moved from the boat to the net.

Mr. Tate said, "As soon as we get this mess strung up on the posts, we'll be done for the day."

"Mr. Tate, can I ask you something?" He grunted in response. Henry paused before reaching for the next handful of sponges. "Mr. McHugh always dried his sponges laid out on the roof. Why don't you?"

Mr. Tate snorted. "Cause these bones are too old to go climbing on the roof."

"You have me now. I could do it for you."

"Who's to say you're coming back tomorrow?"

Henry blustered in protest.

"Make's no never mind. This method works better. In a few days when these are dry, all I have to do is take the net down to the water. Don't have to handle 'em again."

Henry could see the efficiency in Mr. Tate's method, but it still seemed to him that a single layer on a hot roof would dry faster than a strung up bundle.

When the last sponge was in the hammock, Mr. Tate once again threaded the ends of the net together. They carried it outside where it was strung between two posts in the sun forming something of a hammock.

Mr. Tate lifted his gaze to the sky. "Don't have to worry about a storm carrying 'em off neither."

"What about the one's in the middle? How do they get sun?"

"You've got smarts, that's for sure. I shake 'em up in the net every day to take care of that."

The sun was dropping below the trees as Henry trudged home. He was tired but happy with what he had learned today. Mr. Tate's comment about the world discovering the quality of Key West sponges kept spinning in his mind. It confirmed his opinion and bolstered his confidence in his plans. He wanted to get his own boat and gear to start his own business. Eventually, he wanted to have several hookers working for him so he could build up to be a large supplier to a market like New York. It was a grand scheme.

Henry reached home and went directly to the wash station outside the kitchen to clean up as best he could before entering the house. While he was scrubbing his arms, his mother appeared in the kitchen door. Her nose wrinkled. "How was your day?"

"Everything I hoped it would be. Mr. Tate has taken a liking to me. He's teaching me how to hook sponges. Well, actually, hooking them is the easy part. He's teaching me how to find them while standing on the boat instead of diving under the water."

"And how did you do?"

Henry smiled as he rinsed the lye soap from his hands and arms. "Pretty well, I think."

Betsy handed him a towel to dry off. "Come inside. I have supper waiting for you."

Henry was expecting to fend for himself knowing the family ate their meal a while ago. He forgot how nice it was to have his mother take care of him. He kissed her temple. "Thank you." He sat on the kitchen stool and bowed his head to pray before tucking into the salted fish, beans and rice she placed before him.

Betsy lingered in the kitchen not wanting to give up this rare moment alone with Henry. She ran her hand over the table reminiscing of a summer afternoon, long before she married Theodore, when she showed a very young Henry, who was kneeling on the same stool on which he now sat, how to harvest a conch. Her nostalgic eyes lifted to the young man before her. "Your father said you and he had a good conversation yesterday."

Henry finished chewing before answering. "We did." He recalled all he and his father had discussed, particularly how he had hurt his mother. He reached for her hand. "I want to apologize to you for the way I left. I should have waited as father asked. Then he would have been home, and you would not have been left alone."

Betsy placed her free hand on top of his. "I should have explained my feelings rather than being argumentative."

"I doubt I would have listened. My mind was pretty well set on leaving. I'm sorry I was so selfish and uncaring of your needs and concerns."

She turned her bottom hand over and squeezed his between hers. "It's all water under the bridge. You're home now and you're safe, and you seem to be happy. In the end, that's all that really matters to me."

Henry leaned forward and kissed her cheek. "I am so fortunate to have you for my mother."

Betsy closed her eyes and shook her head to contain her emotions. When she opened them again, she pulled her hands from Henry. "Eat. You must be starving. Do you think you will be gone all day tomorrow?"

"If the weather's fair, yes."

"Then, I'll make you up a lunch pail to take with you."

"Thank you, Mother." While he finished his supper, Henry watched her move about the kitchen gathering bread, cheese, and dried meat for the pail and refilling his canteen. She set them on the middle of the table.

"There you go. All ready for you in the morning."

"You didn't have to..."

"I wanted to." She took his empty plate to clean.

He waited till she was done, and together they returned to the house. He spent an hour visiting with his family in the parlor before turning in early.

The following day began the same as the previous until the wind kicked up mid-morning making it difficult to see underwater. Henry volunteered to dive for the sponges, which at least filled the boat half way before another storm chased them to shore. He and Mr. Tate strung up a second fishing net filled with the day's catch and then he released Henry.

The storm crossed the reef but the island was untouched leaving a sultry sunny afternoon. Henry returned home to retrieve his sketch book. Today, he stepped over the low wooden fence in the backyard and walked to the soggy edge of the tidal pond. It was halfway between tides, and the water was receding. He followed the edge of the pond around to the string of houses at the far edge of the settlement. He intended to make his way into the interior hammock looking for something of interest to draw.

As he walked, he contemplated his time on the island so far. He was feeling hopeful and optimistic. He had work in hand and a plan for his future. The weight of his father's disappointment was lifted, and after apologizing to his mother, his soul felt healed after so many years of carrying his shame. He was finally at peace with himself. Being back on the island gave him a measure of peace as well. Despite the increase in buildings and population and the congestion of Front Street, he still loved the wild nature of the island and the waters surrounding it. Turning his back to the pond, he looked past the houses of Caroline and Eaton Streets to the uncleared trees and the various shades of green in the untamed hammock beyond. He was anxious to wander again amongst the white mangrove, gumbo limbo, lignum vitae, pigeon plum, and the silver buttonwood that dared to be different with its silver-green leaves. They were the refuge of his youth, and they called to him now.

He took a determined step towards the trees, but his movement was arrested by a familiar feminine voice calling his name.

* * *

Not having anything better to do, Emily agreed to accompany her mother on a midwife visit to Mrs. Watlington who was *enceinte* with her fifth child due in about six weeks. Emily was sitting on the porch talking with Hannah, the Watlington's eldest daughter and a few years her junior, when Henry came into view. The house faced in the direction he was walking so Henry's back was to them. He not only didn't notice them, but Emily was able to watch him unguarded for a few moments until he turned towards the woods giving her his profile.

She hadn't seen him since his arrival, so his unexpected appearance was a pleasant surprise. Not wanting to lose such an advantageous moment, she rushed to the railing and called out, "Henry." She turned to her companion. "Hannah, wait here. I'll be but a moment, I promise." Impatiently, she lifted her skirts and raced down the steps, anxious to catch up to him.

She waved to Henry as she made an effort to slow her pace to something more dignified. Her heart fluttered as she reached him. "Hello." Belated modesty cast her eyes downward followed by a blushing heat in her cheeks.

Amusement tinged his voice. "Hello."

"I didn't expect to see you here." Their voices collided, and they both laughed as they realized they had said the same thing.

Emily tossed a glance over her shoulder. "I'm visiting the Watlington's with my mother."

"Oh." He gestured with his book. "I was just on my way to do some sketching."

"Do you still do a lot of drawing then?"

"Not as much as I would like, but every chance I get."

The breeze turned and Emily caught a whiff of the odor clinging to his clothes. She waved a hand in front of her nose to dispel it. "Is that sponges I smell? They wouldn't hire you on at the fort?"

Henry's lips tightened. "Actually, I was offered a job at the fort, but it's not what I want to do. You mark my words, Emily Eatonton, sponging is going to be big business one day, and I'm going to be part of it."

"You told me you wanted to fish for them instead of cleaning them. Does this mean fishing is smelly work too?"

"I'm afraid until I build a large enough business of my own, I will have to do both jobs."

"I feel sorry for your wife."

Henry's brow creased. "I don't have a wife."

"Not yet, but I'm sure some pretty girl like Louisa Geiger will catch your fancy before long."

"What if one already has?"

Everything - her heart, her thoughts, her very breath - was arrested by his question. When they restarted doubts assailed her. Who had captured his attention? How had she lost him already? Barely more than a breath did she whisper, "Who?"

Their eyes collided as she waited for him to answer, unsure if he had even heard her question. Then his eyes moved away, looking to the porch behind her as it registered that her mother had called to her.

She glanced back over her shoulder and called out, "Coming, Momma." She turned back to Henry. Desperate to ask the question again, she opened her mouth and struggled to find her voice, but too scared to know the answer, she closed it again. She noticed the amusement in his eyes. Could he be teasing her? She didn't have time to figure it out. "Good day, Henry."

"Have a good day, Emily. Tell your mother I said hello."

"I will." Reluctantly she turned from him and walked to her mother. As they turned towards home, she glanced back to find Henry standing in the same spot still watching her. She waved, and he returned it. She turned forward and bit her lower lip resisting the urge to look at him again. She considered the possibility that he may have been referring to her. Did she dare to hope she was the one to catch his fancy? She certainly had been dreaming of it since before he left and even more so after he sent her the miniature. What man would do that, unless he had tender feelings?

* * *

Henry called himself all kinds of a fool for practically declaring himself to Emily. How had his feelings for her grown in such a short amount of time? Here he was exposing how he felt to her when he hadn't even realized it himself. He knew he found her attractive from the moment he first saw her all grown up, but when had attraction become more? The thing of it was, now that he was consciously aware of it, his feelings were even stronger. With awestruck wonder, he realized he could well be on his way to falling in love with Emily.

His veiled declaration shocked her. He just wasn't sure if it was in a good way or bad. They had always been friends. Could she see him as something more than a friend? He didn't know if she was courting with anyone else. He may have overstepped his bounds, but yet, she didn't seem offended, only surprised and confused.

He dropped his gaze from her retreating back and made his way into the hammock. A short while later, he ducked under the web of a spiny-backed orb-weaver spanning between tree branches to take a seat on a fallen log, having spotted a nearby box turtle foraging in the decaying leaves. He opened his sketch book to begin drawing the turtle. Instead, when he held the charcoal pencil to the page, his mind was filled with Emily's blushing face and soft smile. Giving in to his thoughts, he began drawing her image from memory. When he finished, he began another image of her and yet another, trying to capture her true essence and failing miserably.

* * *

Henry sat bolt upright in bed and for a second he had no idea what had awaken him until he felt the small body wriggling into bed beside him and a little voice murmur, "Henry, I'm scarsed." Henry smiled at his little brother's mispronunciation as he wrapped his arm around James and helped him to crawl under the covers. Another flash outside the window was rapidly followed by a crack that made them both flinch. It continued into an ominous rumble sounding as if it was only mere feet above the roof of the house. James cowered into Henry's side. He soothed his little brother as best he could. Another flash made him clasp James tight in anticipation of the coming explosion of thunder. The storm was right over top of them.

Fortunately, he was able to ease James back to sleep in mere moments. Sometimes being the big brother felt good. He was glad James no longer treated him like a stranger. Since his return, he had worked to build the trust between them, engaging James in play whenever he could. Last night he read him to sleep.

The door creaked open and Betsy peeked in to check on her young son. Seeing his empty bed she turned to Henry's and smiled. "All is well?"

"Yes, ma'am."

She came into the room and smoothed the hair back from James' forehead. She leaned down to kiss his cheek. She then kissed Henry's too. "Thank you."

He smiled. "You're welcome."

Quietly she left the room.

The storm continued its fury, occasionally making James flinch, but he didn't waken. Henry, on the other hand, was having trouble going back to sleep. The steady beating of the rain on the roof brought to mind the time he and a friend were wandering deep in the hammock near the salt ponds while unbeknownst to them, Emily was trailing behind. She must have been five or six years old to his eight or nine.

A sudden downpour overtook them, and he and his buddy started running back home. It came as a surprise to hear a frightened voice scream his name. He turned around to find Emily sprawled in the leaves and muck, having tripped over some tangled tree roots. He helped her up and brushed off her knees, but she whimpered in pain trying valiantly to hold back her tears. She had badly sprained her ankle, and even with his support, it was too much to walk. He sent his friend to bring help while they waited getting soaked to the skin. When Emily started shivering, he bundled her close to him. After a few minutes, he tried to carry her. Not being able to see the ground he was treading, he stumbled a few times. His energy soon gave out, so they huddled under the large leaves of a pigeon plum and waited for help to arrive. Listening for sounds of someone approaching, they didn't speak. He remembered being mad she had followed them, but he was also impressed by her bravery.

He must have fallen asleep for the next thing he knew, it was morning and the birds were calling loudly outside his window. He was late. He sat upright, disturbing James, but then he heard the soft patter of rain and relaxed. They couldn't sponge fish till the weather cleared, and Mr. Tate would take care of any of the other tasks needed. Besides, it was Saturday. He laid back down, taking a few moments to enjoy lingering in bed listening to nature's melody until James stirred and woke. His little brother sat up on his knees and then giggled, collapsing across Henry's chest. Henry tickled him to keep him laughing, and then he climbed out of bed carrying James under his arm with his limbs dangling towards the floor. James squirmed in protest until Henry put him down. "Let's get you dressed little man."

Henry pulled open James' dresser drawer to get his clothes, but a plump little hand pushed him away, "I do." Henry smirked at the almost four year old's independent spirit. He stepped away to await his turn at the dresser. James pulled out a shirt, knee breeches, and socks before struggling to shut the drawer. He finally got it closed and scampered over to his bed. Henry opened his drawer and was surprised to find a new pair of trousers and shirt waiting for him. It was easy to see they were handmade by his mother who used to be the town seamstress until she sold her shop to devote all her time to her children. They were meant to be work clothes to supplement what he had so the laundry wouldn't have to be done as often, but he couldn't bear to ruin something so new. He glanced out the window at the overcast sky. The rain had stopped, but it still dripped from the leaves of the lime tree. He would wear his old clothes just in case the weather cleared, and he ended up fishing.

Henry had to help James buckle his shoes, but otherwise, his little brother dressed himself. When done, he raced down the stairs. Henry followed behind in time to see James launch himself into his father's arms for a bear hug. Henry felt a stab of jealousy for the open affection displayed between them. There had always been affection between Henry and his father, but never so freely expressed.

When he was James' age, his father was grieving for his first wife, Henry's birth mother. To cope, his father focused on his work. Henry understood that now. When they moved to Key West, his father became involved in reporting on the Seminole War which kept him away from home, often six months at a time or longer. His half-sisters felt the effects of his absence the same as him. It seemed as if they were always trying to get reacquainted or saying goodbye to their father. James was born after the war ended, making his relationship different. Henry certainly didn't begrudge him their father's attention, he only wished to have had the same knowing how special it was from the few moments of closeness he could recall.

Theodore looked to Henry. "Come join us for breakfast. Your sister made griddlecakes."

After the family meal, Henry left with sketchbook in hand, headed to Mr. Tate's warehouse. He found the old man sitting on a barrel whittling. He confirmed Henry's assessment. There was no work to be done until the sky cleared. It was not worth the risk of getting caught in a storm. Freed once again from responsibility, Henry went on the hunt for something to draw.

* * *

Emily and her cousin Laura were strolling about town ostensibly to stretch their legs, but Emily hoped the gray skies would lead her to a meeting with Henry. His question of yesterday still haunted her. If he had already found a lady of interest, she wanted to know who it was before someone else told her.

Laura drew her towards the milliner's shop to look at a new hat in the window. Emily obediently stepped to the glass to see what had caught her cousin's fancy. When Laura declared she must take a closer look, Emily distractedly told her to go in without her. She had spotted Henry walking towards them from further down the street. When he got closer, Emily casually walked to the post supporting the roof overhang and pretended to be adjusting the fit of her glove while keeping a surreptitious eye on him. She was pleased when he noticed her presence saving her the embarrassment of calling out to him again as she had done yesterday. It simply wouldn't do to appear too forward.

Henry tipped his hat in greeting as he paused to speak with her. "Good morning, Emily." He nodded towards the window behind her. "Have you been shopping?"

She smiled good-naturedly. "Good morning to you. No, that would be my cousin."

Henry stepped close to the boardwalk in front of her bringing him eye level to her. "I remember a time when hats and frivolities were beneath your notice." His gaze traveled over her from the brim of her straw bonnet to the toe of her polished boot peeking from beneath her ruffled hem and back to her face. His eyebrows rose. "My how things have changed."

Flustered as she had never been before, Emily retorted, "You sir, are no gentleman."

Henry smiled. "While you are now every inch a lady."

A nervous laugh escaped her. "I cannot tell if you mean to insult or compliment me."

"That would be because I have yet to decide if I prefer the tomboy or the lady."

The warmth of his gaze and the hidden smile twitching the corner of his lips discomposed her, and she realized, with some surprise, he was flirting with her. As she was trying to come up with a suitable response, he changed the subject.

"Would you care to walk with me? I want to draw you and here is not a suitable setting."

She frowned not sure if his request was contrived or serious. "I suppose..."

Laura stepped out of the shop diverting his attention. "Hello, Henry. It's nice to see you again."

Henry tipped his hat to Laura. "Likewise, Miss Bennington."

Emily's chin dropped in surprise and envy. He didn't use Laura's given name even though Laura had used his, and she was younger than Emily. If anyone should be referred to as 'miss' it should be her, not Laura.

Henry looked from one lady to the other. "I was just suggesting a stroll to Miss Eatonton to find a suitable location to draw her portrait. Would you care to join us?"

Laura's gaze swept to Emily. Her eyes widened in curiosity.

Emily's ire was soothed by Henry's use of her surname but contradicted by her immediate preference for the intimacy of her given name. What had gotten into her? It was unlike her to be so wishy-washy and emotional.

Wishing to keep his attention to herself and dang the consequences, Emily turned to her cousin. "Laura, didn't you say you have some packing to do since you are leaving in a few days?" She pleaded with her eyes for her cousin to give them space.

"Why yes, I do. When shall I tell Aunt Abby you will return?"

"In an hour or so." Emily kissed her cheek and whispered, "Thank you."

"Don't take too long."

Laura turned away, and Emily cast a brilliant smile to Henry. "Where would you suggest we go?"

Chapter 5

A lift of wind and faster spin
To dance across the Atlantic

Henry cast a glance to their surroundings, looking for a suitable background for her portrait. "I'm not sure yet where we should go."

Emily was flattered he wanted to do her portrait. She, too, looked around them for ideas. She recalled stories from older girls of how boys would trick them into walking the foot bridge across the pond as an excuse to put their hands on their waists, supposedly to keep them from falling. Wanting to test this idea with Henry, Emily considered what location she could suggest. "The Porter house has a very grand front porch."

"Where is it?"

"Across the pond. You walked past it yesterday. It used to be Judge Webb's house."

"Oh yes, I know the one. It does have a nice porch. If you don't think the Porter's will mind..."

"I don't think so. They are nice people."

Henry held out his hand for her to grasp as she stepped down from the boardwalk. They made their way between the buildings, ducking between overgrown bushes and wading through tall grasses. They arrived at the edge of the tidal pond with the footbridge to their left. Henry turned to the right. Clearly, he intended to walk the long way around, defeating her purpose.

"Henry, why don't we cross the bridge?"

He turned and gave first her, and then the bridge, a skeptical look.

Emily cajoled. "It's a much shorter walk."

"I assumed you would not want to risk crossing it in your long skirts."

Emily smiled. "I daresay I can manage."

He shrugged. "If you wish." He followed her lead.

Emily grasped her dress with both hands to lift her hem and stepped up onto the planks of lumber spanning between rock piles. The boards couldn't be much more than two feet wide. Emily had to admit it was easier to manage years ago when her hem fell just below her knees, but she was not about to turn around now. She held one arm out to keep her balance and took a few steps forward. She wobbled as she felt the boards shift with Henry's added weight, but it was well worth it when she felt his hand touch her side just above her waist to steady her. He quickly dropped it again. It was just past high tide and the water level in the pond was high. Even so, Emily knew the deepest point wasn't much past a foot deep. There was no real danger to her person, only her dress and her dignity, should she fall. She took a few more steps forward but didn't feel him move. She glanced back over her shoulder to see him tucking his sketch book into his waistband against his back, securing it under his suspenders. Now both his hands were free. She turned forward again, and bit her lip as she grinned in anticipation.

Not wanting to seem too obvious, she took a few more tentative steps. She could feel him right behind her. About halfway, she pretended to lose her balance and even though it was her goal, when both of his hands landed on her waist, the shock of the intimacy almost made her lose her balance for real. She felt the heat of his touch through the layers of clothing. His breath stirred the wisps of hair along her nape like a caress. His closeness made her feel lightheaded and giddy, like the first time she drank a full glass of wine.

Henry leaned forward to whisper in her ear, "Steady now."

The closeness made her breath shallow and rapid. She knew, placed as his hands were, he would notice. Perversely, she did not want him to know how he affected her, so she stepped forward breaking the contact. She made a point of focusing her attention on her foot placement to distract her from the lingering feel of his touch and the tingling in her neck from his warm breath. It was almost a relief to step once again on solid ground.

Now they walked side by side but not touching. Emily broke the silence that had descended between them. "I forgot to ask. Why do you want to draw me?"

Henry kept his eyes forward. "You have a pleasing profile."

Her cheeks flushed with the unexpected compliment. "I thought you drew landscapes and animals."

"I do, but I've found an interest in people too since being out west. It started with this old Indian at Fort Gibson. He was a warrior with a strong, proud profile. Every day he would sit still for hours in the sunshine for no reason that I could discern. I found myself itching to draw him." He turned to look at her. "I don't suppose that makes sense to you."

"What? Itching to draw him?"

Henry nodded.

"It does. You couldn't resist trying your hand at capturing his likeness on paper and testing your talent."

"Yes, that's exactly it. So one day, sketchbook in hand, I sat a little ways from him hoping to keep him unaware of my intentions and started drawing." Henry pulled his sketchbook out from under his suspenders and started flipping through the pages at the beginning. When he found it, he passed the book to Emily.

"I see what you mean. He does have a very proud bearing, and his wrinkled skin gives him lots of character. This drawing is good." She looked up at him. "Do you think you captured him faithfully?"

Henry's shoulders lifted slightly. "I did better than expected for my first attempt at a person, but to answer your question, no. I didn't capture his spirit. He just looks old on paper, but in person, he had vitality, as if he would stand and fight again if needed."

They had reached their destination, but Emily didn't return his book just yet. She admired the image on the opposite page. "You seem to have captured the spirit of this horse. I see loyalty in his eye."

Henry smiled, but it was tinged with sadness. "He was very loyal."

She heard the possessiveness in his voice. "Yours?"

Henry nodded. "Cisco. I hated having to leave him behind."

"You couldn't bring him with you?"

"I couldn't afford his passage on the ship. Besides, what would I do with a horse here?" He gestured with his chin to their surroundings. "Cisco would have hated it. He loves running across the open prairies."

"You miss it too. I can see you riding him at a flat out run and loving the freedom of it."

Henry nodded. "When I first got out west, I had to learn to ride. I was too young to learn in New York, and of course, a horse isn't needed to get around here. Turned out I was good with horses, which got me a job as a stable lad. I was saving my money to buy my own horse." He smiled at Emily. "Did you know I gave all my sponge cleaning earnings to my mother?" Emily shook her head. "I did. I thought she needed it with my father gone all the time, and all the talk about how the war was hurting everyone. I was so proud to be contributing to the family. She saved every penny of it, and she sent it me. Even after I left the way I did, she still sent it to me." Henry paused, still overwhelmed by his mother's generosity.

Emily quietly waited for him to go on.

"Well, it was enough to buy a little colt newly weaned from its mother. He was a brown and white paint, and I named him Cisco. I raised him big and strong and trained him every day. Everyone said how good I did, especially not knowing anything about raising horses. Took me a while to earn my own saddle, and when I did, I set off for Texas to join the rangers. Did you know rangers have to have their own horse and weapons? The government doesn't provide it like they do for the army. Anyway, Cisco did me proud and saved my life more than once. Hardest thing I ever did was sell him. When it came time to turn over the reins, I almost jumped on him and hightailed it back to Texas."

"Why didn't you?"

He hadn't meant to tell her so much. He wasn't sure he was ready to answer her question. Partly because he was afraid she might not believe him. "Are you saying I shouldn't have come back?'

Emily frowned. "Of course not." She let his deflection of the question stand. Whatever his reasons for coming home, they must have been profound and very private. As she handed the sketch book back to him, the pages flipped in a giant cluster giving her a brief glimpse of a page with her likeness. It was of her face, but with a soft look she had never seen reflected back from the mirror. *Is that how he sees me?*

Henry took the sketchbook from her and gestured to the porch stairs. "Stand about halfway up the steps and gaze towards your house."

She did as he directed and was dismayed to see Christoff and Thorn almost upon them. Caught up in their conversation, neither she nor Henry had noticed their approach.

Thorn reached them first. "Emily, Momma wants you to come home right now."

An angry Christoff walked directly up to Henry as if they had never been friends. "I saw you making fresh with my sister."

Henry stood his ground but said nothing. He certainly couldn't deny putting his hands on Emily.

Emily's eyes widened in disbelief. Her younger brothers were taking the over-protective guardian role too far. She had heard of them acting in such a way behind her back, but this was the first time they had done so in her presence. She put her hands on her hips and addressed Christoff from her elevated position. "What do you mean accusing him of making fresh with me?"

Christoff turned his gaze to Emily. "All the boys know you entice a girl across the foot bridge for a chance to lay hands on them. That's what his intentions were taking you across the pond, and he succeeded too. I saw him."

Emily smugly replied, "You're wrong. It was my idea to cross the pond, not his."

"Then you should be ashamed of yourself."

She hated the way he sounded like father but at least she could argue her defense with him. If father had said that to her, she would have had to bite her tongue. She moved down two steps and kept her voice deceptively calm as she took on a battle of reason with Christoff. "Why should I be ashamed? Just because I wanted to take the shortest route?"

Christoff's eyes narrowed. "Why were you crossing in the first place?"

Emily knew he was trying to prove Henry manipulated her. "To come here."

"And whose idea was it to come here?" His head tilted towards Henry in anticipation of her answer.

Emily smirked. "Mine."

Christoff's eyes narrowed as he turned to face her direct. "Why were you coming here?"

Emily lightened her features and tone to convey innocence. "So he could draw my portrait."

Christoff's face gleamed in triumph. "His idea. Right?"

She wasn't about to let him win this argument. "No. It was mine." She crossed her arms over her chest and dared him to call her a liar.

Christoff turned from her to Henry. "Is that so?"

Henry wasn't sure what to do. He couldn't lie, but he also didn't want to confirm Emily was lying. He lifted his gaze to hers and saw her pleading look.

Emily felt Henry's reluctance and sought to divert Christoff's attention. "What does Momma want?"

Thorn was quick to answer. "She said you should know better than to be alone with a boy, and we was to bring you home right away."

She faked a lighthearted laugh. "That's silly. Why can't I be alone with Henry? He's like an older brother to me."

Henry didn't like the way she declared him an older brother. He wanted, needed her to feel something more. Her antics on the foot bridge gave him cause to hope, but perhaps she really had wobbled.

Christoff glared at his sister. "That was before. Now you're soon to be seventeen and he's twenty. You can't act like you did before. It's not proper and well you know it."

Checkmate. She never could win an argument against Christoff. She glared at her brother. "You should be a lawyer."

He grinned with pride. "I plan to one day."

A sudden thought made her shrewdly study him. She turned her attention to Thorn. His earlier answer sounded rehearsed. She descended the remaining steps and approached Thorn, firmly holding his gaze. "Did Momma really send you?" Thorn dropped his eyes to the ground and shuffled his feet. Emily sent a glaring look at Christoff and put her hand up when he started to speak. "I don't want to hear it from you. Thorn tell me the truth. Did Momma send you?"

Still looking down, Thorn shook his head.

Emily looked to Christoff. "I thought not."

Christoff walked towards her stopping a pace away. His face was tight with outrage. "No, she didn't, but she would have if she saw what I saw."

Henry stepped between the two siblings and spoke to Emily. "Your brother is right. We can't behave as carefree as we once did."

"Fine. Then Thorn can stay as chaperone." She saw Henry was about to speak, and she cast him a pleading look. "Let's stay. I still want you to do my portrait, and heaven knows when you'll have another free day." She tilted her head but refrained from batting her eyes at him. "Please."

Christoff had ruined the moment for Henry, but if Emily still wanted him to draw her, he would. Since they were children he hadn't been able to deny her anything when she added her eloquent 'please' with her pleading gray eyes. It tugged on his heartstrings and made him willing to do anything she asked.

Emily saw Henry give in and sent a glaring look of dismissal to Christoff. "There, are you satisfied little brother?"

He flinched at her intentional reminder of his filial status, but he wasn't done yet. "Are you sure you want me to be first to tell the story?"

Emily's eyes flared. Christoff hated being bested, and she knew it was likely he would get her in trouble just for spite, but giving in would show weakness he would later use against her. Meddling brothers could be so frustrating. Hiding her true feelings, she casually said, "Henry, I don't believe this is the right place after all. What do you think of the view from our cupola?"

Henry smiled in relief. He didn't have to lie and jeopardize his friendship with Christoff nor put himself on the wrong side of Emily's father. Plus, he actually liked the idea of the treetops and sea for a backdrop with the wind blowing her hair. "Your wish is my command."

* * *

Henry put the final touches on the drawing and then handed the book to Emily for her approval.

"You are quite the artist, Henry. Are you sure you wouldn't rather do this for a living?"

"I think if I had to draw, it would take the pleasure out of it."

She smiled. "Maybe so." She handed the book back to him and watched as his hand moved to grasp the edge of the page in order to tear it from the book. She placed her hand atop his to stop him. "No. Keep it. It's for you. It's only fair you have a likeness of me since I have one of you." She wished she could step closer to him, but Thorn's presence on the other side of the cupola playing with a lizard kept her feet from moving.

Henry said, "Thank you for the portrait and the lovely afternoon. I should be going now."

Emily mutely nodded, frustrated that she couldn't think of a reason for him to stay longer. He had already turned down her mother's invitation to dine with them.

* * *

The following day, Emily dressed for church in high spirits, anxious to see Henry again. As their family joined others in the street walking towards church, her excitement grew. The Whitmore's pew was behind theirs, so she was assured of seeing Henry soon.

Henry walked with his family to St. Paul's Episcopal Church. The foundation was begun before he left and he discovered the church to be still incomplete upon his return. The steeple was just one of many things yet to be realized in the construction, the others being finishing touches on the inside. Lack of funds was the main reason for the years it had taken to build, and the current delay. Until the bell was ordered, they didn't have the dimensions needed to complete the steeple. Impatient to occupy the new larger building, the congregation chose to begin holding services in the new church as soon as it was covered. Fortunately, despite the missing steeple, a temporary roof kept rain from getting into the building.

As they walked the short distance from home to church, Henry was constantly nodding a greeting or stopping to speak with the other townspeople; which was not uncommon on a Sunday morning when almost everyone was walking to one service or the other. What made today unusual was the extra attention he was receiving due to his long absence. His father, especially, was eager to share the news with everyone of his return. It nearly made them late for service.

The incomplete building was not the only change. The congregation, once boasting all the most prominent townsfolk, had dwindled to a small number. When asked, his father said the new Methodist minister Reverend Richardson, had lured many away. It wasn't difficult as he was there to officiate for the Methodists while they were as yet still waiting for their new pastor, Reverend Adams, to arrive. Their Episcopal congregation had endured more than a year without benefit of regular clergy. Henry's family remained steadfast having paid for their pew and preferring not to be involved in the political maelstrom that lately befell the Methodists Church with the split between the northern and southern factions. At least for Key West, there was a positive result from the break in divisions with the departure of the unfavorable Brother Graham. His replacement, Reverend Richardson, was heartily embraced by the community at large making it understandably hard for the Episcopals to remain in a leaderless church.

Reverend Richardson's flock soon outgrew the small twenty by thirty chapel on the outskirts of Eaton Street. They built a larger stone structure on Caroline Street. Ironically, its roof was also incomplete, but this was due to time instead of funding.

Henry was last to enter their pew. As Brianna took her seat, the space where she had stood was filled with Emily's beaming face turned towards his, arresting his movements and disrupting his breathing. For a few moments, her beauty bewitched him. The spell was broken when Christoff elbowed Emily, pulling her gaze from Henry's. He became aware of Brianna tugging on his sleeve to get him to sit down. His father sent him a warning glance as well.

Not long into the service, Henry had trouble focusing on the readings. His gaze kept straying to the appealing profile to his left, to follow the curve of her cheek, the line of her nose, her plump lips and square chin, and the slope of her neck peaking from underneath the heavy copper coil at her nape. The harsh sound of a clearing throat brought his attention back to the reader. Several more times, he fought to keep his gaze and his mind from drifting. Afterwards, he hoped he would not be asked about the service, for he could not recall a single word.

After services, the greetings from townsfolk continued. Mayor Maloney, Marshal Browne, Custom Collector Stephen Mallory, Sheriff Coslin, Doc Weeden, Dr. Whitehurst, young Captain Curry and old Captain Romer, Mr. Patterson, the jovial Captain Geiger, John Bartlum and his friend Tuggy Roberts, Gideon Lowe, William Wall, and of course, their wives and children. Henry's head was aching from trying to place all the faces and names with those he remembered from the past and those that were new to him. And of course, the war with Mexico was on everyone's mind. He was plastered with questions as soon as they learned of his involvement with the Texas Rangers.

It was even more frustrating because all of this attention kept him from seeking out Emily. By the time he was free, she had long since returned home.

Christoff doggedly shadowed Emily preventing any chance of her speaking privately to Henry, much less have a moment alone with him. She was beginning to feel confined like a story she once read of a medieval maiden trapped in a tower. Heaven help her if it crossed Christoff's mind to keep her in her room. She had no doubt he would press their mother to do so. Just wait till he had a sweetheart; she was going to give him back every bit of the grief he was giving her.

* * *

That evening, while Emily was helping her mother wash dishes, her frustration boiled over. "Why must I be the only girl in this house full of brothers?" To her way of thinking, if she had more sisters, Christoff wouldn't be so focused on her whereabouts. Her father too might not be so intimidating to all the boys who had shown an interest in her. He was likely to run Henry off as soon as he discovered her feelings towards him.

She glanced up at her mother in time to see a ghost of pain cross her face. Emily put down the plate she was drying to lay a hand on her mother's arm. "What is it?"

Abby brushed away her unexpected tears triggered by Emily's concern. The pain of her loss could still catch her by surprise sometimes. Memories flooded her mind. She sighed, knowing it was time Emily knew. Grief made her voice soft. "I did have a second daughter." Her unfocused gaze sharped on Emily. She took a fortifying breath. "You had a sister, Catherine Ann."

Reverently, Emily whispered, "Why don't I remember her?"

Feeling the need to touch her, Abby brushed a wisp of Emily's hair from her face. "You were so young, not long past babyhood yourself." She lightly shook her head. "We never told you because she died at birth."

Emily was finding it hard to believe her family had such a deep secret. "When?"

"Do you remember the first time you and Christoff stayed overnight with Betsy?"

Emily nodded. "Yes, but when we came home you had Thorn."

"No, the first time was before that. You would have been three."

Emily thought back to those days and began sorting out the different images that came to her. In her mind, she had jumbled the two occurrences together, but now she could tell them apart by the difference in

Christoff. She whispered almost to herself, "And you never told us."

"We would have, if you questioned us, but you never asked why there was no baby. I suppose it didn't occur to your young mind to question my decreased belly, and it swelled again soon enough, I suppose."

"Did you bury her? Did we go to the funeral?"

Abby pushed away the harsh grief of that painful day. "Yes, she is buried in the cemetery, and no, you didn't go. No one did. Your father and I wanted to bury her alone with only Mr. Whitehead to say the blessing over her tiny coffin."

The heartbreak on her mother's face was so strong one would have thought it had happened yesterday. Her mother looked as if she could burst into a torrent of tears, but she didn't. She turned back to scrubbing the dirty pan in the sink. In a few moments, her voice returned to normal. Emily regretted her rash words that opened such a raw wound for her mother. She promised herself tomorrow she would go lay flowers on her sister's grave.

* * *

It was two days later, and late afternoon, before Emily was able to get away from the house. The day following her mother's confession, her father announced the *Abigail Rose* had returned from England and would leave again the next day for Mobile, Alabama with Max as captain to return Laura to her family home near Montgomery. Christoff was going with them to learn more of the family business of merchant shipping. Yesterday was a flurry of preparations and this morning the family had gone down to the wharf to wave them off. The mid-day meal with her mother, Thorn, Nate, and Jacob was a solemn affair. Her father's absence was a usual occurrence, but Christoff's empty chair was disquieting especially for their mother, and after months of Laura's cheerful presence, they all keenly felt the loss of her company.

* * *

Emily stealthily left the house in order to elude her brothers. With Christoff's departure, Thorn and Nate were now her self-appointed chaperones. If they followed her on her errand it would lead to uncomfortable explanations she would rather avoid. Hoping to remain unseen, she kept close to the houses on her side of Whitehead Street, passing under trees and bushes growing profusely at the front edge of each yard to further conceal her passage. She was headed towards the cemetery on south beach, knowing the one near the Marine Hospital had not been used except by the military since shortly after she was born. As she passed the courthouse at Jackson Square, she cast a quick glance over her shoulder, relieved to find the street empty. She walked freely now and soon passed the last house. Whitehead Street faded into nothing more than a cleared path leading to the beach.

It was a pleasant walk, if one ignored the constant annoyance of mosquitoes. The trees and underbrush soon gave way to open coastline. She glanced to the right, taking a moment to admire the lighthouse. She then turned left. She had only been in the cemetery a few times paying her respects when members of other families were buried, never knowing she had a sister in eternal slumber.

She climbed the sand ridge and looked over the sea of markers. Even though the cemetery had only been in use the last fifteen years, there were enough graves to make her search difficult. She stopped at every stone and wooden cross to read the inscription. Most of the names she recognized and she could even recall the faces of many of them. She paused when she found the headstones of Agatha Perry and Madalyn Whitmore, Henry's great aunt and baby sister. It struck her as odd to now know, after all this time, they both had sisters buried here. There were wilted flowers on the graves. She guessed they were placed there recently. She wondered if Henry had done so but thought it more likely one of his parents had. She found the grave she sought close by. Seeing the name and date carved in the polished limestone made the sense of loss, heretofore unknown, seem real.

Catherine Ann Eatonton
Born & Died the 18th of March, 1833.
Beloved

Emily carefully laid the flowers on the stone marker. She wondered what it would have been like to have a sister had Catherine lived. Would they have gotten along or fought as bitterly as her brothers sometimes did? Would she have minded sharing her room? A smile tilted the corner of Emily's lips. She certainly wouldn't have minded sharing the chores.

She said a prayer for her sister's soul and turned to leave. Henry's quiet presence at the graveyard's edge startled her. In his hand were small branches supporting clusters of bright orange flowers obviously cut from the tree in Captain Geiger's yard. She paused as she came along side of him.

Henry asked, "Can you wait? I'll be but a moment."

"Yes." She turned to watch the water gently lapping against the shore to give him some privacy. A few moments later he approached, tossing the wilted flowers into the water.

"Can I walk you back?"

The afternoon sun glinted off his dark blond, wind ruffled hair and illuminated the caring concern in his piercing blue eyes. "Of course." She would follow him anywhere.

They both turned and casually began walking towards the lighthouse as if both of a mind to prolong the rare privacy of the moment.

Henry glanced at his companion. "I saw the flowers. I don't think I knew you had a sister."

"I didn't either until day before yesterday."

"How could that be?"

Emily shrugged. "I was only three when she died." Wanting to change the subject, she asked, "How is the sponge fishing? You don't smell today." She inhaled deeply the scent of sea and his own musk.

"We harvested more sponges this morning, but none are ready for cleaning yet." He looked down at her and smiled. "I forewarn you, tomorrow I will be unpleasant again."

She laughed lightly. "Then you may call on me the day after." She meant it as a *repartee,* but she saw the light in his eyes change from mirth to speculation.

He stopped walking and turned fully towards her when she did so as well. "Does that mean you would like for me to call on you?"

Emily was first to break eye contact as she decided what to say. This was the moment of her dreams, when Henry finally saw her as more than a friend, but now that the moment was at hand, she was at a loss as to how to respond.

Her silence made him feel the need to persuade her of his true intentions. "Somehow, since I've returned, my feelings for you have changed. I no longer want to be just your friend... or an older brother."

Her gaze lifted to his, but she remained silent.

He felt like he would burst if he didn't confess his true feelings to her. He could no longer hold back the words. "I think you had my heart a long time ago. I just didn't realize it until I came back. I love you, Emily."

Tears pooled in her eyes. "Oh, Henry."

"Please tell me you feel the same."

Mutely, she nodded.

"You love me?"

His hopeful doubt helped her find her voice. "Yes. I love you too. You must know, I always have."

He tucked a stray tendril behind her ear and softly asked, "Now what do we do?"

Emily had to look away from the intensity of his gaze to garner a clear thought. "Well, I think you have to ask my father for permission to court me, but he left this morning."

Henry shook his head as he chuckled. "I never have done well at timing."

"I suppose we must keep our feelings a secret until such time as you can speak with him."

Henry made a mental note to ask his father about proper courtship. Although he was well versed in what wasn't allowed with a proper lady, he had no idea what allowances were made for courting. Later, hopefully, there would be an engagement, but he must take one step at a time.

They resumed walking in silence and soon turned to enter the cleared path leading back to town. Henry took note of their complete isolation from everyone else on the island. The trees hid them from all, including the elevated view from the lighthouse.

He grasped Emily's hand and gently pulled her to a halt. He desperately wanted to kiss her, but he would not dishonor her by breaking the bounds of propriety, at least not so far as kissing her lips. He settled for lifting her hand to his mouth and placing a kiss against her knuckles. Her bare skin was warm. He smiled, pleased that she wasn't wearing gloves.

Emily's heart jumped. She took a step closer, lifting her face to his. She wondered how she hadn't noticed her head barely reached his chin or how the crystal blue of his irises darkened at the edges. His eyes dropped to her mouth. She licked her suddenly dry lips hoping he would kiss them. She saw the flash of desire in his eyes before he shuttered them.

He took a step back and reluctantly released her hand. "We best get to moving before your brothers come looking for you."

She was disappointed he didn't kiss her but excited by their encounter. Her dreams were finally coming true. Henry cared for her as more than a friend. She shyly cast smiling glances his way as they made their way back to town walking a respectable two feet apart. Already her mind was spinning in an effort to arrange a similar tête-à-tête. Maybe next time he truly would kiss her.

* * *

Henry left the house after supper with no particular destination in mind. His hoped for conversation with his father was delayed as Henry was loath to pull his attention away from playing games with his siblings before supper, and afterwards his parents retired to the parlor deep in conversation. Feeling too uneasy to sit still with his churning emotions, Henry decided to take a walk. Without conscious thought, he made his way to the western shoreline. To his left, the two story Marine Hospital rose up from the sand. In front of him, the sun was low on the horizon creating a rosy glow on the dark water dotted with fishing smacks riding anchor, their crews long since done with the day's work. Cloud wisps hanging low on the horizon intensified the ever changing colors in the sky. It had been more years than he could remember since he last stood in the quiet splendor of a Key West sunset. It was a fitting end to a day such as his.

It was the last conscious thought he gave to God's beautiful work. Though Henry's eyes absorbed every detail of His canvas, Henry's mind was full of Emily. Her soft looks stirred his soul like no other. His hand ached to sketch her square determined chin, her full lips turned upward in a hint of a smile, and her caring eyes that reached into his soul and drew him to her. He longed to see her tresses set free of their restraint to flow about her shoulders as they used to when she was younger. He wanted to know if her thick copper hair was as luxuriant as he recalled.

His mind drifted back to the afternoon's encounter and the

sweetness of her upturned face expectantly waiting. Denying them both the kiss they so badly wanted was the hardest thing he had ever done, but he would not dishonor Emily. For in that moment, it became fixed in his mind she would be his wife. And in that decision, there was one more question he wanted to ask his father. Could he ask Captain Eatonton straight away for Emily's hand in marriage, or must he go through a courtship first?

What would Captain Max say to either question, courtship or marriage? Henry supposed her father's first concern would be if he could support his daughter. And there was his first hurdle. At this moment, the answer was a resounding 'no'. His agreement with Mr. Tate was hardly enough for him to get his own sponging business started in a year. He certainly didn't want to wait that long for Emily. He felt desperate even now, hours later, to kiss her.

He needed to earn more money and fast. Once he had his own boat, he could begin earning enough to eventually build a small house for them. There were many jobs to be had in the community for menial pay but only one well-paying job. His gaze drifted over the water to the men walking the wharf from the barely discernible fort to shore, ending their toil for the day. Signing on with the army would be a sacrifice, but it would greatly decrease the wait to marry Emily. Anything else would take much longer.

He would speak to Captain Dutton in the morning.

Henry's jaw dropped, stunned by his decision. He had arrived on this island a few days ago unsure how long he would visit, but fairly certain he would leave again. Now, here he was planning a business, a wife, and a home. He couldn't say exactly when the decision was made to stay. It was an unconscious result of his growing feelings for Emily. He smiled. He supposed there were worse places to call home than a verdant jewel of an island set between the Gulf and the Atlantic.

Chapter 6

With wild abandon, spinning ever more
Ocean's child learns to play

Henry's mind was far from the task at hand. Captain Dutton ordered him and John Flynn to take an inventory of their remaining building materials for his report to the Corps of Engineers. The dwindling supply of granite blocks was a huge concern. If replenishment didn't arrive soon, it was going to bring a halt to their progress on the fort. But counting the neatly formed stacks of bricks before him slipped Henry's mind when he caught sight of Emily walking past the fort camp with Louisa Geiger and Hannah Watlington ostensibly on their way to the lighthouse. For a moment, he had a clear view of them between the piles of stacked timber. Just before they passed out of sight, Emily happened to look back and wave. Henry doffed his hat in return.

Flynn caught the movement and walked over to see what had distracted his partner. The path was now empty. Henry hoped that would be the end of it as he resumed his counting. Flynn walked out into the clearing and came back grinning. "Which miss has caught your fancy?"

"I was only being polite returning her wave."

"Which one waved?"

"Never you mind. Get back to work."

"I'm guessing it's not the Watlington girl, she's too young for you."

Henry started his count again having lost his place in trying to discourage Flynn's curiosity.

"Is it Louisa Geiger?" He paused to gauge Henry's reaction. "Nah, she's too shy to wave first. It must be Emily Eatonton. That one don't have a shy bone in her body."

Henry's shoulders tensed at the mention of her name, and his jaw clenched at the unintended slur against her character.

"Ah ha! 'Tis the lovely Miss Eatonton what's caught your eye. More's the pity."

Henry's head snapped up to meet his companion's grin. "What do you mean by that?" *He better not further insult Emily.*

"You haven't a chance with the likes of her. Her pa and brothers keep a sharp watch on that lass. Many's a lad that's tried to woo her and failed."

Henry's momentary relief that Flynn meant nothing against Emily was quickly replaced by wary concern. "What do you mean?"

"Most boys she won't bother to give the time of day, but those she has given a chance, like yourself, if they can make it past her brothers' defense, find themselves refused by her pa. My advice, you better get on his good side first 'fore you go asking to step out with his daughter. The other way 'round will do you no good. No good a 'tall." Flynn slapped him on the back, chuckling to himself as he walked past to resume his work.

Henry's spirits sank. Captain Max returned days ago from his sail. Emily was expecting him to speak with her father, but he was having trouble working up the courage to do so. Flynn's words increased his vacillation. What would he do if Captain Max refused to allow him to court her? He was going to have to gather his courage soon before her father sailed again.

* * *

Emily was frustrated to say the least. She was trying hard not to take it out on her younger brother. Jacob was being obstinate about cleaning his room today, and she couldn't leave for her daily walk until he did.

It was Henry's fault, this restlessness in her. It had been weeks since their walk home from the cemetery. Weeks since he had kissed her hand. Weeks of dreaming of him giving her a real kiss. Weeks of trying to see him, much less have a clandestine moment. She shook her head as her breath hissed out through clenched teeth. After emphatically telling everyone he didn't want to work at the fort, he went and signed on with them as a day laborer. She didn't understand it. Why now? At least while he was sponging there were odd times he could slip away. Now, he worked six days a week from sunup to sundown for the army, and he spent Sunday afternoon's cleaning sponges for Mr. Tate. If not for church, she would never see him. As it was, those moments were brief and guarded before service. Afterwards, he was always dashing off to eat and get to the sponges.

Darn blasted sponges! What in the world was his fascination with them? She was sure she would never understand it.

She thought they had come to an understanding during their walk. When her father returned a few days ago, she expected Henry to come calling. His continued absence was concerning her. Maybe he changed his mind. Maybe he found another girl. Maybe she misconstrued his intentions. Emily shook her head to release the morose thoughts. Likely, he was working so hard he wasn't aware of her father's return. Well, if that was the issue, she could do something about it. But how?

The last two days she and her friends had strolled past the fort on their daily walks. The first day she didn't see Henry. Yesterday, she caught a glimpse of him at the last moment, but all she could do was wave. He was gone by the time they were walking back. If she didn't see him today, maybe she could send him a message. Surely there was nothing wrong with a message from one friend to another.

Jacob whined. "I don't wanna clean my room."

"I know, but Momma says you have to, and you don't want to make her mad, do you?"

"No."

"Then pick up your things." He gave her a cajoling smile. Emily shook her head. "It doesn't work on me." She tousled his strawberry blond curls. "Start with gathering up your dirty clothes."

"I don't want to."

"Please, Jacob. I'll buy you a treat."

His blue eyes lit up.

"I'll buy you a piece of licorice if you clean this room in five minutes, AND you don't tell Momma I bribed you. Promise?"

"I promise."

"Good."

"How are you going to know how long it takes?"

"I will count the seconds in my head."

Jacob frowned. Five minutes was a long time. Seconds were short. "How many seconds do I have?"

"Three hundred."

His concern lifted. "That's a lot of seconds. I can do it."

Emily impatiently watched him as he made a production of going around the room haphazardly picking up dirty clothes and putting away his toys. When he began to slow down, she started counting out loud. "One hundred and two, one hundred and three, one hundred and four...." Jacob scrunched his eyes at her in annoyance, but he picked up his pace. When she reached two hundred, he turned to her for approval. She shook her head. "You have to make your side look as good as Nate's side of the room." Jacob cast a disparaging look at Nate's neatly made bed and not a thing out of place. Emily fought to keep her laughter to herself. It took him until two hundred and ninety seven, but he was finally done.

Emily smiled proudly for Jacob's accomplishment and for her ingenious motivation to get him there. "Well done, baby brother." He stuck his tongue out at her. He hated being called baby.

She left the room and jauntily descended the steps. As expected, Louisa and Hannah were waiting for her on the front porch. The three linked arms and started out on their afternoon walk. It worked perfectly for Emily that Louisa had set her cap for Miguel Mabrity, making her more than willing to walk all the way to the lighthouse each afternoon on the off chance she would see him. This made passing the fort a given without Emily revealing her secret desire to see Henry.

Today as they approached the fort camp, Emily was both excited and dismayed to see several men working onshore. She hoped one of them was Henry, but even if he was, there were too many others around to have a private conversation.

* * *

Flynn nudged Henry's shoulder. "Take a looky yonder."

They were loading bricks in wheelbarrows to take out to the fort. He dropped the stack he was carrying and turned to follow Flynn's gaze to find Emily and her friends walking past. He tried to act nonchalant by pretending to ignore them. He kept his head down as he picked up another stack of bricks.

Flynn had no such compunction. He doffed his sweat soaked hat. "Good afternoon, ladies."

The heads of three other fellows working with them snapped up. They smiled broadly as they also called out greetings. Henry's gut tightened. He didn't want them paying attention to Emily. It was settled. He was going by her house after supper. Even if he didn't ask her father to court her, he would tell her to quit walking past the fort. It was unsuitable to put herself on such display.

Once the ladies were out of earshot, Flynn spoke to the group. "Our friend here has a soft spot for Miss Eatonton."

A tall lanky worker, a year younger than Henry, smirked. "Good luck, my friend. Her father doesn't think anyone is good enough for his girl."

The short, squat man next to him said, "My brother tried asking for permission to court her. He said Captain Eatonton nearly scared him senseless."

Henry's gut tightened even more. How was he ever going to work up the courage needed to get permission to court Emily? He smiled as he realized there was a silver lining to Captain Max's reputation. At least his competition was all but extinct. He wiped his brow and went back to work with a smile on his face. She was going to be his, one way or another.

* * *

Emily trudged on to the lighthouse feeling hurt and disappointed. Henry hadn't acknowledged her presence at all. She was sure he had seen her. What did it mean, his ignoring her? The other men had called out greetings causing her companions to blush nearly to the point of swooning. They quickened their pace in flustered embarrassment pulling Emily along with them.

Henry didn't look her way today. Maybe he did have a change of heart, and that's why he hadn't talked to her father. Her companions seemed not to notice her dispirited responses to their conversation. Her disposition further plummeted upon reaching the lighthouse. Much to her friend's delight, Miguel was outside doing chores when they arrived. Louisa and Miguel's animated conversation was hard for her to watch. She left them with Hannah as chaperone and wandered down to the shore on the pretense of looking for seashells.

Twenty minutes later, she returned to find Louisa and Hannah enjoying refreshments on the front porch with Miguel's mother, Barbara Mabrity. Emily was surprised to see her. The family matriarch was normally asleep during the day as she spent her nights tending the light. She was Key West's official lightkeeper having taken over the position when her husband died just six years after the lighthouse was built. It had been her job for the past fourteen years. Miguel told Louisa she was grooming him to take her place soon as she would be turning sixty-five next year.

Mrs. Mabrity rose and walked to the edge of the porch to greet her. "There you are, Emily. Come share some lemonade with us. Did you have a pleasant walk?"

Emily climbed the steps to greet her host. "I did. Your beach is the best on the island. She opened her hand to display the two shells she picked up to further her ruse.

"Those are pretty ones."

"Thank you." Emily gave her a weak smile as she let the shells slip from her fingers into her skirt pocket. "I hope we didn't disturb your slumber."

"Oh no, not at all, dear. I was just telling your friends, I am leaving tomorrow to visit Nicholosa in Tampa. She had twins, you know, last year."

"How exciting. How many children does she have now?"

"Nine with the twins, and I haven't seen the last four of them."

"I can see why you are excited."

"Yes, yes I am." She suddenly regarded Emily more closely. "You look so much like your mother when she first arrived on the island."

Emily feebly smiled feeling a little awkward to be under her scrutiny.

Mrs. Mabrity continued, unaware of her discomfort. "And you're about the same age now as when your father brought her to visit the first time. They were so sweet on each other. Anyone could see it as soon as they set eyes upon them. Was never a doubt those two would marry. Although, there was a brief spell right after when they couldn't seem to get along, but they got past it right enough. It will be your turn soon." She turned to the others. "All of you girls will be married before long. Enjoy these days now. They'll be gone before you know it."

Hannah stood up. "I think we've kept you long enough, Mrs. Mabrity. I'm sure you have more packing to finish."

"Yes, I do."

Emily and Hannah insisted on taking their glasses to the kitchen, following Mrs. Mabrity inside the outbuilding, while Louisa slipped away to say good-bye to Miguel.

On the way back, Louisa's excited chatter masked Emily's melancholy. She parted ways with her friends hopeful they were none the wiser to her misery. As soon as supper was over, she went to her room with the excuse of a headache. She tried to write in her journal but soon succumbed to heartsick tears.

* * *

Henry stood on the front porch of the Eatonton house trying to work up the courage to knock on the door. He could hear the murmur of voices floating through the open parlor window. At least he knew they were finished eating supper. He waited an extra hour before leaving his house to be sure he wouldn't catch them at the table. Henry raised his hand several times and let it fall to his side again just as many. He didn't have anything to offer in the way of a suitor. At least not yet. Was the promise of his future enough to satisfy Captain Max? Against his will, the stories he was told earlier today of the other men who had tried and failed to court Emily came to mind. It caused him to lose what little confidence he had found to bring him this far.

He couldn't risk being turned down. He didn't yet have what it would take to knock on the door. He needed to earn a few more weeks of pay from the fort to begin investing in his sponge fishing. Once he had his own boat and hook and a warehouse, then he would be in a position to ask Captain Max for permission to court his only daughter.

He turned around and cringed at the loud creak of the floor board under his foot. He was hurrying down the steps when Emily stuck her head out the window and called to him.

"Henry, wait."

He had no choice but to turn around and wait for the door to open. He expected to see her sweet face on the other side, so he was quite startled when it turned out to be her father who greeted him.

"Henry, come in. What brings you by?"

Henry hesitantly said, "A visit, sir."

"Always good to see you. How is your family?"

"Good, sir." As he followed the broad shoulders of Emily's father into the house, Flynn's words replayed in his mind: *better get on his good side first 'fore you go asking to step out with his daughter.* It was sound advice but how to go about it? He entered the parlor and made a point of greeting Mrs. Eatonton before giving a brief nod to Emily and each of her brothers. Christoff happened to be standing closest to him. Henry clapped him on the back. "How was your first merchant sail?" Flynn's advice would be best applied to her brother too.

"It went smooth as butter, and I learned a lot." He added in a whispered aside to Henry, "Not the life for me."

Henry kept his face placid so as not to give away Christoff's confidence. To the main conversation, he asked, "Are there plans of another sail?"

Captain Max said, "We leave again in a week. Would you care for something to drink?"

"No thank you, sir."

While her father was relating the details of the next voyage, standing just beyond his shoulder, Emily cast a pointed look in Henry's direction. Faced as he was, Henry had to wait until Captain Max looked away to give a quick shake of his head at Emily. She frowned, and he could clearly see the question in her eyes: *Why?* He hoped he would have a chance later to explain his plan. Tonight was about setting the groundwork for his eventual request.

She would have to learn patience.

When Captain Max finished speaking, Mrs. Eatonton gestured to the settee. "Please have a seat."

"Oh, I hadn't planned to stay long."

Captain Max said, "Surely long enough to have a decent conversation."

Remembering his purpose, he realized it wouldn't do to make a hasty exit. Henry took the seat. Emily was quick to join him, forcing him to stand again until she settled herself, and then he sat beside her. Unnerved by her nearness, he did his best to hide it from her parents by trying to pretend it was like days gone by. She was simply his tomboy friend, but instead of a well-worn bland day dress, she was wearing a pink confection and smelled like the sweetest of flowers. He shifted uncomfortably, cleared his throat, and cast about for something to say. Emily's scent brought to mind the bushes on either side of the front porch. "Mrs. Eatonton, I noticed your roses are looking quite healthy."

"Thank you, Henry. They are blooming well this year."

Emily impatiently squirmed next to him. He dared not look at her for fear of giving away his feelings.

Captain Max said, "I hear you are working at the fort. What do you think of its construction?"

Henry smiled and relaxed. Here was an easy subject to talk about. Every aspect of the fort fascinated him. He had already exhausted his family listening to him. "It is a modern marvel of design and is being built so sturdy it will surely stand for centuries. I bet it will last even longer than Fort Marion in St. Augustine."

"Have you seen the plans?"

"Yes, sir. It is to be trapezoid in shape. The longest side will face the shore and be used for barracks. The other three sides will house cannons facing all the channels leading to the island."

Mrs. Eatonton shook her head. "I don't see the need for such protection. This island is not that valuable."

"I beg to differ ma'am. We are in a strategic location to control shipping between the Gulf of Mexico and the Atlantic Ocean which is vital to our country, and being one of the richest cities, there is much to protect here."

Captain Max laid a hand on his wife's shoulder. "He is right, dear, and with the fort we'll have nothing to worry about from our enemies should they decide to make war."

"Surely we will not be going to war again."

"I doubt we will with England, but Spain and Mexico are not content with us. It is only prudent to be prepared. Besides a fort will keep the military here, and that is always good for Key West."

"I suppose you're right."

Emily nudged Henry's shoulder with hers attracting the sharp eye of her father. He pulled away but froze as she spoke, "Henry has something he would like to ask you father?" She turned to smile at him. His gut sank as if he had swallowed stones.

He turned his head away from the room and harshly whispered in her ear, "Not now." He turned back to find Captain Max studying them closely. Henry swallowed hard when the captain rose from his seat. "Perhaps you would be more comfortable speaking in my study?" He held his hand towards the door. "Shall we adjourn there?"

Knowing it was a statement and not a question, Henry rose on shaky legs and preceded him out the door. As he left the room, he heard Mrs. Eatonton address Emily in an admonishing tone. He hung his head. This was not how he wanted this conversation to go. He couldn't imagine what Captain Max must think of him. He turned into the study and stepped aside for Captain Max to enter the room. He waited for him to indicate if Henry should sit or stand. Silently, the captain moved to the sideboard and poured two drinks, handing one to Henry.

"You look as if you need this."

Henry accepted the drink and braced his shoulders. Showing weakness would not bode well, no matter how this meeting proceeded. He needed to take this conversation in hand if he hoped to ever win her hand. "Captain Max, Emily believes I'm here to ask your permission to court her, but that is not the case."

"It's not? Then why are you here? If she has such ideas are you toying with her affections?"

"To be honest, sir, that was my original intention, but I've come to realize I need to further improve my circumstances before I can consider a wife." He held Captain Max's gaze as he waited for his response, resisting the urge to fidget as the seconds ticked on the grandfather clock behind him.

Captain Max said, "Emily is headstrong and impatient."

Henry held his smile in check. "Yes, sir."

Max continued. "Most men would consider that a flaw in a wife to be beaten out of them."

Henry failed to hide his shock. "I would never, sir. Most of the time, I like those qualities in her."

"Except when they land you in situations such as this."

Sheepishly he nodded. "Yes, sir."

"What are your intentions?"

"I was planning to wait until I earned enough to get my business going before asking your permission to court Emily. I then hoped to be able to at least rent a house if not build one before asking for her hand in marriage." Captain Max's eyes widened as he said the last. Clearly her father was not expecting the seriousness of his intentions.

Captain Max swallowed hard before speaking. Avoiding the more sensitive subject of marriage, he asked, "What business are you starting?"

"Sponge fishing. I believe Key West can compete in the larger markets once the industry is built up enough to supply the demand. We have superior sponges. I need a few more weeks of working at the fort to get started, first on my own, but eventually, I intend to have a crew of hookers and cleaners."

"You have purpose, and you're being sensible." He crossed his arms over his chest and ran his fingers over his mustache before speaking again. "What are your feelings for Emily?"

Henry frowned unsure what he was asking. "I want to marry her, sir."

"You've said as much. Is that why you returned?"

"No, sir. At least, I didn't think so at first." A thought occurred to him. *Was this why God called him home?*

Max said, "What do you mean?"

He wasn't sure how much he wanted to tell this man. Would the truth sound silly to him? Maybe it was best not to reveal God's calling, at least not yet. "I returned for my family. Until I saw Emily, I had no idea I was harboring tender feelings for her."

"Whereas, Emily believes she has loved you all her life."

Henry was too surprised to hide his shock. "She has?"

Captain Max remained silent.

Suddenly, Henry understood what Captain Max was waiting to hear. Carefully, he set down his untouched drink and faced the captain with all the bravery he could muster. "Sir, I have come to realize I love your daughter. I want to give her a lifetime of happiness. I wish for her to be my wife if you will give your blessing."

After a heart-stopping moment, her father's face relaxed into a smile. "Henry, one day I will be proud to claim you as a son-in-law, but for now, you only have permission to court my daughter. An engagement will wait according to your own plans until you can truly support her. Emily will have to learn patience." He raised his glass for a toast.

Henry picked up his glass and held it aloft.

Captain Max clinked his glass to Henry's. "To true love."

"To true love." They both took a sip. "Thank you, sir."

Max gave the young man a piercing look. "For the sake of peace for both of us, I suggest you mention nothing of marriage to Emily until you have met at least the first of your goals. It will be our secret."

"Yes, sir."

"And since you are only courting, you will act accordingly."

"Yes, sir." Henry clearly understood his meaning. No kissing – at least not on the lips.

"I suppose we should call it a night. I expect to see you Sunday to walk Emily to church."

"Yes, sir."

Captain Max walked him to the door. Henry wasn't sure if he was hurt or relieved not to speak to Emily again. Tomorrow was Thursday. He would have to wait until Sunday to see her again. He smiled as a thought occurred to him. Come Sunday, everyone would know Emily was his girl simply because he had her father's approval.

Emily was fidgeting something fierce by the time she heard Henry and her father leaving his study. She impatiently waited for their appearance to learn what had been said. The opening of the front door and her father's dismissal of Henry made her heart sink. He must have refused Henry. She watched as her father calmly entered the room, kissed her mother's cheek as if nothing major had occurred, and settled in with his paper.

"Father!"

Max lifted his eyes to his daughter while keeping his smirking grin hidden behind the paper. "Yes?"

"How could you?"

He shook his head. "How could I what, sweetheart?"

Emily flounced to her feet. "How could you refuse him?"

Abby gave her daughter a stern look. "You are too old to be throwing a tantrum. Calm yourself."

"How can I be calm when father has refused the man I love?"

Max lowered his paper. "I was not aware you were in love with anyone, especially not an old chum like Henry."

"But, I am. And now you've refused him." She was close to tears. "I don't think he will ever work up the courage to ask again."

Abby said, "If you think so little of his courage then perhaps you should reconsider your feelings for him."

"Oh Momma, how could you understand?"

"I understand more than you know."

Max sighed. His daughter needed to learn patience, prudence, and obedience if was to make a good wife one day. "Emily Rose, first you are being disrespectful to your parents. Second, if you were patient you would have soon learned what you wished to know. Since you are sadly lacking in that virtue, you will now have to wait until I decide you have learned some patience to discover what has been decided, and since you seem to be struggling with decorum as well, I think it best if you do not leave this house again until Sunday services to give you time to ponder what all it means to be a lady."

Emily opened her mouth to voice her complaint, but a stern look from her mother kept her silent. Her impetuous impulses had got her into trouble again. All she could do now was meekly obey. "Yes, Father." She resumed her seat and picked up the handkerchief she was haphazardly embroidering. She got little accomplished in the way of stitches with her mind disturbed by all that had happened this evening. The scene kept replaying over and over in her mind with the same conclusion. She dearly wished she had not spoken up and forced the issue between Henry and her father. Perhaps Henry understood something she didn't which made him reluctant to speak. In any case, she had to find the patience to wait until Sunday before she would learn anything from her father or Henry. Hopefully, she would have a chance to speak with him before church services.

Chapter 7

Frenzied and erratic, fickle as a sailor's heart
A mercurial wanderer drifting about the equator

Sunday morning dawned bright and beautiful to match the buoyancy of Emily's spirits. Today ended her isolation. The punishment for her impetuous behavior was difficult for her to bear, making today seem as special as a birthday, which hers happened to be tomorrow. Besides, her mother always said, 'happiness is not the absence of problems but the ability to find joy despite them,' and she was determined to be joyful.

Tomorrow she would be seventeen. Usually there was a special family supper to celebrate birthdays. Perhaps she could persuade her mother to invite Henry's family to join them. It was part of her campaign to win her father over to Henry. Before going to sleep last night, she replayed Wednesday evening over and over in her mind along with her encounter with Henry at the cemetery. Knowing Henry, she believed his feelings were true and would not change simply because her father refused permission to court her. They would simply have to find a way to convince her father to change his mind. Her birthday celebration was the first step in her campaign.

Since her maid, Lydia, had the day off, Emily chose a buttercup yellow dress that buttoned up the front, so she could dress without help. It had a rounded neckline dipping low enough to show her collarbone; a little too much skin for church, but not so much her mother would make her change. It was her favorite dress. She wanted to look her best when she saw Henry again. She was afraid he may be cross with her for forcing the conversation with her father.

She had just finished pulling her hair up in a chignon when her mother called the family to breakfast. Emily gave a last look in her vanity mirror, pinching her cheeks for color. She spun from her reflection, skipped from her room, and lightly descended the stairs. She passed her father seated at the head of the table and paused to kiss his cheek. She tousled Jacob's curls, and took her seat with a happy smile.

Her mother placed a platter of fluffy eggs in the center of the table to join the covered basket of biscuits and bowl of sawmill gravy; her father's favorite breakfast. She then took her seat and bowed her head of age streaked auburn hair for the blessing.

As they all said 'amen', Emily lifted her head and looked around the table at her family. For some reason she felt the need to take a moment to count her blessings. Of course, there was food and a roof over her head with a very well-appointed house underneath. Her family had servants to help cook and clean every day except for Sunday. She had a maid to help her dress in the morning, and to undo the hard to reach buttons and corset strings at bedtime. She was thankful for all of that, but especially for her family.

Her parents sat at either end of the table and were lightheartedly bantering with each other as they usually did at mealtimes when her father was home. Often, he was gone for weeks at a time sailing one of several merchant ships he inherited from her grandfather who passed away two years ago. Emily noticed the deepening laugh lines around her mother's eyes and lips as she smiled, and the silvery gray mixing in with her father's blond queue tied with a strip of leather. His hair was not usually so long. It wouldn't surprise her if her mother insisted on cutting it before he left again.

Next to her father and looking more like him every day, her fifteen year old brother, Christoff, wolfed down his eggs like a starving hound. Growing up she fought with him the most, but he was also her closest companion. In her youth, she preferred to run loose about the island tagging after her younger brother and Henry rather than doing girl things. This was probably because there were no other girls her age. There were many girls on the island, but they were either a few years older or younger than her. Being the tomboy that she was, she could find little common ground with any of them. Christoff may have protested, but he suffered her presence with patience and often humor. Her favorite thing about Christoff was the way he made her laugh.

Sitting next to Christoff, Hawthorne was quick to remind everyone he would be twelve in two months. They had called him Thorn since birth, dubbed so by a two and half year old Christoff who had trouble saying his full name. Before their two youngest brothers came along, Christoff often referred to his two siblings as 'Rose and Thorn'. A moniker which annoyed the recipients but amused most everyone else. Thorn was her serious brother, which made it fun to tease him. He, of course, was also studious and could be found more often than not with his nose in a book, especially if it had anything to do with science or engineering.

On her left was nine year old Nathanial. He was the sweet natured one of the bunch. Emily was sure he was her mother's favorite even though she would protest to her dying breath she loved all her children the same. Nate had bright blonde, curly hair, soft blue eyes, and could charm his way into getting almost anything he wanted, but he was tempered by polite reserve to keep him from being troublesome. That role was filled by her youngest brother, Jacob, sitting on her right. He could be needy and demanding. He was blessed with his father's dimples and sparkling blue eyes framed with strawberry blond curls. He figured out the power of his smile before he was one, and now that he was six, he practiced it on every matron on the island which provided him with an endless supply of penny candy in his pocket. Even as annoying as he could be sometimes, she adored her littlest brother.

She could honestly say of the four of her brothers, she didn't have a favorite. She couldn't imagine life without any one of them.

Her eyes swept to the foot of the table where her mother presided, smiling indulgently over her family. These days, she and her mother butted heads often, mostly concerning what was and wasn't expected of a young lady, but it in no way diminished the pride Emily felt for her. Her mother was often called upon as town midwife and nurse to the sick. Her skills were in high demand now that Mrs. Mallory was getting on in years. Her mother was doing her best to pass on her skills to Emily, but as the sight of blood turned her nauseous, the lessons were not going well.

The servants didn't work on Sunday, so Emily helped her mother clear the table after their meal. They piled all the dishes on a tray to be left by the kitchen sink. They would wash them upon their return from church rather than risk soiling their Sunday clothes before services. Finally, the family was gathering in the foyer preparing to leave. Emily was anxious to get to church to see Henry and gauge his feelings. She hoped it would not take much to persuade him to forgive her for being impetuous, that is, if she even had a chance to speak with him.

A knock at the door startled them all except her father. He strode forward as if expecting someone, but who would he be expecting on Sunday morning?

Max opened the door wide. "Good morning, Henry. Do come in."

Emily's jaw dropped. *What was he doing here?*

A glance passed between her father and Henry, and at her father's nod, Henry approached her. "May I have the honor of escorting you to church, Emily?"

Belatedly, she became aware of her gaping mouth and shut it. She glanced from Henry's serious and hopeful expression to her father's barely hidden mischievous grin. In a flash of understanding, she realized Henry had managed to ask and was granted permission to court her during his visit the other night, but because of her impatience, her father refused to tell her. Irritation threatened to control her words for the briefest of moments until her eyes collided with Henry's pleading ones. She smiled, realizing no matter how it came to pass, she was grateful to have him before her, patiently awaiting her reply. "Nothing would make me happier."

Relief drew Henry's smile wide as he lifted his arm towards the door. "Shall we go?"

Emily nodded and preceded him out the door but waited for him to join her at the top of the porch stairs. He held out his arm. She placed her gloved hand properly on the back of his gloved hand turned palm down. She hoped he couldn't feel her tremble with jittery excitement. Happily, she strolled down the street and proudly nodded to those who greeted them. She surreptitiously cast a glance at her first real beau and their eyes caught.

Henry leaned closer to almost whisper, "I gather your father didn't convey to you the outcome of our conversation the other night."

Emily looked to the ground to hide her blush. "No, he did not, but it was my fault. It was part of my punishment." She bravely raised her gaze to his. "I owe you an apology."

"For what?"

"For not allowing you to speak to my father in your own time."

Henry snickered. "I wonder how long we would still be waiting if you had? I do not need your apology, but I accept it."

She frowned in bewilderment. "You don't think I was improper?"

He chuckled. "I didn't say you weren't improper. I have known you for a long time and realize impropriety is part of your character and usually part of your charm."

"But certainly it is not a becoming trait for a wife."

He looked down at her. "I am not overly concerned. Maturity has a way of curing us of our childish shortcomings."

She laughed. "You are too generous by far."

"Would you rather I did mind?"

"No, because I imagine if you did, you wouldn't be interested in me."

His eyes went soft. "You're wrong. I am interested in spite of any of your failings." He smiled in accompaniment of his teasing note. "And you have several."

"Oh! Failings indeed. I know for a fact your mother taught you it isn't polite to insult a lady."

"Yes she did." His eyes roamed from Emily's head to her hem and back again. "And you are a lovely lady." He paused a moment before quietly adding, "My lady."

Emily's heart fluttered. She liked the idea of being his lady.

They were approaching the other parishioners lingering outside the nearly completed St. Paul's Episcopal Church. She was startled by her father's voice calling out a greeting to Mr. and Mrs. Whitmore from behind her. She had been so entranced with Henry, she had forgotten her family was following them. Henry laid a calming hand atop of hers. The warmth of his fingers heated her blood. To distract her growing physical response to him, she focused on those gathered in the sun's warmth.

Several young ladies cast envious glances in her direction. Emily stiffened her spine, proud to be on the arm of the handsomest, most sought after boy on the island. Nay, man. For he was certainly no longer a boy, and today she didn't feel like a girl. She was living her very own fairytale and couldn't wait for the happily ever after part to begin, but she would content herself with the happiness of here and now. She smiled up at Henry and was rewarded with his charming grin. He led her to a group of friends but they had time for little more than greetings before the visiting reverend called them in for service.

They passed through the entry of the steeple-less church. Emily expected Henry to join his family in the pew behind theirs, but much to her delight, he took his seat next to her. It was distracting having him so near. She had a hard time keeping her focus on the reverend's homily about being good neighbors.

After the service, both families walked together since they were headed in the same direction. Emily couldn't help her delighted grin as her mother issued an invitation to Mrs. Whitmore to join them for supper the following evening to celebrate her birthday. Henry turned his palm up and squeezed her hand causing her cheeks to warm. As the families parted ways in front of her house, Henry lifted her hand to his lips and said, "Until tomorrow."

Emily couldn't contain her broad grin as she watched him walk away. Tomorrow couldn't come soon enough. Christoff nudged her shoulder hard with his as he passed her to climb the porch steps. She thought she heard him whisper something about a fool in love, but she was too happy to mind him.

* * *

Monday morning, September twenty-eighth, Emily awoke to an overcast sky, not that she gave it any notice. Today, she was seventeen, and Henry was courting her. She was in love. She doubted she would notice if the sky was falling. Exuberantly, she flung open the doors of her wardrobe to contemplate her choice of dresses. Now she wished she had not worn the buttercup one yesterday. She was left to choose between her second favorite dresses, a heavy navy, or a light weight pink the style of which felt much too young for her now. She pulled it off the hanger and held it up, recalling how tight it was across her bosom the last time she wore it. Perhaps, it would be best to give it to Brianna. Emily laid the dress across her bed and turned back to her remaining choices. The navy dress was too hot to bear today. She pulled a white shirtwaist off the hanger and paired it with a light blue calico skirt with a wide matching blue ribbon around the middle of her waist. It was everyday and common, but it would have to do. She dressed quickly and hurried downstairs to help her mother finish making breakfast.

Shortly after the midday meal, her three closest friends, Louisa, Hannah, and Brianna, came to wish her a happy birthday and entice her out for a walk. Of course, Louisa was most anxious to walk to the lighthouse. It was easy enough to agree since it suited Emily's purpose to pass the fort camp. The girls chatted about fashion and boys as they made their way to the shoreline. Emily was disappointed in her quest. All the workers were on site, far from shore, as they passed the fort. She was not even afforded a glimpse of Henry.

Louisa interrupted her thoughts. "Are you and Henry soon to be engaged?"

Brianna frowned. "They are not engaged."

Emily heard the defensive tone in Brianna's voice. Was she against a match with her brother? She would have to find a way to delicately ask her about it. She and Brianna were friends. She would hate to lose that over

Henry. To Louisa, she said, "My father gave Henry permission to court me. That is all for now."

Hannah stopped walking to enthusiastically grab Emily's hands. "Oh, how exciting for you. You have a beau." Her face grew serious. "Will you marry him if he asks?"

Emily threw a concerned look at Brianna. Her closed expression was not encouraging. "I don't know, but I doubt I have to concern myself with an answer anytime soon."

Louisa quickened her pace leading them to the lighthouse. "I sure wish Miguel would ask permission to court me."

Brianna shook her head. "I don't see what all the fuss is about getting married. I would rather have my independence. Who needs a man underfoot telling you what to do?"

Emily breathed a sigh of relief. Maybe Brianna was only against marriage in general and not specifically hers to Henry.

The girls had a brief visit with Mrs. Mabrity. Louisa was disappointed not to see Miguel as he had worked long into the morning taking care of the lighthouse and was still sleeping upon their arrival. Emily, however, was excited to see Henry working in the camp on their way back. He then gave her a thrill when he excused himself from the company of the other men to come speak with her.

As Henry approached the group of girls, he doffed his hat to all, but his eyes were only for one. "Good afternoon, ladies." They murmured their greetings in return. As he stepped forward to take Emily's hand, Brianna stepped between them.

Brianna linked her arm with Henry's and turned him back towards the fort. "Show me what you are working on today."

Henry cast a bewildered glance at Emily before facing the fort. "We are building up the foundation with granite blocks. Today we are working on the far curtain wall. Soon it will be high enough you'll be able to see it from here."

Hannah said, "I find it fascinating you can build underwater."

Henry turned to answer her. "We aren't actually building underwater. The sea is held back by breakwater and cofferdams. The water was pumped out once those were in place, giving us a somewhat dry place to work." He turned away from the fort. "Well ladies, I best be getting back." He smiled privately for Emily. "See you for supper, birthday girl."

Emily jauntily waved at him as she trailed behind her friends, reluctant to leave his side.

They had tea upon their return to the house. When they were done, Louisa and Hannah declared it was time to leave. At the door, Emily took Brianna's hand. "Can you stay a little longer? I have something for you."

Brianna nodded. "Of course."

Emily waved goodbye to Hannah and Louisa, and then led Brianna up to her room. She picked up the pink dress she laid across the bed earlier and handed it to her friend. "I can't wear this anymore. I thought you might like it."

Brianna held it to her chest and smoothed the skirt against her legs. "It's lovely. Thank you."

"You're welcome." Emily took a deep breath for courage. "Can I ask you something?"

Brianna lifted her large blue eyes to Emily's gray ones and waited for her to say more.

Emily tossed about for a way to phrase her question. It was not as easy as she thought it would be to ask Brianna how she felt. "Earlier you sounded... upset, I suppose, at the notion of Henry being engaged."

Brianna's mouth thinned, and she inhaled sharply.

Emily hurried to finish before she spoke. "I was wondering if you object to him marrying me, or is it to the idea of him marrying at all?"

Brianna cast her eyes to the floor. Her breath slowly released.

Emily anxiously awaited her answer.

Brianna lifted watery eyes. "He has only just returned. I didn't know he asked to court you. It took me by surprise today. I was, and still am upset over the idea of him leaving home again. It doesn't matter the reason. Of course, if you two decide to marry I'll be happy for you. How could I not be? My best friend and my brother."

Emily rushed to embrace her with tears in her eyes too. "Oh thank goodness. I don't know what I would have done if you were against us."

"How could I be against having you as my sister-in-law?"

"Brianna Kate, you are putting the cart before the horse. He hasn't asked yet."

"No, but he will. One day." Brianna pushed away from Emily. "Thank you for the dress. I'm afraid I must be going. I promised to help mother prepare our contributions for tonight's supper."

"What are you bringing?"

"It's a surprise. I can't tell you."

"Don't you dare show up without cinnamon bread."

Brianna's face fell. "Oh no. It's too late to start making it now."

Emily shook her head. "It's alright. I was just teasing."

* * *

At quarter till seven, Abby received the signal all was ready and shooed her daughter upstairs to change. "You want to look your best for dinner and you have flour all over you."

Emily took her apron off and looked down in dismay. "I have no idea what I am going to change into. I wore my best dress to church yesterday."

"I'm sure you can find something appealing."

Emily hung her apron beside the kitchen door. She sighed heavily as she walked the short distance across the yard to the back door and into the cool house. She took the back stairs up to her room as she mentally reviewed the remaining choices in her closet. Nothing was suitable. She had to admit her wardrobe was deplorable. It was filled with dresses that were too old or too tight. As much as she abhorred the idea, she was going to have to take the time to have a fitting and order more dresses. She had avoided it for too long now.

She opened the door to her room and halted mid-stride. Her hand flew to cover her mouth. There on the other side of her room, hanging from the door of her opened wardrobe, was a beautiful new silk dress of light emerald green trimmed in ecru lace. There was nothing childish in the design. It was a true honest-to-goodness ladies ball gown. Instead of the typical ruffles around the skirt, this dress was decorated from waist to knees with unique horizontal pleats on the front and back skirt panels. The full skirt blossomed out wide enough to encompass the new hoop skirt resting on the floor next to it. It was nearly sleeveless, the neckline of which, edged in delicate lace, draped low from the shoulders and would leave most of her neck bare. Her cheeks pinkened imagining herself in such a décolletage. For certain, her father would never approve. But yet, only her parents would give her such a gift.

Emily felt her mother's hand rest gently across her back. She turned to her with tears glistening. "Thank you. It's beautiful." She embraced her mother then turned back to gaze once more upon her lovely new dress. "Father will never approve of such a dress."

Abby smiled. "Leave your father to me. Happy birthday, Emily."

"I love it, but whenever shall I wear it?"

Abby smiled mischievously. "I suggest tonight."

Emily was horrified. "Oh no. I couldn't risk ruining it at a family dinner and then not be able to wear it to the next party."

Abby's smile grew. "But tonight is the next party. We are hosting a ball in your honor."

Emily's face went blank with incomprehension. "A ball?"

"While you were helping me fix supper, the house was being prepared for our guests."

Emily was confused. "But it takes weeks to plan a ball, and just yesterday I heard you invite the Whitmore's to supper."

"All a ruse to surprise you."

She laughed. "You have surprised me." She looked from the dress back to her mother's smiling face. "A ball? For me? Tonight?" She couldn't imagine why they would make such a fuss over her birthday.

Her mother nodded. "It's been too long since we celebrated anything. I thought your birthday made a good excuse."

Emily could hear guests arriving as Lydia put the finishing touches on her coiffure. Several small sections of hair in front were braided and wrapped around her crown, accentuating the thick coppery plaited coil piled high atop her head interwoven with thin ecru ribbon. Her mother returned wearing a dusty rose gown just as the final pins were put in place. She took Emily's hand, pulling her to her feet to stand before them wearing only her corset, pantalettes, and new green silk slippers. She was helped into the large hoop skirt. Then her mother and Lydia lifted her new dress over her head and settled it over the hoops. Lydia buttoned up the back of her bodice while her mother fussed with straitening the décolletage.

Abby stood back to admire the results. "You look stunning... and so grown up."

Emily stepped towards her dressing mirror. She didn't recognize the woman who looked back at her. The dress draped perfectly over her caged crinoline and the bodice was snug, but not tight, accentuating her womanly figure. Above the neckline, her alabaster skin glowed. The mirror showed her chest to be adequately covered, but when she looked down she saw the hollow valley gaping back at her. Her hand flew to cover it as her panicked eyes searched for her mother's. She felt indecently exposed.

Abby smiled. "I assure you, your dress is considered quite proper for a ball in England, but your father would agree with you, so I brought this to fix it." She shook out an ecru lace fichu and leaned forward to drape it around Emily's neck and knot it above the gentle swell exposed above the dress.

Emily looked in the mirror to study the results. It was better, but still more skin than she had ever shown. She was handed her elbow length gloves and turned towards the door. Her mother gave her arm a gentle squeeze. "It is time to greet your guests."

Emily's father joined them in the hall. His eyes swept over her before glancing at her mother, whom she guessed gave him a warning, before returning to hers with a smile of approval. "You look lovely. May I escort you down?"

"Thank you." Emily took her father's arm. They descended the wide front stairs together, her parents on either side of her. All the candles were lit on the five tier chandelier bathing the foyer below in a soft yellow glow. Indeed, the whole house was suffused in candlelight. Her mother must have borrowed every floor candelabra on the island. Every table surface was adorned with huge bouquets of tropical foliage and flowers. The stair railing was festooned in pink ribbon and bows. She turned to her mother. "The decorations are beautiful."

At the bottom of the steps, she was greeted by the early arrivals, the first of which was the Whitmore family. She graciously accepted their compliments and well wishes. Mrs. Whitmore promised a whole loaf of cinnamon bread, just for her, was safely tucked away in the kitchen for tomorrow's enjoyment. Henry approached last. His adoring admiration deepened her blush. She was not used to such attention.

Henry curled his hand into a fist to keep from brushing his fingers across her rosy cheek. Besides being inappropriate, with her parents flanking either side of her, it would not go unnoticed. The hint of rose water wafting from her bare shoulders was not helping matters. He had to settle for bowing low over her hand. He suppressed the urge to kiss it. Rising, he caught her eyes and tried to convey the fullness of his feelings while polite and acceptable words passed his lips. "Happy birthday, Emily. You indeed will be the belle of your own ball." He handed her a single yellow and white plumeria blossom stolen from his mother's prized plant.

Emily's blush deepened. She lifted the luxuriant petals to her face to lightly breathe in the heady perfume. "Thank you, Henry."

"Could I have the opening dance with you?"

Max cleared his throat. "The opening dance is mine. You may have the second, if Emily wishes it."

Henry accepted his decree and looked to Emily for confirmation.

"It will be my pleasure to dance with you."

With a smile, Henry turned to Abby. "Mrs. Eatonton, would you honor me with the first dance?"

Abby returned his smile. "I would be delighted."

Henry nodded in acceptance and cast one more glance to absorb Emily's loveliness before stepping aside to allow her other guests to greet her.

It was common in Key West for everyone to take advantage of any reason to celebrate. Her parents issued an open invitation for any who wanted to come. Another common trait was for guests to bring food to share. All were welcomed and directed to place their offerings on buffet tables set up in the dining room. Emily stood between her parents for the next half hour greeting most of the town dignitaries along with friends and neighbors. Many complimented her appearance, but Brianna, Hannah, and Louisa especially gushed over her new frock.

Once the receiving line was done, she floated on her father's arm to the yard outside where musicians had set up under the canopy of the mahogany tree. The dancing was opened with a quadrille under a darkened sky. She and her father took their place at the head of the lead square with her mother and Henry opposite. Two other couples joined to make up the sides of the square. Nearby four more couples formed another square including Thorn and Brianna. The dance began with bows to the partner and the corner. The movements of the dance allowed her to briefly dance with Henry. Her pulse leapt every time his hand touched hers. She couldn't keep her eyes from his handsome face causing her to misstep more than once, but her father didn't comment.

At the end of the song, they applauded the musicians and fellow dancers. Henry stepped forward to claim her for the second dance. Emily's heart fluttered as the band conductor announced it would be a waltz. Henry slipped his arm around her waist to lightly splay his hand against her back. Tentatively, she placed her right hand in his upraised left hand. Her left hand settled on the breadth of his muscular shoulder. Otherwise, they maintained a respectable arm's length of distance between them. She, of course, had seen the waltz danced before, but this was her first time in the arms of someone other than a pretend partner. Her heart thudded in her chest aroused by Henry's nearness. She could feel his breath brush her cheek, and her stomach fluttered. Words were hardly spoken between them but much was conveyed in their locked gazes.

Too soon, the song ended, and Henry was forced to relinquish his hold on Emily. Her hand was quickly claimed for the next dance while Henry retreated to the sidelines. With so few ladies and so many men, he did not feel obligated to dance with anyone else.

Supper was served after the fourth dance. Everyone filled their plate and found a place to sit or stand and sample the fare. Henry made sure he was close at hand to escort Emily to the food and thereby eat with her. A few other young men tried to do likewise, but a harsh look from Henry was enough to discourage most of them. He smiled when Emily's obvious preference for his company discouraged the rest. It gave him a thrill and scared him too. He didn't want anyone else laying claim to Emily, but he wasn't sure he was ready to publicly announce his intentions towards her. It was all moving too fast, but he had only himself to blame. He simply couldn't control his feelings when he was in her presence.

He watched Emily bite into a plump, pink shrimp and his gut tightened. His desire to kiss her increased with every passing minute in her company.

Emily saw the raw look in Henry's eyes as he watched her. She now recognized it as desire for it mirrored her own yearning. He wanted to kiss her. She wanted to kiss him. Unconsciously, she licked the buttery brine from her lips and saw his pupils flare. She cast about for something to say to divert them both. "I can't believe my parents went to all this trouble for my birthday."

"Why not? You are their only daughter."

"But seventeen is nothing special."

"Perhaps not, but you are special." His voice mellowed, and his gaze pierced hers hoping to convey all he was feeling for her.

A soft smile played about Emily's lips. She couldn't miss the message in his warm eyes. The connection pulled them towards each other. Their shared feelings tightening around them like unseen rope tying them together.

The spell was broken by the approach of friends. Eventually, they were pulled apart by conversation though they remained physically close to each other.

Supper was followed by more dancing. Emily was a much sought after partner, but they managed to have the last dance together. It was another waltz. Henry slid his arm around Emily much more confidently than the first time. Her hands moved to him with surety of placement. They moved gracefully in tune with each other, oblivious of the other dancers.

Betsy and Theodore danced past them and smiled, happy their son had found a reason to stay on the island. A few turns later, they noticed the look on Brianna's face as she danced by in the arms of Thorn. Their eyes met in shared concern.

Abby's eyes misted over as she watched Emily gaze adoringly at Henry. Max tightened his hold in response. It was the same look Abby still gave him in their more private moments. If he had doubted the strength of his daughter's feelings before, watching her with Henry now, removed them.

Abby leaned back in his arms. "Is she ready for marriage?"

Max met her concerned gaze. "You don't think she is?"

"She seems less mature than I was at her age."

"She is, but you have to take into account you were motherless and running a house before we met. She will rise to the occasion when the time comes."

He kissed Abby's temple and rested his head against hers as they moved to the strains of the waltz. He knew she was feeling sentimental and melancholy knowing it wouldn't be long before their daughter would be married and starting a family of her own. The days of Emily residing under their roof were dwindling, and they were both feeling the sadness of the impending loss even if it was tempered by joy over her found happiness. The ball was Abby's way of distracting herself from all that she was feeling. It was too bad the distraction couldn't last longer.

Those watching Henry and Emily could clearly see how the young couple felt about each other. Speculation began on how soon a wedding would be announced. The islanders were ever on the lookout for a reason to celebrate and weddings were favored above all else.

Chapter 8

Drawn to warmer water in a feeding frenzy
Twirling ever faster
Caribbean bound

Two days later, Emily was sitting on the front porch before supper hoping to see Henry pass by on his way home from working at the fort. The day was overcast with occasional wind gusts and now as she watched, the clouds were building with the threat of an evening storm. Not that she really noticed. Her thoughts were occupied with reliving her ball, especially dancing in Henry's arms. She felt like the loveliest lady at the party, and the most cherished. Her father had always made her feel loved and protected. Henry did too, but he also made her feel important and special to him. She supposed it was the same way her father made her mother feel. It certainly looked like her mother felt that way when Emily watched them dance the last waltz.

Her reminiscence was interrupted by the approach of a colored man with broad shoulders, muscular arms, and nappy dark hair salted with gray. He was the friendly first mate of her father's wrecking ship, the *Mystic*.

"Good evening, Mr. Thomas."

He removed his cap and held it against his chest, crushed in his large hands. "Evening, Miss Emily. Is your pa home?"

The absence of his infectious grin warned her this was not a pleasant visit. Something was horribly wrong if Thomas wasn't smiling. She rose from her seat. "He is. Let me take you to him." Thomas followed her into the house. She led him to her father's study where the old friends greeted each other warmly despite the strain and concern in Thomas' eyes.

Curiosity made her want to eavesdrop on their conversation, but a movement in the hall reminded her she couldn't do so inside without being observed. She returned to the front porch and carefully took a seat in the wicker chair next to the window of her father's office.

"How did it happen?"

"He gots his leg tangled in a rope one of the new hands left about the deck 'bout the same time the ship rolled. Doc says it's broke, and he has to stay off it."

"So the *Mystic* is short her captain for a spell."

"That be the gist of it Capt'n."

"Thank you for coming to tell me Thomas. Tell Captain Keats not to worry. I'll be by to visit him later."

"Aye Capt'n."

She heard Thomas leave the room. She was going to get up from the chair, when the murmur of her parents' voices made her wait.

Her mother asked, "What are you going to do?"

"I don't know."

Thomas came through the front door, startling Emily. She held still hoping he wouldn't turn and notice her. If he did, her presence would be revealed. To her relief his long strides took him off the porch without betraying her.

Her mother's plaintive plea reached her ears. "You promised."

"I know I did but to leave the *Mystic* at anchor deprives her crew from earning money for their families. Six other livelihoods are at stake here."

"Surely, there is someone else."

"I can think of no one I can trust."

Silence followed. Emily could well imagine the speaking looks passing between them.

She gathered the *Mystic* needed a temporary captain, and her father had promised her mother he would no longer captain a wrecker.

Max watched Abby walk from the room, in dejected silence. They both saw the inevitability of the situation. He was going to have to break his promise. The *Mystic* must have an able-bodied captain. Thomas didn't want the position and there was no one else he could trust with his ship. While he hated hurting Abby by breaking his promise, the adventurer in him was leaping for joy. At least for a few weeks, he could return to doing what he loved most on the ship he loved best.

Trying to temper his enthusiasm with reason, Max walked to the window, his mind full of preparations he needed to make before leaving. Namely, replacing himself as captain of the *Abigail Rose*. A flutter of movement caught his attention. He turned his gaze to find Emily sitting in the chair beside the window. She normally preferred to sit on the other side of the porch telling Max she had been intentionally eavesdropping. He stepped through the open window to confront her.

Emily nearly jumped out of her skin as her father's leg appeared over the window's ledge. She rose from her seat to flee but froze as she was confronted by the full form of her angry father. They took each other's measure for a moment, neither speaking. Her guilt made her first to break eye contact.

Max inhaled sharply. "What do you have to say for yourself?"

She knew better than to play innocent. It was better to own up to her misdeed. She could only hope her reason would make her punishment lenient. "I could tell from Thomas' demeanor something was wrong. I imagined the news to be much worse than it was. I am afraid concern overcome sound judgement."

"More like impatience. Emily, you know better."

She hung her head. "Yes, sir."

"What did you hear?"

"Captain Keats broke his leg. The *Mystic* needs a replacement captain until he is healed."

"And?"

"It most likely will be you." She raised her eyes to his. "Will you really break your promise to Mother?"

Max blinked. How did she do that? He was confronting her with her guilt and now she was confronting him with his. For a moment, he clearly saw the woman she was becoming standing before him. He was proud of her but not ready to face her. He blinked again and in the confusion he saw in her gray eyes she was once again his young daughter. "That is none of your concern."

Emily grimaced. It wasn't and yet it was. "I have never known you to break a promise. How could you do that to her?"

Max wanted to yell at her, but Henry's approach made him hold his tongue. In a low voice he said, "Sometimes there are things beyond our control and promises, no matter how well intentioned, become casualties of the situation. Your mother understands. Now as for you, no more eavesdropping. Next time, there will be consequences."

Emily bowed her head. "Yes, sir."

Henry noted the pensive conversation between father and daughter. He hesitated to approach until Emily caught sight of him and smiled. A rumble of thunder heralded his arrival and drowned out his greeting.

Max nodded. "Good evening, Henry. How it the fort work progressing?"

"Laborious, sir. As always."

"I'm sure it is."

"May Emily go for a walk?"

She waited with breath held for her father's decision.

Max looked to the piling thunderheads with significance. "Perhaps you should stay on the porch. Besides, I'm sure supper is almost ready."

"Of course, you're right. It was ungentlemanly of me not to consider the risk of getting caught in a downpour."

"Come, have a seat." Max moved to the chairs outside the parlor window and held the back of one in a clear indication for Emily to be seated. Once Henry and Emily were settled in the wicker chairs bracketing either side of the window, Max nodded to them and went inside.

Emily expected Lydia to be sent out as a chaperone and was puzzled when she failed to appear, distracting her from Henry. Voices drifted to her from inside the parlor reminding her they had an audience nearby. She could well imagine her father was keeping an eye on the window. She finally turned her full attention to Henry with a smile.

Henry returned her smile with a grin. "There you are. I was beginning to wonder if I should leave."

Emily's face fell. "I'm sorry. I didn't mean to ignore you."

"Is something the matter? You and your father seemed to be having something of a serious discussion."

"Captain Keats broke his leg. It places a burden on father to find a replacement for him while he mends."

"I'm sure he will."

Emily smiled sardonically and nodded. "He already has." Eager to change the subject, she recalled the memory she had been toying with earlier in the day. "Do you remember the time we got into your mother's Madeira?"

Henry laughed. "I do. Christoff had a fit, but we knew he would never tell on us."

"You were acting so silly."

"Silly? How so?"

"You couldn't walk straight. You were bumping into all the furniture. I think you were pretending to be an Indian. I couldn't understand anything you said."

"You were the one who couldn't stop laughing. Everything was funny to you. Until Aunt Aggie found us." Henry gaze turned away, and his face sobered. "I miss her." He shook his head. "I miss the family dinners we used to have."

"Even the silent ones?"

"Yes, even those. I miss all the good and bad that was Aunt Aggie. I regret all the family dinners I missed while I was away."

Emily looked intently into his eyes. All trace of humor left her voice. Somberly, she asked, "Did you find what you were looking for?"

Henry took an uneasy breath. It was as if she was staring into his soul, and he responded with all the depths of his emotions. "I discovered it was here all along." She looked at him with trust and hope and longing. He knew the same feelings were reflected in his eyes.

Emily was drowning in his gaze. His open sincerity tugged at her heart. The seriousness of the moment overwhelmed her. She had to take shelter from it. To lighten the mood, she snatched the sketchbook he had been holding in his lap. He reached to take it from her, but she batted his hand away.

"Emily, no."

She looked up at him with a playful smile. "What are you hiding Henry Whitmore?" To her surprise, he didn't respond, simply settled back in his seat, resigned to let her see what she would. Her hand hovered over the cover, now hesitant to open it. A crack of lightening made her jump. She caught the book as it nearly slipped from her lap. And then the rain let loose. She stood and Henry rose too. She tried to hand him back his book. "I suppose you need to get home."

Henry didn't take the book. "I think I'll wait until the worst of it passes." He gestured towards the chair.

Emily sat down and allowed him to open the book in her lap. He turned the pages past the old Indian and his horse Cisco. The next was a landscape scene.

"That is the Neosho River at Fort Gibson."

Emily took over turning the pages. The next several drawings were different views of the fort and some of the Indians.

Emily looked up at him. "I can see your skills improving as I turn the pages."

Several pages later the scenes and people changed to documenting his time with the Texas Rangers.

She pointed to a haunting landscape. "And this one?"

"That's the Rio Grande River. Mexico is on the other side."

"It forms the border between us and Mexico."

"The disputed border."

"Is that why we are at war with them?"

He nodded. "One of the main reasons, anyway."

The next drawing was of the fanciest horse-drawn carriage Emily had ever seen. "Where was this? It's beautiful."

"In the French Quarter of New Orleans. I wanted to add more of the ornate buildings behind it, but I didn't have enough time."

"Your drawings are good. I feel as if I have travelled with you. Thank you for sharing these."

Henry's pride swelled with her praise. Now, he waited with baited breath for her response to the next series of drawings.

Emily turned the page and inhaled sharply. Covering the next two pages were several images of her face including the one she caught a glimpse of days ago with the soft look in her eyes. He made her look beautiful and more womanly than she felt. She turned the page and revealed the drawing of her in the cupola with the water behind her. He caught the motion of the wind lifting her tendrils. She started to turn the page again, but he laid his hand on hers and then turned back a page.

"Do you like them?"

"Is that how you see me? I hardly recognize myself. I mean they are good, really good. They look just like me, but they have a quality in the expression that I don't see in the mirror." Henry frowned, so she tried again. "You make me seem older and sweeter than I see myself."

"Then yes. That is how I see you."

The front door opened. Henry straightened from leaning over her.

Thorn stuck his head out. "Supper's ready."

Emily nodded. "I'll be right there." His head disappeared, and the door shut behind him. Emily looked to Henry. "Will you stay to supper?"

"I should be getting home. The rain has eased now."

"I suppose so." Emily flipped through the last few pages quickly. They were mostly drawings of the fort construction, birds, and animals. She handed the book back to him and rose from her seat. The rain had slowed to a drizzle.

Henry glanced around them. No one was in sight. He moved them into the privacy of the space between the window and the door. He leaned in to press a quick kiss against her cheek, and then with a smile, he turned from her. She watched him hurry down the street before turning to go inside.

* * *

The following evening Max made the announcement to the family at supper. "I will be taking Captain Keats place for a few weeks aboard the *Mystic*. It means I will be able to come home every other week for a few days instead of being gone so long. How does that sound?"

Christoff's face lit up. "Oh boy! We're going wrecking."

Abby turned to him in horror. "Your father may be but not you."

Christoff knew better than to contradict her. He turned his pleading gaze to his father.

Max turned from his son to his wife. "We will discuss it later." His look asked her not to say any more in front of the children.

Thorn was silent.

Christoff said, "Which reefs will you patrol?"

"The Dry Tortugas."

Nate said with boyish enthusiasm, "Are you going to chase storms?"

Abby grimaced.

"Not if I can help it, son."

His tone held a final note they all recognized. The subject was closed.

They adjourned to the parlor after supper as usual, but their parents soon left the room to go outside. From the open window, they could occasionally hear a harsh whisper, but their words did not carry to the house. A short time later, they returned to the room. Expectant faces all turned their way. Max gave a nod to Christoff who grinned in return. The look on his mother's face kept his more enthusiastic response held in check.

Early the following morning, Abby walked Max and Christoff to the front door. She hugged her son tight. Embarrassed by the display of affection, he slipped from her arms and hurried out of the door.

Max looked down at Abby trying to convey all of his feelings to her, and there were many; sorrow to be hurting her, pride in her for letting him go despite her fears for their safety, thankful for her understanding, and the over-all enduring love he felt for her.

Abby placed her hands on either side of his face and raised up on her toes to kiss him. "Come home safe."

"Aye, aye Wife." He left the house before emotions could get out of control.

Abby watched them walk down the street, father and son, until they disappeared from her sight.

* * *

Saturday, October 3rd, Henry left the fort camp with three and a half weeks' wages in his pocket and spirit in his step. He now had enough to buy his own boat and hook. He only wished he would have more time to use them. It didn't make sense to buy a boat now when he could only work the sponge grounds one day a week. Better to save his money and wait for a more opportune time. If only finding sponges could be done in the evenings, but alas, it took the bright light of day to see clearly under the water. Unfortunately, he spent the sunlight hours six days out of seven at the fort.

It was hard to believe he had been home a month already. The time had flown. Especially when he considered how much his plans had changed since he set foot ashore. He arrived with a vague notion of a short visit; a few weeks to see that all was well, and then he would return to the Rangers. But here he was now, with no plans to leave - ever - and holding the funds to start a business, a home, and a family of his own.

Henry walked into the house and was pulled from his thoughts by his father's request to join him in the study. Usually the family was gathered in the parlor at this time of day, and indeed, he could hear the rest of them talking and laughing from down the hall. He followed his father into the room inhaling the pungent aroma of cigars. He turned to take a seat in one of the chairs facing his father's desk and was surprised to find Mr. Tate already occupying one of them.

"Hello, sir. How are you doing?"

Mr. Tate slowly rose to greet Henry with a nod. "Not well, I'm afraid."

Theodore laid a hand on Henry's shoulder. "I will leave you two to talk."

Henry's concern grew. "What is wrong Mr. Tate? How can I help?"

His elderly friend twitched, fitfully turning his hat in his hand. "I've received a letter from my youngest sister in Jersey. Her husband passed away. She needs someone to take over his fishing boat to provide for her young 'uns. There's no one but me to do it."

"I'm sorry to hear about your troubles and my condolences for your brother-in-law."

"We didn't ever see eye to eye, but he did take good care of my sister, Lizzy." His gaze shifted to the window. "I'm going to hate leaving this place, but I couldn't live with myself if I let my sister down in her hour of need." He shuddered. "I really hate New England winters."

"Couldn't they come here to live?"

"She refused my offer, not wanting to further upset her children by uprooting them."

"Oh. How soon do you plan to leave?"

"I have passage for day after next."

"Is there anything I can do to help?"

"Actually, that is what I'm here for. I obviously can't take my boat with me. I know you be wantin' to start your own fishin', so I'm offering to let you buy me out of boat and tools. I already talked to Asa Tift. He'd be willing to let you take over the lease on the shed, and my buyers are willing to deal with you once I assured them you were a natural at sponging. I got your share of the last sale of sponges in my pocket. I'll sell you everything for the price of your share, if you're interested, or I'll pay you now, and we'll call it square."

Henry stood there shaking his head still trying to absorb all his mentor had said and was offering. "Your offer is too generous." His take of the last set of sponges was certainly not equal to what Mr. Tate's whole business was worth. Henry smiled at the old man. "And too good to refuse." He pulled his army wages from his pocket and held it out to Mr. Tate. "Sir, I insist you take this and my share of the sponges as fair trade for your business."

Mr. Tate pushed his hand away. "If I had married and had children, I would give this business to my son, but God didn't see fit, or I failed to take notice when I should have, and so I have none. These last few weeks working with you, teaching you my trade, have been the closest I ever had to feeling like a proud papa. I would out right give it to you if I could." He patted his pocket. "But I'm afraid I need this for traveling money. It's enough for that, so don't you go insulting my good feelings by offering me your money."

Henry slipped the bills back into his pocket and held out his hand to Mr. Tate. "Thank you, sir. I learned a lot from you, and I'll put it to good use. Just you wait. One day you'll see Key West sponges for sale in New Jersey."

Mr. Tate nodded sagely. "I'll be watching for them. I know you can do it. You've got gumption, and that's what it'll take to make it in the big markets."

"Would you care to stay for supper, Mr. Tate?"

"Nah, thank you though. I've got to get back and finish sortin' out my belongings. Here's the key to the lock on the shed. Good luck, son."

Henry turned and followed Mr. Tate to the door. "Good luck to you too, sir. Thank you again... for everything."

Hearing the front door close, his parents entered the foyer and looked at him expectantly.

Henry shrugged still in shock over all that had transpired. "It seems I now have my own sponge operation."

Theodore proudly squeezed his shoulder. "Congratulations."

Betsy asked, "Will you be quitting your job at the fort?"

Henry frowned. He hadn't thought that far ahead. It was good pay and interesting work having a hand in the fort taking shape. "I think I'll stay on, at least for a while. I'll see how well I do on my own fishing on Sunday after church and cleaning the sponges during the week as I have been."

Theodore said, "It sounds like a wise plan not to jump right in, but to go about it gradually. The only fault in your plan is breaking the Sabbath. What about selling the sponges? You can't do that on Sunday nor in the evenings."

Henry's frown deepened. "I'm not sure, but I have time to figure it out. I won't have enough sponges ready to sell for at least a few weeks."

Chapter 9

From tropical heat and lofty chill
Strength and speed gather
Tightening to a center well formed
A child now grown

Henry knew he had to leave. The sun was drifting past its zenith. He had lingered too long already. He shouldn't have agreed to dinner after church with the Eatonton's, but it took a stronger man than he to resist the temptation of a hopeful Emily offering Mrs. Baxley's famous fried chicken. He eagerly accepted Emily's invite to prolong his time with her. Escorting her to and from church was all the time he had for courting. He really should have grabbed a quick bite to eat and been out on the reef, but he was enjoying her company, and now that the meal was at an end, he still did not want to part from her. His heart was firmly anchored to hers. Each smile she cast in his direction seemed to remove another link in the chain limiting how far he could drift away from her.

He wiped his mouth and placed the fine napkin, now stained with grease, on the linen covered table. "Mrs. Eatonton, thank you for a delicious meal."

"You're welcome, Henry."

He really should get to the sponges, but he was reluctant to leave Emily, especially when he likely wouldn't see her again till next Sunday. Besides, he wanted to share his good news with her, preferably in private. A bold idea came to mind and he lifted his eyes to Emily's in speculation. Would she accept his offer and more importantly would her mother let her? Henry absently listened to the voices ebb and flow in conversation around the table as he worked up his courage. Courting was one thing, but it wasn't likely Emily's mother would give permission to the idea stirring in Henry's head. But then again, Emily often said she took after her mother, giving him hope.

He inhaled deeply for courage and took the risk. "Mrs. Eatonton, it is such a nice day, I was wondering if you would give permission for Emily to go sailing for an hour or so?"

"I don't see any harm as long as Thorn accompanies you."

Henry held his grimace in check. "I'm afraid my boat is not so large. It is only a two man craft."

Abby's first inclination was to say no. She could well recall the trouble she and Max got into going off on their own before they were married. The look in Emily's eyes said she would likely go along with whatever Henry suggested.

Henry saw her disapproval coming. *In for a penny, in for a pound.* He must try to assure her. "We will stay near the island. Anyone from Whitehead or Front Street who cares to look will be able to see us." He knew full well she would head up to the Captain's walk as soon as they left the house. Situated as their house was on Whitehead Street, she would be able to keep them in sight.

Abby wavered. She knew Henry to be honorable; besides, he and Emily were courting. Maybe it was best to see how they would handle a little privacy. Her gaze went to Emily. Abby saw the same excitement burning in Emily's eyes that she once felt for Max. She knew its intoxication and part of her didn't want to deny Emily the feeling. There was little trouble for her to get into staying visible from shore in full daylight. "Very well."

Emily nearly squealed in delight.

Abby gave Henry a stern look. "As long as you keep to the shore as promised."

Henry bowed his head. "Yes, ma'am." He turned to Emily. The excitement shining in her eyes made asking her if she would like to go a moot point. He stood up and walked over to pull out her chair. As soon as they were out of sight of the dining room, he eagerly reached for her hand. At the front door, he paused long enough for Emily to retrieve her parasol, and then it was all he could do to keep his pace in check with hers as they walked to the other end of town.

Emily wistfully asked, "What was Texas like?"

In his mind, he compared Texas to Key West in considering how to answer her. "There is a great feeling of space, even in the towns. Whereas here our temperatures are steady, there the weather can change drastically from morning to night and day to day. The terrain is very changeable too. It has prairies that go on further than you can see with nothing but tall grass and thorny brush and plains with only tumbleweeds to break the monotony."

"What are tumbleweeds?"

"It's a dead plant that the wind has broken from its roots and blown for miles. It sometimes looks like it is rolling across the ground, hence, the name."

"It sounds desolate."

"It is. But between the flat lands is an area of tree covered hills that can be peaceful when you're not worried about bears, wolves, or mountain lions."

Emily turned to him in horror. "You mean to say you slept outside with those creatures?"

He nodded. "They generally leave you alone as long as the campfire burns. Sometimes, in the darkness we could hear the wolves howling or a mountain lion kill its prey."

"You are teasing, trying to frighten me just like when we were children."

"Not this time. They were very real. But it wasn't all bad. There is nothing prettier in spring than a grassy hillside covered in blue bonnets."

"What are those?"

"Flowers bluer than the sky. It was pretty." He turned his head to look at her. "But not as pretty as you." She blushed further proving his words. He drew his eyes away with some difficulty. "I saw many rivers and streams except in the regions that were arid and dry and home to rattlesnakes. At the end, when we were camped in the Rio Grande Valley preparing to fight Mexico, it was closer to the coast and felt more like home with the palm trees."

"You sound in awe of the territory but you don't sound like you miss being there."

Henry considered her perception. "You're right. I don't miss being there." He chortled. "I thought I would, but I don't."

"I wish I could see it."

"Maybe one day you can."

She hoped he was thinking he would take her there one day.

Henry pointed to the dilapidated structure they were passing. "I can't believe the Pirate Shack is still standing."

"There has been talk of tearing it down. Remember how you scared my brothers with stories of John Gomez coming back to kill anyone who tried to dig up his treasure."

"They were so gullible, I couldn't resist."

Beyond the shack was the Curry house. They waved to Mrs. Curry sitting on her porch. A few moments more and they reached Henry's boat. He dragged it to the softly lapping water and held out his hand to assist her.

* * *

Abby left the maid clearing the table to make her way to the covered cupola atop the house. Open walkways extended out to the right and left of it along the ridge of the high pitched roof giving her a grand view over the surrounding rooftops and trees. She watched the couple disappear around the corner onto Front Street. It would take them five minutes or so to reach his boat beached at the other end. It would take another ten minutes or so before they sailed into view, if Henry was true to his word.

Minutes after the couple passed Henry's house, Betsy emerged and headed her way. When her friend glanced up, Abby waved for her to come up.

It wasn't long before Betsy's head appeared above the hatch door. "When I saw Henry walking alone with Emily, I thought I might find you up here. Do you know what he is up to?"

Abby looked to Betsy in amusement. "Not exactly. He asked to take Emily sailing. I would guess he is wooing my daughter. Not that wooing is necessary. She has been in love with him since she was two. What I am wondering is what his intentions are?"

Betsy didn't think Abby meant to offend her, but she still felt the need to defend her son. "Honorable, I am sure."

Hearing the slightest edge of hurt in her voice, Abby turned to her friend. "I am sorry Betsy. I meant no offense. I know Henry is honorable. I only wondered if today is an innocent outing, or if there is something more serious afoot."

Betsy hadn't considered the idea. "No. He wouldn't be proposing to her already. Unless... Has he asked Max for his blessing?"

"As far as I am aware, he has only asked to court her, and he would ask Max first for her hand in marriage, wouldn't he?" Abby relized it was a rhetorical question and relaxed a little.

Betsy nodded in agreement but felt the need to add, "He will propose eventually."

"I know. I did not expect to face this so soon, but then they are of age as hard as that is to fathom. They seem too young to be old enough to marry."

"Will you accept Henry as a son-in-law?"

Abby was surprised. "Of course! Why would you doubt it?"

"Just feeling a bit overprotective, I suppose." She felt ashamed to have questioned her best friend, so she quickly changed the subject.

* * *

Emily trailed her hand in the cool water, letting the pattern of the current mesmerize her in an attempt to keep her gaze from Henry's strong arms pulling on the oars. The boat glided smoothly across the sun-sparkled, cyan surface. Henry seemed to be headed somewhere particular. She didn't bother to ask where. It didn't matter to her. She was simply happy to prolong their time together. She adjusted the tilt of her parasol to keep the sun off her face. True to his word he kept them close to the island. Emily turned her questioning eyes to his when he suddenly stopped rowing and pulled the oars into the boat. A glance at shore assured her they were within view of her house albeit too far to clearly see if her mother was watching. She waited for Henry to explain.

Henry eagerly peered into the water around them. "I have something to show you Em."

His excitement was contagious. Emily looked as well but could see nothing out of the ordinary to cause such enthusiasm.

"Just wait a moment." Henry suddenly stood, rocking the boat, and then stepped up on the seat. "Hold on."

Emily didn't need his warning. She was already gripping both sides of the boat, her parasol all but forgotten in her sudden concern of turning over. "What in the world are you trying to do?"

Henry worked to restore their balance. "Hand me that hook, please."

Emily grasped the handle he was pointing to and lifted it up so Henry could take it.

As he pulled, the hook caught on her skirt. "Careful now."

She freed her hem from the wicked looking prongs. 'What is that for?"

"You'll see."

"Dang it all Henry, why must you be so mysterious. Tell me what this is all about."

Henry was too preoccupied to answer right away. He held the hook over the water and peered into the shallow aquamarine depths as they floated over sand and coral. Emily wanted to look as well but with his precarious position she was scared to move least she turn the boat over. In the next moment, he found what he was seeking. The hook went 'kerplunk' into the water and came back up with his prize. Warily, Emily watched him remove the round muckish object from the tines and gleefully drop it in front of her. She reflexively reached out to catch the squishy thing in an attempt to keep the watery mess away from her skirt, just as he planned, judging by the grin on his face. "Henry James Whitmore! What on earth are you doing?"

"Showing you our future."

* * *

Abby lifted her spy glass to peer towards the couple in the little row boat a few hundred yards down the shoreline and another thirty from shore. She lowered the spyglass, confused by what she thought she was seeing. "What is he doing?" She lifted the spyglass again. "Henry is standing on the seat. Is he trying to turn the boat over?"

Betsy held out her hand. "Let me see."

Abby handed her the telescope.

"I'm not sure... Oh, I see, he has a sponge hook. Why is he sponge fishing with her in the boat?"

* * *

Emily looked to her dripping hands. "A sponge? Pray tell, what does a sponge have to do with our future?" The thrill of hearing Henry speak of their forthcoming life together overruled her disgust at holding the slimy sea creature or plant or whatever it was.

Henry stepped down into the boat and returned to his seat, carefully putting the hook in its resting place. "I have heard some say our sponges are the best in the world."

She handed over the sponge and wiped her hands on the rag he offered her. "They are the nicest I have ever owned."

"Exactly!" His excitement grew. "I mean to build a business selling them. This boat is the start. It's mine, Emily! Mr. Tate has to return north. He gave me everything; the boat, the hook, the nets, his buyers, and the warehouse lease. I now have what I need to get started. Later, I can expand once I have more experience in the trade. I am sure I can make a fine living for us. I have done some ciphering and with hard work and a little luck I believe in a year or so I can start building our house." Exuberance made Henry throw caution - and decorum - to the wind. He dropped down to one knee in front of her bringing his face within arms distance of hers. Looking upon the endearing face of the only girl he had ever loved, he smiled, sure of her answer. "Can you wait a year?"

The suddenness of his move shocked her only slightly less than the dawning of his intention, and in return, she couldn't resist teasing him. "A year for what?" Besides, she wanted to hear the words.

"A year for what? To marry me, of course!"

Laughing she said, "Dear Henry, you call that a proposal?"

He dropped to both knees and scooted forward till he met the resistance of her knees. He then picked up both her hands from her lap, and after working all traces of humor from his visage, he earnestly peered into her eyes. If she wanted a full-fledged vow of devotion he was more than willing to please her. "Dearest Emily Rose Eatonton," he paused till the merriment in her eyes gave way to solemnity. "Would you do me the honor of taking my hand in marriage, to be my lifelong love and companion, to bear my children, and allow me to indulge you in every way I can think of for the rest of our days?"

Emily's overwhelmed mind could only think two words - *Oh my!* She would have pressed a hand to her chest but he was holding them both. A moment ago, she was enjoying girlhood and flirtation. In the space of a few heartbeats, Henry's serious proposal of marriage, not to mention child-bearing, made her suddenly feel too grown up, too soon. She stared at him wide-eyed as she struggled to breathe. She couldn't flippantly answer. His question deserved a serious response from her, but was she ready for this? At least he was proposing a yearlong engagement. It would give her the time she needed to acclimate to the idea of babies and the more disconcerting prospect of how babies are made. One thing she was sure of – she only wanted to share those experiences with Henry. She could not imagine another in his place, which made her answer a little easier to give.

She finally exhaled the breath she had been holding with her shaky answer. "Yes." She gave him a tremulous smile to ease the anxious concern she saw in his eyes.

"Are you sure?"

She could only nod in reply, but she did so vigorously.

"Can I kiss you?"

Emily's heart jumped. *Oh my goodness!* She was still recovering her wits from the first shock. Now here was another. Finally, her first kiss. She had been waiting for it ever since she stepped out of the mercantile to see him standing in the street. Throwing propriety to the wind in favor of ravening curiosity, she gave a slight nod and waited.

Henry's heart was racing as he tentatively moved closer to her. Unless he counted the dirty barmaid in Texas who kissed him on his twentieth birthday – which he didn't – this was his first real kiss. He was on his knees in front of her holding her hands. Over her shoulder, the ruffled edge of the forgotten parasol fluttered in the breeze. The sun warmed his back, but his attention was for her alone. He leaned forward. Only a hair's breadth remained between his chest and her bosom. He let instinct take over.

Emily's pulse was racing in anticipation. His eyes dropped to her mouth. She watched as he leaned slowly towards her. Unconsciously, she licked her suddenly dry lips. He halted for a heartbeat before resuming.

Henry tilted his head, puckered his lips a little, and pressed them gently to hers. His eyes closed of their own volition.

Her eyes closed as his lips lightly touched hers.

He held still for a mere moment, then pulled his head back.

They both opened their eyes at the same time to look at each other in wonder... and confusion. They both had the same thought. *Was that all?* Something was missing. It had to be. The kiss was too bland.

Henry spoke first. "Can we try again?"

Emily nodded. "Please do."

Henry let go of her hands and placed his on the boat on either side of her for leverage. This time he brought his warm lips to hers with more surety, and though he was still gentle, he did increase the pressure and lingered longer before reluctantly parting.

She smiled in answer to the query in his eyes. "Much better." That was more like what she imagined when she practiced kissing her hand in the solitude of her bedroom. Her eyes pleaded with him to kiss her again.

He brought his head down to hers without hesitation and this time varied the pressure. After a lingering moment, their lips parted with a smack causing them both to giggle in modest embarrassment.

Henry couldn't help himself. He impulsively kissed her again and again.

Emily placed her hand on the center of his chest and pushed him away. "Enough Henry! Someone could be watching." She cast a nervous glance towards shore. "You know my mother most likely is on the Captain's Walk with her spyglass in hand."

"Your mother has a spyglass?"

"Of course."

The notion sent Henry scuttling back to his seat.

* * *

Abby was having trouble believing what she was seeing. "The nerve of him!"

Betsy's head snapped at Abby's tone. "What has he done now?"

"He kissed her! He's kissing her again!" Surprise turned to displeasure. "And again."

Betsy looked to the figures in the boat. They were too far to see any kind of details, but they were certainly merged together. Her son was headed for trouble.

Abby turned to Betsy. "You don't think he meant for us to see this? He told me before he left, as if he knew I would be watching, that anyone from Whitehead Street would be able to keep an eye on them."

"I am sure he would not flaunt her in such a way. He merely forgot himself." Which she realized was not much better.

* * *

Emily discretely touched her lips with her fingertips wishing to hold on to the wondrous sensations of her first real kiss – kisses, actually. They were all she had dreamed of and more. The breathless excitement of his lips on hers was something she wished to repeat again, and soon. She smiled, watching him as he rowed the boat further south, wishing he would stop and kiss her again but knowing he wouldn't.

Henry wasn't paying any attention to their heading. He was rowing in order to keep his hands occupied and off of her. He liked the way her lips felt under his. He liked it a lot. Those blissful moments of kissing lingered warmly under his skin. He never imagined simply kissing someone could wreak such havoc on his being. His palms sweated, his breath was erratic, his heart thundered, and his senses were reeling. And that was just from kissing her. How did a person survive doing more than kissing? His lips curved upward. He couldn't wait to find out, but wait he would.

As if sensing the direction of his thoughts, Emily asked, "Have you spoken with my father?"

Henry gave her a sheepish look. "Yes and no. We spoke of a future engagement, but he truly only gave his permission for courting."

"Oh Henry, now we'll have to keep our engagement a secret until you get his permission."

"It will be hard to hide how happy you have made me, but I suppose you're right."

They drifted for some time each lost in their own thoughts before Emily broke the silence. "Aren't there already a bunch of spongers in Key West? How are you going to make a lot of money when there's only so many people around here in need of sponges?"

"True. Key West sponges are currently only selling from St. Augustine to Havana. I plan to sell them up the eastern seaboard and eventually around the world. I just have to find the right person to help get them to market."

"And when you do, how are you going to have enough to sell all by yourself?"

Her interest heartened him. "I plan to have a crew of spongers and a larger boat towing several smaller boats, so they can go further and stay out longer allowing the collection of more sponges in the same amount of time."

"How will you find the person to help sell them?"

"My father has connections in New York. I can start there. I'm sure once discovered, people will demand our sponges, and then the brokers will come looking for me."

Emily smiled broadly. "It sounds like a grand plan. If anyone can make it happen, I believe you can."

Henry grinned. It felt good to have her confidence in him. The sudden tug against the oar demanded his attention. A glance at the now distant shore confirmed he was getting into the stronger currents past the southern point of the island. The lighthouse was now in his view instead of behind him. It was time to get Emily back home anyway. Smoothly, he turned the boat in the water and rowed them back to the western shoreline.

A half hour later, they paused to say farewell at the Eatonton's front porch. Emily faced Henry. "Thank you for spending time with me today. I know it kept you from gathering sponges."

"It was worth it." He glanced at the sun's position. "I still have a few hours left." He lifted Emily's hand to his lips. "Until next Sunday."

"I wish it could be sooner."

"Me too." He kissed the back of her hand again and turned away before his will to leave was tested any further.

Emily entered the house with a dreamy smile still hovering on her face. It was settled between them even if she would have to wait to share her joy with everyone else. She drifted towards the stairs. One day she would be Mrs. Henry Whitmore. No longer just a wish written in her diary but a dream come true. It was more exciting than she imagined it would be.

"Emily Rose Eatonton."

Belatedly, Emily realized her mother must have called to her several times already to have used her full name. She turned to follow her into the morning room, relieved to find they were alone. The tone of her voice sounded as if she had likely seen her and Henry in the boat.

Abby shook her head. "Have you forgotten yourself?"

Unsure to what her mother was referring to, Emily kept silent.

Abby was beside herself in disappointment in her daughter. "Kissing in public. Kissing at all. Have you no self-respect? No proper young lady would *ever* allow a boy to kiss her unless she were engaged and rarely even then."

Emily stoically listened to her mother's reprimand, but she failed to completely hide her smile at the word engaged.

Abby saw the corner of Emily's mouth lift. Whatever else she was going to say was lost as understanding of its implication took hold in her mind. Her jaw dropped. "Have you two spoken of marriage?"

Unable to lie to her mother, Emily mutely nodded her head.

"When?"

"Today, out on the boat. It was as if we couldn't help it. He was telling me of his plans for his sponging business, and how he could soon provide for our future." Wonder bloomed across her face. "In the next moment, he was down on his knees asking me to be his wife." Replaying the unbelievable joy of the moment in her mind brought a full, far-away smile to her face.

Abby floundered as she saw the beauty of happiness radiating from Emily. Of course, she wanted her daughter to be happy, but Henry was pulling her away too fast. "But he only has permission to court you." She was sure Max would have told her if he had given permission to marry.

Emily absently answered, "He said he and father spoke of a future engagement."

Abby's anger returned, strengthening her tone and capturing Emily's full attention. "I doubt your father meant the future to be so soon. Until he returns to say otherwise, you are forbidden from being alone with Henry. You must always have a chaperone, and you will speak no more of marriage. And absolutely no more kissing. Is that understood?"

Emily hung her head. "Yes, mother."

Chapter 10

Pushed due north
Land in sight

Standing at the wash station outside the kitchen, Betsy handed Henry a towel to dry his face feeling a little bit of *deja vu*. Years ago, she had done the same when he came home reeking of dead sponges, and she insisted he wash up more thoroughly before joining them for supper. Fortunately, today he only smelled of sea and sweat. "Did you do well sponging this afternoon?" She smiled while his face was covered with the towel. She had learned some finesse in the years he was gone. That day long ago had ended in an argument when she directly confronted him with his tardiness. Today, she started with easy conversation intending to gently coax from him the answers she was seeking.

Henry dried his hands and lifted his face to hers. "Well enough for the short time I had left."

"Why was it short?"

Henry sighed. "I was enjoying Emily's company too much to leave right after dinner."

"She is a sweet girl."

Henry's gaze went faraway. "Yes, she is."

Betsy bit her lip wondering just what in particular he thought was sweet. She would be surprised if he was thinking of anything other than kisses. "I went to visit Abby this afternoon."

Henry's stomach dropped. He had a sneaking suspicion there was a very good reason she was mentioning her visit. He tried to hide his distress with nonchalance. "Did you have a good visit?"

"The view from the Captain's Walk is always amazing, but today had added interest. Do you know we saw two people kissing in a boat?" She shook her head. "It is surprising what people will do in public nowadays."

Henry swallowed hard. She knew. Mrs. Eatonton knew. He wondered how many others had seen them. He let the passion of the moment overwhelm good reason. He would make sure it did not happen again. He couldn't allow Emily's reputation to be marred by his folly.

Betsy smiled gently. "I believe that's all that needs to be said about public displays of affection. I hope you understand, kissing is not part of courting, not even in private."

"Yes, ma'am." His brow furrowed. "What...How... Was Mrs. Eatonton much upset?"

Betsy sighed. "Yes, as any mother of a well brought up daughter would be. I imagine Emily is receiving a reminder lesson in the proper decorum of a lady."

Fear made it hard for him to get the words out. "You don't think she will forbid her from seeing me again, do you?"

Betsy took the towel from his hand. "I don't think the consequences will be that harsh, but you would do well to tread lightly. You must have patience, now more than ever. I know it's hard to do so when you are in love, but, think of it as a necessary test of the strength of your feelings." She looked deeply in his eyes. "I can see your love is strong enough. Max and Abby will see it too when the time is right."

Henry ran a frustrated hand over his head. "It would be easier if I knew how long that would be."

"You must find patience, but that being said, I have something for you when the time is right. Come with me." Betsy led him to her room. "Would you mind getting Aunt Agatha's jewelry box from the top of your father's chest of drawers?"

Henry pulled the box down and ran a hand over the dusty lid before handing it to his mother.

"Aunt Agatha spoke to me the night before she died. She wanted me to make sure to give you your mother's wedding band." She sat on the bed with the chest and reverently lifted the lid. She was surprised to see a folded missive resting on top of the contents and even more surprised that it was addressed to her. With a trembling hand, she picked it up, unwillingly reliving that last night with Aunt Agatha.

Henry patiently waited for his mother, but when she continued to sit still with the parchment in hand, he grew concerned. "Mother?"

Betsy brought her mind back to the present. She laid the envelope aside to read later in private. She shifted the contents until she found the engraved gold circle. She placed it on Henry's open palm.

Henry reverently held the ring, feeling the importance of the tenuous connection it represented to his mother and tried to imagine Emily wearing it. He thought she would like it. Carefully, he placed the ring back in the box. "I think it would be best to leave it safely tucked away until I have Captain Max's permission to ask her to marry me."

Betsy absently nodded her agreement.

Henry leaned over to kiss her check. "Thank you, Mother."

After Henry left the room, it took a few minutes before Betsy worked up the nerve to open the envelope. Aunt Agatha must have added the letter sometime after they talked. She hadn't opened the chest since that night, not even when she cleaned out Aunt Agatha's room to turn it into a much needed nursery.

Betsy reached into the box and lifted the rose cameo necklace Aunt Agatha always wore. It now belonged to her. She left it in the box when Aunt Agatha gave it to her as she couldn't imagine ever wearing it. Now, years later, she felt a desire to honor her memory but hesitated, wondering how Theodore would react. She let the black silk strand sink back into the box and picked up the missive.

This letter was Aunt Agatha's last act on earth, these her last words, and they were addressed to her – not her nephew, Theodore, or her grandnephew, Henry, but her. Betsy couldn't imagine what the old woman felt was so important to say. She hoped it wasn't criticism. Aunt Agatha dispensed enough while she was breathing, even if it was well meant.

There was only one way to find out.

Betsy took a deep breath to steady her hands as she slipped her finger beneath the wax seal. She unfolded the yellowed parchment and felt a chill as she read the words penned years ago.

> *Dear Betsafina,*
>
> *I wanted you to know the last few years of my life have been the happiest since Captain Pary's passing. You and your island welcomed this old bitter woman into your midst and accepted her as your own. For that I am grateful. I may not have shown it, but I believe you are the best wife for Theodore and mother for Henry. You are a God-given blessing to us.*
>
> *I see a long life together for you and Theodore once this Florida War is over.*
>
> *Don't cry for me. These tired bones are ready for their rest. I lived my life as I chose and my only regret is I will miss seeing your children grow.*
>
> *With love,*
> *Agatha Whitmore Pary*

Tears rolled down her cheeks as Betsy quietly folded the letter and laid it in place of the pendant. She closed her hand tightly around the piece of jewelry and closed the lid. Her hands came to rest on top of the sleek wooden chest.

That was how Theodore found her minutes later. He stopped short when she lifted her face to his, and then rushed to her side to envelope her in his loving embrace. His care brought on her tears in earnest, and she clung to him as tightly as she clung to the cameo.

When her crying stopped, Theodore leaned back to see her face. He let her go only long enough to wipe the tears from her cheeks before returning his arms to her waist. "What is it, my love?"

Betsy opened her hand between them so he could see the cameo resting on her palm.

"Aunt Agatha." He smiled as his eyes grew moist. It hurt him still that he wasn't home to say goodbye to her or to comfort his family. It was his second biggest regret in life. The first was not being home when Madalyn died. Maybe if he had been....

Betsy raised her luminous gaze to his. "Teddy, would you mind if I wore this? She gave it to me the night before she died. I couldn't imagine wearing it then, but I would like to now."

Theodore didn't trust his voice, so in answer, he lifted the black silk cord from her hand and tied it around her neck. He stared at the delicately carved ivory rose set against black onyx in a silver filigree setting. He would always see Aunt Agatha in his mind when he looked at it, but he was pleased to note it looked right on Betsy. He kissed her once to let her know he was fine with her decision, and then he kissed her deeply with husbandly adoration.

* * *

It was barely nine o'clock, Friday morning, and Henry had already lost count of the number of times he had crossed the pier from camp to fort and back again. He was hauling bulky granite blocks so heavy they could only be moved one at a time in a wheelbarrow. Captain Dutton was pushing the brick layers hard to finally finish the block foundation in an attempt to make up for time lost due to rain delays and supply shortages. They had one more course to lay on the western curtain, and then they could begin the brick walls. Everyone was excited by the prospect because it meant their work would finally be visible from shore. More importantly, the bricks required less back breaking labor than the blocks.

Henry paused to wipe the sweat from his brow while the water beneath the pier taunted him with its crystal clarity. The weather was so clear and bright, it was an excellent day to hook sponges. If only he wasn't obligated to the army. Frustrated tension tightened his shoulders as he picked up the wheelbarrow handles. It was his own fault he was stuck here since he willingly signed on to this project and chose to stay rather than turn in his notice as soon as Mr. Tate gave him the boat. At the time, one more months' pay seemed sensible, but the pure, startling blue dome overhead mocked his decision.

He reached the work site and impatiently waited as two strong colored men lifted the heavy stone from the wheelbarrow. Henry turned around to retrace his steps while they continued the difficult task of moving the heavy stone to the fort wall. Captain Dutton stopped him on his return to camp.

"Mr. Whitmore, I need you to run an errand for me."

"Yes, sir."

Captain Dutton handed Henry a roll of drawings. "Run these back to my room at the barracks and bring me back the set laying on my desk."

"Yes, sir." Henry gladly left the camp and checked his normal brisk pace to enjoy the walk.

* * *

Emily was restless. It was a beautiful day, and she wanted to do something other than needlework.

Abby raised her gaze to Emily, but the knitting needles in her hand kept moving. She was working on a blanket for a neighbor expecting her first child. "What is it dear?"

Emily sighed. "I'm feeling restless."

"Would some company help? You could invite your friends over for tea. I could make some scones and invite Betsy too." Their parting the other day was strained by Henry's actions. She needed to assure Betsy she carried no ill will.

Her mother's suggestion didn't satisfy her need, but Emily didn't have any better ideas. "I'll go invite them now."

Noticing her less than enthusiastic response, Abby pondered how to make afternoon tea more appealing. "What if we set up a table in the garden?"

Emily's smile brightened and she nodded. "I'll hurry back to help you." She picked up her parasol on the way out of the door considering which way to go first as the three houses were in three different directions. She turned left headed towards Louisa's near the corner of Front Street.

It was a quick stop to issue the invitation to Louisa. She had just closed the door behind her when she heard her name called. Surely the sound of Henry's voice was purely her imagination. She lifted her gaze and was pleasantly surprised to find Henry hurrying towards her. Her face split into a grin. Here was the true answer to her anxious feelings. "Hello!"

Henry's grin broadened, "Hello, Em. I've missed you." He had a hard time not reaching out to take her hand mindful they were right in front of the Geiger's house. "How have you been?"

"Good. Better now. I've been missing you too."

"I'm on my way back to the camp with these drawings, but I can walk you back to your house."

"Actually, I was headed to your house to invite your mother to tea."

"She'll enjoy it. My sisters too."

They began walking back the way she had come.

"Mother suggested we serve tea in the garden."

"It is a lovely October day for a garden party."

"Yes, it is."

"I can't remember when last I've seen the sky so deeply blue."

Emily heard the longing in his voice and knew he wished to be out on the water. She started to reach out her hand to touch him, but pulled it back as she recalled her mother's admonishment. "Patience, Henry. We must both have patience."

He lowered his voice to a whisper even though no one else was in sight. "Mother told me she and your mother both saw us kissing. Did you get into much trouble?"

"Just a reprimand on proper behavior and a reminder that we are only courting, not engaged." She winked at him. "At least not officially engaged."

Her audacious flirtation made it impossible for him to resist kissing her. He clamped his jaw, balled his fist, and turned his face forward futilely searching for patience and restraint.

Emily instinctively understood his silent battle. She smiled to herself taking mild joy in the power she had over him. It made their relationship feel equal as he held her desire and emotions with the same power.

Henry suddenly leaned down to pick a wild flower from the side of the road. He presented it to her with a bit of a flourish. "A token of my love."

"Thank you." She lifted it to her nose. It had an earthy smell. She brushed the soft petals against her chin.

They walked on in silence, both aching to touch the other, but grateful to be in each other's company, if only for a moment. She could see he wanted to kiss her. She wished he would steal a kiss. She wanted him to so desperately, she didn't care who might see. Well, honestly, she did care, but it would be worth it. He didn't though.

It was disappointing to them both when they reached his house.

Henry lifted her hand to his lips and kissed it. "One day, my love..."

Emily smiled. "It's so hard to be patient."

Her eyes unknowingly pleaded with him to kiss her. It took all his fortitude to resist. "I must get back to the fort."

Emily tightened her hold to keep him from releasing her hand. "I love you."

Henry smiled. "And I love you." He sighed. "One day we will share our lives. For now, I must be off. It takes money to build a house for my future bride."

She smiled. "I would willing live in a hovel if it meant we could be together sooner."

Henry laughed. "I'll keep that in mind. Now, really, I must go. I'll see you on Sunday."

"Yes, Sunday."

Henry began walking away, but a few paces later, he turned and jauntily waved to her.

She waved back. Too soon he disappeared from her sight. Though grateful for the few moments they had, Emily's spirits dropped again with Henry's departure. She climbed the porch steps and knocked on the door. It was answered by Brianna. Emily declined to enter. She issued the invitation to tea and made her way around the fenced back yard and pond to invite Hannah.

Returning home, she found her mother in the backyard setting out chairs while Mrs. Baxley smoothed a yellow damask tablecloth on a round table placed under the edge of the mahogany canopy where the ground was less disturbed by roots. The dappled shade was a pleasant retreat from the bright sunshine. The spot was also chosen for the nearby Beauty Berry bushes her mother cultivated for their ability to repel mosquito. She was crushing some of the leaves between her hands to further release the scent and scattering them on the ground around the table.

Abby looked to Emily. "Is everyone coming?"

"Yes."

"Would you like to make the table arrangement?"

"Yes, I would. Do you have a preference?"

Abby smiled. "Your choice, Emily."

Emily wandered around the yard. Being late in the year, the flowers were limited. The most prolific blooms were on the bougainvillea climbing along the side fence and the roses by the front steps. Emily went inside the house to retrieve a white bone china vase from her mother's china cabinet. She took it outside to the kitchen work table and then retrieved the kitchen shears and a basket since both of her flower choices had thorny stems. She first cut some small palm leaves to give her arrangement added texture before moving on to purple bougainvillea. The flowers were actually very tiny and white, each nestled inside the center of three purple, tissue thin bracts. She cut a multitude of long stems to give an airy feel to the arrangement.

Lastly, at the front steps, she cut five of the nicest roses she could find. Her mother cultivated the thick, healthy bushes from cuttings from her father's childhood home. They and a pocket watch her father always carried were all the reminders he had of his family, as his parents died of scarlet fever when he was a boy. Neighbors burned the house down to prevent the spread of the disease. Her father found the pocket watch in the ashes. The cuttings were taken shortly after Emily was born when her parent's made a trip to New England. They stopped by her father's old home and found the ruins of the house. Surprisingly, the rose bushes were healthier than ever and blooming profusely. When her father told her mother how they were his mother's favorite she insisted on taking cuttings. It was only through Abby's determined efforts they survived the trip and adapted to their new home in Key West. They were considered a local miracle since they shouldn't have survived much less thrive in the limestone soil.

Twenty minutes later, Emily stepped back from the kitchen table to admire the results. The milky white roses with hints of pink were evenly nestled in the draping, deep purple bougainvillea supported by the palm branches. She took the arrangement out to the table, pleased with her color choices against the yellow tablecloth.

Emily next helped in the kitchen making sweetened lemonade for the younger children while her mother pulled the freshly baked scones from the oven. By the time their guests began to arrive, the table was set with cups, saucers, and dessert plates. Blended black tea was steeping in a heated tea kettle beside the platter of scones and a dish of pigeon plum jelly. Upstairs, a tray of lemonade and biscuits waited in the nursery for the younger children who would be looked after by Lydia and Mrs. Baxley.

Brianna was thrilled when Mrs. Eatonton invited her to join the ladies in the garden. Agatha showed her displeasure at being left behind by sticking her tongue out at Brianna when their mother wasn't looking. It was the first time Brianna was included with the older girls and the adults. It made her feel special. Almost as special as when Thorn asked her to dance at Emily's birthday party. This was her first formal tea. She did her best to mimic her mother's actions.

After greetings and gushing over the table setting, the six ladies settled down to enjoy the fragrant tea and scones with light-hearted banter consisting of reminiscing over Emily's birthday ball, dress styles, favorite flowers and songs, and the occasional bit of friendly gossip. Emily had to admit the tea party was a good distraction.

They were discussing current needlework projects when two ruby-throated hummingbirds flew over the table violently striking each other. The buzz of their darting flight mixed with angry chirping and their clashing beaks stunned the group into horrified silence as they watched the two female's fight to claim the red blossoms on the nearby Mandeville. The chase swung around the yard before one flew off and the other returned to feed on the coveted nectar. The group remained silent, watching the tiny glimmering green body flit from one cherry trumpet to the next. A moment later, the nemesis returned. They once again mimicked a floating sword match around the yard. When the contestants flew away, talk resumed around the table.

Hannah said, "Isn't the sky an exceptionally bright blue today?"

They all looked up.

Betsy murmured, "It is beautiful."

Abby nodded. "Yes, it is. Max would call it a weather breeder. There will be a bad storm somewhere soon." Instantly, her thoughts shifted to worries of Max and Christoff's safety.

Hannah and Louisa sent worried glances to each other and Emily grimaced. "You don't think it could be another hurricane, do you?"

Abby smiled encouragingly. "I hope not but only time will tell."

Brianna cast a worried glance at her mother. She well recalled how frightened she was two years ago when the last hurricane struck them.

Betsy noted the troubled looks on the young faces around the table. "Chin up. There's no sense borrowing trouble. If a hurricane it will be, we've survived many before. Today is a gift, and we should enjoy it to its fullest."

* * *

Henry walked the length of his father's bookshelves for a second time looking for anything to distract him from thoughts of Emily. He finally accepted defeat. Nothing peaked his interest.

Supper ended over an hour ago. His parents were engaged in backgammon, Brianna was doing needlepoint, and James was playing with a toy horse and wagon. Emmaline and Agatha had finished the dishes and returned to the parlor to do needlepoint and read. Soon it would be their bedtime. There were still several hours left in his evening, and he needed a distraction from thinking of Emily.

The cameo his mother was wearing didn't help either. He noticed it as soon as he saw her. She smiled and said, "I hope you don't mind. Things are to be enjoyed in the moment not saved for a special day that may never come or hidden away." She was right, but the reminder of Aunt Aggie only increased his disquiet.

Earlier in the day, Flynn invited him to have a drink after work. At the time, he turned him down, but now the idea held some appeal.

To the room he announced. "I'm going out for a walk. I'll be back in an hour or two."

Theodore looked up from studying his next move. "Take care, son."

Henry made his escape and strolled through the gathering twilight to the far end of Front Street. He saw Flynn sitting at the bar as he passed the front window of the grog shop. He walked through the open doorway into the large open room. Cigar smoke lingered in the air from two gentlemen in the corner playing cards. The barkeep was busy refilling drinks for the three fishermen lined up on stools to one side of Flynn. Henry slid onto the empty stool on his right. Flynn nodded to acknowledge his presence, and turned his attention back to the fishermen. From the sounds of it, they were trying to outdo each other with tales of epic fishing.

The barkeep stepped in front of Henry. "What can I get ya?"

"Whiskey." A glass tumbler was soon placed in front of him with two fingers of amber liquid. He took a sip and felt the heat ease down his throat. He idly turned his attention back to the fishermen.

The closest one held up his hands shoulder width apart. "I tell you it was that big if it was an inch."

The far end said, "Psh, one big one ain't nothing. I was hauling in fish faster than I could reset the lines. Thank goodness I came in early. Dropped off a whole mess of fish at the market ahead of Nelson. I heard he was filled to the brim too."

The third man somberly said, "Fishin' this good only means one thing."

His pronouncement hung in the air like a death threat. He and his companions took a moment of respectful silence. Henry looked to Flynn who shrugged his shoulders. Henry addressed the fishermen, "What does it mean?"

The closest man set down the glass he almost had to his lips and slowly turned to Henry. "Big gale coming."

Henry's brow furrowed. "How does good fishing mean a storm is coming?"

The old fisherman shook his head. "Don't know why. Just be so."

Henry turned his gaze back to his drink. He hoped it would be just a gale and not a hurricane. Henry remembered riding out one when he was a boy. He remembered helping get the house ready, sitting inside all day listening to the wind roar, and cleaning up all the fallen debris afterwards. The scariest moment was when a cocoanut broke the upstairs window. As a kid, it was something of an adventure. He doubted he would feel so now if he had to go through another one. He hoped the fishermen were wrong.

Chapter 11

Land Ho!
Jump the mountain peak to the other side
Tangled and tripped
Greedy hunger leading onward

Saturday, October 10th, 1846

Henry noticed the sky had an ominous red glow as he walked to work in the early dawn. The eerie light revealed darker nimbus clouds sweeping across the overcast sky. It brought to mind the fisherman's prediction. Clearly there was a brewing storm headed their way.

The red faded with the full light of morning, but the clouds continued to come and go. A smattering of misty rain hit his back, hurrying him along. He was one of a dozen men moving wheelbarrow loads of red brick out to the fort. In the next moment, his concerns mocked him with patches of blue sky. By the time, he reached shore for another load it was growing overcast again.

As the morning passed, the intermittent rain increased. When a worker nearly fell from the rain slickened boards Captain Dutton was forced to call a halt to the day's work. There were no complaints from his soggy workers. Unable to sponge fish either, Henry washed his face and hands at the fort camp and headed off to visit Emily.

Mrs. Eatonton was standing on their porch studying the sky. She smiled in greeting at Henry's approach, but it did not reach her eyes. He could see her growing concern, but then he remembered Captain Max and Christoff were out wrecking. Perhaps her concern was more for them than how bad the approaching weather might be for the islanders.

"Hello Henry."

He rushed up the steps to get out of the drizzling rain. "Hello, Mrs. Eatonton."

Her gaze was drawn back to the bands of clouds. She already noted their movement swept from east to west. She didn't need Max to tell her it was a bad sign. She had been through enough storms on the island to know. She couldn't believe it was happening again. This would be the second time Max was out on the *Mystic* while she carried the family through a hurricane. Last time he sailed home four days later with a broken mast. How bad would it be this time? She would do best to put her worry for them in God's hands. There was nothing she could do for them and plenty she needed to do here. Her mind was working on a list of things needing to be done in preparation. She turned her gaze back to Henry. "Are you here to visit Emily?"

"Yes, ma'am."

"I suggest you make it a quick visit and get on home. Would you mind sending the boys out to help me get the house ready for the storm?"

If he needed any more confirmation trouble was on the way, her request was it. "Yes, ma'am."

Henry walked into the house and called out, "Emily." She soon appeared at the top of the stairs. "Are your brothers up there?"

"Yes."

"Your mother needs Thorn and Nate to help her with the house."

Emily turned back towards the bedrooms and returned with her brothers. They flew down the stairs ahead of her. Thorn nudged Nate's shoulder. "See. I told you it was going to be a hurricane." They brushed past him and out of the door like their own storm.

Emily stopped on the bottom step. Despite their brief encounter yesterday, it felt like it had been too long since last she saw him. The dreary weather could not dampen her spirits for she was too happy to be in Henry's company.

Henry stepped forward to the bottom step so that they were nearly eye level with each other. Softly he said, "Hello, Em."

She smiled. "Hello, Henry."

"I can't stay. I need to go help my family prepare for the storm, but if I can, I'll visit later."

"I hope so."

He leaned forward and kissed her cheek before turning smartly and going back out the front door. The way the rain came in pelting bursts and could dwindle to nothing in between strengthened the notion it was more than just a rainy day.

Henry arrived home to find his father securing the last shutter on the house, so he went to the backyard to help bring in any loose items around the house. Outside the kitchen, he grabbed the bucket and basin from the wash station and deposited them inside on the kitchen table where he found his mother gathering food and water. Next, he pulled in a bench and the work table they used for cleaning fish. He then helped his father move his mother's potted plants inside.

After depositing two more plants in a corner, Theodore looked at the pile of food on the table. "Betsy, be sure to gather everything edible without cooking. I would rather have too much than not enough." She silently nodded her agreement and returned to her task.

Henry entered the room from the opposite door with a potted peony.

Betsy pointed to the upper shelf. "Would you mind getting down those two baskets?"

Dripping wet, Henry stretched to reach them and placed them on the table where Betsy began quickly loading them with food. On his return with another plant, she asked him to take one of the baskets to the house. Theodore soon followed behind with the second.

From the kitchen doorway, Betsy glanced around the yard for any treasured plants they might have missed. Finding none, she secured the doors on either side of the kitchen and dashed through the rain to the house.

Henry was waiting for a chance to let them know his plans.

Theodore wiped his face with a towel and passed it to Betsy.

Emmaline came into the room and eyed the baskets of food. "Are we giving away all our food?"

Betsy laughed. "No, sweetheart. We're going to have an indoor picnic later."

Emmaline gleefully smiled and ran off to tell her sisters and brother.

Theodore cast a glance at Henry. "We should go see if help is needed to secure the churches and government buildings."

Henry could have groaned at the added delay in returning to Emily, but he knew his father was right. They made their way down Whitehead Street, splitting up at the corner of Eaton Street. His father went forward to Jackson Square to help with the public buildings. Henry turned left to help with the churches.

* * *

While Henry headed off in the fitful rain with his father to help the town, his younger sisters were upstairs in the nursery explaining the storm to James.

Brianna turned from the window to face her siblings. "Momma and Poppa won't say it because they don't want to scare us, but I'm old enough to know this is a hurricane."

Agatha and Emmaline's eyes grew wide. They remembered the hurricane of two years ago; the hours of screeching wind that hurt their ears, the endless pelting rain, things crashing about outside, and having to help clean up all the palm branches and leaves strewn about the yard afterwards.

The earnestness in his sister's face concerned James. "What's a hairy-cane?"

Agatha turned to her little brother proud to share her more worldly experience. "It's a monster storm that tries to shake the house down."

Brianna rolled her eyes. "Aggie you're going to scare him to death." She moved to kneel in front of the round-eyed toddler. "It is a very windy storm. It will rattle the windows, but we'll be safe in the house."

"With Momma and Poppa?"

She smiled. "Yes. Momma and Poppa will keep you safe."

* * *

Theodore held the board in place over the jail house window with his shoulder while holding a nail with the same hand. He hammered it in quickly and reached for another nail from his pocket. He was a veteran now at prepping for these storms and could efficiently manage the preparation of the buildings. He wished he could face the storm itself as calmly as he covered the windows. After going through many of them since moving here, they still had the power to make him nervous. On a small island, there was no escape. One couldn't retreat further inland or take a train somewhere else like you could on the mainland. By the time a storm revealed its strength, it was not safe to leave by water.

He looked up from his task surprised to see Stephen Mallory approaching in what appeared to be his Sunday best.

Mr. Mallory stepped up quickly to give him a hand holding the board. "Here, let me help."

Theodore nodded. "Thanks." Another pair of hands certainly made the job easier. He reached for another nail and cast a sideways glance at his companion. "A bit overdressed for storm preparations."

Mr. Mallory looked down at his clothes and shrugged. "I came straight over from celebrating Mass at City Hall. A priest from Havana is visiting long enough to say Mass and perform sacraments before sailing on to Charleston with high tide."

"You probably should have changed first."

"I was worried about the buildings. It didn't cross my mind."

"Is City Hall taken care of?"

"Yes. I left several fellow parishioners seeing to it."

"Good. Judge Marvin and Marshall Browne are seeing to the Court House."

Mr. Mallory nodded. "That's good. I came to help and to make sure the official papers were secure."

Sheriff Coslin arrived in time to hear the last. "Ah good. I was worried I would have to do this on my own. I'll take over, Mr. Mallory, so you can see about those papers."

Mr. Mallory traded positions with Sheriff Coslin and clapped him on the back. "Thanks."

The sheriff nodded and watched him walk away. In a few hammer strikes, Theodore had the other side secure so Sheriff Coslin could let go. Together they finished nailing the board and started on the next window. The windows on the front being done, they moved to the sides which were higher. Fortunately, Sheriff Coslin had the height to reach them so Theodore held the boards. In no time, the task was complete. With the government buildings secure, Theodore and Mr. Mallory walked back to town with the rain pelting on their backs.

Mr. Mallory looked at Theodore questioningly when he kept walking past his house.

"I need to board up the newspaper office."

"Of course. I'll help if you like."

"I would be much obliged."

"We'll call it even, if you help with my house."

"Deal. What about the custom house?"

"I surely could use your help with that too."

* * *

Henry and several other young men helped secure the steepleless St. Paul's Episcopal Church. With several of them working at it, the storm shutters were soon closed and latched over the multitude of windows. They moved on to the incomplete First Methodist Episcopal Church South to do the same, although without a permanent roof, Henry wondered if it wasn't a futile effort.

When they were done, Reverend Richardson called them all together. Huddled under the entry overhang he said a quick prayer for the safety of all. He dismissed them with a reminder to be good stewards by looking out for their neighbors and taking care of those in need.

Henry was hungry and ready for dinner, but first he had to go down to the wharf to secure his boat and sponges. He took the shortcut across the pond, carefully traversing the slippery narrow walkway. More than once the gusting wind tried to knock him off balance, but he managed to get to shore without falling off. He ran the rest of the way past his warehouse and down to the water.

He debated pulling in the sponges from the soaking line in the water. The normally calm water was wildly undulating from the approaching storm front. Would the sponges be safe riding in the waves? He finally decided he didn't want to take the risk of stronger tides pulling the nets loose and robbing him of all his hard work. He pulled the net in and hauled the bundle of half decayed sponges to the boat. He dumped them in and dragged the boat up the beach, stopping to add the bundle of sponges he had left strung up to dry. The boat was now piled so high he struggled to keep it from spilling over. He finally pulled it all into his warehouse. The weight and effort of doing so left him breathing hard. He stood in the open doorway a moment catching his breath while watching the gusting sheets of rain. He didn't linger long. As soon as his breathing returned to normal, he stepped out and securely latched the door. He ran a quick glance over the building noting the sound construction. He could only hope it would stand if the wind and water turned violent.

It was well past midday now, and he was starving. He decided it was best to head home to eat before returning to Emily's.

Betsy rose from her seat on the porch to greet him with a smile and a towel to dry off. "I saved you a plate in the dining room."

Henry warmly returned her smile. "Thank you."

He found his father already seated and working ravenously on his meal. "Is the town ready?"

Theodore's mouth was full so he nodded.

"Good." Henry bowed his head and silently prayed over his food before starting in with the same dedication. Father and son downed their food and water in silence. When they were almost done and feeling better with nourishment a childhood memory settled over Henry and made him laugh.

Theodore looked up at the sound. "What's so funny?"

"I was reminded of all those silent meals we shared with Aunt Aggie because she didn't like conversation while she was eating, and then I recalled the first time, around this very table, when you defied her. We had company and you had just returned from a trip to visit an Indian camp."

"Hmm. I remember. I had just returned from Charlotte Harbor with William Whitehead."

"That was before the war, wasn't it?"

"Yes."

"You told her it was your table, under your roof, and you were going to share your story. She puckered up in displeasure, but did you notice, by the time you had everyone else at the table laughing about missing forks and knives, she was hiding her smiles?"

"I did notice, but she held her tongue until she was done eating even though she had questions."

Henry's smile faded. He lifted sad eyes to his father's. "I miss her."

"I do too, son."

Betsy entered the room to check on them. She cast a questioning glance at Theodore.

"We miss Aunt Agatha."

She smiled tightly and moved her gaze from Theodore to Henry. "As do I. She was cantankerous, but I do believe she meant well."

Theodore reached out and squeezed her hand. "That she did." He rose from the table to kiss her cheek. "Thank you for the food. It couldn't have been easy to make with everything crowded into the kitchen."

Betsy smiled and picked up Theodore's plate. "There are worse things than preparing a meal surrounded by plants. Now that your stomachs are full, you should both change into dry clothes."

Henry stood and handed her his empty plate. "Thank you, Mother." He looked from one parent to the other. "If you don't mind, I'm going to visit the Eatonton's. I may not return till after supper."

Betsy set the plates down on the table. She saw the determined look in his eye and held her words. It would do no good asking him to stay and even less telling him to stay. She kissed Henry's cheek and then laid her hand against it. "Be careful."

Henry gave her a nod. "I will."

Theodore followed Henry out to the porch. The rain was almost constant now and the wind continued with sporadic gusts. He cast a worried look at the sky. Coming to the same conclusion Betsy had, he brought his gaze back to Henry's. "Keep an eye on the weather. If the wind picks up, I want you to come home."

"Yes, sir."

Theodore watched Henry lope off into the downpour with mixed emotions flowing over him; pride, sadness, nostalgia, but mostly grateful his first-born had returned, and it appeared to be for good.

* * *

Henry arrived at the Eatonton's drenched to the skin and chilled. Thorn opened the door and stood back for him to enter. Emily soon appeared handing him a towel to dry off.

Abby went to the foyer to see who was calling in this weather. She was not surprised to find Henry dripping on the rug. "Henry, you're soaked. Thorn, take him to your room to change. He can borrow some of Christoff's clothes."

Henry was going to protest, but the determined look in Mrs. Eatonton's eye made him hold his tongue. He returned less than ten minutes later carrying his bundle of wet clothes thinking he should leave them on the front porch.

Abby saw Henry hesitate at the bottom of the stairs. "You can hang your clothes on the pegs in the back room to dry."

He wasn't surprised by Mrs. Eatonton's direction. He had always been treated like family, not a guest, in this house. She was also one of those women that believed it was better for a person to do for themselves than to do it for them.

Emily stepped forward holding out her hands. "I'll take them for you."

Henry felt his cheeks get hot. His smallclothes were in the bundle too. The idea of Emily seeing them... or touching them... Now his ears felt hot too. He emphatically shook his head. "No, I'll do it." He quickly turned from her and left the room as fast as he could walk.

Baffled, Emily watched him leave the room.

Thorn stepped up to her shoulder. "He's embarrassed."

Emily looked over her shoulder. "Whatever for?"

"He didn't want you messing with his underclothes."

"But I'm sure his sisters have done his laundry, and I've washed yours before."

Thorn shrugged. "It's different when it's a girl you're smitten with."

The practical side of Emily still didn't understand. Thorn walked away, so she put herself in Henry's shoes and thought of him hanging up her chemise and... Her cheeks went pink picturing Henry holding up her bloomers. She turned away from the room to hide her face which got even hotter when she heard Thorn snickering until her mother declared, "Enough."

Emily followed them into the parlor and resumed her earlier seat in the Queen Anne chair. She picked up her needlepoint sampler while she waited for Henry to return.

A few moments later, Henry appeared in the parlor doorway to find

Nate and Thorn standing over the gaming table debating between playing chess or backgammon. Jacob was kneeling on the heart of pine floor exposed between the room's area rugs building a tower with his wooden blocks. Mrs. Eatonton and Emily were settled in the matching Queen Anne chairs strategically placed in front of the window to capture the natural light for needle work. With the dense storm and closed shutters, there wasn't much light to be had today, so a lamp flickered on the small table between them. He chose the settee adjacent to them for its closer proximity to Emily.

The boys finally decided on a game of chess and were quietly involved in setting up the pieces when Jacob decided to topple his tower. The resulting cacophony of wood striking wood brought the ladies heads up only to smile and once again resume their work.

Emily lifted her gaze to Henry. "Would you like to play a game? Backgammon or cards, perhaps?"

Henry shook his head. "It's been a busy day. I'm content to sit quietly for now."

"Were you helping prepare for the storm?"

"Yes. After our house, I helped with the churches, and then secured my boat and sponges in the warehouse. I hope it holds if this storm gets really bad."

Abby paused from crewel stitching a fern on the edge of a tablecloth she intended as a Christmas gift for Betsy to glance at the weather glass hanging on the wall nearby. She nervously noted the water's progression up the spout of the glass indicating another drop in the air pressure. She still didn't want to say it out loud and upset the children, but they were definitely in for a hurricane. The concern tightened her features. She couldn't be sure, but she thought the pressure might be lower than it was before the storm in 1844. That one was so bad several houses were severely damaged and the Revenue Cutter Vigilant and her crew went missing from the harbor never to be seen again. It was going to be a long night waiting and praying.

Henry noticed Mrs. Eatonton's distress. He followed her gaze to the weather glass and felt the tendrils of fear tighten around his spine. He had never seen it look like that. His eyes collided with Mrs. Eatonton's and in them he could see her plea to keep silent for now. He gave a slight tilt of his head to acknowledge her request and turned his attention back to Emily. He missed most of what she said, but fortunately, his attention returned in time to hear her question.

"Would you draw something in my scrapbook?"

Henry mutely nodded. She got up to retrieve it from her bedroom. While she was gone, Henry listened to the pattering rain. His father's words came back to him, so under the pretense of seeing how the chess game was progressing, he casually stood in front of the window on the adjacent wall. The gusts did not sound any worse than before, but he supposed he should only stay another hour or two before heading home.

He met Emily in the center of the room when she returned. He carefully took the large book from her and followed her to the settee. He sat beside her and opened the book, so it lay across both their laps. He quickly took advantage of the situation by secretly holding her hand beneath the open book. Emily turned her head giving him a blushing smile before awkwardly turning the first page with her left hand. She showed him her collection of messages, poems, copied quotes, lockets of woven hair from friends and family, magazine clippings, drawings (some quite good), ribbons, and fancy doodles. Pages here and there captured events in her life with journaling of attendees, food and drink. A page or two she quickly turned, not giving him a chance to read. Her pinkened cheeks made him curious, but he said nothing. When they reached the blank pages she let go of his hand and pushed the book towards his lap.

"Do you have a pencil I can use?" He usually carried his supplies with him, but due to the rain he had left them at home.

"I do and I have some pastels if you would like to add color."

Henry carried the book to the round, tea table set in the middle of the room with four chairs. He settled in as Emily brought him a box of pastels.

"What would you like for me to draw?"

Emily sat next to him and shrugged. "I don't know."

"What is your favorite animal?"

"I love the sea turtles, and dolphins, and hummingbirds, and pelicans, and roosters, cats, and lizards–the small ones with the blue tails more than the large green ones."

Henry chuckled. "I should have remembered." She looked at him quizzically. "You love all creatures."

She bounced her head from side to side with a closed smile. "Yes, I suppose I do."

"Since you named it first, I will draw you a green sea turtle swimming in the water."

She nodded her head. "I would like that." Emily quietly watched him as he went to work.

About twenty minutes later, Henry was putting the finishing touches on the outline of the turtle when a heavy rustling noise moving down the side of the house disturbed the room's occupants.

Abby hurried to the window to peer through the cracks in the shutter slats. "I think it was a torn palm branch." She turned to the room and in a cheerful voice said, "Boys, I want you to go to your room and drag your bedding down. We're going to sleep downstairs tonight. Henry, would you mind helping them?"

"Yes, ma'am."

In no time, all their bedding was arranged in the centermost point of the house. Abby turned to Henry. "I think it best if you go home now."

Henry nodded. "I agree." He hated parting from Emily and thought of Mrs. Eatonton by herself. "Are you sure I shouldn't stay since Captain Max isn't here?"

Abby smiled. "He usually isn't here. We'll be fine. Your parents will be worried and may need help with your sisters."

Emily said, "Wait." She dashed off down the hall to return a few moments later with Henry's clothes in a bundle. She handed them to him.

Suddenly, the possibility of what they may be facing gave Henry an unsettled feeling. What if...he couldn't think it. He wouldn't think it. Still, the worry made a simple goodbye impossible. He hugged each of them, holding Emily a little tighter and longer than the rest, and daringly kissed her cheek right in front of her mother. Bravely he said, "I will see you tomorrow." He gave a jaunty wave as he opened the front door and stepped out into a blustery wind that pelted him with water before he even cleared the porch.

He walked northwest on Whitehead Street towards home. Between the houses, the wind gusted against his back. Right now, it was an unpleasant rain storm. How much worse was it going to get? He ran up the front porch steps glad to be home and out of the weather. It was going on five o'clock but the diminished light made it feel much later.

"Thank goodness you're home!"

Henry smiled indulgently as his mother rushed to greet him at the door as if he had been missing for days. His father trailed behind, no less grateful, but more sedate in showing it. His mother hugged him tightly and then linked her arm in his pulling him along to the parlor where the rest of the family was gathered in the gloom of the storm shuttered house.

"How is Abby doing?"

Henry brought them to a halt in the hall and quietly directed his answer to both of them. "She is concerned. Have you checked the weather glass?"

Theodore's jaw clenched. "I have. It concerns me too."

Henry nodded. "Before I left, she had us pull all the bedding downstairs so they could sleep in the foyer away from the windows."

Theodore nodded. "A sensible idea. We'll do the same."

Betsy looked from one to the other. "But we don't have a room without windows."

Theodore tilted his head towards the front of the house. "We'll sleep in the study. It will be tight but less chance of being hurt by flying debris."

Betsy looked up at her husband. "Why is that?"

"The wind is blowing against the back of the house. Anything airborne will strike the back and east sides of the house making the front west corner the safest."

"That seems sensible."

"Betsy, you and Agatha gather our provisions and move them to the study. Henry, Brianna, and I will bring our bedding down."

They entered the parlor and Betsy let go of Henry. "Girls, we need your help. Emmaline, you're to mind James. Keep him out of our way. Agatha, we're going to move the food and water and a few more lamps to the study."

Theodore stood in the doorway. "Brianna, you'll help move our beds downstairs."

Emmaline stood rooted in place, her eyes wide as saucers. "Mama is it a hurricane?" The monster Agatha teasingly spoke of to James was becoming very real to her.

James started a rhythmic clapping. "Hairy-cane, hairy-cane, hairy-cane."

Agatha was quick to shush him, afraid her mother would find out about their earlier conversation.

Betsy turned to Theodore. He saw the distressed look in her eyes. Putting his own fear aside, he smiled reassuringly for her. He stepped forward to place his hand on the back of her head in a loving caress and kissed her forehead before entering the parlor. He picked up James and settled in a straight-back chair by the tea table. "Girls come here." Agatha and Emmaline came to stand on either side of his knees. He looked into their anxious eyes and his heart went out to them. *How could he ease their worry without lying to them?* "Yes, it looks as if this will be a hurricane." Emmaline's gasp tore at his heart. He pulled his little Emmie-Grace to his side. He couldn't do the same for Agatha with James on his knee. Instead, he opened his hand for her to grasp. Betsy came to his aide. She knelt between the girls and wrapped her arm around Agatha. "We don't know how bad it will be, but you don't have to worry. We're right here to protect you. We're not going to let it hurt you, but you need to be good girls," he looked down, "and boy, and do exactly what we tell you to do with no questions asked. Is that understood?"

Both girls mumbled. "Yes, Poppa."

He gently smiled. "It's going to be all right and fun, even. Once we get our chores done, we'll play games and have our picnic supper in here on the floor. Later, we'll all go to sleep together in the study. And we won't worry about the big ol' storm outside because we'll be tucked safe and sound in this good strong house." A glance at Betsy's concerned eyes and the skeptical looks on the girls' faces made him realize they needed more than his assurances. He lifted his gaze to the doorway. "Henry, Brianna, come join us, please."

Sensing his father's thoughts Henry led Brianna into the room and knelt between his mother and Emmaline. Brianna took the space on the other side of Agatha. The family joined hands and bowed their heads.

Theodore spoke softly. "Dear Lord, we know not what is to come or what your plan is for us, but we rest easy in your assurance that faith in you will bring us through whatever may come. We ask for your protection not only for our family and friends but for everyone in our town and all who are in the path of this storm. Give us strength to face it with faith and courage. And may my family live in the words of our family verse from your servant, Joshua. Have not I commanded Thee! Be strong and of a good courage: be not afraid, neither be thou dismayed: for the Lord thy God is with thee whithersoever thou goest. Amen."

His family echoed him. "Amen."

"Now, let's continue our preparations with faithful hearts."

And they did. The tasks were quickly done. They picnicked on smoked fish, cheese, and walnuts. They played every active game they could think of that was safe for inside to wear out the younger children so they would go to bed peacefully. In the study, the desk was pushed up against the wall and covered with their supplies. In the corner by the hallway, the three youngest were sleeping together. Brianna and Henry would share a mattress on the other side of the door. Betsy and Theodore placed their bed next to it. A small pathway ran the center of the room from the doorway to the window.

Betsy tried to close her mind, to stop listening to the wind and rain. Waiting for a gale's arrival, wondering how severe it was going to be, was tedious, but she knew once it was upon them, the hours were to be endured until it passed.

The noise of the storm was muffled by the full bookcases banking each wall and the closed heavy drapes. They were snug from the storm, but the air was hot and stifled, making it difficult for the adults to find sleep.

Eventually, they all dozed fitfully.

Chapter 12

Renewed on the Florida Straights
To even stronger strength

Sunday, October 11th

Abby awoke in the early hours unsure what had disturbed her slumber. The room was dark. She could barely make out the shapes of her sleeping children, even Jacob, curled up as he was with his back nestled against her chest. She carefully slipped away from him to stand beside the table. She felt for the matches she placed there the night before. Years of practice made it easy to remove a match from the box and set the tip inside a folded piece of sandpaper pulling it out briskly. As the flame flared and settled, she lifted the glass chimney from the ceramic oil lamp and touched the flame to the oil-soaked wick. When the light strengthened, she lifted the lamp to illuminate the portico table clock forgetting she had moved it out of the room to keep the quarter chimes from disturbing their slumber. Quietly, she made her way to the parlor to discover the clock hands pointed at five minutes to three o'clock.

The sounds of the storm were muted in the foyer but here in the parlor near the eastern outside wall, she could hear the wind blowing against the house. It still wasn't a gale but it was certainly stronger than when they retired. In a way she could never explain, she felt the building menace of the approaching storm. Further attempts to sleep would be useless. *Poseidon's strength had effectively banished Morpheus' hold.* Abby laughed softly at her fanciful musing.

The reverberance of a heavy tree limb crashing in the yard startled a scream from her. She cast the light towards the weather glass on the wall and nearly dropped the lamp. The water was dripping out of the spout. This hurricane was going to be a much worse than any before it.

Her concerns grew. She knew this house was soundly built but others on the island were not. People were going to be in need of medical care, especially after the storm, and what about the patients now at the Marine Hospital? It was normally short-staffed overnight, especially on the weekend. It was likely by morning most of the doctors and nurses would not be able to leave their homes. It would be too dangerous.

She felt God urging her to go. Her skills would be needed, and she was close. The hospital was less than a thousand feet from her back door. If she left now, she could easily make it there. But... she couldn't leave the children. It didn't even bear thinking. She could not be separated from them at a time like this. God's answer was clear in her mind. *Take them with you.* Still, she argued against it. It was pouring rain outside and the wind would make it difficult for Nate and Jacob. They would all be soaked to the skin before they got out of the yard. God mocked her excuse with silence. Abby closed her eyes and took a fortifying breath. She knew better than to argue with Him. He knew best. Maybe they would be safer at the hospital with its heavy brick foundation, even if it was right on the water. She would heed His command.

With the decision made, Abby moved on to practical matters. She hated the idea of waking her sleeping family and dragging them out into the storm, but there was really no other choice. She would have to do it now before the storm got any worse or more dangerous. She returned to the foyer and met Emily's concerned gaze. "Good, you're awake. I'm taking all of you with me to the hospital. Quickly, wake your brothers."

"Why are we going to the hospital?"

Firmly and without emotion, Abby replied, "Emily, now is the time to act without question."

"Yes, mother." Emily turned to do her bidding, starting with Thorn, then Nate, and saving Jacob for last. She had no idea why her mother would want to move them now. If she was needed at the hospital, why didn't they go there last night? Emily shook Thorn's shoulder. He grumbled and complained until their mother called him to help her gather supplies. Nate was always sweet-natured no matter how much he was annoyed to be woken in the dead of night. Jacob couldn't keep his eyes open, so she let him sleep. She would wake him again when it was time to leave. Fortunately, they had all went to bed pretty much still dressed because of the approaching storm. She slipped her feet into her boots and buttoned them. She then did the same for Jacob while he continued to sleep.

Abby filled a basket with all the food she had previously brought in from the kitchen. She covered it with oilcloth and handed it to Thorn. She checked the downstairs rooms for anything else they might need. Seeing the mattresses on the floor, she worried about flooding. Time was of the essence so rather than take them all the way upstairs to the rooms, she had Emily and Thorn help her move them partway up the stairs. Deeming them ready to leave, Abby lit two covered lanterns, handing one to Nate. She led them to the back door where Emily was waiting with Jacob who was rubbing his eyes and trying not to whine. Abby handed Emily one of the umbrellas by the door. She took the other one and looked them over. "Ready?"

Thorn shrugged. "As ready as we can be." He opened the door and waited for the others to pass before closing the door behind him. Fortunately, the back of the house was in the lee of the winds. Under cover of the portico the ladies opened the umbrellas. Abby looked down at Jacob. "Hold on to my arm and stay close." He tightly grasped her arm holding the umbrella. In her other hand, she held the lantern aloft. They stepped out into the yard and were soon pushed along by wind and driving rain.

Emily and Nate huddled together under the second umbrella. Just before stepping out from under the cover, she tossed a look back to Thorn. He shook his head. The covering was only large enough for two. He had already decided to run ahead of the group. He was confident he could find his own way in the dark and move quicker unencumbered.

Emily grimaced at the heavy wind-tossed water pelting against her left side and back. The umbrella was doing little good. She was still getting soaked by the cold rain. A few steps ahead of them, her mother and Jacob had just reached the other side of the outdoor kitchen when a hard gust turned their umbrella inside out. Her mother tossed it into the open kitchen. The door must not have been lashed tightly. The wind had already torn it from one of the hinges. She grasped Jacob's hand and hastened her pace. Emily looked to Nate and at his nod she tossed their umbrella into the outbuilding as well. Together, they dashed ahead, soon catching up to their mother and Jacob. Thorn was out of sight in the darkness. They only had to cross three lots to reach the hospital, but it now seemed a very long way.

Shivering from her cold, wet clothes, Emily held her hand to her face to shield it from the sheets of windblown rain. Nate held the lantern aloft although it did little to light their way in the encompassing darkness. His other hand tightly grasped hers rather than protect his face. Around them, the eerie silhouettes of trees and bushes erratically danced in the gusting wind. Every so often the gusts were strong enough to push them sideways and they struggled to keep their footing. At least the way was familiar, and the yard behind theirs was fenced giving them a guide.

Emily didn't understand why her mother felt it was so important to uproot them from a warm dry house in the dead of night. She only hoped the reason was worth what they were going through to get there. She shivered again and noticed Nate did too. They had come to the end of the fence. Now they had to pass the house, cross Thomas Street, pass one more house and an empty lot, and they would reach Emma Street and the hospital. As if in slow motion, yet moving as fast as they could, they managed to do just that. Her skirts grew heavy as the water penetrated the layers of her dress, crinoline, and chemise.

Finally, the two-storied, white-washed brick and windowed facade of the Marine Hospital loomed in front of them. They passed through the gate in the white picket fence and raced up the crushed stone walk. They climbed the many steps to the front door which Thorn opened for them. Behind him the hall welcomed them in with a bright yellow glow.

Thorn pushed the door closed against the wind as they stood huddled in the entryway making puddles on the floor. Abby looked at the long faces of her soaked children and berated herself for not thinking to bring dry clothes with them. She knew they would get wet, but she expected the protection of the umbrellas to at least keep them halfway dry. She leaned down and briskly rubbed Jacob's arms to give him some warmth. The approach of hurried footsteps brought her attention to a young lady with dark hair and a welcoming smile coming down the hallway with an armload of towels. Abby rose to greet her. "Millie, thank you."

Millie handed out the towels as she spoke, "Abby, I can't believe you came out in this weather, and with your children no less, but I'm glad you did. The storm is making some of the patients restless. We could use your help."

Abby smiled inwardly. *The Lord knows his people's needs.* "I am happy to help." She turned to her children. "You remember Nurse Millie?"

Four voices overlapped as they greeted the nurse wearing a large plain white apron over an everyday navy dress.

"Good morning children... I think I may be able to scrounge up some dry clothes. Come this way. There's an examination room you can use for privacy. We can hang your clothes to dry."

Abby wrapped the towel around her shoulders. "That would be nice Millie. Thank you."

Emily followed the tall brunette down the bright hall, with its lingering smell of cut lumber, into the foul air of the dimly lit, open ward occupied by a dozen patients taking up about half the available beds. She buried her nose in the towel in retreat of the horrid mixture of body odor, used chamber pots, laudanum, camphor, and other things she couldn't identify. *How could her mother stand working here?* She glanced over her shoulder at her family trailing behind her. Jacob's wrinkled nose was the only indication the smell bothered any of them. At the far end of the building, they came to a short hallway with two doors facing each other.

Nurse Millie opened the one on the left and stepped aside. "You can use this room. I'll be right back with whatever clothes I can find."

Emily stepped inside the examination room to find a large, tall heavy table in the middle with a foot stool at one end. To the side was a chair and a smaller table being used as a desk with an assortment of instruments neatly arranged on its surface. In the far corner was a dressing screen. The unlatched storm shutters made a staccato sound as the wind beat them against the building. Her mother cast a quick glance about the room and purposefully strode forward to open the window. A blast of watery wind tore past her. She ruthlessly pulled the shutters closed and latched them, closing the window again. She then turned to her children. "Thorn and Nate, I have a task for you to do before you get dried off. Come with me."

Abby led the boys to a storage room and began handing them all the buckets she could find. She dragged a small, oval shaped bath tub into the main room. "I want you boys to fill this tub with water from the cistern and then fill the buckets." It wouldn't be enough if the hospital's cisterns were flooded with salt water, but at least it would be some water. With the boys busy, she returned to the room to find Millie laying out some clothes on the table. "What did you find?"

Millie turned with an apologetic smile. "Only some shirts for the boys. I'm afraid we don't have anything for you or Emily."

Abby nodded. "It will do. Thank you for trying." When she left the room, Abby turned her gaze to Emily. "We can at least wring the water out of our clothes and dry our skin before putting them back on less the crinolines. That may help us dry out. You should go first." She followed

Emily to the screen and undid her buttons. "Hand me your clothes over the screen." Abby pulled a bucket out from under the small table and set it onto the big table. While Emily was undressing, she helped Jacob change into a dry shirt that was way too big for him and then had him remove his pants. She wrung the water out of them as best she could, gave them a few shakes, and returned them to Jacob. He grimaced as the cool wetness touched his skin.

He whined, "I don't want to wear these."

Abby saw the warning signs of a coming tantrum. He had been so good up to this point. She decided best not to push him. "Fine. You can leave them off and wear your shirt like a dress."

He scowled at her. "I'm not a girl. I'm a big boy."

"Then put your pants on." He started to argue further. She gave him her sternest look. "Jacob! Wear the pants or not, that is your only choice. There are no dry ones for you." To her relief he put his pants back on.

Emily stood behind the screen shivering in nothing but her chemise and bloomers. They were damp too but she couldn't bring herself to strip completely naked in this strange room. Besides she didn't think wringing them would make them any dryer. She undid her coiled braids letting the saturated auburn strands fall freely to her waist. She squeezed the water from her hair as best she could and towel dried it while her mother wrung out her dress. Water dripped from her crinoline draped over the dressing screen slowly increasing the puddle on the floor. Her boots and silk stockings lay in the corner. Both were wet through and through. She dreaded donning them again. With the humidity in the air, it would be hours before she felt dry.

Her back was to an outside wall. The wind battered against it and every now and then she heard something brush past it.

Her mother handed her the dress. Emily slipped it over her head and couldn't help the shiver that raced down her spine as the coolness of the damp fabric settled around her. She turned so her mother could do up the buttons running up her back. She then unbuttoned her mother's dress and helped her out of it before taking it to the bucket to ring out. It took all the strength in her hands to twist the layers of fabric releasing the absorbed water. When she was finished, Emily shook it out and helped her mother dress again sans the crinoline now dripping beside hers.

When her mother sat in a chair to put her shoes back on Emily cast another loathing glance at hers. "Must I wear them?"

Abby gave Emily's request consideration, inwardly grimacing as she laced up her own wet boots after pouring out the excess water accumulated inside. Emily's feet would be warmer barefoot and would keep her from catching a cold, but on the other hand Emily was a lovely young lady, and the ward was full of disreputable sailors. She eyed her hemline. Without the crinoline, Emily's skirt brushed against the floor. It was long enough to keep her feet hidden when standing still or sitting but what about walking?

"Emily, pace the room please."

Emily did as asked. She walked from one end to the other under her mother's keen observation.

"Very well, you may leave them off for now."

Thorn and Nate appeared in the doorway dripping from head to toe. Thorn said, "We've done as you asked."

"Very good." Abby ushered them into the room and shooed Emily out into the hall. "Both of you change into the dry shirts on the table. There are pants too if you can find a way to make them work, otherwise wring out your pants as best you can. You may leave your shoes off if you like. Come find me when you are done." She held her hand out to her youngest. "Come along, Jacob." Out in the hall, she paused to whisper to Emily, "Keep in mind these men are not to be considered gentlemen. You must maintain a respectable distance at all times."

Emily's eyes flared in surprise. "Yes, ma'am." Her father was a captain. She had been around sailors all her life. She knew how to behave around them and while, yes, some would take advantage of a girl given half a chance most were quite pleasant company. She didn't need her mother's reminder as if it were her first experience with seamen.

They walked back into the open ward and once again Emily's nostrils were plagued by the horrific mixture of strong odors. A bank of shuttered windows flanked either side of the room. The muted sounds of pelting rain and rushing wind penetrated the room. Even though she had just come in from the storm, she wished she could see what was going on in the pitch black night.

Nurse Millie was bending over one of the patients wiping his brow with a wet cloth. She straightened at their approach.

Abby said, "What can we do to help?"

"Would you mind if Emily took over here? Mr. Donovan has a fever I'm trying to bring down."

At her mother's nod, Emily stepped forward and took the cloth Nurse Millie passed to her.

Two beds down a man lifted up on his elbow. "I gots a fever too needs tending." A stern look from her mother had him laying back down without another word.

Abby turned to Nurse Millie. "Who else is here?"

"Mary is upstairs sleeping until her shift starts. She came in after supper just in case the storm got worse. I'm afraid it's just the two of us."

"And how many patients?"

"Thirteen."

Abby nodded, thankful so few of the sixty beds were in use. "What have you done to prepare for the storm?"

Millie's forehead wrinkled. "Done? Why nothing except close the shutters in the ward." She shook her head in bewilderment. "What was there to do?"

Abby recalled Millie had only recently moved to Key West from

Charlotte, North Carolina. She laid her hand on the younger woman's shoulder and spoke earnestly, trying to convey the seriousness of the situation without causing too much alarm. "Millie, this isn't just a storm. It's a hurricane, and it's going to get much worse." She turned to her daughter. "Emily, would you please check all the windows on both floors to make sure the shutters are latched and the windows are closed?"

Emily rose and handed the wet cloth back to Nurse Millie. "Of course, mother." As she walked away, she heard her mother say to Nurse Millie, "Why don't you tell me about each of these patients?" Emily picked up one of the lit lanterns at the end of the room and turned up the flame. She would deal with the resulting soot later, right now she needed the extra light. The rest of the downstairs rooms proved to be secure, so Emily climbed the darkened stairs to the second floor. Before she reached the top, she knew it would not be the case up here. She not only could hear the storm more clearly, she could feel its energy swirling in the air.

This floor had the same layout as below with a central room filled with patient beds and enclosed rooms flanking either end. A quick glance in the four rooms near the stairwell with the lantern lifted high revealed closed shutters. She walked down the hall to the main room headed for the open windows on the windward side of the building facing the water. There were three open sashes with puddled water beneath them. The shutters were closed so she shut and latched the windows. The reduced noise in the room brought her attention to the ruckus flapping of an unlatched shutter. She found it a few windows down. Dreading the rain spattering she would receive the moment she opened the window, she peered out in the darkness unable to see anything other than the splattering of wind tossed water against the glass.

How bad was this hurricane going to get? Her mother appeared outwardly calm, but Emily could see the tension tightening her shoulders and jaw, and the worry in her eyes. If her mother was worried... At least, the peak would likely hit them during the daylight hours. It was better than at night.

Bracing for the onslaught of water, Emily opened the window and stuck her head out reaching first for the right shutter and then for the left. She brought them together but now stood in a quandary. She could feel the wind tugging the wood from her grasp. If she let go of either one to secure the latch the shutter was going to fly open again.

"Hold on, Emily."

She glanced over her shoulder to find Nurse Mary rushing to her. In the moments she waited for Mary's help, Emily became aware of the unusual sound of waves crashing against the shore. Situated as the island was inside the reef, the ocean normally caressed their coast with gently lapping water. Tonight, the reef was no match for the restless water being pushed ahead of the storm. It sounded ominously close in the dark. Fascinated, Emily opened the shutters a few inches to see, but the night was too dark. Disappointed, she pulled the shutters closed. At least this building had a tall foundation, hopefully they wouldn't have to worry about flooding.

Mary slipped her slim fingers into the slats of the right side shutter. Emily was then able to settle the latch in place. She turned to greet the petite, sweet-natured brunette she had known for years. "Thank you. I would have had a time figuring out how to do that alone."

Mary smiled warmly. "You're welcome." Her smile faded. "It sounds as though my prayers have gone unanswered."

"What did you pray for?"

"For this not to be a hurricane." Mary's smile returned. "Come. Let's see what we can do to help downstairs." When Emily glanced to the far end of the room, Mary added, "I've already checked them."

Since she had the light, Emily led the way down the stairs to the main room. She returned the lamp to the side table where she picked it up from on her way upstairs. She turned down the wick so it would burn cleaner. Her mother asked her to return to tending Mr. Donovan's fever. As she mopped his perspiring brow, Emily wondered how Henry and his family were faring.

* * *

Whitmore House

Henry awoke disoriented for a moment in the dark room. As his eyes adjusted to the weak light of a single candle burning on the desk, he could make out the various members of his family sleeping around him in his father's study. In the corner, his parents were sitting with their heads together whispering. He only knew this from observation. The heavy sound of the raging storm obliterated their hushed tones. He jumped at the scratching of a broken tree branch brushing past the house and saw their concerned looks fly to the window as well, even though nothing could be seen beyond the darkened shutter. He realized the intensifying storm must have woke him. He wondered if his parents had slept at all.

His family had weathered many a hurricane, especially his mother. He remembered his first experience, eleven years ago. His mother lived on the island many years before he, his father, and his aunt arrived. She calmly kept them entertained while they huddled for hours in the living room as a hurricane passed by them. He wondered for a moment why they hadn't been in this room until he recalled on that day, the wind blew from a different direction.

Henry flinched again as something else hit the far side of the house. By the heavy thump, he guessed it might have been a cocoanut.

Henry's worry deepened. His mother was anything but calm this time.

His thoughts drifted to Emily. He wondered how she and her family were faring. He hated not knowing. He wished both families had taken shelter together.

* * *

Marine Hospital

A crash in the back office brought Emily's head up and her back erect. She must have dozed off while tending Mr. Donovan. Her mother flew past on the way to investigate the noise. The howling wind reaching inside the building told Emily at the very least a window was broken. Looking around the open ward, she noticed the blackness beyond the shutters had given way to a gunmetal gray morning. Nurse Mary was moving around tending patients, but most everyone else had been sleeping until the noise woke them. A moment later, her mother closed the door to the room and hurried back into the main ward.

Emily rose to intercept her. "What happened?"

"One of the side trees fell and a branch came through the window." Abby cast her eyes across the expanse of shuttered windows and the beds lined up in front of them. Their proximity was disturbing. If a tree fell through one of these windows, it could hurt someone. "Emily, we must get all the beds to the center of the room." She raised her voice. "Everyone, we need your help."

Her sons and the nurses came quickly. They worked together to get the beds moved. It was easy enough with the sailors who could stand, but it took four of them to move each bedridden patient.

Abby saw the deep concern on Nurse Millie's face mirrored around the room in some of the sailors and especially Nathaniel's. They needed a distraction. She pulled a chair in front of the center bed and took a seat facing the men. "As some of you know I'm originally from England. We don't have these kinds of storms there. I remember the first time I experienced a gale. It was on my father's ship sailing over just before we reached Jamaica. I was tossed about so violently in my bunk, my whole body was bruised." She got a few nervous chuckles at this statement. "I was told later we only clipped the edge of the hurricane. It gave me a good respect for them and taught me I would much rather be caught in one on land than on sea."

A lot of nodding heads met her pronouncement and just as she hoped it began the sharing of tales distracting them all from the tempest sweeping across the island.

Emily's thoughts flew again to Henry. She could imagine him huddled with his family playing games to pass the time. Perhaps later when there was more light he would sketch. She wished she were at home. At least then she would have more options for keeping her hands busy and her mind distracted. As it was, the stories were not holding her attention. Instead, she found herself focused on the rise and fall of the wind gusts, comparing the intensity of each one and trying to decide if it was the same or stronger than the last. If Henry were here, she wouldn't notice the wind.

* * *

Whitmore House

Henry was feeling restless. He couldn't sit any longer listening to the wind raging around the house. It filled his ears and his head. If there was any way to get away from it, even for a few minutes, he would do so. It felt like agonizing hours since they moved from the study into the hall to huddle under the staircase away from all the windows and yet not quite an hour had passed.

Earlier, he and his father moved the two Queen Anne chairs from the parlor into the hall. Two of the mattress were taken from the study and now leaned against the walls. Henry didn't understand their purpose. When he asked, his mother whispered, "In case the worst should happen." He was still puzzled, but her eyes pleaded with him to say no more for fear of upsetting his younger siblings. His mother settled in one of the chairs trying to sooth a fussy James. At her feet, his sisters were bickering over a card game they were playing. His father was in the other chair reading by the light of an oil lamp when he wasn't admonishing the girls. Tempers were on edge. The storm was getting to them all.

A rapid banging commenced against the upper story of the house. Grateful for any excuse to move and even more so for a chance to glimpse what was going on outside, Henry jumped to his feet. "I'll check on it." He gave his parents no time to gainsay him.

Theodore called out to Henry's retreating back. "Be careful!"

He took the stairs two at a time. In the upper hall, he followed the sound to his parent's room and the window facing northwest. The wind pressed the right shutter against the window but the left one was open and flailing against the house. Henry stepped to the glass panes. The tempest outside captured his attention. Not only was the sky dark gray with angry, swift moving clouds, but the very air was heavy with moisture obliterating his view of all but the back yard. It was as if the rest of the island ceased to exist. His gaze fixed on the rain-blurred palm trees. All the fronds were blown to one side looking like a flag snapping in the wind or an umbrella turned inside out. A shingle blew past striking the side of the house, making him jump. It snapped him from his reverie. Images flashed in his mind of fall leaves scampering like little children across the streets of New York, tumbleweeds blowing across the Texas plains, and summer storms whipping up frothy waves on the shallow waters around the island. These were child's play compared to what he witnessed now as the ever-increasing winds were tearing apart not only the trees and bushes but the houses as well. He had witnessed some harsh storms during his time riding with the Texas rangers, but nothing compared to the power and ferocity of these winds. The heavy gusts were visible airborne waves of water. He hoped the storm would soon pass.

Bringing his mind back to the task at hand, he opened the window and was blasted with wind driven rain. He leaned out to grab the errant shutter and nearly lost his balance as the full force of the gale tried to push him back into the house. As soon as he had his hand on the shutter, he realized the problem. The latch was broken and the bottom hinge was torn free from the house. The shutter was hanging by a single hinge. He let it go and closed the window. Turning, he cast about the room for a solution. Not finding one, he recalled some twine left in his knapsack that he used for traps. He raced down the hall to retrieve it and then back to his parents' room.

He opened the window again and with great difficulty pulled the dangling shutter to him. As he hoped, once he got the shutter pulled towards the window the wind direction was in his favor pushing the shutter towards him. He worked the string around the bottom half of the frame lacing it between the slats. He then pulled the other shutter closed and laced the cording through both shutters leaving enough slack to work his hand between them. When he ran out of excess twine he pulled the lacing tight, bringing the shutters together, and tied the ends. It may not last the storm, but it would hold for a while at least. He closed the window with a smile of accomplishment.

He turned to leave and realized his front was soaking wet. He returned to his room and quickly changed into a dry shirt. He grabbed his drawing supplies and slowly descended the stairs reluctant to return to the safety of the stairwell. He would much rather be on the front porch absorbing the power of nature's fury.

At Henry's return, Theodore looked up from his reading – more like his attempted reading. "Was it a loose shutter?"

"Yes, a hinge and the latch broke on the rear window of your bedroom. I tied the two shutters together. It should hold for a while but not if this gets much worse. Hopefully this storm will blow past soon." He caught the worried look his parents shared and gave up the slim hope this ordeal was almost over. He settled on the floor and leaned against the side of his father's chair to share the meager light from the lamp and began sketching what he had seen from the window.

Chapter 13

Wild and free
Twisting the atoll
Tighter and tighter the dance

Marine Hospital

Emily screamed and instinctively covered her head even though she was in no danger. The glass window behind her shattered, struck by a flying board now lodged in the broken shutter. Millie, Mary, and Nate echoed her distressed cry. Emily was tending Mr. Donovan who didn't even stir at the noise so deep was he in his fever induced sleep. She laughed at herself for being so skittish.

Her mother soon appeared with a broom in hand to sweep the glass shards to the wall and out of their path. Not wanting to risk being close to the windows any longer than necessary, she didn't bother with a dustpan or discarding the shards in the trash. She then gave Emily a pointed look towards her hem and quirked her head in the direction of the offices where her shoes were piled with her brothers. Emily gave a nod of understanding. She dutifully left to put her shoes back on, grateful when she found them somewhat drier than before. She then made sure Thorn and Nate did the same.

The wind was still increasing.

Emily could hear it picking up the edges of the shingles which snapped back into place, creating the sound of a strident drum. There was no escaping the noise. The only thing to do was try not to focus on it. She was failing miserably. The harder she tried not to notice, the more she heard every detail. How she wished Henry were there to help her. She hoped he and his sisters were having less of an ordeal. But what if they were not....

* * *

Whitmore House

The wind kept increasing as the morning wore on, as did the sound of debris hitting the house. It was happening so frequently now they were no longer startled by each occurrence. Every time Henry thought the hurricane couldn't get worse, it did. When he first woke up the wind was howling around the house. By the time the family moved into the hall it was screaming. Sometime after the shutter incident, it escalated again to a shrieking sound the likes of which he had never heard before. Now it had a deep tonal moan. They could hear the slate shingles being pulled from the roof but most disturbing, especially to Agatha and Emmaline, was the house seemed to be breathing. It didn't make much difference to the girls when their father explained the walls were flexing from the changing air pressure. It was already fixed in their minds there was a monster outside causing the house to quiver. Henry watched them huddle together for comfort and even Brianna seemed to be struggling with worry. It was strange that James, having taken a nap earlier, was the calm one. He was quietly playing with a wooden wagon filled with blocks in between the chairs.

When Henry's gaze went back to the girls, Emmaline was crying. Agatha was turned away, so he couldn't see her face. Henry moved closer intending to pull Agatha and Emmaline into his embrace when he heard Agatha telling little Emmie, "The monster is trying to get us. He's going to tear our house apart." Emmaline's cries turned into hysterics.

Betsy was crocheting, enjoying the freedom of not having James in her lap. She was more than happy to let him get down after his nap. The warmth of the closed up house had made them both sweaty. As Emmaline's panicked cries reached her ear, she dropped her needles and yarn to the floor to open her arms, inviting Emmaline to climb into her lap. Her little girl was not so little anymore. Betsy missed the days of snuggling with her. Emmaline practically ran into her arms and was soon settled on her lap. Betsy ran her hand over her hair as she held her head to her chest and tried to soothe the tears away. The only word she could make out of Emmaline's sobbing was 'monster'. Betsy supposed to a child a hurricane would seem like a monster.

Emmaline huddled against her mother's chest but kept a wary eye on the ceiling. Because of Agatha's taunting, she truly believed there was a big hairy monster outside trying to get into their house. The louder it got the more she believed it was going to be able to reach in and grab her.

Henry was grateful his mother realized Emmaline's distress. Not to be outdone, Agatha crawled into their father's lap. Brianna scooted closer to Henry. He put a comforting arm around her, pulling her close. The churning storm matched Henry's unsettled emotions. His family may need him, but he ached to be with Emily. He imagined she and her brothers were huddled together too, trying to find comfort in each other as the outside world was torn apart.

They all jumped as the swirling winds sent forth a cocoanut cannon crashing through a window in the back wall of the house, hurtling across the floor in a diagonal path in front of them to land in the parlor to their left. Glass shards scattered across the floor, and the moaning winds were even louder now that there was a hole to pass through.

James crawled out from between the two chairs, rose and took several steps forward intending to get to the cocoanut. All three adults reached out to stop him, but Betsy was closest. Poor Emmaline was dumped off her lap as she lunged forward to grasp James' britches and pull him back to her side. Even within inches, she had to yell to be heard. "DO NOT leave my side." Betsy knew he didn't understand the danger, but her tone was enough to widen his eyes and leave him silent.

As they all resettled, Henry became aware of another imminent threat about the same time his father discovered it. In the rush to catch James, the lamp was knocked off the side table. The glass chimney shattered and oil leaked out from around the wick in the tin base, bursting into flame just as he and Henry both moved into action and forcefully bumped heads. Henry pressed a hand against the pain in his temple reeling with pinpricks of light bursting behind his eyelids. He was sure his father must feel the same.

While they recovered, Brianna stepped forward desperately trying to untie her apron from around her waist preparing to do battle. Henry recovered his wits and, knowing the apron was inadequate, he rushed to grab the closest floor rug in the parlor. He dashed back and dropped it on the growing flames. The blaze was instantly smothered.

Theodore laid his arm across Henry's shoulders and pulled him close. No words were said. As relief turned into thankfulness, he further pulled his son into a tight hug, grateful for his quick thinking and action. Theodore choked back his tears. Their ordeal was not over with yet. He had to remain strong.

Henry breathed deep trying to calm the nervous energy flowing through him in response to the crisis. His father stepped back and nodded as he swallowed hard. Henry understood all he wanted to say but didn't. They turned to find the rest of the family huddled around Betsy with wide frightened eyes.

Henry now appreciated his mother's insistence for putting their shoes on this morning. The broken glass and fire were good reasons. He gathered up his sketching materials from the floor where they had miraculously escaped the spilled lamp oil and fire and placed them on the sideboard in the parlor.

Theodore glanced at the broken window and quickly decided there was nothing they could do to block the wind flowing through the house. Now they needed more protection. He spoke into Henry's ear to be heard. "Help me move these chairs." He leaned down to Betsy. "You and the children sit with your backs against the wall." They placed the chairs in front of the family and leaned the mattresses against them forming a makeshift wall in case anything else should be hurtled inside the house. Theodore lifted the mattress edge and climbed into their improvised bunker.

Henry hesitated to follow suit. He took a step backward so he could see out the broken dining room window. As he watched, shingles, siding, and all manner of greenery flew past. The hurricane did seem like a giant monster ripping their island apart. He had never seen such raw power. The thin walls they hid behind seemed inadequate protection from the fury outside. Resigned to it, Henry made his way under the opposite side of the mattress to huddle with his family in the stagnate air of their meager fortress. He hated the cave like feel of it and wished again there was a safe place from which he could watch the storm's passing.

Betsy knew they were in need of distraction. She guessed it was close enough to midday to have their meal, so she pulled the basket of food out from the corner and began setting out canisters of nuts, dried bananas, and crackers. Brianna unwrapped a wedge of sharp cheddar cheese.

Theodore smiled, thankful to have Betsy as his wife and helpmate. She seemed to instinctively know what their family needed and right now food was a good distraction. He looked around at his children. As they met his eyes with expectation, he bowed his head and spoke as loudly as he could. "Lord, thank you for the sacrifice of your son. Thank you for the sturdy roof over our head and the food laid out before us. Bless it to our nourishment. May my family, and all of those in the path of this storm, take shelter in your protection." As he began the familiar verse the voices around him joined in. "Have not I commanded Thee! Be strong and of a good courage: be not afraid, neither be thou dismayed: for the Lord thy God is with thee whithersoever thou goest. Amen."

* * *

Marine Hospital

The relentless noise all around made Emily want to scream at the world to make it stop. The heavy storm winds seemed to be growling at her like a living thing. The sound was unlike anything she had ever heard. And as if the now constant wind was not enough, the slate shingles had started flying off hours ago, several of the windows were shattered, trees were breaking, unknown objects were constantly being hurtled into the sides of the building, and the flapping of loose shutters added to the cacophony. After so many unending hours, and knowing many more were likely ahead of her, Emily was finding it hard not to fall apart. Tears sprang to her eyes as she rolled clean bandages.

She looked around the room to gauge how the others were fairing. It was easy to see she was not alone in her struggle. Some were huddled and rocking. Others had their hands pressed tightly to their ears. Some were pacing the room. A few had gathered not more than ten feet from her trying to out sing the storm with Amazing Grace. Only sporadic notes carried to her ears. Most were drowned out by the wind that felt like it was trying to rip the very building apart.

Abby saw her daughter struggling and went to her. She pressed her forehead to Emily's temple. "Focus on the task at hand. Block out everything else."

Emily kept her head downcast to hide her shameful tears. "I'm trying."

"I know." Abby patted her shoulder. She looked around the room and saw many others feeling the same way. Playing a game would help them all but the frustration of yelling to be heard would defeat the purpose. She turned back to Emily. "Try thinking of a happier time like your birthday party or your favorite place. I'll see if I can find something more challenging for you to do than rolling bandages."

Abby had taken no more than a few steps from her daughter when the strident ripping of metal nails rapidly pulled from wood drew her gaze upward.

Emily rose to her feet with her eyes trained on the ceiling. The basket of bandages fell unheeded to the floor, some unravelling across the wood planks.

Nathaniel raced to his mother's side to be enfolded in her embrace with his eyes tightly shut and his cheek pressed against her still damp dress. Thorn trailed behind holding the hand of a wide-eyed Jacob who was obviously trying valiantly to be braver than he felt. The reactions of those around him scared him more than this latest noise from outside. Until now, he thought he was safe inside the building. He reached for his mother's hand wishing they were home where he could hide with his blanket under his bed.

Mary and Millie straightened from their tasks. The patients who could sat bolt upright in their beds. They all listened to the banging rafters and silently prayed the roof would hold.

Several minutes passed before those in the room let their tension ease, but there was still a hesitancy about them as if they were ready to flee at any moment.

Thorn was the oldest able-bodied male in the building and to his way of thinking, being 'man of the house' so to speak, it was his responsibility to do what his father would do in this situation. He approached his mother. "I can go upstairs and check the damage."

Abby's fear for his safety made her answer more forceful than she intended. "No."

Anger instantly flared, showing in his furrowed brow, sparking eyes, compressed lips, and tense jaw. He hadn't meant it to sound like a request. He meant to tell her he was going, but now that she had told him 'no' he would be disobeying her if he went.

Abby turned Thorn away from the patients and spoke into his ear. "Thank you for offering but you won't see anything from the second floor. It is unwise to go climbing into the attic. The roof could be torn off at any minute."

His cheeks flared as he reluctantly accepted her wisdom.

Emily approached. Abby looked from one face to the other at a loss as to how to keep them busy.

Jacob pulled on her apron. "Momma, I'm hungry."

Abby lifted her timepiece from her apron pocket to find it was half-past the noon hour. Anxiety had kept her from feeling hungry, but her youngest had yet to miss a meal in his life. She ruefully ruffled the curls he inherited from his father, bringing to mind her worry for Max and Christoff. She sent another prayer heavenward for the safety of her family. Resolutely, she turned her mind back to the task at hand. Jacob's request had solved at least one problem. She tasked Emily and Thorn with offering food and water to the patients.

Surely this was the worst of it, and the storm would soon pass.

* * *

Whitmore House

Betsy was sitting cross legged with her back against the wall and Emmaline in her lap. Theodore sat on her left, their hands entwined, his thumb caressing hers. Agatha was on his lap leaning against his chest. Brianna was on her right with her knees pulled up to her chest and her head leaning against Henry's shoulder as he sat on her other side. James had crawled under one of the chairs bracing the tilted mattress.

She closed her eyes and focused on her mental list of things to be done when the storm passed. It was something to occupy her mind. First she would clean up the broken glass and open the shutters. Next, they should empty the plants from the kitchen so she could make them a hot meal. Theodore's sleeve had a hole that needed mending.

She felt Agatha place a hand on her leg as she leaned over to speak to Emmaline. The storm was too loud to hear much of what was said but Betsy did hear her say monster. She opened her eyes to see James and Emmaline further distressed.

"Agatha!" She gave her a warning look.

Theodore pulled Agatha away from the others and spoke to her.

James and Emmie both climbed into Betsy's arms to be comforted. "Shh. It will be alright. There's no monster. It's just a very bad storm."

Eventually, they settled down again.

Theodore had restrained from looking outside all morning, other than a glance out of the broken dining room window, but he could no longer bear it. He had to see. Besides, he needed to stretch his legs. In the meager light of the room, his eyes met Betsy's. She nodded her head in understanding. He sent Agatha over to Brianna and ducked out from the mattress. It felt good to stand up tall elongating his back.

Henry peered out from behind the other side of the mattress wall, and seeing his father was not intending to use the chamber pot, he quickly left the shelter to follow him. If his father was going to look outside, so was he.

Theodore glanced back in surprise when he felt Henry's presence behind him as he stepped out onto the porch but said nothing. They braced their backs against the house in the modicum shelter of the leeward porch. All the wind battered houses across from them were missing shingles and siding.

As they stood there some of the shingles from their roof were ripped away and flung across the street striking Betsy's old shop. Henry supposed they were very fortunate the pond was behind them limiting the amount of torn housing the storm could hurl at their house. He looked down Whitehead Street towards the Eatonton house even though he couldn't see much past the neighbor's yard. He was worried about Emily. Their house was not so well situated. He prayed her family was safe.

Theodore squinted trying to better see Betsy's former home and seamstress shop, a small single story house with a porch directly across the street. He couldn't be sure but he thought it was leaning a bit away from them. He hoped it would survive the storm. Fortunately, it was used only as a shop now and no one was inside, but it would still be a loss to their friend and current owner, Esperanza Keats.

Having satisfied his curiosity and knowing Betsy would worry, Theodore pushed Henry towards the door but they both swung around as they heard a horrifying new sound above the wind. It was the cracking and splintering wood of the seamstress shop as the roof was pulled away and in a matter of minutes the swirling air ripped the rest of it apart. As they stood there watching it collapsed in a heap as if in slow motion.

Henry stared at the wreckage. His mind was flooded with the memories of spending afternoons with Betsy in her little house while his father was away reporting on the Seminole War. It was in her parlor he learned the alphabet. And now it was gone.

* * *

Marine Hospital

Emily straightened from adjusting the pillow of a soldier with a broken collar bone. She hated causing him more pain in doing so but was relieved to see he was now resting more comfortably. She noticed something in the hallway had caught his attention. She turned to find a neighboring family standing there. The noise of the storm had drowned out any sound of their entry. She knew how hard it had been for her family to face the gale before dawn when the winds were only beginning to build. The strength of it now would seem impossible to traverse, but here they were standing in front of her, haggard and soaked to the skin. She could only imagine how exhausted they must be from the effort to reach the hospital, and she wondered what could have possibly happened to their home to force them to such a desperate act. She grabbed the last clean towel and rushed to Mr. and Mrs. Garcia with their daughters aged ten and twelve. She handed the towel to Mrs. Garcia. Knowing the parents spoke little English, she turned to Claudia and Elena. "What happened?"

Elena dropped her head to hide her tears.

Claudia wrapped her arm around her younger sister. "Our house fell down."

"The whole house?"

Claudia and Elena both nodded vigorously.

Emily had never heard of such a thing. A roof damaged, windows broken, wall boards torn away, but never a whole house.

"However did you manage to get here?"

Tears welled in Claudia's eyes. "We had to fight the wind. Sometimes it wouldn't let us move." She choked up, unable to say more.

Abby reached them and with broken Spanish told the parents the two empty beds at the end of the room were for their use. Next, Abby sent Thorn to move the changing screen they had used earlier into the hallway between the offices so the family could have some privacy to dry off away from the danger of the windows.

Thorn finished setting the screen up in the hall and looked longingly at the closed door to the stairwell. He turned to eye his mother. She was busy getting the new arrivals settled. He was sure he could get back before she noticed he was missing. The need to see what was going on outside overwhelmed obedience. He took advantage of his mother's inattention to sneak into the stairwell, closing the door behind him. He wanted to see what damage had been done to the roof, and he wanted a chance to look out the window without his mother's strident call to move away from the glass.

Inside the stairwell, the haphazard thumping of the loose rafters was amplified. He climbed the stairs and at the top boldly opened the door to the second floor. Here the storm's fury was even louder, assaulting his ears with a deafening dissonance. He moved to the bank of western windows on the leeward side of the building facing the water. He pulled the casement panes open, unlatched the shutters, and pushed them open. He was not prepared for what met his eyes. When he walked to the hospital this morning, it was too dark to see much but he knew it was nothing like it was now.

The world outside was whited out. Beyond a hundred yards nothing could be seen in the swirling winds. Heavy, sporadic sheets of rain moved across his view. The palm trees on either side of the building were bending low, the fronds extended like hands desperately reaching out for rescue. Down below, the beach now stretched wide as if abandoned by the water. The wind had pushed the tide back leaving several extra yards of exposed shore. A small boat hung partially over dry ground suspended from its tether to the pier. Beyond the end of the pier, all was a blur of whitish-gray. It looked like a world gone mad.

A sudden unexpected gust in his direction ripped the shutters from his hands and sent them crashing against the wall of the building. He threw up his arm for protection against the onslaught as he closed his eyes and turned his face away to avoid the stinging force of the wind driven rain. As quick as it came, it was gone. He had seen enough. He pulled the shutters closed and latched them. As he was closing the windows, another burst fought his efforts despite the aide of the shutters in diffusing its strength. With the windows latched, he stood for a moment listening to the winds torment the loose roof boards and beat against the building. The wind was no longer blowing strictly from the northeast. Did that mean the storm was changing direction? Whatever it was doing, he sure hoped it was moving away from them. It certainly couldn't get worse.

He searched the rooms for entry to the attic. He was disappointed when he found a small access door and no ladder with which to reach it. Knowing he had been gone too long already and soon his absence would be noted, he gave up the idea and returned downstairs, slipping back into the room undetected.

Emily took a tray of food and water to the new arrivals. They had dried off as best they could and now sat huddled together on the edge of the two hospital beds they had been offered. The drooping eyes of the girls attested to the taxing effort it took getting here. It appeared sleep may win out over nourishment. She handed the tray to Mrs. Garcia who murmured, "Gracias, señorita." Emily gave a nod. "De nada." She then turned away to seek out her brother.

"What did you see?"

Surprised by Emily's voice behind him, the dipper fell from Thorn's fingers to splash into the water bucket. He turned to find a knowing grin on her face. He tried for innocence. "What do you mean?"

"I mean, what did you see upstairs? Did you go into the attic?"

He sighed. He should have known someone would notice. He was thankful it was Emily and not their mother, otherwise he would be getting a lecture now. "No. I couldn't see much. The storm is so thick it has whitewashed the air around us."

Emily frowned. "You couldn't see the island?"

"I couldn't look in that direction. It's windward silly. I did look out to sea. The water has been pushed away from shore. It was very strange. And the wind seems to be turning."

She breathed a sigh of relief. "Good. Maybe this is almost over. It surely can't get worse."

"I had the same thought." Thorn's gaze sharpened. "Does Momma know I went up there?"

"I don't think so. She's too busy with the patients."

"But you noticed."

She smiled. "It's what I would have done if the situation were reversed."

Thorn grinned. "Yes, you would."

An hour later, there was no doubt in anyone's mind the wind had changed direction. It now battered the rear of the building with increased ferocity; something none of them thought was possible. Clearly the intensity of this hurricane was more than any of the islanders had ever experienced before, and the strain of it showed on their faces. The only ones sleeping now were the Garcia girls from sheer exhaustion. Everyone else tried to find other things to occupy their hands and minds, but the truth was, the tempest would not allow it. It viciously held their captive attention as it worked to loosen the boards on the other side of the roof.

An hour or so later, the roof finally gave way with an awful tearing sound leaving the full force of the storm raging overhead with little more than the ceiling and plank floor of the second story for protection. Millie screamed, Mary fainted, the patients were in various states of distress, Nate and Jacob came running to their mother. Without the roof for protection, they could feel the uncomfortable air pressure pulling upward. An unspoken worry passed over them all. Was the building in danger of imminent collapse?

Thorn took off for the front door now on the leeward side of the storm. He had to see it. He skidded around the corner, flew down the front hall, and opened the front door in time to see the roof tumble on its long end after touching the ground. The wind hurtled it on end a few more yards before it rolled again tearing it apart and destroying the fence they had passed this morning before crashing into the side of the house behind theirs. Thorn had to hold onto the door frame. The air pressure was pulling him outward. As the roof's movement ceased, Thorn noticed everything else. Palms were bent over so low they were nearly touching the ground. The older ones snapped under the pressure. Hardwood trees were uprooted. Bushes were stripped bare. Off to his right, shingles were peeling away from the roof of an outbuilding. A board flew past as if an arrow shot from a bow. It would be impossible to walk in this tempest, and even if a person managed to remain upright, so much was flying around in the air, the chances of being struck and killed were high.

He leaned out the door trying to see down Front Street. His mother's hand on his shoulder startled him. Words were useless, so she pulled on his shoulder. Thorn relented and with a final glance around him, he reluctantly moved inside the hall and shut the door.

Abby leaned close to tell him. "If you must do something, go make sure the doors are secure to the stairwells on either side. Do not go upstairs." She saw him contemplating. "Thorn! I mean it. Do not go upstairs."

Emily waited at the end of the hall, watching her mother and brother. She too wanted to see what was going on outside, but Nate was holding tightly to her arm. Thorn would tell her. His face was mutinous when he turned towards her. Maybe later she would ask him. Her mother reached her first and turned her back to the ward while Thorn went in the other direction. Curious, she looked over her shoulder to watch him.

"He's checking the doors to the stairs. We need to figure out something for you to do."

Emily had to lean close to hear what her mother said. The noise, annoying as it was before, was now overwhelming. Her mother squeezed her hand. "Emily, we will endure." It sounded as if she was trying to reassure herself more than Emily.

* * *

Whitmore House

Betsy was standing beside the mattress when Theodore and Henry returned from the porch. "What did you see? What was that awful noise?"

Theodore grimaced. He inferred rather than heard what she asked and would rather not tell her, but he knew how tenacious his wife could be. He yelled to be heard. "Your shop is gone."

Betsy's saucer blue eyes grew even wider. "What if that happens to this house?"

Theodore gathered her in his arms. "Shh, that's borrowed trouble. We are only going to worry about what is right in front of us."

Betsy nodded, knowing he was right.

They settled down behind the mattress and for many moments nothing more was said until the change in the wind captured their attention. All of them cautiously left the safety of the mattress to listen to it ominously swirl around all sides of the house. Betsy lifted concerned eyes to Theodore before ushering the children back behind the mattress.

Theodore and Henry stepped closer to the broken dining room window watching in awe as the tempest twisted and turned outside. They returned to the mattress knowing Betsy needed help with the younger children. Eventually the wind began to steadily blow from the opposite direction with even more intensity. Now the storm was throwing debris against the front of the house with the porch receiving the brunt of the windward force. The broken dining room window was now in the lee of the storm. Father and son left their shelter and dared to step closer.

Henry's eyes were riveted on the pond. He had never seen waves on the shallow water before, but now the wind whipped it into a frenzy and the water was high. The edge of the surge was several yards closer to their house than the bank's normal boundary.

Another crash upstairs had Theodore pulling Henry back to the mattress knowing Betsy would fret over them.

* * *

Marine Hospital

It wasn't long after the roof was gone before water began seeping through the upper floor, adding further discomfort to their misery. A drop or two at first, soon became a constant dripping. Nowhere in the building could they escape this latest annoyance. It was one more hardship to be endured in a day of hardships. Water dripped around every board in the ceiling onto heads and shoulders, the sick and wounded, soaking into blankets, bedding, and pillows. There was no avoiding getting wet any more than there was escape from the clangor. Thorn found a hammer and nails to tack sheets to the ceiling over the sickest of patients, but it was only a temporary reprieve at best. Eventually, the water soaked through the sheets to relentlessly drip on the floor.

Emily mindlessly watched the droplets form and release to splash in the puddle below. Despite the increasing anxiety, she, like most of the others around her, was growing numb from exhaustion. The storm had been upon them for twelve hours now.

Chapter 14

Frivolous youth untamed
Whirling with giddy abandon
Unfettered and unchecked

Marine Hospital

It was late afternoon and everyone was miserable. Hour after hour the hurricane raged, fraying nerves and sparking tempers. Abby's attention was focused on the needs of those around her. It was her way of trying to keep her thoughts off the noise of the storm and worry for the missing roof, not to mention fretting over her decision to move the family to the hospital and fearing she may have put them in harm's way. For a moment, it all began to overwhelm her. She retreated to an empty chair in the corner of the room and bowed her head. A moment of prayer restored her strength and reminded her to leave her worries in God's hands.

When she stood up, Millie approached to ask her about a patient's treatment. Abby's eyes scanned the room checking on her children. Emily was treating Mr. Donovan's fever. Nate was talking with a young cabin boy who had broken his ribs after his first attempt at climbing rigging. Thorn was keeping Jacob entertained with a card game.

Emily dabbed the wet cloth against Mr. Donovan's forehead. Suddenly, he reached out to painfully squeeze her wrist. His light brown eyes opened and sought hers. "I hear rushing water."

Emily started to shake her head in denial, but then she discerned it too. The added sound underneath the menacing wind gave rise to another threat. Her head came up and her frightened gaze sought out her mother's comforting presence.

Abby turned from conferring with Millie. Her attention was drawn to Emily feeling the instinctual need of a child for its mother. The horrified look on Emily's face had Abby rushing to her side. Fear made her heart race while her mind tried to reason what could have caused such a reaction. There was no blood visible so she wasn't hurt. Did Mr. Donovan accost her? No, he wouldn't. He was a good man. What could it be?

Emily rushed forward to meet her mother. "We heard water."

"Water?"

"Outside. Rushing water. Like the tide has reached the building."

Confusion gave way to dawning horror. Abby placed her hands on Emily's shoulders. "Keep calm and say nothing to the others. We are in a brick building eight feet above ground. There is no need to alarm them.

Quietly go back to what you were doing."

"Yes, ma'am."

Abby squeezed Emily's arms in reassurance. She then turned and made her way to the offices on the southern end of the building determined to face the storm's wrath if necessary to see how high the water had risen. She wasn't surprised to find Thorn close on her heels. They opened the windows of the corner office and felt the blast of spray hit their face. It took all of Thorn's strength to push open the shutters against the formidable wind. They were both shocked when the left shutter was torn from his hand to disappear in the swirling tempest. Without the shutter's protection, they were blasted with the full force of the storm's fury.

Thorn couldn't believe what he saw. Whereas earlier the beach was unusually low, it was now submerged.

Abby held up her arm to shield her eyes as she leaned out the window to gauge the water's height against the foundation. Foaming waves rushed against the base of the building. The island was indeed being flooded. So far she would guess it to be four or five feet deep and could still be rising.

Forced to leave the right shutter flapping against the building, Abby and Thorn closed the windows, but remained there a few moments longer watching from the spattered glass. They were surrounded by angry surf. Dry land was gone. Even the boards of the wharf were underwater.

Abby's eyes grew wide. Blindly she reached out for Thorn as if needing the feel of him to keep from drowning in the nightmare playing out before her eyes. She saw the wharf torn from its pilings. It now floated towards them on the waves with the menace of a raging bull. Hope that it would be carried past them soon ended. They backed away from the window as a large wave brought it crashing against the brick wall beneath them, not once but several times. Horror filled her as the mortar between the bricks opened into a crack running up the height of the wall. Abby turned Thorn towards the door hurriedly pushing him out of the room. The window shattered as she slammed the door behind them.

They returned to the main ward to find its occupants in hysterical chaos. Millie and Mary looked to her as she entered the room. Abby tried to convey a calmness she was far from feeling. If that wall collapsed, what would happen to all of them? The Garcia refugees who came counting on the security of the solid brick walls to shelter them now appeared ready to take flight again. Abby rushed forward to calm the family. The young girls were huddled together wailing.

Abby bowed her head and prayed for their safety as she never had before. She prayed that her husband and son were far from this storm even knowing it was more likely they were sailing into it. How the salvagers managed to sail in one of these tempests let alone save ships was beyond her comprehension, and why her husband loved it, even more so.

Emily had to leave Mr. Donovan's side to tend to a sailor several years younger than her. Whatever had caused the crack and shudder of the building had sent him into a panic. Having nowhere to flee for safety, he was in danger of hyperventilating. She grabbed his hand and faced him. "You're safe. Take deep breaths." She did so too, hoping he would mimic her actions. His darting eyes refused to hold hers. "My name's Emily. What's yours?"

"W… w...Willie."

Firmly she said, "Willie. Look at me." She shook his shoulder. "Look at me." His piercing blue eyes finally settled on hers. "It will be all right. Willie, breathe with me." She took a deep breath and was relieved when he did the same. In her peripheral, she saw her mother give her an encouraging nod. "Just breathe, Willie. Something hit the building, but it's made of brick. We're safe here." At least she hoped they were safe. Her mother and Thorn had come running out of the room from where the sound originated. Though they tried to hide it, they were both shaken. Once Willie was calm enough to settle back in his bed, she sought out Thorn.

She found him in a corner animatedly describing something to Nate. She couldn't hear his words until she was close enough to touch him. She wasn't surprised he was telling their younger brother the story she wanted to hear.

"Then a big wave carried the remains of the dock right for the wall where we were standing. We backed up as fast as we could, and then it crashed."

He threw both hands up high and back nearly smacking Emily, unaware of her eavesdropping. She ducked out of the way and then came into his line of vision.

"It was the dock?"

"Yes."

"How high is the water? Has it reached us?"

"Reached us and gone around. We're neck deep as far as I can tell, maybe more."

Emily saw the fear in Nate's eyes and laid a reassuring hand on his back. "This building is strong. We'll be fine."

Thorn gave them a mischievous smile. "It may be better than wood, but it is not impervious. That dock cracked the wall all the way up to the ceiling."

Emily's eyes flew from Nate's head to Thorn's gaze checking for honesty or tommyrot. It wouldn't be the first time he embellished a story to frighten his siblings.

"Honest it did. The brick is cracked and the roof is gone. Bet our house isn't even standing anymore."

Nate cried out in distress. Emily pulled him to her as she cast a scornful look at Thorn. "You should be ashamed of yourself." There was no need for him to add more to their worries even if it was very likely true.

She pulled Nate with her as she walked away from their brother. At least Thorn told her what she wanted to know. The water was high and flowing all around them, and the loud noise they heard was the dock crashing into the side of the building.

Abby met them as they crossed the puddled floor to the beds. Her face was flushed with concern and her gaze flitted between them. "Are you all right?"

Emily nodded.

Nate muttered, "Thorn said the hurricane knocked down our house."

Abby took Nate's hand and headed towards Thorn. "Nathanial, we will pray our home is fine, but it is possible the storm was too much for it."

Her mother would deal with her brothers, chastising one, and comforting the other. Emily wandered back to Mr. Donovan.

The storm was driving her mad. She was tired of worrying over things she couldn't control. Tired of the constant dripping from the floor above. Tired of the discordant wind. Tired of looking at her concern mirrored on all the faces around her. Tired of waiting for an end that seemed would never come. She was weary of the waiting and the worry. Weary of the fear of losing the safety of this building, fear of losing her home, and fear for everyone else on the island caught in this tempest. How many were in this wicked weather right now fleeing from their homes? Where would they go? Where was Henry and his family? Were they huddled in their house praying or worse? What of Lydia and her family and so many of their friends and neighbors? So many questions. So much to bear. When would this hurricane end? Only time would bring her answers.

Emily tried to do as her mother suggested and focus on the task at hand. Mr. Donovan was sleeping fitfully, still burning up with fever. She dipped the white cotton towel in the cool water, wrung it out, refolded it, and dabbed at Mr. Donovan's brow. It wasn't enough to divert her mind. Her mother also told her to think of a happier place.

Henry.

The image of his face never failed to make her smile.

Her mind drifted back to that wonderful September day he walked back into her life. She had been teasing Laura about the stock boy who had caught her eye as they exited the mercantile. For a moment the bright afternoon sunlight blinded Emily as she stepped through the door. When she could see again, her gaze found Henry's. The surprise of it made her stop and stare. He looked just as she imagined he would having spent hours dreamily staring at the miniature portrait he had sent her, and yet, he looked so different. He was certainly more mature in feature and deportment, but it was something else that made her feel uncertain and excited. He seemed manly. He left more a boy than a man in so many ways but returned a man grown. Although, she had caught glimpses of the boy she once knew, and it was endearing. Just as she began to wonder, standing in front of the mercantile, if her feelings for him might have changed, he spoke. He only said her name, but it felt like a caress to her soul. The resonance of his voice unexpectedly set her heart aflutter. The tone was deeper and stronger than she remembered. It made her insides go weak with longing.

A longing she soon learned he shared when they later met at the graveyard. She still found it hard to believe Henry really loved her. It wasn't just a dream she would wake from and find he still roamed the wilds of Texas over a thousand miles away from her. He was here, and he was planning their future together. A giddy grin spread across her face at the thought. As she became aware of it, she cast a furtive glance about the room to make sure no one else had noticed. She sobered her expression but continued her thoughts.

A home of their own and privacy to share all the kisses her heart desired. She couldn't imagine how it would feel to lie in his arms. It was something she had never even contemplated until now. Was she ready to take on the duties of being a wife? It was daunting enough to think of running her own house. The other wifely duties made her stomach flutter. She only hoped they would be as enjoyable as kissing. The feel of his lips pressed against hers...

And while Emily relived kisses, the hurricane raged, momentarily unnoticed.

* * *

Whitmore family

A new sound garnered the huddled family's attention. It was not airborne but ground level and coming from the front of the house. Theodore and Henry made their way to the front door, cautiously opening it. The air pressure pulled the handle out of Theodore's hand, sending the door crashing against the wall. What they saw outside shocked them. The collapsed shop was now riding on incoming waves of surging water, battering their front porch. The tide was lapping at their porch floor.

Henry stared in horror.

His family may no longer be safe in the house. It was in immediate danger of flooding or worse, collapsing like the shop. But what could they do? As the next wave roughly pushed the debris against the porch, Theodore and Henry struggled to shut the door. Henry looked to his father and found the same concerns written in his wrinkled brow and troubled hazel eyes.

Theodore could only shake his head in dismay. Leaving the shelter of the house was unthinkable, but the possibility of it falling down on top of them was just as frightening. He turned and walked back to his family. He needed to share his concerns with Betsy. Together they would decide what was best.

Betsy could easily read the seriousness of their situation on Theodore's face. She met him in the foyer so they could talk without raising the children's alarm. Deciding she wanted to see for herself, Betsy brushed past Theodore and Henry. She opened the front door a crack and was thankful when Theodore reached over her to grab the edge to help her hold it. The pile of floating debris that was once her shop rushed to greet her on a surge of water. She stepped back and slammed the door as it crashed into the porch railing and water seeped under the threshold. Sounds of moving water could be heard under the house. Betsy raised her panic filled eyes to Theodore. "Do you think the house can hold together?"

"I don't know. So far it is."

"Momma!"

Betsy and Theodore both raced to the children in response to the panic in Agatha's voice. They didn't even realize they were splashing through water until they reached the children and Brianna, holding Emmaline, pointed to the watery floor boards. Betsy wrapped Agatha in her arms and ran her hand over her head in a soothing embrace. "It will be alright sweetheart." Her eyes met Theodore's as he picked up James. She hoped she was telling them the truth.

Henry walked to the broken window and wasn't surprised to see the coastal surge licking its way towards the swollen tidal pond. What would happen to them when the two waters met? How much worse would it get? Were they safe to stay in the shelter of the house? Where would they go if they left? The questions were furiously spinning in his mind. Underneath was the concern Emily and her family were likely facing a similar situation.

The water was definitely still rising. As he watched, the land between the pond and the surge was rapidly disappearing. A bucket floated on the rising tide bobbing in the doorway of the outdoor kitchen. His father joined him at the window still holding James. Creaking wood brought Henry's stricken gaze to meet his father's.

A shriek pulled their attention back to the girls as Betsy admonished Emmaline. "Calm down. It's just water." Her questioning eyes met Theodore's.

Henry looked down to see the water was covering their feet. He raised his gaze to his father's. "What do we do now? Go upstairs or out in the storm?"

They both turned to again look out the window. The hurricane was still raging. The land was almost covered over. Off to the left, they could see other people fighting their way through the wind and the water in search of higher ground. Theodore couldn't wait much longer to make a decision. The deeper the water got, the harder it would be to get his children through it. On the other hand, perhaps the house would hold. He just couldn't see leaving the shelter of the house for a wet and treacherous walk through the pelting rain to questionable safety.

How could he purposefully lead his family into the bowels of such a wicked storm? Besides the dangers of the debris-filled wind and the rising water, where would they go? Even if they could fight against the wind to get to one of the brick buildings, they were all located closer to the coast and would be even more flooded. As fast as it was rising, the water would be over their heads before they got there. If they headed for higher ground, the only shelter would be the trees, and they seemed to be no match for the wind. For now, the safest risk was staying where they were but moving upstairs. Morbidly he thought, if the house fell at least they wouldn't be crushed beneath both stories.

As Theodore came to this conclusion, the shop debris pushed past the porch railing to crash into the front wall of the house, shifting it from its foundation and forcing him to do the unthinkable. "Betsy, gather what you need. We're leaving the house. Now!"

As if to confirm Theodore's decision, changing air pressure caused a door to slam upstairs. They all flinched. It seemed very likely the storm could blow the house apart as easily as it could topple it over. Theodore gathered his family together at the back door. He said a quick prayer for their safety before opening the door to the tempest outside.

Henry was first into the thigh deep rushing water carrying a food basket in one arm tucked tight against his chest. Horizontal wind lashed at him even though the house protected him from the worst of it. He turned to give his other hand to Agatha. She hesitantly descended the steps covered in swirling gray salt water filled with everything torn from the island. Her grip tightened as she left the last step and the water enveloped her to her chest. Henry gave her an encouraging smile. He understood her fear. This maelstrom was nothing like the waters around the island they so intimately knew and loved.

Brianna followed behind Henry and Agatha with three canteens full of water hung around her neck. She huddled into herself instinctively trying to seek refuge from the onslaught of wind, rain, and flying objects, but even with her head down, the water still hit her face, blown up from the surging tide and carried on the horizontal wind. Never before had she questioned her father's decisions, but surely, they would have been safer in the house.

Betsy finished tying her bonnet. She held Emmaline's hand as together they walked down the water covered steps. On the bottom step, Emmie refused to move. The water was up to her waist. Betsy stepped down to the ground and turned to face her. She saw terror on her daughter's face. If only she could carry her, but Emmaline was too big. Betsy lifted her young daughter's chin with her free hand and leaned in till their faces were almost touching. "Emmaline, we have to do this. I'm scared too, but we have to face our fear and move past it. One step at a time. I'll not let go of you. I promise." When she still didn't move, Betsy abandoned reason for command. "Now, Emmaline." She gave her hand a tug and Emmie stepped down.

The tide came up to Emmaline's chin. Fear made Betsy grip her hand even tighter as she hurried them forward to shallower water. Betsy's torso was instantly soaked to the skin by the wind-driven rain. She gritted her teeth. They would have to resign to being wet for the duration of the storm. She continued to fret over Theodore's decision to leave the house. She would have rather taken their chances going upstairs. She turned back, blinking against the rain-soaked wind, to tell Theodore she changed her mind. The moan of the house being pushed from its foundation had her turning forward once again, hurrying Emmaline along.

James anxiously watched his family leave the house. He didn't understand why they were going outside where the hairy-cane could get them. Brianna had promised him they would be safe from the monster as long as they stayed in the house. He didn't want to leave. He didn't want to be out with the monster. He turned to flee back into the house.

Theodore bent to pick up James but he slipped away. He held back a growl of frustration as he chased his young son back to the mattress. He caught and swung him up into his arms, kicking and screaming. His tantrum grew more frantic as they left the house. One shod foot made sharp contact with Theodore's rib. He roared, "James. Settle down." Obedience was instant. So was the startled look on James' face that was soon followed by crocodile tears.

Theodore had never used that tone with his youngest son before. His quiet authority was normally enough to subdue any misbehavior. He felt contrite for causing James' tears and hugged him close in an effort to convey his feelings and protect him from the onslaught. James hesitated before wrapping his arms around his father's neck as they left the shelter of the house. The little boy's face was plastered with sea spray and gusting wind, taking the breath from him. He turned his face forward and tried to find shelter under his father's bearded chin.

Henry saw the way James clung to their father. He remembered doing so at his age and feeling secure, but then came all the long absences when he did without his father's security. He had forgotten the feeling until now. Putting the memory aside, he turned to lead his family to higher ground. The violence of the hurricane took Henry by surprise. Seeing and hearing it from inside the house was nothing compared to feeling the full force of nature's wrath. It rendered him insignificant and powerless. He waited for Brianna and Agatha to catch up so he could take Agatha's other hand. As they moved around the kitchen and away from the windbreak provided by the house, the gusting wind pushed at their backs with such violence, twice it knocked Brianna off her feet. Agatha would have went down too if not for her tight grip on Henry's hand.

As they stumbled forward, Henry was at least thankful the storm was at their backs. It would have been impossible for them to move in the opposite direction. That was not to say the wind was blowing in one direction. It was strongest from the northwest, but it hurled at them randomly from all directions. During the more ferocious gusts, they were forced to stop walking and huddle together. Leaves and fronds pelted their backs and littered the water's surface. While the wind buffeted them from above, the surging water pushed at them from below.

They came to the wooden rail fence in the backyard. Henry helped each of his sisters to climb over before handing the food basket to Brianna and doing the same. Henry focused on reaching the land still exposed between the rising tide they were trudging through and the swollen pond. Wind picked up heavy water droplets from the water's surface and flung it at their faces adding to their misery. Just a little further and they would be free of the tide.

Henry tried to look behind him to check his family's progress. The wind-blown water-filled air stung his eyes making it impossible to look westward for more than a second, but it was long enough for him to see a heavy branch skim over Brianna's head. He ducked pulling Agatha down. She stumbled to her knees and the branch splashed into the pond a few yards in front of them. Henry helped his sister regain her feet. Brianna's hand on his shoulder brought his eyes to hers. They shared a look of relief.

It was short-lived.

Another incoming rush of water swirled around them, once again raising the water level and covering over the last of the exposed land as it finally collided with an incoming wave from the pond. With renewed urgency, Henry led them forward moving as fast as Agatha's short stride would allow but then he changed his mind. He decided it would be best to wait for the rest of the family to catch up before crossing the pond. He stood with legs braced apart, back against the wind, providing shelter for Agatha. Brianna soon reached his side, turning sideways to the wind to better stand her ground.

Brianna held a hand to her eyes for protection but still could do no more than glance behind them. Fear assailed her when all she saw was a whiteout of windblown water. There was no sign of their parents. She leaned into Henry and yelled into his ear. "I can't see them."

Henry turned his head to yell back. "Don't panic. They'll be here." He forced himself to believe his own words and prayed for their safety.

The three of them huddled close for warmth and anxiously waited, looking forward. On the other side of the pond, Henry could make out blurry outlines of the houses on Caroline Street. He couldn't tell how close the pond had risen towards them nor could he see clearly enough to tell if they were damaged. They at least all seemed to be standing. Beyond Caroline Street, the houses on Eaton Street were hidden in whitewash. To his right, the colliding waves of the pond and the western shore covered over the bridge at Whitehead Street. As the water rose above her knees, Agatha wrapped her hands around Henry and pressed her face against him. Today was the first time he had ever seen her show fear. He embraced her with his free arm and ran his thumb over her shoulder in a soothing motion. It was the best he could do for her.

Gusting winds blew over them with incredible strength. Henry's legs were tightening with the strain of holding still against them. He prayed his parents would reach them soon. He didn't want to have to make the decision to go on without them. A shingle flew past them. They were in constant danger of being struck by flying debris. Henry lifted his eyes to the houses across the pond. He was debating which of them to head towards when he saw the roof pulled off one of them followed by a trail of torn rafters and attic items. Was there anywhere safe for them to go?

Chapter 15

Dizzy drunkenness unbound
Limitless to destroy

Henry and his sisters, Brianna and Agatha, waited at what was once the edge of the pond for the rest of the family to catch up. The water was still rising behind them. It wasn't long before they were standing past Agatha's waist. Henry kept questioning his decision to wait.

He had just decided they should move on rather than continue to huddle in the midst of the gale when Brianna leaned in to exclaim, "I see them." Relief washed over him as profoundly as the wind was battering him. Above all else, he felt their family needed to stay together to survive whatever was to come before the hurricane's end.

It seemed to take an inordinate amount of time for their parents to reach them. Several times, Henry cast quick glances over his shoulder to gauge their progress. In only a few moments, the water had risen from his ankles to past his knees and was steadily moving upward. He could feel the push of it against the back of his calves adding to the pressure of the wind against his back. Several times he stumbled forward under the onslaught.

When finally the family was all together again, Theodore decided it would be best if he led the family across the swollen pond. Betsy insisted he should carry Emmaline through the turbulent water, fearing the child's waning strength would not be enough to fight its current. She took James from Theodore.

Henry watched his parents begin sloshing forward. They were crossing the flooded pond at what should be the shallowest point. He, Brianna, and Agatha followed close behind. A board broken loose from the boardwalk over the middle of the pond floated towards them. As best he could tell in the swirling whiteness, the crossing was completely submerged. He was thankful the wind was at their back, but the air was filled with water carried by the storm and spindrift from the pond, making it difficult to see in any direction. With the water, the wind also carried all manner of objects, heavy and light, turned deadly by velocity; tree limbs, palm fronds, shingles, and even unwary birds torn from their perch. They huddled close to the water's surface trying to avoid being struck by most of it. Torn vegetation swirled in the angry currents and clung to them. The water steadily deepened with every step forward. Danger was everywhere. Henry longed to reach the relative safety of one of the houses ahead of them.

Agatha slipped. Brianna moved her between them. The water was soon up to Agatha's neck. Henry prayed it didn't get deeper. He thought they were almost to the middle.

Suddenly, in front of them, his mother tripped over a submerged branch. She fell face first in the water unable to save herself for holding James out ahead of her to keep him from going under. She choked on the water screaming for help as James went under. His father rushed to catch him with Emmaline in his arms, but he missed. Henry dropped the food basket and pulled free of Agatha's grasp to race towards his floundering brother. He caught his arm just as he went under a second time. Henry pulled him to his chest. He was sputtering and crying, but thankfully safe. He held him tight, shocked to realize warm tears were running down his cheeks too, in profound relief. In the next moment, they were both wrapped in their mother's embrace and soon joined by Brianna, Agatha, Theodore, and Emmaline. Henry's eyes met his father's. They both realized this day, indeed this moment, was the reason God called him home. His family needed him.

The urgency of their situation ended the emotional moment. Feeling another rush of incoming water push past his legs, Henry reluctantly gave James back to Betsy so he could take the heavy food basket from Brianna. She had fortunately rescued it from sinking when he cast it off to save James. The family now linked arms and moved forward together as they slogged and finally sloshed through the far side of the pond to emerge near Whitehead Street.

Theodore paused for a moment undecided about heading towards one of the houses behind the pond or heading for higher ground further inland. He knew his family was growing weary of battling the storm but as he watched the water's edge reach towards the Watlington's house, it appeared heading for one of their neighbor's would only be a brief respite before they were forced to retreat again. He looked to Betsy and saw her longing for shelter. Her eyes widened in fear and then the world went black.

Betsy gasped in disbelief as she watched the man she loved crumple in a heap before her. A slate shingle struck Theodore's temple, narrowly missing Emmaline.

Emmie crawled out of his lax arms, sobbing, and for the first time in her young life, her mother ignored her distress. She turned to watch her mother frantically tend to her father. His inert form scared her more than the fall to the ground. She gratefully turned into Brianna's offered comfort which she soon shared with Agatha and James.

Henry once again dropped the food basket and rushed to join his mother at his father's side. Fear's hold on him made it hard to breath. Betsy tore off a strip of her water-logged crinoline and held it to the bleeding cut on the side of his father's head. Rivulets of crimson ran into his wet hair and down his cheek. Henry wasn't sure what to do, but with the water still rising, staying here wasn't an option. He slid his hands under his father's shoulder intending to lift him, but Betsy made him stop.

Over the roar of the storm, she yelled, "I've got to stop the bleeding first."

Henry shook his head. "We can't stay here."

"Take the others and go." She pointed to the Watlington house.

"Come back with help."

Henry hesitated. He didn't want to leave them, especially with his father unconscious. He glanced towards the pond to find the water was almost upon them again, but he also saw others struggling through the water. One of them was leading a mule and cart.

He got to his feet and leaned down to tell his mother, "I'll be right back." He left his family and forced his way against the wind and tide and stinging rain by sheer determination. He held his arm over his face to shelter it from the scouring sand particles carried in the wind. When he finally reached the cart, it was with great relief he turned his back to the tempest. He now could see the man leading the cart was Mr. Mallory with his wife, daughter, and mother inside. Henry sent a thankful prayer heavenward. Mr. Mallory's mother, Ellen Mallory, not only ran the boardinghouse but also cared for the sick and infirm. She could help his father, and right now Mr. Mallory looked as if he could use Henry's assistance getting the mule and cart through the chest deep water.

Henry nodded to Stephen and pointed to his huddled family in the distance. He yelled, "My father needs help." To his relief, Stephen nodded and turned the mule in their direction. Henry was impatient to reach his father. The cart inched along, the seconds ticking into minutes that seemed like hours.

As soon as the mule stepped from the water, Henry ran around to the back of the cart. As if sensing the situation, the elder Mrs. Mallory was already there. Henry helped her to the ground. She moved purposefully to Theodore's side.

Betsy relinquished the cloth to the matron's caring hand and watched as she carefully checked the bleeding and the severity of the wound.

Stephen bent down to his mother. "We need to move." He nodded towards the trees.

Ellen nodded in understanding. She wrapped the cloth around Theodore's head and knotted it. Her caring eyes looked into Betsy's. "He needs stitches, but he'll have to make do without them." Her words were lost in the wind. Ellen stood and made gestures indicating Betsy should move back and Theodore should be moved to the cart.

As Stephen leaned down to grasp his legs, Henry lifted Theodore by his shoulders. The jolt of movement brought Theodore back to consciousness. Feeling Theodore's limbs stiffen, Stephen lowered his legs and moved to his shoulder.

Theodore's head hurt like the dickens. He opened his eyes and raised his hand to investigate. At the same time, he realized where he was and that Henry and Stephen Mallory were supporting his weight. He got his feet under him and felt a wave a dizziness wash over him. His limbs went weak for a second before it passed and he was able to stand.

Betsy gave a deep sigh of relief when she realized Theodore had regained consciousness. Her heart still hurt from her initial fear when he crumpled to the ground. She thought she had lost her husband. Learning he was still alive had eased the constriction, but true relief came when she looked into his hazel eyes. She moved her head next to his to be heard. "How do you feel?"

"What happened?"

"A shingle struck you."

He swallowed against the rising nausea. "I'll be all right." He pulled his arm from Mr. Mallory's, but Henry refused to let go. Theodore took a shaky step forward, testing his balance. A gust of wind made him stumble. Henry's grip tightened and kept him from falling. Determination to get his family away from the pond kept him moving forward. By the time he reached the cart, pride was put aside. He allowed Stephen and Henry to help him onto the wooden bed. Mrs. Mallory was lifted in next to him. She moved to his head to check his wound.

Henry mouthed his thanks to Mr. Mallory who gave a nod in return as he took James from Betsy and handed him up to his wife in the cart. Henry lifted Emmaline in as well. Seeing the cart was crowded, Agatha shook her head when Henry turned to her. Brianna gratefully relinquished the heavy food basket.

Mr. Mallory led the mule past the houses, headed for the highest point on the island. Henry, Betsy, Brianna, and Agatha walked beside the cart using it as a shield against the buffeting wind. Henry glanced back occasionally to his family noting the haggard weariness in their faces and the grim determination to keep moving. The pieces of debris flying about in the air were getting larger. Heavy tree branches, torn siding, and fence pickets flew about them. They all were in imminent danger of being struck down. The fear of flood waters encroaching from behind kept them trudging onward. Every once in a while the air would clear enough to see other nearby families flanking them.

The constant battle against blasts of wind and the battery of flying debris made the trek slow and agonizing. Henry's back and legs were aching. Agatha was tiring out and leaning on him for support. The wind had worked her braided hair loose and whipped it against her face and his side. She gave up trying to contain it and now just tried to keep its stinging slap out of her eyes. Henry glanced back over his left shoulder to check on the others behind him. Their tired faces reflected the same misery.

Mr. Mallory led them deep into the trees at the edge of the settlement where they found small pockets of relief from the unrelenting wind although now they had to also avoid being hit by wind-whipped branches. Relief filled Henry when he felt the ground sloping upward. Here the trees were taller. Ahead a copse of white mangrove surrounding a large mahogany beckoned him. It would be as good a shelter as any they were likely to find. Not to mention, the cart wouldn't be able to go much further as the undergrowth increased. Mr. Mallory had come to the same conclusion for he brought the cart to a halt.

Henry positioned Agatha in the lee of the wide mahogany trunk. She was soon joined by the rest of his younger siblings. They huddled together for warmth. Henry and his parents encircled them adding further shelter. They were joined by Stephen Mallory, his wife, daughter, and mother. Young Maggie Mallory made her way into the center of the huddled mass to join Agatha and Emmaline. Ellen Mallory made a point of positioning herself next to Theodore so she could check the dressing on his head wound. Henry anxiously watched as she tested the water and blood soaked bandage for fresh bleeding. Seemingly satisfied, she stepped away but not before Henry saw the concern in her eyes.

* * *

Other families soon joined them, some having crossed the pond by boat. They, too, gathered behind the largest trees they could find holding onto each other as an anchor in the storm. Here and there a tree would crack under the pressure causing them all to look upward in fear.

Nearby, a man squatted against the gnarled trunk of a lignum vitae. His hands were pressed tight over his ears to block out the menacing, never ceasing, battering, shrieking wind.

Reverend Richardson was in another group with his head bowed in prayer, but if he prayed aloud the wind carried it away from their ears. Beside him a woman was on her knees with hands over her ears, rocking her torso. She appeared to be screaming.

Henry sympathized with them. He was weary of the storm sounds filling his head.

They all were waiting for the hurricane to pass, for the warmth of the sun. Waiting for the waters to recede. Waiting for rescue from the nightmare.

Betsy and Theodore clung closely to each other to share body heat. The unseasonable warmth of two days ago was but a distant memory. She tried to control the shiver that overtook her as the wind gusted across her back. A glance at her husband's face gave her a new concern. Fatigue was stamped across his features and pain reflected in his eyes. He caught her gaze and gave her a weak reassuring smile. She returned it, hoping to share some of her strength with him in the simple but powerful gesture. She wondered what time it was. It was going on five o'clock when they left the house. Now she noticed the storm shrouded gray skies were darkening. Night was approaching. The ground was too wet to sit down. How long could her family remain huddled in this madness? How long before Theodore's strength gave out? How much longer must they endure this maelstrom? What would be left of the island when it was gone?

Henry was wondering the time as well. He watched as Stephen momentarily pulled his arm from his wife to check his pocket watch. His grimace after flipping open the cover didn't surprise Henry. The timepiece likely stopped working when it got soaked as Stephen brought his family through the pond. Judging by the waning light, Henry guessed it was approaching sunset making it about two hours since they left the house. Two tortuous hours. As a strong blast pushed against his back, it occurred to him the wind was once again coming in gusts instead of the constant buffeting they endured upon leaving the house. He felt sure it was a good sign they were on the backside of the storm. Henry offered a silent prayer asking that it soon pass. He wasn't sure how much longer his family could endure the open exposure. He wondered again if they shouldn't have remained in the house despite the risks or at least taken shelter with one of their neighbors behind the pond. A flooded house was better than being exposed out here in the wilderness.

Betsy's attention was pulled to her daughters in the midst of an argument. Emmaline was nearly in tears and Maggie was fiercely frowning. She bent over the girls having to yell to be heard. "What is it?"

Agatha looked up. "God doesn't love us." She had to repeat it louder for her mother to hear.

Betsy leaned close to her ear. "Yes he does. Why would you say that?"

Agatha sobbed. "Because of this." She gestured wildly with both hands nearly knocking Emmaline in the face. "Why would he do this if he loved us?"

Betsy's heart lurched. How could she explain God's love in the midst of a gale? She knelt before her daughter in total disregard of the soggy ground. She pulled a wide-eyed James in front of her and then took up first Agatha's and then Emmaline's hand, pulling them close to her sides. She waited for Maggie to complete the circle. "God loves us. He is not punishing us. He is testing us. Testing our faith. And when we are tested we pray. Right?" At their nod she said, "Say it with me." Their voices joined hers and when the words drifted to them, Theodore and Henry did too.

"Have not I commanded Thee! Be strong and of a good courage: be not afraid, neither be thou dismayed: for the Lord thy God is with thee whithersoever thou goest."

Betsy squeezed the girls' hands. "We'll be alright. This too shall pass." She wished she could tell them they would be home soon. Was their home still standing? She put the thought from her mind. There was nothing she could do about it now and worry was just borrowed trouble. She had plenty of trouble to face right now. She hugged her children to her as Angela Mallory took Maggie into her embrace. For now, Betsy could offer comfort. She leaned back from the girls and said, "Let's sing! We can sing louder than this storm." She started singing the first song that came to mind. "Joy to the world, the Lord is come." She was pleased when the girls picked up the tune each trying to outdo the wind. Theodore helped Betsy to her feet and smiled approvingly as he joined in the second stanza.

The energy required to sing above the storm soon waned. After only three songs, the group once again lapsed into silence as darkness descended. The storm was obviously dying down but not fast enough. They were all wet, cold, hungry, thirsty and tired. At least two of the issues could be addressed. Henry left the group to retrieve the basket from the cart. One of the canteens was passed around with the caution of only one swallow per person. Until they knew how many cisterns were damaged, they had to consider the water they carried to be all they would have for days. Betsy pulled a jar of dried fruit from the basket which was also passed around their group. It came back to her with two pieces left. She gave it to Henry and with a nod indicated he should take it to the family of four huddled closest to them.

Henry returned from his delivery and walked around the Mallorys to his parents. He leaned in between his father and Stephen. "I'm going back before it gets any darker to see if there is a house left we can shelter in."

Theodore nodded in agreement. Stephen moved to go with Henry, but Angela tightened her grip on his arm holding him back.

Henry shook his head. "I can move faster alone."

Theodore squeezed his forearm. "Hurry back."

* * *

Marine Hospital

Over the last few hours, Emily and most of the others had grown used to the muffled sound of heavy debris striking the building with the flowing water. Few flinched anymore even though they all were worried about the missing roof and cracked wall from the dock collision.

She was so weary of it all.

So many hours.

So many hours of listening to howling winds and rushing tide outside, and dripping water inside. So many hours confined to a building now in danger of collapse. So many hours of nothing to do but listen to the relentless hurricane, trapped in her own thoughts. It made Emily want to scream at the world. She would if it would help, but it wouldn't.

A loud crack filled the air and the floor shuddered beneath their feet.

Emily and everyone else jumped, startled by the unexpected disturbance.

It came from the northeastern side of the building. Something else very large must have hit the building, hard. Thorn went running to the offices on the far end to investigate. Once again the occupants of the hospital were in varying states of distress. Emily was pleased to note Willie was taking deep breaths instead of hyperventilating this time, saving her from having to run to his side. She gave him a nod of encouragement.

She watched Thorn return to the room to meet their mother. Emily hurried to join them followed by Millie and Mary.

"It looked like timbers from the fort camp. The wall is cracked." Thorn flinched as a particularly strong gust of wind made the building shudder. "This place could collapse any minute. Do you think we should stay?"

Abby facetiously asked, "Where would we go?"

Millie said, "We can't move all these patients in this weather."

Thorn turned away, feeling foolish.

Of course no one else in the room could hear what was said over the noise, but it was clear by their expressions they understood what Thorn found was not good. Varying emotions from concern to terror were reflected in the faces around the room.

The wind and water beat unmercifully all around them causing the unstable structure to shudder despite being made of brick. Panic spread like wildfire from the refugees to the nurses and to the patients. Emily felt its hold tighten around her. She knew they were all thinking the same thing. How much longer must they endure and would the building hold?

Her mother pulled them together as a group to pray. She spoke loudly over the wind asking God for his protection. The momentary lull of wind as she prayed helped calm their fears.

* * *

High Ground

Henry found it easier to travel now that the wind was dying down. It still was gusting hard enough to make him stop and hold his ground but that was only every ten minutes or so. In between, he ran as fast as he could through the dense brush. He had to find shelter for his family and get back to them before it became too dark to see. He burst from the trees into the clearing behind Eaton Street. He was greatly relieved to see houses still standing in front of him. He headed to a modest one in the middle he knew belonged to Jonathon Keats and his wife Esperanza.

As he rounded the front of the house, he could see the high water mark did not quite reach these houses. Even better, the water was starting to recede. He turned to approach the Keats' front door only to find his way blocked by the fallen front porch. He circled back to the rear door and knocked heavily. It was soon answered by their eldest son, Gabriel. He beckoned Henry to come in.

Henry found Mrs. Keats in the living room with her children gathered round. Captain Keats tried to rise awkwardly on his broken leg. Mrs. Keats sent her husband a look that made him return to his seat. She came forward to greet Henry with her soft Cuban accent. "Why you're soaked through and through!" She turned to her eldest daughter. "Maria, bring a towel for Señor Henry."

Henry shook his head. "No time. My family is out in the woods. I came to find a safe place for the night. Can I bring them here? My father is hurt. The Mallory's are with us."

"Si, of course. We will make room."

"Thank you, Mrs. Keats. I must hurry and bring them back before it gets any darker."

"Here, take this with you." She picked up a glass enclosed lantern and quickly lit it with a taper from one of the nearby burning candles. She passed it to Henry. "God speed."

Henry nodded gratefully and was gone. Esperanza turned to her children and set them about gathering dry clothes and towels, food and water, in preparation for their forthcoming guests.

Henry raced back to his huddled family as darkness descended. The decreasing winds made the journey easier but periodic gusts were a strong reminder the hurricane was not done with them yet. In a fraction of the time it took to reach the trees the first time, he made it back. As the adults all turned at his arrival, his smile conveyed his success. He could see their relief.

At Ellen Mallory's insistence, Theodore was forced to ride in the cart. He held James and Emmaline in his lap. Agatha agreed to ride with Maggie. They perched on the oilcloth covered crates holding the custom records Stephen insisted on taking in case the custom house flooded or worse, was destroyed.

They soon set off for the Keats. Others taking shelter nearby were quick to follow them. No one wanted to spend the night in the cold, wet, darkness. Their progress was hindered by a few fallen trees they were forced to go around. By the time night had fallen, they were drying off in the protected shelter of the Keats' home.

The children were chattering like magpies sharing their stories of the day's events. Esperanza passed out small cups of tea to the shivering adults, sparingly using their dwindling water supply. She gave Mrs. Mallory the requested bowl containing the remaining heated water from the kettle and a clean cloth.

Ellen Mallory carefully unwrapped the bandage from Theodore's head. She didn't want to cause any more bleeding than necessary to stitch it up. Past experience told her Theodore had a strong constitution. He was going to need it. Otherwise, she would have argued when he turned down Esperanza's offer of laudanum. Gently, she cleaned the inch long gash in his temple revealing the beginnings of bruising. The swelling didn't appear to be bad enough to hinder her sewing. Ellen accepted the small sewing needle from Esperanza and held it for a few moments in the flame of the candelabra she had pulled close to provide light. She picked up the piece of thread that she left soaking in the hot water and threaded it. She stepped up to Theodore. "Are you ready?"

Esperanza silently handed him her wooden spoon. He started to refuse and then thought better of it. He laid it on the table when Betsy offered her hand. He held it lightly and gave her a reassuring smile before turning his gaze to Mrs. Mallory. He gave her a firm nod. She took a step closer. Theodore's back was to the room so the children couldn't see his face. He knew he could stoically remain silent so as not to alarm them. He only hoped he could hold his grimace as well. He turned his gaze to Betsy's and held it.

Ellen pulled the skin together and set the needle to her task. Theodore winced at the first pass but then resolutely held still and quiet. Her only clue of his suffering was in the beads of sweat that appeared across his brow. Quickly she completed nine neat stitches, dabbing away the blood between each one. She wrapped his head with a fresh piece of linen. Betsy saw that he was settled on the couch.

* * *

Marine Hospital

Abby was exhausted. She was struggling to stay awake despite the storm. The wall clock read half past eight when she sent Emily and Thorn around with water and food. It was the last of the food, but at least the water supply was holding. She was sitting in a straight back chair set against the interior wall under an overhead plank. It was the driest place in the now dimly lit room. The other occupants were shadowy figures laying upon the beds or moving about tending patients.

Her eyes flew open to find Emily shaking her shoulder offering her some freshly cut cocoanut meat. Abby smiled and accepted the bite of food. As she chewed she became aware of the murmur of voices. She could still hear the wind outside, but it was finally beginning to abate.

Glory be!

Emily noticed the relief on her mother's face and nodded. They both grinned. The worst was finally past.

Abby's thoughts turned to Max and Christoff. She prayed again for their safety, fearful they might be tackling the storm head on to save another ship. If only she could have persuaded him to keep to his promise. But then again, a merchant ship would be no match for the storm they just endured.

Emily stole away from the group to peer out one of the darkened windows overlooking the harbor. She chose the one with the torn shutter but it mattered little. She couldn't see much beyond the reflection of light from inside the room. The storm was easing but its noises still hurt her aching head. She pinched the bridge of her nose and rubbed her forehead trying to ease the pain. It didn't do any good. She was worried. Worried if their house was still standing, worried if her father and brother were safe, and mostly worried for Henry and his family. Her mind conjured horrible images of them being trapped and drowned under the rubble of their home.

Her mother would tell her to keep busy to distract her thoughts and fears. She turned away from the window deciding to make some willow bark tea for her headache. Maybe there were others who needed it too.

* * *

Keats House

After being cleaned up, changed into borrowed clothes and fed, the Keats, Mallory, and Whitmore children were put to sleep on makeshift pallets spread across the living room floor. Betsy turned away thinking they were settled but little James came from behind her to crawl into his father's lap.

Theodore lifted him up. "It's way past your bedtime son."

James reached up his tiny hand to pat his father's cheek. "Don't worry poppa... We're safe from the monster now."

Theodore choked up. He was worried, and he wasn't hiding it well if his little boy noticed. He smiled for him. "You're right, and soon the monster will be gone." He kissed his forehead and set him down. "Off to bed with you." Theodore's gaze caught Betsy's tearful one. For her he whispered, "We'll be fine."

Henry felt the poignancy of the moment shared between father and son.

The adults quietly talked around the table reliving their ordeal and sharing what they had seen. When talk turned to how bad the damages might be, Angela Mallory broke down sobbing. Stephen drew her in his arms. They were still reeling from the loss of their two year old son only a month ago. Now they faced the possible loss of their home.

Angela soon pulled herself together and apologized to the group.

Esperanza offered her another cup of tea.

"No thank you. If you don't mind, I think I would like to lie down. It has been a trying day."

"Of course. Come with me. I put fresh sheets on the children's beds."

Angela, Ellen, and Stephen retired for the evening. Esperanza soon followed suit. Betsy, Theodore, and Henry were still too keyed up to sleep. Jonathon kept them company at the table until close to midnight when the hurricane finally dissipated.

Not long after, they gratefully found places to sleep where they could, knowing they would need their strength to face the light of morning, for tonight it was enough to be safe and dry. Before he turned out the lamp, Henry saw the worried look that passed between his mother and father. Would morning light prove his family to be homeless?

* * *

Marine Hospital

Emily breathed a sigh of relief. Several hours ago the wind dropped from a constant roar to regular gusts and now those were growing further and further apart. It was almost over and the hospital was still standing. The dripping water from the ceiling diminished. They were fortunate the rain was not more substantial as with other hurricanes. The wind brought enough trouble pushing the tide inland and whipping the water about in the air. As it was, it rained enough that all the bedding was wet, the food was gone, and clean water was dwindling. She hoped the rest of the island was not as devastated as she feared. What would they do if it was? She shied away from contemplating such a daunting outcome. Weariness settled about her. Sleep soon followed.

Abby awoke with a start. Those around her were asleep. Millie and Mary were in chairs next to her propped against each other. Emily and Nate were curled together on a hospital bed. Only half the lanterns were still glowing. She checked her timepiece. It was after one in the morning. A soft clatter at the far side of the room drew her attention. Thorn had returned to the room with an oil can to refill the lamps. She suddenly realized what had disturbed her sleep. It was the absolute quiet outside. The hurricane had finally passed.

She walked to the bank of windows facing her house, sidestepping the broken glass on the floor to open one of the unbroken casements. She unlatched the shutters and flung the right one open wide. She couldn't see far into the blackness. Clouds still obscured the moon and stars. She wouldn't know how bad the damage was until first light. The sound of moving water brought her gaze down to the foundation. The tide still swirling around them. She guessed it to be a foot or two high, but at least it was receding. She decided to leave the window open to allow fresh air to circulate in the ward.

She walked past each of the beds checking on the patients. She was pleased to note Mr. Donovan's fever was gone. At least something good had come from the day. She squeezed Thorn's shoulder to show her appreciation for his help and then returned to her chair. Her eyes closed as she sank down to the seat, and she slept.

Chapter 16

Gulf waters ahead
Fight not to slow

Monday, October 12th
Keats House

Wearily, Henry waited for the first light of dawn. His mind was too full of concern for Emily to sleep. He hated not knowing if she was safe, if there was still a roof over her head, or if she was wet and shivering. Aside from Emily, he worried if their house was still standing. Had they done the right thing in leaving it? In the rush of things, Henry had done no more than glance at his nearby sketch pad and charcoals. His haversack was upstairs. There was no way to carry them and help his family escape to higher ground. Their possible loss was not even a consideration in the moment, but now in the quiet, he could lament the decision. It hurt to contemplate his work at the very least would be water damaged. That all might be forever forfeit, even harder to bear. His possessions were few. His family had much to lose, the house being the biggest. What would they do if the worst had happened?

Until it was light enough to move about, he couldn't have answers, and it was several hours before dawn. Henry sighed heavily with frustration.

The storm blew itself out over the last few hours. All was eerily quiet now except for the soft sounds of the children sleeping about the room on makeshift bedding. He occupied a chair by the front window of the Keats' house. Across the room, his father slept fitfully on the sofa. His discomfort as likely from the head injury as from being propped up at an odd angle with his feet hanging over the arm. Mrs. Mallory said they needed to be concerned if he showed signs of imbalance or nausea. Otherwise, she expected he would be fine except for some bruising and a headache. His mother and the Mallory's were occupying the children's' beds.

Henry's deep sigh drew Theodore's glance. Besides the headache from his injury that kept him from sleeping, he was as worried as his son about their house and their neighbors. How many stayed in their homes? How deep had they flooded? How many had survived–homes and people? What would they find when daylight came? How would they recover if it was as bad as he feared? The questions circled endlessly in his mind increasing the headache and his restlessness. But underneath the worry, he was profoundly grateful for the safety of his wife and children.

He must have finally drifted off to sleep. A few hours later, Theodore awoke to the annoying sound of squawking birds adding to the pain of his headache. He lifted his hand to his temple and grimaced. His wound was too tender to touch. His gaze caught Henry's on the other side of the room. Between them lay all the children of the three families sharing the dwelling.

The need to relieve himself had Theodore rising from the couch only to sink back down as a wave of dizziness passed over him. Henry was by his side in a heartbeat. Theodore waved him off. The feeling quickly subsided. Cautiously, he tried rising again, slowly this time. He waited a moment and was relieved to find his legs steady enough to move forward. He and Henry made their way to the back door in the faint light of early dawn.

Henry opened the door as quietly as he could so as to keep from waking the children.

They stepped out into a foreign and yet familiar land.

Henry's heart wrenched. The first thing he noticed beyond the soaked ground was the yard littered with shredded island vegetation and torn building materials. Dazed, they walked down the steps and into the detritus.

Words failed them.

The forest beyond the yard was stripped of greenery. Many trees were broken or uprooted to lay haphazardly against their more sturdy neighbors. Those still standing were blackened as if scorched by fire. Overall, there was an uncomfortable sense of brown that would increase to overwhelming proportions in the coming days when all the torn greenery began to wither and decay in the hot sun. The unbelievable power of wind and water left their island looking as close to an apocalypse as Henry could imagine.

What he saw only heightened his concerns for Emily. He walked to the corner of the house where he could look towards the pond and town. His view was blocked by the partially standing houses on Caroline Street. He wanted to run and find her, but his father's call forced him to wait. In the Keats' backyard, the kitchen was still upright, but the outhouse lay on its side blown a few yards from its setting. His help was needed to right it before he could go to Emily.

* * *

Marine Hospital

Weak rays of morning sun filtered into the hospital when Emily stirred from a light sleep. She rubbed her eyes and looked around getting her bearings. Few others were awake yet after the long ordeal of yesterday. She rose and walked over to the closest window facing the street. She opened the casement and unlatched the shutters pushing them open wide.

She gasped at what she saw before her.

She naively thought getting through the storm was the worst of it. She was so mistaken. Daylight revealed the narrowness of her thinking. Now, was the worst of it.

Her island lay in ruins.

Nothing in her life prepared her for this; this total devastation of her hometown. The cleanup from past storms had taken days. What she saw before her would take months, if not years, to overcome.

She ran across the open floor and down the hall to the front door. Outside she stood on the landing taking in all of the destruction from the elevated height of the front entry. The vegetation, the buildings, and the islanders had taken a beating. The neat and tidy streets were now littered with... everything! To her right, Mr. Fielding Browne's house was, thankfully, still standing, but the street was clogged with huge piles of timber from the fort construction camp. Some of it now lay haphazard between houses, and worse, a few timbers were driven into one of them. The houses she could see had various amounts of destruction, but all of them were damaged. None had escaped the hurricane's wrath. To Emily's left and further down the street was more of the same with the added oddity of a fishing boat perched in a broken tree. How many were alive or dead?

Others from inside the hospital joined her on the stoop including her mother and Thorn coming to stand on her left. Molly reported that the outbuildings behind the hospital were gone as was the dock which they knew had struck the wall during the storm.

Emily's gaze moved back to the right, once again taking in all the devastation. Her heart squeezed tighter. She looked past the debris filled street to the stand of denuded trees in the distance and the clear sky beyond. Her eyes went back and forth above the barren trees tops. Something was dreadfully wrong. Something more than the sad sight of the storm beaten palms. Panic bloomed in her chest as she struggled to understand what her sight was telling her. Her breath grew short and shallow as realization dawned on her.

It came out as a croaked whisper. "The lighthouse is gone." She turned her stricken gaze to her mother and brother in desperate need for them to tell her she was wrong.

Thorn turned to look at her with confusion.

She tried again with more strength in her voice as the release of tears flowed down her face. "The lighthouse is gone."

Thorn's eyes went over her head searching in the direction of Whitehead Point. He stepped around her just as her mother, having heard her this time, came forward to fold Emily into her embrace. Emily's heartbroken sobs burst from her. It was all more than she could take.

Abby's heart lurched. She knew Barbara Mabrity was visiting her daughter in Tampa and had left her son Miguel in charge of the light with a hired assistant. She looked to Thorn. "Miguel may need help. Go see what can be done and try to find more help on the way."

Thorn nodded, readily accepting the mantel of responsibility. He wasted no time lifting a good-sized tree branch off the steps and tossing it over the side so he could be on his way to those in need.

Fear of what he might face made Abby call after him. "Hawthorn, be careful."

* * *

Keats House

Anxiety was gripping Henry's insides. He couldn't wait another moment to find Emily. It seemed to take hours to find the tools they needed. Mr. Keats shed was ripped apart. They ended up borrowing neighbor's tools and his assistance in exchange for shared use of the outhouse. The neighbor's was obliterated.

As soon as Henry finished helping his father prop up the fallen down outhouse as best they could, he took off at a run for Emily's house. He ignored the scoured and confused chickens wandering about nor did he pay much attention to the damages of the other houses he passed. He doggedly made his way over and around fallen trees and windblown debris to the Eatonton house.

It was with great relief he found the house intact, even the cupola. It appeared to only have a few missing shingles and siding boards. He raced up the steps and knocked on the door, shuffling as he waited for it to be answered. Impatiently, he knocked again. When the silence continued, he moved down the porch to look in the broken parlor window. The house was silent.

After a moment's hesitation, he opened the front door and stuck his head inside. "Hello?" His voice was lost in the emptiness. *Where could they be?* He turned back to the street looking towards town, and then it occurred to him. *Of course!* Mrs. Eatonton would have gone to the hospital and probably took Emily and her brothers with her.

He skirted around the house, headed for the coast. He stopped short when he found a torn wall in his path forcing him to finally take notice of his surroundings. His peripheral awareness of the destruction sharpened into focus. His jaw dropped in dismay. He trudged slowly forward. His gaze swung from one horror to the next, not paying attention to his path, until his foot caught. He freed himself from the tangled branches and stopped walking to gape at what was left in the aftermath.

All of the houses were damaged, some severely. He was sure at least one house was missing all together. Not only was the ground littered, but wet leaves and palm fronds were plastered to windows and walls. The houses still standing were missing large amounts of shingles and in many cases sections of the roof. A few houses were partially collapsed. Henry turned his gaze to the right, in the direction of his house. He couldn't see it from where he stood, but what he did see left him with little hope it was still standing. Curiosity pulled him to investigate, but it was overruled by the need to know that Emily was safe.

The residents were beginning to emerge from their torn dwellings. Their faces were dazed and they moved slowly as if walking out of a dream into a waking nightmare. Some looked around blankly not knowing what to do but most investigated the ruins and checked on neighbors.

Henry continued onward.

At the next house, Mr. Young was struggling to right his outhouse. The tightly built structure was intact, but like the Keats, it was blown off its base. Henry helped him set it upright. He wiped the sweat from his brow, shook Mr. Young's hand, and set out once again to reach his beloved.

Ahead he could see the Marine Hospital was still standing, but the roof was gone. He hurried forward, anxious to reach Emily. At the next step, a muffled sob stopped him. He turned towards the sound and found a gray-haired lady cradling her husband's head in her lap. The pallor of his skin told Henry he had died sometime during the hurricane.

Memories of cradling the body of a fellow ranger after his first Indian battle swamped Henry's mind. The sudden death of a man who had become a good friend had cut him deep. The echo of pain in his mind gave him great empathy for the new widow.

He approached her softly and gently placed a hand on her shoulder. She looked up with tear-reddened eyes. Henry's heart lurched as he recognized the Eatonton's housekeeper, Mrs. Baxley. She had fed him more cookies in his youth than he could ever count.

Mrs. Baxley's voice drifted on the wind. "He went out in the storm to find our dog and never came back." Her words ended with a heart-wrenching sob.

Henry squatted down in front of her, unsure how to help.

She ran a blue-veined, shaking hand over her husband's head. "I think he was struck by something. See the blood on the back of his head. He won't wake up." She lifted her faded blue eyes to Henry's again. "Can you wake him?"

Henry's throat tightened as he sadly shook his head. He reached forward to take her hand. "Mrs. Baxley, he's gone. Will you let me help you up?" She didn't say anything as he gently moved Mr. Baxley to lay on the ground. He then helped her to her feet. Shakily, she reached behind her to untie her stained white apron. Henry was puzzled for a moment when she handed it to him but soon realized her intention. He bent down and placed it over Mr. Baxley's face.

Now he stood wondering what to do. Should he walk her to her house or take her to the hospital with him? Henry breathed a sigh of relief as Mrs. Young came rushing over to them followed by Mr. Young. She placed a caring arm around Mrs. Baxley's shoulder and with a nod of appreciation to Henry turned the grieving widow back to her house.

Mr. Young took his hat off as he looked down at his neighbor and friend. "I'm not sure what to do with him. It will be some time before a funeral can be arranged."

Henry shuffled on his feet. He was obligated to help take care of Mr. Baxley, but he was still anxious to get to Emily. What if something like this had happened to her or her family? Fear tightened his chest. He glanced towards the hospital. He was so close and yet...

Mr. Young sighed. "I suppose moving him to his porch, out of the sunlight, is the best we can do for now. You take his shoulders and I'll get his feet."

Relieved by his suggestion, Henry quickly bent to the task. With Mr. Baxley taken care of, he nodded to Mr. Young and resumed his path.

He climbed over a haphazard pile of timbers in the street. He recognized them as the ones belonging to the fort construction. He paused to look in the direction from whence they came. The distance was too great to tell how much damage had been done, but it was sure not to be insignificant if the lumber was relocated by almost half a mile. Henry shook his head. He couldn't worry about that now. He made a zig-zag sprint around the rest of the debris between him and the hospital and up the steps.

He burst through the front door and slowed to a brisk walk as he left the entry hall to enter the main ward. His gaze immediately fell on Emily as she deposited a tray on the end of a bed. He didn't notice anyone else. He had eyes only for his beloved. Perhaps if he had seen the others, he wouldn't have done what he did next. In long determined strides, he reached her. He saw her surprise change to happiness as he approached and shock as he enfolded her in his arms. His relief in finding her unharmed was so great it overwhelmed all reason.

It was the most natural thing to do...

He kissed her.

Kissed her without one concern as to who might be watching.

The sailors grinned and nodded, one even whistled in good-natured approval. Mary and Millie smiled at the reckless display of young love.

Abby turned at the commotion and grew livid. *How dare he!* Her red-headed emotions flowed strong as she strode forward ready to pull Henry away from her daughter.

Henry broke the kiss and whispered in Emily's ear, "You're safe in my arms." It took another heartbeat to register that she was trying to push him away. An angry Mrs. Eatonton appeared in his peripheral, as he let Emily slip from his embrace. His smile faded as soon as he got a good look at his future mother-in-law. He took a step back and held his hands up. "I apologize."

Abby glanced at her daughter whose cheeks were flushed bright red and whose eyes were cast to the floor. She would deal with her later. Despite his being a head taller than her, Abby firmly grasped Henry's arm and led him back to the front door. Outside on the stoop, she faced him with fire flashing in her eyes. "What in the world were you thinking to treat her like a common trollop in public?" She shook her head. "Have you no respect for her?"

"Please, Mrs. Eatonton. I can explain."

She crossed her arms over her chest and waited, refusing to let his remorseful pleading soften her heart.

"I wasn't thinking. I was so relieved to find her unharmed after worrying for so long. I was so overwhelmed with joy, the only way to express it was to kiss her." He shrugged with a charming self-deprecating smile. "I was concerned for you too. Are the boys good? Thorn? Nate? Jacob?"

She saw the sincerity in his eyes but held her expression firm. "You must promise me here and now, you will never kiss her in public again. Ever."

Flippantly he said, "Not even on our wedding day?"

Anger flared anew. "Henry James Whitmore..."

He held his hands up in surrender. "Yes, yes, of course, I promise."

Abby took a deep calming breath. "Is your family safe?"

"Yes. We had to leave the house in the middle of the storm, but they are all fine. Poppa was struck by a flying shingle which cut his temple." At her indrawn breath, he hurried to add, "He's fine. Mrs. Mallory stitched it closed. We passed the night at the Keats' house. I left them to make sure your family was safe. I looked for you first at your house. It still stands, by the way. Just some minor damage." His eyes drifted away as emotions rolled over him. He swallowed hard before returning his troubled gaze back to hers. "Most of the houses I passed are in bad shape and not everyone survived. Mr. Baxley is dead."

Abby's hand flew to her chest. "Mrs. Baxley?"

"She is with Mrs. Young."

Abby nodded solemnly. After a moment she said, "This hurricane was severe. It will be a miracle if there are not many injured like your father. Does your family need you to return right away?"

"I don't think so."

"The lighthouse is down."

Henry turned around to stare at the emptiness where the lighthouse once stood against the blue sky.

"I sent Thorn to see if help was needed. You should be able to catch up to him."

Their eyes met, silently sharing the fear they both held for the Mabrity family.

"I will."

Abby watched him go down the steps two at time and head off down the road. She sent a prayer for the safety of Miguel and whoever else may have taken refuge in the lighthouse. Her gaze once again took in all the damage surrounding her. If anything, it looked worse now than when she first saw it. Tears pricked her eyes. Her island lay in ruins like she had never seen it before. How many lives were lost or broken? How were they going to recover? How would they have enough fresh water if all the cisterns and fresh water lenses were flooded? How would they feed everyone if kitchens were destroyed and food stores spoiled by salt water? How many of them would be without a dry bed tonight? Or any bed at all?

174

She must try to get away in a little while to check on Mrs. Baxley. Her heart ached for her friend. How was she going to get on without her devoted husband? The thought made Abby turn her eyes towards the water. Where was Max and Christoff? She could only pray they had avoided the storm and would return home soon. She refused to let her imagination run with the alternative. She could only move forward by having faith in their safe return. Contemplating anything else would emotionally cripple her.

* * *

Henry debated if he should follow the coast or Whitehead Street out to the lighthouse. Based on his experience fleeing the floodwaters of yesterday, he was leaning towards Whitehead thinking any survivors would have sought higher ground, but Thorn didn't have that knowledge. His friend may be following the coast for expediency. Wanting to see the fort made up Henry's mind. He would go by way of the coast.

He started out at a jog but slowed down as he began to see what was left of the fort camp. Even after all he had witnessed so far, the scene in front of him still shocked him. Everything that once made up the camp, the flooding water had carried towards town. It didn't matter how heavy the item. The equipment, the timbers, the bricks, the buildings; they were all strewn along the path between the town and the fort.

He saw disheveled men moving around the debris, beginning to pile salvageable goods. And beyond them, alone at the base of the still standing flag pole, Captain Dutton was raising the flag. The stars and stripes fluttered in the gentle breeze, pure and clean, having been kept safe from the storm. The other soldiers paused in their tasks to salute the flag. Henry watched it for a moment, letting the sight fill him with hope for their recovery.

Concern for Miguel had him moving forward again.

From the direction of the stable, now some two hundred feet closer to town, one of the army soldiers stumbled in his direction. As he drew closer, Henry recognized Flynn. He looked a sight. His uniform was soiled and torn and his red hair was matted to his head from dried salt water.

Flynn clamped him on the back. "Good to see you, mate."

"You too." The words they spoke were the same as said on numerous other days, but today, the meaning behind them was poignant.

"Not all of us made it, I'm afraid."

Henry's eyes tightened.

"A bunch of men didn't show for roll. There is talk some went to the lighthouse for shelter before the flooding started. I haven't seen Bradley, Angus, Harper and Harley since the waters wiped us right out of our tent." He gestured back towards the other soldiers. "They be looking for bodies. I managed to get hold of a cannon carriage wheel. Just held on tight. Found myself washed up half way to the hospital. The animals went for a ride too. Amazing thing. They all made it. All five of them horses and one stubborn mule still in their stalls though they be quite skittish this morning. I was just trying to figure out how to get them some water. Cistern's salted. You here to help?"

"Not exactly. The lighthouse has fallen. I'm on my way to see if they need help. Have you seen a boy of about twelve pass this way?"

"Nah, but I've been with the horses the last little bit. Could have missed him. Go see the captain. I think he was sending men to look for survivors."

Henry gulped. Survivors. It put his mission into perspective. He was assuming he would find Miguel, injured perhaps but somehow alive. He hadn't let himself consider that may not be the case at all. He gave a nod to Flynn and sprinted over to Captain Dutton.

"Hello sir."

"Hello Henry. Your family secure?"

"Yes, sir, but I'm afraid the lighthouse is not." He gave a nod towards the missing structure. "I'm on my way to help. Maybe you could send a few men just in case..." Henry faltered unable to finish the sentence as his mind conjured digging his friend out from under piles of brick.

"I sent a group of men about a half hour ago. I plan to head that way in a moment."

Henry nodded. He took off running now.

A glance towards the water showed the wharf leading out to the fort was washed away. From shore nothing could be seen of the stone walls they had spent so much effort building. Indeed, it was impossible to know if any of the construction remained. A year's worth of hard labor undone in a day. Would the army spend the money to start building again? Henry shook his head. The thought was irrelevant at the moment. He had to get to the lighthouse.

As he rounded the outward bend of the coast, he saw a figure up ahead. He called out as loud as he could. "Hawthorne." The wind whipped the sound back in his face. He ran faster trying to catch up to him, not wanting Thorn to face what was ahead alone. He stumbled once but caught himself and kept going. He was breathing hard. The southern point was just ahead. Thorn was slowing down. He stopped just as Henry finally caught up to him, laying a hand on his shoulder, and bending over almost double as he tried to catch his breath. The rigidity of Thorn's shoulder communicated itself to Henry.

Neither of them expected what they found.

Together they stared, trying to make sense of what they saw or rather what they didn't see.

The rise of sand upon which the lighthouse was built was swept clean. It was gone. The lighthouse and the keeper's cottage. Gone. Only a few iron posts from the lantern remained, half covered in sand.

Thorn trudged into the churned up water and Henry followed. There was nothing visible under the murky surface.

Thorn turned his troubled gaze to Henry's. "Where is it?"

Henry could only shake his head.

Henry turned them back to shore. They could hear the soldiers searching the woods. He hoped they would find something of his friend.

Captain Dutton appeared. His men returned to report having found only a few bricks about a hundred yards inland. Realizing there was nothing to be done, the captain ordered his men to return to camp. He then approached Henry. "I'm sorry son. Did you know them well?"

Henry swallowed hard, thinking of all the times he and Miguel had played together growing up. "Yes." Henry laid his arm across Thorn's shoulders turning him away from the emptiness. "Let's get back to your mother."

Captain Dutton soon left them behind to walk at their own pace. Thorn and Henry were too numb to hurry. Neither of them felt like talking so they trudged onward in silence.

After rounding the bend where the shore turned back on itself, Henry became aware of the ocean debris strewn upon the beach. He was so focused on the lighthouse, he didn't notice it on the way out, but now he couldn't help but register this latest evidence of destruction. It was as if the ocean had thrown up all over the shore. From amongst the broken coral torn from the reefs, dead fish, strewn seaweed, and bits of shells, Henry stopped to pick up a sponge. Many more lay nearby. He looked out over the water. Would there be any left to harvest? How long would it take the sponge beds to recover? Had the storm destroyed his hope and dreams for the future too?

Chapter 17

Abundance gone
Desperately moving on

Keats House

Betsy awoke to a child's whimpering cry. She opened her eyes to find James standing beside the bed, rubbing his tear reddened eyes. She sat up on the side of the bed and lifted him into her arms. "Did you have a nightmare?"

James nodded and then snuggled his head into her neck. She rubbed his back soothingly. While part of her gloried in the rare joy of cradling her youngest as he was hardly a toddler anymore, the other part of her was remembering yesterday's ordeal and thinking of all the worrisome things she would face today. She stood up and walked with James to the window in time to see Henry hurrying past. She could easily guess he was on his way to see Emily. She watched him leave the yard and then turned her gaze to find Theodore contemplating the damages to the kitchen.

Judging by the light, the sun had risen an hour ago. It was the only thing normal about today. Everywhere she looked sunlight revealed the destructive wrath wrought upon the island. Feeling her tension, James whimpered. She turned from the window and took a deep calming breath.

In the bed beside hers, Ellen Mallory still slept. She set James down and whispered, "Shh. Don't wake Mrs. Mallory." He solemnly nodded with his innocent wide-eyed gaze. She couldn't resist kissing his sweet forehead. Quietly, she dressed grimacing as she slipped her dirty, ragged dress of yesterday over her equally dirty chemise. She wished she had a change of clothes or could borrow some, but alas, Esperanza was too petite to borrow one of her dresses. Until they could get back to their house, she would have to make do. Betsy ran her hands down the rumpled dress making it as presentable as she could, ignoring the torn hem. At least the rest of the family was able to borrow clean clothes.

She carried James out of the room to find the other children still asleep on the living room floor. Esperanza appeared from her room. They met by the table to exchange whispered greetings. It was a wasted precaution. One child stirred and in moments they were all awake and chattering. Betsy put James down to join them.

Esperanza said, "I'm going to see what I can find in the kitchen."

"I'll go with you." Betsy conveyed with a look for Brianna to watch James.

Both ladies halted outside the back door. Although having seen it from the windows, they were still shocked by what surrounded them. Overwhelming devastation everywhere. Betsy had weathered many storms and even flooding over the years, but this one was far and away the worst she had ever seen. Recovery seemed like an insurmountable prospect.

Dear Lord, give us strength.

The outhouse was upright, if tilted a bit. One of the kitchen walls had given way making it unsafe to enter. Theodore met them at the steps.

"I just checked on your neighbors. They are all fine and their houses are mostly intact."

Esperanza smiled. "Thank you."

Theodore inclined his head towards the outbuildings. "I have an idea of how to fix the kitchen, but it will require your help."

Betsy nodded. "You shall have it, after we eat."

"Hmm."

Taking that as agreement, Esperanza led them into the house. She moved to the sideboard and pulled a basket towards her. "We'll have to make do with what's left in here for now."

Betsy helped Esperanza put together a meager breakfast of cheese, biscuits, fruit and water. Coffee would have to wait until they could access the stove in the kitchen. Jonathon shuffled into the room on makeshift crutches. Esperanza left her task to scold him for being up. Ignoring his protests, she helped him to a chair and propped up his broken leg.

Betsy and Theodore hid their grins. It felt good to smile after the seriousness of the last two days, and the hardships they were facing.

Esperanza admonished Jonathon, "Stay there. I'll bring you food."

While the ladies returned to their task, Theodore took a seat next to his friend.

Jonathon huffed. "I hate being like this. Especially now."

Esperanza said, "I know you do, but remember, Dr. Weeden said you would make it worse if you didn't stay off of it."

Theodore said, "I have an idea of how you can help repair the kitchen." He caught Esperanza's frown and looked to her as he added, "While seated in a chair."

They were distracted by Stephen, Angela, and Ellen Mallory entering the room. Jonathon and Esperanza insisted on sharing their food, overruling the Mallory's reluctance to dwindle their resources.

Breakfast was eaten quickly. After their meal, Esperanza's eldest was left in charge of James and the Keats' youngest. The other children began cleaning up the yard, piling up the debris to be burned. They did so without being told as it was their task after every storm. Meanwhile, all of the adults worked together to reset the kitchen wall. Jonathon helped by holding a support line while seated in a chair. When they finished, Theodore announced he was headed into town for news. The Mallorys followed, headed to the boardinghouse. They left their daughter, Maggie, with the Keats. Esperanza and Betsy set to work cleaning up the kitchen and taking stock of the food supply.

Despite her busy hands, Betsy couldn't keep her mind from worrying about the state of her house. She was hoping for the best but feared the worst. Would there be anything left to save? Had they lost everything? Nervously she played with the ruffle at her throat.

A horrified gasp made Esperanza turn towards her friend. "What is it?"

"Agatha's cameo. It's gone."

"Calm down and think. Are you sure you were wearing it in the storm?"

"Yes. No. I don't know."

"I didn't see it when you arrived here. When was the last time you remembered seeing it?"

"We went to bed in our clothes. We slept downstairs." Her eyes brightened. "But I changed into this dress beforehand. I put the cameo in the jewelry box. I wasn't wearing it." She breathed a sigh of relief and then her face fell. "But our house... I don't know if it still stands. It could still be lost along with everything else."

* * *

Marine Hospital

As Emily moved about the room offering water to the patients, her emotions fluttered between elation and embarrassment over this morning's kiss. Henry had taken her completely by surprise. She knew the affectionate display was detrimental to her reputation. Some of the soldiers were still giving her sly looks behind her mother's back, but she rejoiced in the fact that Henry's emotions ran so deep he couldn't help his outward manifestation of relief.

But these thoughts were only momentary between the worry and concerns for the suffering around the island. She worried for all but especially for those closest to her like Henry and his family and Lydia. Her mother told her of Mr. Baxley and fears were high for Miguel Mabrity. She worried what Thorn and Henry would find when they reached the lighthouse. Fortunately, the gruesome images her mind conjured were interrupted by the arrival of refugees.

Abby rose to greet the tired father and children standing forlornly in the opening of the foyer.

Emily, anxious to follow her mother to the door, dropped the ladle in the almost empty bucket of water and left it on the floor between the soldiers' beds, ignoring their shouts of thirsty protest. The next patient picked it up, drank his share, and passed the bucket on to the next proving the task was her mother's idea of busywork. Emily noted with some surprise as she passed the longcase clock it was not quite eight in the morning. It felt much later.

Abby greeted the weary father. "Mr. McCreary, come in." He was followed by three of his four children; Sadie, Jeremy and Meredith.

George McCreary ran a hand over his head. "I'm sorry to burden you. I didn't know where else to turn. Our house is gone and the children need shelter and care." He had to pause to restrain his emotions before continuing. "They have lost their mother and my youngest."

Abby inhaled sharply. "I am so sorry for your loss."

Mr. McCreary bowed his head.

Abby said the first thing she could think of to move him past the emotional moment into practical matters. "I'm afraid we don't have any dry clothes."

George lifted his stoic face to hers. "I didn't expect you would. But could I ask a favor, Mrs. Eatonton?"

"Certainly."

"Could you keep an eye on my youngsters while I go see what can be done about my house? Others may need my help too. The sun will warm me quick enough."

"Of course I will keep them. They will be fine here. And you are right. The sun would warm all of you right up. You should all go sit on the front steps." Abby opened her arms wide herding them back the way they came.

The eldest, Meredith, sat down on the top step with her hands primly folded in her lap.

George looked down at Sadie. "You stay here with your sister."

Sadie tightly grasped her father's trousers. "I want momma."

Abby inhaled sharply in dismay. Tears sprang to Meredith's eyes. Jeremy's shoulders tightened as he stoically watched his father bend down to his little sister.

"Sadie girl, your mother... isn't here. I need you to be a big girl and stay with Mrs. Eatonton."

"I don't want you to go."

"I don't want to leave you, cherub, but others need my help."

Sadie began sobbing making it difficult to understand her. "You said we were safe in the house."

George pulled her into his embrace. "Oh Sadie. It was supposed to be safe. It just happened and now we have to find the strength to overcome it."

Big fat tears rolled down her cheeks. "I don't want to overcome it. I want momma, and I want to go home."

George rubbed her back soothingly as he fought his own tears. "I know child. I do too."

Meredith was silently sobbing. Emily sat down next to her and pulled her into an embrace while Abby laid an arm across Jeremy's stiff shoulders.

George pulled back to look into Sadie's eyes and placed his hands on her shoulders. "I need you to be strong for me. Your momma would want you to be strong now."

Meredith wiped her eyes and turned to reach out a hand to her sister. "Sadie, come sit with me now so father can go. He will come back later for us."

George nodded and smiled. "I will come back. Can you be a good girl and keep your sister company until then? Maybe Mrs. Eatonton can find something for you to help with."

Abby nodded to George. "I am sure they will be a big help to me."

George placed a kiss on each girls' forehead and stepped away. "I'll be back as soon as I can."

Jeremy called out to his father before he had descended more than a few steps. "I want to help."

George pondered for a moment if his son would be more of a hindrance than help, but the determined look on his face overruled any doubt. A single nod of approval had the boy scrambling down the steps. George looked to Abby again. "I noticed the foundation is cracked on the front corner."

"It was struck with debris from the rise and egress of the storm surge."

"I'll walk the building to make sure there are no major concerns."

"Thank you."

Jeremy trotted after his father as he circled the perimeter. When they came back to the front, George reported, "There is a twenty-five foot crack on the southwest corner and about sixteen feet high on the northeast side. Of course the roof is gone as I'm sure you're aware. The building's stable for now but we'll need to get that roof fixed pretty quick. I'll try and round up a crew."

Abby nodded. "Thank you, Mr. McCreary."

"No need. From the looks of things this town is going to need every bit of good shelter to be had."

Abby's gaze followed his progress towards town, once again taking in all the devastation. Every building for as far as she could see had some kind of damage.

It was going to be a long day.

Nate appeared at her side. Abby turned to hear what her son came to tell her. She hoped it wasn't another disagreement between patients.

"Momma, you wanted me to let you know when we were down to the last bucket of water."

"Yes, I did."

"Should I get some more from the cistern?"

"Put some in one of the empty buckets and bring it to me." As he rushed off she called after him, "Don't drink it." He waved a hand to let her know he heard her. She smiled. Nathanial's enthusiasm could always brighten even her darkest day.

She remained standing outside gazing at the purity of the storm-washed sky for a few more moments needing to absorb its beauty in order to face everything else. Inside there were bed pans to empty, bandages to change, medicine to dispense, and a myriad of other tasks. Mary and Millie could take care of most of them. Lack of fresh water was soon to become a crisis and right behind that would be food, not just for the occupants of the hospital, but for all of the islanders. Abby wanted to leave the hospital and find out how bad the situation was everywhere else, but she was tied here by the children; hers and Mr. McCreary's.

A sharp cry of pain brought her attention to the street to find two men helping an injured man. Even from this distance she could tell he was losing too much blood. Abby raced down the steps to intercept them. Upon reaching the trio she saw the splintered piece of wood protruding from the man's thigh. There was no time to get bandages. She leaned down and tore a good strip from the bottom of her chemise. When she straightened, she looked the injured man in the face. He was sweating and pale but still conscious. She wasn't sure how long that would last. "This is going to hurt something awful." She didn't give him a chance to respond. She grabbed the protruding end of the wood and pulled it out as straight as she could. She tossed the blood soaked fragment from her and quickly wrapped and tied the torn linen around the wound as tightly as she could manage. She glanced at his face, not surprised to find he had passed out. She led the men back to the hospital.

Emily and the McCreary girls quickly moved aside for them to enter. Abby brusquely told her daughter, "Come with me."

Emily rose and followed behind the men.

Inside, Nate handed Abby a half-full bucket. She took it from him and continued leading the group to the closest empty bed. As the patient was laid down, Emily watched her mother cautiously taste the water. Her expression was enough to tell Emily it was contaminated with salt water and unfit for drinking. She knew there was only one bucket of water left for more than two dozen people. What were they going to do when the last of the water was gone? Her mother handed her the bucket. She expected to be told to dump it, but of course, her mother was more practical.

"Emily, take this water and set it to heat on the stove. Bring me a basin, a wash cloth, and clean bandages."

She was quick to do her mother's bidding. She poured the water into a large pot and set it on the burner. She stoked the fire and then quickly gathered the requested items. She returned to her mother who was returning from the supply cabinet with items needed to suture the wound. The two men who carried in the injured man had left.

Abby took the items from Emily. "Go back and watch the water. Let it boil a minute and then remove it from the stove and bring it here to cool."

"Yes, ma'am."

As she walked back to the cast iron stove in the corner of the ward, Emily mused on how her mother's instructions were more commanding in nature here at the hospital, lacking the softness of tone she used at home. Emily sat in a chair next to the stove and wiped the moisture from her brow.

She wondered if they would return home soon. She hoped they wouldn't have to stay at the hospital all day. She didn't mind helping her mother, but the sight of so much blood was unsettling. She checked the fire again hoping to get the water boiling faster and sat back down.

Where was Henry now? Was he on his way back or was he still at the lighthouse? Did he and Thorn find Miguel or was he dead? How would Henry handle it if his friend was gone? Stoically, she was sure. In that respect, Henry was quite like his father. Thorn would be stoic too. Thorn was good at doing what was necessary without complaint. But she also knew her brother felt things deeply. He would hide his feelings. Then again, Henry would too. She hoped they would be able to help each other deal with whatever they found.

Pushing aside the morbid concerns, she turned her thoughts to Henry's kiss. A smile hovered on her lips as she recalled the masterful way he took her in his arms and pressed his lips to hers giving her no chance to resist. Not that she offered any resistance. Relieved that he was safe, she melted into his embrace and succumbed deeper still with the passion his kiss invoked. By the time he released her, she was no longer aware the rest of the world existed. The haunting feel of his lips pressed to hers made her touch her mouth in wonder.

The sound of bubbling water broke her reverie. She returned her attention to her task and counted off the seconds. At the minute mark she grabbed a towel and pulled the pot from the stove. Carefully, she carried it across the ward to set it on the floor next to the still unconscious man. Her mother took the towel from her and poured some of the steaming water into the basin to help it cool faster. Emily started to walk away, but her mother bid her to stay and help cleanse the wound.

Pleadingly, Emily asked, "Couldn't Mary or Millie help you?"

"They are both busy. You can do it."

Emily's stomach said otherwise. She took deep breaths trying to control the rising nausea as her mother began undoing the makeshift bandage and then cut away the pant leg revealing the man's naked skin and jagged wound with oozing blood. She turned her head away and swallowed hard as her mother began wiping the laceration clean.

Abby said, "Heaven only knows how but thank goodness it missed the artery." Blood began to flow again as she probed the wound to make sure there was nothing foreign left inside.

Emily noticed the man's head twitch, likely from the discomfort her mother was inflicting upon him.

When the wound was cleansed to her satisfaction, Abby said, "I want you to hold the skin together, so I can stitch it closed."

Emily unconsciously shook her head and backed away.

"Emily, pull yourself together. You can do this."

"No, Momma. I can't."

Firmly Abby said, "Yes, you can."

Even if she could get past the blood trickling from his wound, Emily couldn't imagine touching this man so intimately. "Shouldn't Mary or Millie help instead?"

"They are busy elsewhere. We haven't time for your maidenly modesty. You were bold enough to kiss a boy on the lips not over an hour ago. Now find some of that gumption to help me save this man's life."

Her eyes flared wide. She had never heard her mother speak to her thus.

"Come. Sit. Put your hands here."

Emily sat with one hip on the bed and her back to the man's head. She allowed her mother to place her hands on either side of the wound and demonstrate the required pressure to exert.

"Now you may turn your head."

Emily was thankful to do so as her mother took up a threaded needle. She focused on the clear blue sky outside the window. She did her best to ignore the significance of the slight push and pull she felt against her fingers while taking shallow breaths to combat the nausea caused by the ferrous effluvium assailing her. The moments stretched uncomfortably long.

"There, it is done."

Emily promptly removed her hands with great relief and fled to the open window. The fresh air soon restored her equilibrium, but it was the sight of Henry's return that cleared her mind of the last few moments. Eagerly, she flew to the door to greet him and then sobered as she recalled his errand. The dejected slump of his and Thorn's shoulders said much.

At the top of the stairs, Thorn silently slipped past her with his head down. Henry took up Emily's hands feeling the need to touch her. His sorrowful eyes looked deep into hers. "We only found some iron and a few bricks." His voice was hollow. "There was no one to help. No one to find." He swallowed back the tears that threatened.

Emily nodded trying hard to hold back her tears. She squeezed Henry's hands to convey her sympathy.

Henry looked down the street towards the fort. "Four men were lost at the fort camp." He turned his troubled gaze back to Emily. "I'm going to make my way towards town, see if there's others who need help. There could be people buried under their houses."

Emily nodded as he squeezed her hands, released them, and turned to once again descend the steps. She watched him until he disappeared from her sight before returning inside.

Abby was waiting for her in the foyer. "Emily, you really should be more reticent."

Emily's emotions were too raw to react calmly. Anger colored her retort. "Why should I be deceitful when we are both of the same mind? The storm has done naught but increase the feelings between us."

Calmly, Abby said, "What I mean is, you should not share your feelings so readily in public."

"You are referring to this morning's kiss."

"Yes."

"And did you not observe us now being more discreet?"

"Better, but there was still touching."

"For heaven's sake, mother, he just lost a friend. Besides, we are practically engaged."

Abby's voice hardened. "But you are not, in fact, engaged." She softened her tone. "All I want is for you to cease your affectionate displays. Please remember, you are setting an example, especially for his younger sisters and your brothers."

Suddenly too tired to sustain her anger, Emily murmured, "Yes ma'am."

"Very well. Now, we have much work to do, starting with the bedding. There are many who will be homeless tonight and in need of a place to sleep. We have beds here but they are wet from the dripping water. I want you to lead the other girls in stripping the soaked sheets from all the empty beds and hang them out to dry. I'll have the boys drag any wet mattresses outside and pray the sun can dry them."

"Yes ma'am. What about the patients with wet bedding?"

"Millie and I will take care of those. I hope we have enough clean sheets to go around."

The next hour flew by in a flurry of activity. It was soon realized just taking the mattresses out into the sun would not be enough to dry some of them. The ticking had to be opened and the cotton layers inside spread out to dry as well.

It was as they were involved in this task that a very distraught Petrona Wall approached with her one year old son on her hip and trailed by her wide-eyed six year old daughter. Emily went to meet her. They were a sad looking group with stained and torn clothing.

Mrs. Wall dropped her free hand from her lips to tightly grip Emily's arm. "Please tell me they are here."

The desperation in her voice was unmistakable. Emily's head tilted. "Who are you looking for?"

"My family." It came out as a wail.

Emily glanced at the children in confusion. "I haven't seen Mr. Wall."

"No! My sister and brothers. My niece and nephew. Where could they be? I cannot find them anywhere. Their houses fell down. I called out but no one answers. The lighthouse and cottage are gone. I don't know where else to look."

No wonder they looked so ragged and miserable. Mrs. Wall must have been searching all morning with her children in tow. "Have you tried the army barracks?" Word had reached them that the barracks had survived the storm with almost no damage and the quartermaster had offered them to help shelter the homeless families.

"No."

Emily was at a loss as to what to do to help. "Come inside."

Mrs. Wall shook her head. "I must keep searching."

"Please come inside for a drink of water. It's hot and your daughter needs to rest a moment."

"No. I must find Francis and Faustina. I fear Miguel is lost. Mother is coming home soon. They must be found."

Emily had never dealt with a hysterical person before. Her mother would know what to do. It took a little more cajoling to get the frantic woman to go inside.

"Come Mrs. Wall. My mother is inside. She will help you."

As soon as they entered the ward, Emily waved her mother over.

Abby rushed to Petrona Wall. "Where is Mr. Wall?"

"I haven't seen him since he left this morning. Please help me find my family."

Chapter 18

Folly and falter
Not what it once was

Henry retraced his steps of that morning back to Emily's house. The day was growning uncomfortably warm and humid. Two boys appeared chasing loose chickens. The fowl were a sight with their missing feathers and sand scoured skin. Henry helped them catch one before moving on. He kicked a palm branch from his path. In some places, the ground was scoured clean down to the hard limestone, other areas were riddled with everything caught by the wind and water, and in odd places the beach sand was piled inland. He was pondering the random oddity of it when he stopped short. Under a fallen tree lay a dead pig he hadn't noticed earlier. He felt like he should do something with the animal, at least to save the meat. He looked around for help, but no one was about. A closer look at the carcass showed it was beginning to bloat in the heat. The senseless loss struck him hard since much of the islanders' food was likely destroyed.

Approaching the Eatonton house from the rear, he could now see what he had not in his rush this morning. A section of the roof was missing on the backside along with a small portion of siding and a few broken windows but otherwise the house was good. He moved past it and turned left on Whitehead Street headed towards his house a few blocks away.

It was the lack of presence that first alerted him all was not well. Their house normally loomed over the neighbor's one story. He sprinted the remaining distance past two heavily damaged houses and then stopped short.

Henry fell to his knees.

He stared in horror at what met his eyes. His family's home lay in ruins with its front wall facing upward as if the windows were eyes turned towards the sun. The front yard was littered with the remains of the front porch and the seamstress' shop. Under the duress of the flooding and the heavy battering of debris, the front porch eventually collapsed after they left. At some point, so too did the back wall give way, leaving the house in the crooked heap he saw before him.

His heart ached thinking of all the lost treasures and childhood memories. It was more than he could face alone. Slowly, he rose and trudged around the remains. In a trance, he resumed walking towards the center of town. He stopped occasionally to help neighbors move heavier debris. He followed the sound of voices around the bend of Front Street to find a group of men sharing news gathered at the triangle piece of land known as Clinton Place. He wasn't surprised to discover his father was one of them.

Theodore noticed the empty look in Henry's eyes and cautiously asked, "Did you find the Eatonton's?"

"Yes. They spent the night at the Marine Hospital. It suffered damages but is still standing."

"I heard. Mr. McCreary is recruiting help to repair the roof since it can offer shelter to many in need."

Henry held his father's gaze. "Have you seen our house?"

"Yes." The single word contained a wealth of shared pain.

"How is the rest of town?"

Theodore didn't mind the change in subject. It was easier to talk about the general devastation than their loss. "Everything on this side of the pond and along the west and southern coasts were flooded. I think every structure still standing has some kind of damage from the winds. The new churches were both destroyed and the old Episcopal one carried out to sea. The salt works were also ruined. The custom house is badly damaged. Mr. Mallory said a nine foot board flew like an arrow impaling one of the rooms before the flooding brought it down."

"Guess it was pretty smart of Mr. Mallory to take the records then. They might have been lost."

"It would seem so."

Their conversation was interrupted by a raised voice. "Folks, can I have your attention, please."

They turned along with the rest of the crowd to hear what Mayor Maloney had to say. He stood in front of the gathering flanked by the marshal and the sheriff.

"I'm glad to see you all. It is with a heavy heart I tell you we've already had reports of many lost or missing from our community. Doc Weedon is keeping a list, so report what you know to him. He'll be at the Marine Hospital after this meeting. Our custom collector, Stephen Mallory, has volunteered to help with housing. If you have room to share or are in need of shelter, please go to him. I know we all have our own concerns, but we also need to work together as a community. If you have room to spare, please be generous."

Many began speaking at once. The mayor held up his hands demanding silence. "I know you are worried and our needs are many. Let us join together to help each other and mayhap we will recover faster. Right now our first concern must be our friends and neighbors. I am asking for all able-bodied men to divide into three teams with assigned areas. First priority will be to check every building for anyone trapped or buried. After that work can begin to repair the least damaged buildings so our people may find shelter tonight. Marshal Browne, Sheriff Coslin, and Mr. Mallory will lead these groups. They have each been assigned an area of town and will prioritize the needs of their area. We are in need of tools to do the work. If you can lay hands on some please bring them with you."

A voice shouted out. "What about food and water?" Others chimed in.

Mayor Maloney raised his hands to quiet the crowd. "I realize shelter, water, and food are primary concerns. So far, I am aware of only two good cisterns. We will be rationing water from them until we can have fresh water brought in or restored by rain."

One of the men at the front of the group asked, "What of food?"

The mayor shook his head. "It has not been decided how to deal with the lack of food. I will take any of your suggestions. Hopefully we will have some answers later today. Let us meet here again tomorrow morning to reassess our situation. Go with God."

The mayor walked off and the remaining men began clustering in groups around the three leaders.

Henry turned to his father. "Will you be joining them?"

"Yes, whichever group has the fewest."

"How is the Keats' cistern?"

"Good, but it is small and does not belong to me, so I have not volunteered that information to the mayor. Their food supply is minimal too. I left your mother and Mrs. Keats salvaging what they could."

"Did you hear the lighthouse is gone?"

"No." Theodore's eyes lifted from Henry's distraught face to the horizon over his shoulder.

"I don't think anyone survived."

"You've been out there?"

Henry mutely nodded.

Theodore dropped his gaze back to Henry's and reached out to give his shoulder a supporting squeeze knowing neither he nor Henry would tolerate anything more demonstrative in public.

Henry swallowed hard in the hope his voice wouldn't crack. "I also found Mrs. Baxley this morning holding her dead husband, and four men were lost at the fort."

"I'm sorry Henry. We're they friends?"

Henry nodded. His eyes dropped to the ground unable to hold his father's concerned gaze.

Theodore gave his account. "We are waiting to hear reports from the harbor. It is feared many ships and crewmen were lost. I heard Mr. William Curry tell Mr. Mallory his house was washed out to sea. The family fled to higher ground, but their old slave insisted on staying behind. It is assumed he was taken with the house."

Henry knew the Curry's lived on the north shore not far from his sponge warehouse. If the Curry house was washed away than it was likely his warehouse and all his gear was gone too. He stared wistfully in its direction wishing he could take the time to find out its fate. Maybe later he could take a look. Right now, he was needed here.

Theodore noted his son's expression. "What is it, Henry?"

"Nothing of importance. What are the Curry's doing for shelter?"

"Hmm." Theodore suspected Henry was thinking of his sponging equipment. He again laid a hand on Henry's shoulder. "Have faith, son. It may still be there and if not... the Lord provides. As for Mrs. Curry and the children, they were taken to the army barracks. I saw them this morning –

the barracks that is. They escaped the flooding and have minimal damage. The soldiers were already hard at work repairing them. I don't mind saying, it was a comfort to see Old Glory flying over them."

Henry sighed. "I felt the same when Captain Dutton raised the flag over the remains of the fort camp."

Mr. Mallory soon led his group off towards the far end of Front Street with the intent of repairing the roof of the Marine Hospital after checking the houses for those in need of rescue. Henry would prefer to have joined his group for obvious reasons, but followed his father to the smallest group led by Sheriff Coslin. They were charged with the northern end of Front Street where the dry goods store was deemed most important to repair. Marshal Browne had the area in the middle of town. It was decided, although it was not the least damaged, the Cocoanut Grove House would provide the most benefit to the community.

As the men broke off in groups, Henry noticed conversations were all about each person's ordeals and sharing what they had seen and heard since. Everyone said it was the worst hurricane they had ever experienced.

Soon, axes, saws, and hammers were heard everywhere doing rescues and repairs throughout the town. The youngest boys, including Jeremy McCreary, were tasked with bringing water to the men.

* * *

Keats House

After spending the morning helping Esperanza cleanup her kitchen, Betsy was ready to see what damage there was to her house and kitchen. Theodore, ever the newspaper man, had left hours ago to get the news around town and to offer help where he could. She felt she could do no less.

"Esperanza, would you mind watching James and Emmaline? Agatha can help with the children. I want to take Brianna and see what remains of our house and kitchen and what food we can salvage."

"I don't mind at all. Could you do me a favor in return?"

"Certainly."

"I wish you to check on my neighbor, Mrs. Watlington. Her time is near upon her and with the storm..."

"Say no more."

When Betsy told the children of her plans, James grew distressed and clung to her skirt. In his mind, his sisters promised their parents and the house would keep him safe. They left the house and his father was gone when he awoke. He couldn't lose his mother too.

Betsy dislodged the tearful James and turned him over to Agatha. It hurt to leave him so upset, but Esperanza assured her he would be fine.

Betsy and Brianna donned their damp bonnets against the tropical sun and ventured out anxious to see the storm ravaged island. The Keats hadn't lost much, but Betsy feared what she would find at her house, in her kitchen, and at their neighbors.

They made a brief stop at the Watlington house. Their knock was answered by the second daughter, Sarah. She showed them into the parlor where Mrs. Watlington was ensconced on her sofa knitting, still heavily burdened with the pending arrival of her fifth child.

The visit was kept brief and soon Betsy and Brianna were on their way again. Her mother suddenly stopped walking. Brianna did too and followed her gaze to the other side of the pond. Even from a distance they could tell something was tragically wrong. The house lay in a broken heap. They resumed walking around the pond now well within its boundary. Brianna found it hard to believe yesterday she traversed this same ground covered in several feet of water.

Splintered wood and limbs lay everywhere catching at their skirts. Their hemlines were soaked from the ground moisture and puddled water by the time they reached the edge of the back yard. The fence was gone. Betsy stopped again to stare. Most of the palm trees were still standing though they looked ragged and worn out, much as Betsy expected she would feel by the end of this day.

Brianna quietly slipped her hand into her mother's needing her strength to cope with the horror in front of her.

Silently they took in the wreckage that was once their beloved home. Eventually, Betsy moved closer and Brianna followed. It obviously wasn't safe to look in the house, so Betsy turned her attention to the outdoor kitchen. The building stood at a slant. It probably would have fully collapsed if not for the brick oven and built-in interior shelves. Betsy tentatively pushed against the walls testing for movement. They held fast. The door was caught open leaving space for them to enter. Cautiously Betsy moved inside.

In the dimly lit interior, she found her prized plants overturned, wind burned, and salt water washed. Beneath the verdant carnage lay shattered pottery, crockery, and glass littering the floor. She pushed this newest pain down deep to focus on the task at hand. She straightened her shoulders and purposefully stepped forward. Her shoes crunched on the broken shards irritating her wounded heart like nails dragged across a chalkboard. She picked up a tin of crackers, handing it to Brianna. "Open it and see if they are dry."

To get to the food they would first have to remove much of the mess. Betsy began righting unbroken pots and salvaging what she could of the plants.

"Momma, the crackers are good."

"That's something to be thankful for."

Betsy assessed each plant she pulled from the tangled greenery and handed it to Brianna. Outside the kitchen, the plants they hoped to save were lined up on one side of the door while the other side was a growing pile of the hopeless remains. Fortunately, her favorite plumeria being put inside first was protected by all the other plants piled around it. If it could overcome the saltwater, it might be saved. The hope was enough to bring a temporary smile to her face.

When the plants were cleared out, Betsy inspected what she could see of the shelves looking for any staples to be salvaged. She expected it to be bad, but again, the plants had taken the brunt of the winds, protecting what lie deeper within. A sack of flour was wet to the touch, but on the shelf above the jars of spices, including the coveted cinnamon, dried fruit, and a large canister of oatmeal were unharmed. She handed Brianna a basket she found on the floor. It was placed on the table and filled with the smaller jars.

Betsy stepped to the side of the shelves and crouched beneath the leaning wall trying to reach the hole in the floor where she stored canned goods and root vegetables.

"Momma, I can get to it easier than you can."

Betsy hesitated but Brianna moved forward confidently. She cleared an area to rest her knee and then reached into the water filled hole.

"Be careful. There may be broken glass."

Brianna turned to her with a smile. "The jars aren't broken."

"Still be careful. The water could have pulled broken pieces into the hole."

One by one Brianna began handing muddy jars to her mother followed by a sack of potatoes, another of carrots, turnips, and one of dried corn now soaked. Betsy doubted the corn could be saved under the best of circumstances. She considered trying to clean the root vegetables. If they could get them washed and dried again quick enough... A bowl of dirty water at her feet convinced her otherwise. Even if she had clean water and a way to dry and store them, there was no telling what had been in the flood water for of a certain it was mixed with dejection from the overturned outhouses. As much as she hated wasting food, she wasn't going to take the chance. She discarded the sacks of vegetables along with the flour. There were more than two dozen cans and jars consisting of green beans, stewed tomatoes, pickles, fruit, jelly, honey, peas, dried mushrooms and the like. Not a jar in the hole was damaged and the seals were intact.

Brianna also found the tin of coffee on the floor by the stove but unfortunately a heavy planter crushed the tin of tea allowing water to invade the tea leaves.

They left their finds piled on the table to collect later. Now they turned to face the house. Despair stole over Betsy as she realized all was likely lost. She was assailed by memories of their life in this home. She found love again in this house and gave birth to all her children here.

Brianna's movement broke her reverie. She put a restraining hand on Brianna's arm when she moved forward with the intention of climbing inside. "It's not safe."

Holding back her tears strained Brianna's voice. "What are we going to do?"

The shimmering despair in her daughter's eyes broke her own

closely held indifference. Betsy took a fortifying breath. "Focus on the good."

"What good?"

Betsy turned her daughter to face her. "We have much to be thankful for. Our family is safe. We may have lost our house, but we have shelter with the Keats for now and others will help us just as we will help them. We can also be thankful not all of the food was lost." She tilted Brianna's chin upward. "It could have been worse, so much worse. We could have been in the house when it fell and been hurt or..." She couldn't bring herself to even say the other possibility out loud.

"I know you are right, but it still hurts."

"Yes, it does, but we've only lost things. Replaceable things. Others have lost so much more than we have. They have lost what matters. The house hurts, but it doesn't leave an ache in your heart like losing a loved one. In time, we'll have another house." She paused to tighten control over her own emotions. "Our heart strings may be torn, but we haven't lost everything. We still have our hopes and dreams and our memories. They will help us get through this. We will get through this, I promise you. Together, as a family. Now, do you hear the sound of axes?" Brianna nodded. "Let's take that tin of crackers with us. I think we will find some hungry men ahead of us."

Betsy made a quick check of the cistern before moving on, confirming it was brackish. She doubted any of the cisterns near Front Street would still be fresh. The flood waters were too high.

From the pond to the coast, the damages increased. Here was obviously the worst of the storm's carnage. They walked towards the industrious sounds of saws and hammers to find men working to clear debris from the street and repair the Cocoanut Grove House. It was approaching the noon hour and feeding these men would be a priority. Betsy hoped there was food to be had but that hope fled as she rounded the back of the Cocoanut Grove House facing the beach. The large outdoor kitchen and outhouse were completely gone.

Ellen Mallory and Mayor Maloney were deep in conversation when Betsy and Brianna approached.

Their greetings were tempered by grief for all that was lost.

Betsy laid her hand on Brianna's shoulder. "We have come to help."

Mrs. Mallory nodded. "We could indeed use yer help. Angela is started on de inside cleaning. De mayor and I were just discussing food."

"It looks as though you have none."

"'Tis true."

Mayor Maloney said, "The hospital is in dire need as well. The army has offered a day's rations to meet the needs of the sick and those helping to restore our town, but we need a place to prepare and serve it."

Betsy asked, "Can the army prepare the food they are offering today?"

"I can ask. I don't see why not. They have the least damage."

"Could we set up tables outside the custom house like we do for celebrations?"

Mrs. Mallory smiled. "'Tis a good idea."

The mayor shook his head. "The yard in front of the custom house is a mess. We would have to take men away from repairs to clear it. And then there is the matter of gathering the tables and chairs."

Betsy frowned. "You are right. It is a bit much to do so soon. Do you know what the army has for rations? Perhaps it can be brought to the men where they are working. I'm sure they would be willing to eat as they can."

The mayor nodded. "I will go see what the lieutenant can suggest. That takes care of today. Tomorrow we will need to collect food donations to feed everyone and come up with a plan to bring in more food."

Betsy said, "That sounds reasonable, but who are we to collect donations from? I've just come from my kitchen. I've lost over half my food stores. It appears Mrs. Mallory has lost all of hers. Most of the homes were flooded and will be the same."

Mayor Maloney said, "I understand, but if each can give a little, I believe we will have enough. We will worry about it later. For now, I'll go see what the army has to offer." He tipped his hat. "Good day, ladies."

The trio watched him leave. Betsy turned to Mrs. Mallory. "What do you need us to do?"

"Don't ye have yer own house ta tend?"

"There is naught we can do there. We have salvaged all we can from the kitchen, but the house itself is a pile of wood too precarious to deal with just now."

"Oh my stars, I am so sorry ta hear dat. Where will ye sleep tonight? Ye are welcome here."

"Thank you, but we are settled in with the Keats for now. I am sure there are others who will need your hospitality. What can we do to prepare a place for them?"

"There is much cleaning to be done. The water came in from above and below."

"Then let's get to cleaning."

Mrs. Mallory led them into the Cocoanut Grove House. Angela straightened from brushing off an end table with a dirty rag to look at them with beseeching eyes. "I don't know how to truly clean this without water."

Mrs. Mallory said, "'Tis not possible. We will have ta have it from somewhere."

Betsy sighed deeply, mentally preparing for the monumental task ahead of them. "The cisterns may not be safe to drink, but the water will do for cleaning."

Brianna took in the scene with great dismay. They were standing in the midst of the parlor. Although the flood water had receded with the storm, the wood floors were still shiny with moisture. The white plaster walls clearly showed the high water line at chest height. The curtains too had a soiled demarcation. The island air was always humid, but in the enclosed room it was unpleasantly higher with a sinister feel. Brianna soon found the source as she laid her hand on the back of an upholstered chair withdrawing it quickly as she encountered heavy moisture. Her foot left a soggy indentation on the rug. A dirty residue clung to every surface from her chest down.

Mrs. Mallory, having earlier perused the house and had her emotional breakdown, stoically went about opening windows to let the fresh air flow through the house.

Tears threatened as Brianna was not only overwhelmed by the damage in the room, but as she considered how all of their belongings would be in a much worse state. They may not be able to recover anything of their old lives.

Betsy looked from Angela to Brianna. Their faces reflected the paralyzing dismay she too was feeling. "Ladies, we can't get lost in the daunting whole of it. Focus on the task at hand."

Mrs. Mallory came to the center of the room and looked about with her hands on her hips. "'Tis overwhelming. Most of dis will need ta be taken outside ta dry."

Betsy said, "At least this there is plenty of sunshine for drying."

Mrs. Mallory nodded. "Aye. I'll find some men ta do the heavy lifting. Shall we start upstairs? At least the water coming in upstairs was not contaminated. We can start by hanging the sheets out ta dry. We must do all we can ta have beds ready for tonight."

The Cocoanut Grove House was a beehive of activity as men and boys worked on roof repairs, removed furniture and rugs from downstairs, and wet mattresses from upstairs. Mrs. Mallory was kept busy sorting the various bric-a-brac into keep and trash piles. Sheets were soon fluttering from every inch of porch railing spanning the front and back of the two story hotel.

Chapter 19

Pushed eastward on
Atlantic's son heads home

Henry and Theodore's group had only a few houses to check on this end of town, as most of the buildings were businesses. The houses were deemed empty having confirmed the families safely fled to higher ground. Of the salvage warehouses, O'Hara's was little damaged, Browne and Green's were partly unroofed, but James Filer and Asa Tift's warehouses were a pile of ruins. Most of the wharfs were missing and the rest were in bad shape. A sailor was found in Green's warehouse trapped under fallen shelves of salvaged goods. He was uncovered and taken to the hospital with a broken collar bone and bruised ribs.

Having completed the search for survivors, they began repairing Asa Tift's dry goods store to protect the valuable undamaged food and materials needed to rebuild. Oilcloth from the store's inventory was used to cover over the missing shingles, the broken windows were boarded up, and the weakened wall was braced. The wind and water cavalierly wrecked the inside of the store. The floor and counters were littered with debris but oddly some of the shelves were untouched with cans and jars still neatly arranged.

Henry paused to wipe the sweat from his brow and take the offered dipper of water. He looked at the men around him and saw much the same in their weary gaze. Though it was not yet noon, they were already worn out – emotionally and physically.

Sheriff Coslin's group soon finished the dry goods store and began clearing the street, working their way towards the Cocoanut Grove House to help Marshal Browne's men.

The afternoon heat was oppressive adding insult to injury. There was little breeze and no shade to be found under the tattered trees. The bewildered birds hovered about the ground, their homes too destroyed by the wind. Not only had it ripped the sheltering leaves from the trees, it just as brutally demolished their nests. To make matters worse the mosquitoes were stirred up into a feeding frenzy. Henry shook his head in dismay at the once emerald island now stripped of its beauty.

Theodore approached his son noting the hollow look on his face and intentionally injected a light note in his voice. "Isn't it inspiring?"

Henry's brow rose and chin dropped as he turned to his father. "What do you mean? All I see is ruins."

"Yes, the plants and trees are torn, but they have been before and will eventually recover. The buildings will be rebuilt in time. The loss of lives is heartbreaking, but death is a fact of life. We will grieve, and we will continue on. We will also be thankful for those who live. Don't focus on the bad, Henry. Find the good." He gave a nod to the men walking ahead of them. "What I see is inspiring. A group of men from all stations of society working together to help each other and the community. It may not last, but for today, it is good."

Henry took his lesson to heart.

* * *

Marine Hospital

Emily watched her mother calm Petrona Wall enough to let go of Olivia and baby Fernando long enough to drink some water. She handed the baby over to Emily.

"Will you take the children? Wash their faces and find them something to eat."

"Yes, ma'am." Emily held her hand out to Olivia. She walked them over to where the McCreary and Garcia children were gathered with her brothers. Meredith was eager to help soothe the frightened youngsters.

A few moments later, her mother came to speak with her. "Mrs. Wall is still unsettled and who can blame her. She is coming to accept her brother, Miguel, is gone. What she needs now is to discover what has happened to her other siblings. I am needed here so as much as I hate to put this burden on you, I feel I must. Thorn would be of no comfort to her if the worst has happened. I will send him to find Mr. Wall. I want you to take her to the barracks to look for her family. I do not expect you to find them. It seems to me, if they were merely displaced from their homes, they would have sought shelter with their sister."

"You think they are buried under the houses."

"I am afraid so."

The Wall children were left in the care of Claudia and Meredith. Emily walked beside an eerily silent Mrs. Wall. Everywhere she looked there was destruction. Nothing was left untouched. It seemed bad enough while she was secure in the shelter of the hospital. Being outside surrounded by it was overwhelming. It was all she could do to keep panic from welling up inside. Carrying on a conversation was beyond her as well.

The most direct route to the barracks was nearly due east across the undeveloped backside of the settlement. They passed the court house and jail. Not far beyond them was Mrs. Wall's house. A glance confirmed the house was still standing. Emily looked in the opposite direction down Whitehead Street, but she was too far away to see if her house still stood. They kept to the backyards of the houses on the south side of Eaton Street making their way through the maze of fallen trees and rubbish. As the ground rose, it became drier where the flood waters didn't reach. On they went struggling over and around the strewn debris. Sweat trickled down Emily's back. Branches grabbed at her skirt and scratched her legs. She began to wonder if taking the long way around by way of Front Street and the northern coast would have been better. The walking certainly would have been easier. Not that Mrs. Wall was complaining. She was moving forward with a driven purpose undaunted by heat, mosquitoes, and climbing over and around downed trees. In due time they reached their destination.

Arriving at the military compound was like leaving behind chaos to step into a neat and orderly world, as if Mother Nature had not dared to touch it. The grounds were swept clean of the wind's wrath; a sign of the army's morning toils. Men in uniform were working in small groups to repair damages to the buildings while others were erecting tents on the parade ground.

Emily knew from a previous visit with her father that the two soldier barracks were on the far side of the parade grounds. She led Mrs. Wall past the officer quarters with more confidence than she felt being surrounded by so many men in uniform. They heard children playing as they approached their destination. A group of youngsters came running from behind the buildings. A mother stepped out onto the piazza admonishing them to play quietly.

Emily approached the woman. "We are searching for Barbara Mabrity's family. Have you seen any of them?"

"Not in this building. Try the next one. I haven't had a chance to see who's over there yet."

"Thank you, ma'am."

"God be with you."

As they turned to leave, Emily heard her name. She turned back to see a disheveled young woman running towards her. It took a moment to recognize her neat and tidy lady's maid with her frayed hair and mud splattered dress. "Lydia!" Emily was so overjoyed to see her alive, she embraced her.

Lydia awkwardly returned the unusual gesture and then stepped back. "I'm glad you are safe. And the rest of your family?"

Emily said, "They are all fine. We don't know yet about father and Christoff. And your family, are they safe?"

Lydia's face crumpled. "My mother..." She couldn't speak the words to tell of her mother's drowning.

Emily read the deep sorrow in her eyes. "I am so sorry, Lydia. You have my condolences."

Lydia nodded. "I'm afraid I won't be able to return to my duties, at least not right away. My family needs me. My father..."

Emily put her hand up. "Say no more." She reached out to squeeze Lydia's hand. "Take as much time as you need. Your position will be waiting for you."

Lydia's eyes filled with tears. "God bless you, Emily."

Mrs. Wall impatiently shuffled behind Emily. Learning what happened to Lydia and her family would have to wait for another time. "I must go help Mrs. Wall find her family. Take care, Lydia.

"You too, Emily, and you as well, Mrs. Wall. I pray you find your family safe."

They left Lydia and anxiously approached the open door of the next barrack. From within came the sounds of hushed voices, a woman sobbing, and a baby's insistent crying. Emily led Mrs. Wall up the steps and into the shadowed interior. It took a moment for her eyes to adjust from the bright sunlight.

Before them were the displaced, bedraggled mothers and children of the fallen houses. While their men were out helping others or scrounging to save remnants of their former lives, they were here trying to keep the fear and worry at bay.

Mrs. Wall suddenly rushed past her. Emily followed, hoping she had found Francis or Faustina. Instead, she grasped the hands of another woman Emily soon realized was Faustina's neighbor.

Emily stood back a little allowing the two women to converse.

In answer to her query, the neighbor reached out to hold Mrs. Wall's hand. "Your brother Francis and his family came to Faustina's house early in the morning. I know this because she sent Joseph over to ask if we wanted to go with them to weather the storm in the safety of the brick lighthouse. My husband declined."

Mrs. Wall's voice trembled. "You are sure both families went to the lighthouse?"

"Yes. I watched them leave through the window. I was concerned for them walking so far in the storm." She gasped as Petrona's hand slipped from hers.

As the true nature of her loss hit her, Petrona Wall fell to her knees. Her head bowed to the floor and her arms were wrapped around her torso. Her grief stricken cry turned into a keening wail.

Emily knelt beside her and placed her arm across her shoulders. It did little good. Comfort was not to be had in the overwhelming loss of seven family members. Emily tried to lift Mrs. Wall to her feet, but she was too senseless in her grief to cooperate. Petrona Wall was understandably inconsolable, but she couldn't leave her like this. Emily looked to the faces surrounding them for help.

A man burst through the crowd behind them. Emily gladly stepped aside for Mr. Wall to gather his wife in his arms and carry her from the room. Emily thanked the neighbor for providing answers and left the barracks. She saw Mr. Wall ushered into one of the officer's quarters to console his grieving wife in private. With nothing more to do to help, Emily walked back to the Marine Hospital.

By the end of the day, it was also believed seven workers fled the fort camp to shelter at the lighthouse. Thought to be the safest place on the island, it proved no match for the great hurricane. All together fourteen lives were lost in the disappearance of the circular tower.

* * *

Boardinghouse

Betsy was hanging one of the last sheets on the front porch when she saw a group of men approaching. Her heart leapt to see Theodore and Henry among them. She hurried down the stairs and out to the front yard anxious to greet them. The hours since they parted this morning felt like days. Brianna was right behind her.

Theodore saw the deep turmoil in his beloved's eyes. His Betsafina was a strong woman and he could recall only one other time when her emotions overwhelmed her in public. Now looked to be the second. Her jaw was clenched tight. As she came near, he opened his arms. She walked right into them to hold him tight. The day's trauma made them cling to each other seeking solace and support to face what lie ahead. Neither cared that they were on display. In the next heartbeat, Theodore opened his left arm to include Brianna in the embrace. He pulled her close and kissed her head thankful once again his family made it through the hurricane unharmed. He then turned his head and shared a look with Henry.

They broke apart as one, turned towards the Cocoanut Grove House, and put aside their loss to help as best needed for the benefit of the community.

It was well after noon when several soldiers arrived to hand out hardtack and dried meat. It was a very unappetizing meal but not a complaint was to be heard. It was at least something to feed the hunger plaguing them. It was followed with a half ration of water, not nearly enough, but certainly better than nothing.

* * *

Mr. Mallory returned with the rag tag remains of his group. His team had the arduous job of clearing the majority of the houses. The shock of the extensive damage began to wane as the day progressed. They skipped the houses whose occupants were accounted for and probed each fallen and toppled structure for the missing. Voices grew hoarse from calling out in search of buried survivors. One man was rescued, trapped in an upper room, giving hope to those missing loved ones, but despair followed for the bodies found under the rubble, adding to the emotional brutality of the day.

By the time Mr. Mallory's men were done searching houses, it was getting late and many were too emotionally distraught to offer further help. Their plans of replacing the hospital roof were put on hold. Only a handful returned with Mr. Mallory to the boarding house.

* * *

Progress on the boarding house was interrupted by the arrival of a portly man nearing his fortieth year. Having arrived in Key West at sixteen just after its founding and making a name for himself as a successful wrecker and maritime pilot, everyone knew Captain Geiger. He was walking home after a day spent surveying the harbor and surrounding waters. The men were quick to intercept him, even those on the roof descended to hear what he had to say.

"Gents, it has been a busy morning, I tell you, and the losses are high. The pilot boat *Lafayette* is gone, three of her crew lost in the harbor, along with my *Louisa*, sunk again and only a year since the last hurricane."

One of the men asked, "Will you leave her to her fate this time?" They all knew the ordeal Captain Geiger went through last year to raise his ship from the edge of the Gulf when she succumbed to a hurricane.

"By God, I will raise her again! At least she's not so deep this time."

Theodore asked, "And what of her crew?"

"All accounted for."

A man said, "Praise be!"

Another said, "Only two ships lost is not so bad."

Captain Geiger shook his head. "Tis just the beginning. The shoals of the north shore are littered with ships; some on beam ends, some dismasted, at least four are bottom up, and I'm sorry to say the Revenue Cutter *Morris* is bilged there too. 'Tis said one of those ships was anchored on the Atlantic side before the storm and is believed to have been driven across the east end of the island by the winds and surging tides."

"Across the island?"

Geiger nodded. "She weren't the only one pushed across land. There's a brig left high and dry inland between here and the salt works." He nodded his head to the east. "She's standing perfectly upright without her masts and nowhere near the water."

Silence reigned for a moment as the men were once again forced to recognize the awesome power of a hurricane and their own insignificance. It was only natural their thoughts then turned to their livelihood.

Theodore was first to ask the question. "What of the other wreckers?"

Captain Geiger shook his head. "The ships anchored near Key West were sunk or damaged. It's too soon to know for sure, but we can hope those further up the Keys are unharmed."

Henry said, "And those out at the Dry Tortugas."

Captain Geiger nodded. "Aye."

Stephen Mallory stepped forward. "Are there any ships capable of making sail for water and supplies?"

"There are one or two we might could repair straightaway."

"Then by all means, set about doing so. There's only a few good cisterns and no telling how much food has been lost. We'll need all the able fishermen out again too. Have you seen the mayor?"

"No."

"I imagine he'll be looking to hire a ship soon enough to bring back supplies."

A few moments later the men dispersed, returning to their tasks.

* * *

A few hours later, Theodore and Henry joined a group of men gathered around the marshal and the sheriff in time to hear them report, "Sir, we have run out of usable lumber."

Sheriff Coslin asked, "How much more do you need?"

The lead man consulted with the others and then said, "About twenty feet of board and maybe four dozen shingles."

The marshal and sheriff looked at each other in silence. They had already salvaged all they could from the streets. Anything else would have to come from another house or building. Sheriff Coslin turned to the group. "Does anyone have a suggestion?"

Theodore stepped forward. "You can take it from my house."

Henry opened his mouth to protest but closed it again knowing their house was too far gone to repair. No matter what he said, his father would believe the wood would be better put to use helping the community.

Stephen Mallory approached in time to hear the last. He gratefully shook Theodore's hand. "Thank you for your generosity on behalf of my mother and the community."

"Hmm."

Henry's lip quirked. It was his father's typical response to almost everything, but especially when receiving compliments or gratitude and anything emotional. As the workers gathered tools in preparation of harvesting the needed lumber, his father put a restraining hand on Henry's shoulder.

"Why don't you take this time to go see to your warehouse?"

"Aren't I needed here?"

"We can do without you for a little bit while we get more wood."

Henry started to question him again, but his father interrupted him with a commanding, "Go." He nodded and gratefully took off at a lope for the northern shore.

* * *

Marine Hospital

Emily handed a bed-ridden soldier the last hardtack from her basket. The rations brought by the army a little while ago were just enough to go around. They had also provided two more buckets of much needed drinking water which Nate and Jacob were offering to the patients.

She was still feeling unsettled from her ordeal with Petrona Wall. The mindless tasks she had been performing since her return suited her state of mind. She once lamented the monotony of her life before Henry. Today, monotony would be preferable to the struggles they were facing. She approached her mother who was checking the dressing on the man she stitched up earlier.

"What should I do now?"

Abby replaced the bandage and looked around the ward. All seemed under control. "Perhaps now would be as good a time as any to go to the house."

It was something they all had wanted to do since daylight. The needs of the patients and the townspeople who had trickled in throughout the morning with various injuries had kept her mother from leaving. She refused to allow Emily and Thorn to go without her. Her burdens were eased with the arrival of Dr. Weeden. Now that the time had finally come, Emily experienced a nauseating fear of what they might find despite Henry's assurances to her mother that the house was still standing.

Much to his chagrin, Nate was left behind with Jacob, while his mother, Thorn, and Emily went to see the house. Meredith was deemed capable of watching over them, her siblings, and the Wall children for the short time they expected to be gone.

They had to wend their way through the storm's remains. Walking amidst the devastation was even more traumatic then looking over it from the elevated entry of the hospital. There was so much damage it was overwhelming. Despite her earlier sojourn, seeing the destruction within the settlement was just as devastating for Emily. Concern for their friends and neighbors abounded and recovery seemed like a daunting impossibility. Emily choked back her tears as she struggled to keep up with her mother.

Even though Henry told them the house was still standing, it seemed hard to believe given all the wreckage they passed. To actually see it standing proud against the blue sky was a beautiful sight.

As they came to the backyard, the immediate relief of seeing the house intact gave way to concern for the hole in the roof. One of the lime trees had fallen and blocked the back entrance. Palm branches were piled up against the foundation, leaves were stuck to the siding, some of the porch lattice was broken, but it was the dirty water line marring the bottom two boards of siding above the brick foundation that cause further concern. It was five feet from the ground.

The mahogany tree they sat under for the tea party just two days ago was a sad sight, stripped as it was of all its leaves and wind burned. A curious silence surrounded them other than the sounds of men working. It took Emily a moment to realize it was the birds, or rather, the absence of them.

Before entering the house, Abby tasked Thorn with checking the cistern while she and Emily searched the remnants of the outdoor kitchen. The small outbuilding was also miraculously still standing. She was sure it was thanks to Max's insistence on using mortise and tenon joinery and securing the foundation to the limestone when constructing the house and outbuildings. Unfortunately, the doors on either side of the kitchen normally used for cooling airflow were torn free allowing the storm to wreak havoc with all that was stored within. Fortunately, the food and dishes stored against the back wall were less disturbed. Thorn reported the cistern was brackish.

They walked around the house to enter the front door. Abby sorrowfully noted the bare rose bushes. They were as good as lost, killed not by the wind, but by the salt water. Inside they found the expected damage from flooding. The water had risen almost a foot inside the house. The rugs would have to be taken out. Fortunately, the water didn't reach any of the upholstered furniture. Everything it touched could be cleaned except in Max's study. Water had seeped down from the room above. All the papers on his desk were ruined.

The trio headed upstairs now anxious to see what else they would find. The roof was missing above the boys' bedroom which was above the study. The bedding escaped the worst of it but the center rug was soaked through. The other rooms were fine other than two broken windows. The glass was scattered across the floor along with the water, fronds, and leaves that were blown in. It would be easy to clean up. Emily discovered she had left her scrapbook on the foot of her bed. She picked it up and held it to her chest, thankful the treasured keepsakes within were undamaged. Immediately, she felt contrite in her joy over something so trivial when others had lost everything and when there were families mourning lost loved ones.

Abby climbed the stairs to the attic. Emily and Thorn followed. Here the scene was much different. The torn roof not only allowed in the water but the winds as well, leaving the contents in mayhem. Old clothing, books, and various household discards were cluttered about the room. Abby walked amidst the mess, touching things here and there, trying to determine if anything important was missing, knowing the tornadic winds could pull things out of a roof opening. She stopped when she came to an overturned crate. Sunlight through the open roof illuminated the aged wood slats and the contents scattered in front of it. A few log books were laying open, the pages curling as they dried in the heat of the sun. Abby stooped down and righted the crate. Still inside was a book of poems. She picked it up, rose to stand in a shaft of sunlight, and ran her hand over the spine; a reminiscent smile of a day long past hovered on her lips.

"What is it mother?"

Pulled back to the present, Abby turned to her daughter. "A memory."

"Of father?"

"Yes."

"Tell us."

Abby looked at Emily's eager face and Thorn's mildly interested one and hesitated. It was a very personal memory and a trifle embarrassing.

"Please."

She didn't like it when her children answered her with 'nothing' so she refrained from doing so now even though she would prefer not to elaborate. "You know we met because he was salvaging your grandfather's ship on Loggerhead Reef." She continued as they nodded, "I was left by myself in his cabin while they worked. I was growing restless and noticed this crate of books. They were all logs and journals which would be a breach of privacy to read, but then I found tucked in between them this book of poetry. I picked it up deeming it safe enough to read." She stopped not wanting to share the rest of the story.

Emily frowned at her mother's continued silence. "And?"

Abby gazed into her daughter's eyes so like her own. "I found this inscription." She turned the book so Emily could read it for herself. Thorn leaned over her shoulder.

> *Something to remind you of me on your long voyage.*
> *Your loving wife,*
> *Emma*

Emily's startled eyes lifted to her mother's. "Father was married before you?"

Abby chuckled. "No, but I had the same thought and it..." She wasn't sure what to say as she recalled all the emotions she had felt in that moment.

"It made you feel disappointed."

Thorn walked off having no interest in affairs of the heart, especially his parents.

Abby smiled at Emily. "Yes. Disappointed, hurt, and angry. Mostly angry."

"Why?"

Abby belatedly realized she had backed herself into further uncomfortable explanations. "Because I thought he was flirting with me, and he had no right to be if he was married. It was deceitful."

"But he wasn't married. So who was Emma?"

"She was the wife of Captain Nate Hamilton, the previous owner of the *Mystic*."

"You named Nathanial after him."

"Yes."

"How long did it take you to learn the truth?"

"Not long." She gave her daughter a rueful smile. "You come by your boldness naturally." Abby bent down and began collecting the scattered log books. "I wonder why your father insists on keeping these."

With Emily's help they were soon returned to the crate.

Abby called Thorn to her and tasked him with taking the crate downstairs. She and Emily laid the wet clothes and blankets out to dry in the sunny area created by the hole in the roof. They left the rest of the attic cleanup for another time. Downstairs they laid out the opened logs and journals on the dining room table to dry. Abby hoped that without the direct sunlight the pages wouldn't curl, or at least not as much. The first few books were in Captain Hamilton's handwriting. When she came to one with Max's neat script, her heart caught. She ran her hand down the page where his hand once passed. Tears bleared her vision. Where was her beloved now? She looked out the window towards the sea.

Emily noticed her mother's stillness. "You're worried about Poppa and Christoff."

Again, tears pricked Abby's eyes. It was a comfort to have a daughter who understood and shared her concerns. She held out a hand to each of her children. "We should pray for their safe return."

Chapter 20

*Twisting mass is growing old
But not done yet*

Even after hearing Captain Geiger's report, the actual sight of all those stranded ships was still shocking for Henry to behold. The north shoals looked like a nautical graveyard. Here and there were men actively working to recover a ship, but for the most part, the vessels held an air of abandonment.

Behind him lay all that was left of his warehouse.

While circling the pond, Henry held onto a slim hope that his warehouse would still be standing with all his gear and week's harvest of sponges still intact. He knew it was a slim chance for the area was deeply flooded during the storm, the warehouse was flimsily built, and the nearby Curry house had been swept out to sea. He should have prepared himself for finding the same fate.

The shack was gone but by some miracle his boat was still held fast by the anchor pin he drove into the limestone the day before the storm and when he flipped the battered boat over, he found the sewn net full of uncleaned sponges he had tied inside. His shack was gone, his supply of nets were gone, the cleaned harvest was gone, and all his tools, but at least his little enterprise wasn't a complete loss. He wouldn't be able to get right back to work, but then there was so many other needs to take care of, he wouldn't have been able to anyway.

He walked to the water's edge and stared out at the storm abandoned ships. Their owners had certainly lost more than he had. The gentle lapping of the surf called his eyes downward. Here as with the other beaches it was littered with broken coral, sea fans, dead crabs, sea urchins, and torn grasses but the water in this area was of an unusual clarity. He could easily see all that lay beneath its surface.

He would have to head back soon, but for a moment he watched the fish darting here and there. A wandering crab caught his attention. He followed its path to deeper water where he saw a curious object. He waded in and was delighted to discover it was a sponge hook snagged in the limestone. He pulled it free and lifting it from the water realized with even more excitement that it was his hook. Why such a simple thing should make him giddy with excitement he couldn't say, but it did. He took it back to shore and jubilantly secured it to his boat. He decided to lay his sponges out to dry upon the shore and having finished the task hurried back to rejoin the others in finishing the hotel repairs.

* * *

Boardinghouse

Betsy straightened from her task as Ellen Mallory approached.

"I must thank ye dear from the bottom of me heart for providing from yer own house."

Betsy frowned. "I'm sorry, Mrs. Mallory, I don't know what you mean. What have I provided besides labor?"

Ellen's hand flew to her mouth in consternation. "Oh my, I thought ye knew."

Betsy silently shook her head and waited for Mrs. Mallory to explain.

"We needed more wood ta secure the roof. Yer husband offered ta procure it from yer house."

The words escaped on a rush of breath. "He did." Betsy lips compressed with unreasonable fury which she promptly tried to hide from Mrs. Mallory. "I'm glad we could contribute. Would you excuse me please?" She didn't wait for her to answer but turned away with angry strides taking her from the hotel yard to her house. She was partially aware her feelings were beyond what the situation called for, but she couldn't seem to contain her ire.

She rounded the corner from Front Street to Whitehead and found the men approaching her, returning with their harvest of wood. She blocked Theodore's path and waited for the other men to continue on. One of them took the wood Theodore was carrying to leave him empty handed.

Theodore's brow wrinkled with concern. "What is it Betsy?"

She nearly hissed at him. "You didn't consult me."

His head snapped back as if she had slapped him. He could tell she was angry but hadn't expected it to be directed at him. "I was sure you would agree. Our house cannot be saved and there was no other lumber to use."

"I'm sure I would have agreed but taking from our house... I should like to be asked rather than finding out as I did." Her voice broke as the emotional dam released, and the anger left her in a rush.

"Oh, Betsy, I'm sorry sweetheart." He pulled her into his arms. "Today has been too much to bear."

Her tears were kept in check but she leaned into Theodore for a moment gathering strength from him. "Yes, it has." She stepped back and straightened her shoulders. "What are we going to do?"

"Rebuild, of course."

"Can we afford to do so?"

He sighed deeply. "That is not today's concern. Now, we finish helping Mrs. Mallory. We spend another night with the Keats. Tomorrow we will sort through our belongings and decide from there."

"That sounds like a reasonable plan."

He brushed back a wayward tendril of her dark hair. "Feel better now?"

She smiled weakly. "Yes."

He held his arm for her and she placed her hand in the crook of his elbow. He placed his other hand over hers. "I'm sorry I didn't let you know about the wood."

"Sometimes I think we may know each other too well. We take things for granted. But at the heart of the matter, I think my anger was more because I needed your support than because of what you had done."

"I think I needed these moments alone with you too." He leaned down and kissed her temple as they trailed behind the other men.

After a few moments of silence, Betsy whispered, "There is so much damage."

Theodore's eyes had been roving over the devastation as well. "I know."

"I told Brianna to focus on the task at hand to keep from being overwhelmed, but it's not easy."

"I know."

They paused for Betsy to shake her skirt loose having caught on a jagged board in the road.

"And I'm afraid our problems are just beginning." She looked up at Theodore's earnest profile.

"Hmm."

Agreement. She smiled to herself. She could count the very real blessing that Theodore was still with her to play her private game of guess the meaning of his hmm. Mrs. Baxley's loss reinforced her thankfulness as did the stories she was hearing of families separated as they fled from the flooding and of those who drowned.

Henry came loping up beside them. The spirit in his step made Betsy smile.

Theodore eyed his son. "Am I to suppose you have some good news to share?"

Henry matched their pace and his expression grew reserved. "I lost the shed and all the cleaned sponges, but on the bright side, I still have a boat, a net full of sponges to be cleaned, and I found my hook in the water. It's very odd. The water on the north shore is crystal clear. I suppose it has something to do with the storm surge or perhaps the southern egress of it."

Theodore said, "Aye, likely the egress."

They arrived back at the boarding house and were soon separated, pulled in different directions as they were needed.

* * *

Boardinghouse

As the day wore on the effects of hunger, thirst, heat, and despair made tempers short. Though water was being passed around, it was rationed to half a dipper when normally they would get two. A fight broke out over an accusation of one man drinking more than his allotted share of water. Theodore was quick to step forward with Mr. Mallory and a few others to pull the men apart.

Henry was watching from a distance when he spied a cocoanut on the ground. He smiled at the memory of hot summer days enjoying the milk of a freshly cut cocoanut. He approached his father and Mr. Mallory. "I have an idea."

Both men turned to him. Mr. Mallory said, "What is it Henry?"

"The storm knocked down most of the cocoanuts. If they were collected and opened, they could supplement the water."

Mr. Mallory grasped his shoulder. "Henry that is an excellent suggestion and so obvious I can't believe no one has thought of it already. I suppose this storm has us all muddled and flustered. Could you round up the younger boys to collect them and some of the older boys and knives to open them?"

"Yes, sir." Henry took off to do his bidding.

Mr. Mallory turned to Theodore. "We always knew he was a smart boy." He clapped Theodore on the back. "I'm going to find the mayor and share Henry's idea."

* * *

It was late in the afternoon when the hotel roof was finally done. The men were dismissed to see about their own needs although a few men stayed to help set up a makeshift kitchen in the yard under Mrs. Mallory's guidance. The ladies were still hard at work cleaning the inside.

Theodore approached Henry. "I'm going down to the bight. Want to come with?"

Henry nodded. He knew his father was hoping to get interviews for his next paper. He was sure to find men at the grog shops swapping storm stories. Rather than follow Front Street through town as they did earlier in the day they walked along the churned up brown water of the western coast but soon stopped to stare at the emptiness. The wharves leading from the harbor to the salvage warehouses were washed away, including the one Henry had debarked on not so many weeks ago. Their presence was such a firm and vital part of the town that their absence now was as distressing as the wreckage of their home.

Henry turned his troubled gaze to his father. "Every time I think our losses can't be worse..." His frown deepened. "It's going to be a long time before we recover. If we ever do."

Theodore's chin lifted a notch. "Have faith son. If we all pull together, we will get through even this."

They both noticed it at the same time. Eerie white oddities bobbing in the water. They studied them trying to determine what it could be. Dead fish or birds seemed most likely. Finally, the tide brought them in close enough to reveal bales of cotton.

The corner of Theodore's lip rose. "I suppose there is some irony to be found in wrecked cargo floating into the harbor of a wrecking town without its ship and while the wreckers are wrecked."

Henry gave a half-hearted chuckle, but he saw it more as a somber reflection of their tragic circumstances.

Of an accord, they turned away from the water and made their way between the warehouses and rubble to the drinking establishments. It was not hard to find the ones that were open for business. The ruckus spilling out of their doors was indication enough.

All the men had stories to tell. Every conversation centered on a person's storm experience; where they were, what they suffered, what they had lost.

Amidst the hubbub of sailors and tailored men, they found Lieutenant Pease of the Revenue Cutter *Morris* drinking quietly at the bar. Theodore remembered Captain Geiger saying the *Morris* was one of those wrecked on the north shoals. He motioned to Henry that they should join him.

Henry studied the man in his mid-twenties. They had met on two previous occasions, and Henry noticed he looked rather haggard in spirit. After greetings, Henry said, "I saw your ship."

Lieutenant Pease spoke with a decided New Jersey accent. "Did you now?"

Henry nodded. "Were you originally anchored in the harbor?"

"Aye. At sea is no place to be when caught in a tempest such as we just experienced, but the harbor proved none the better."

"Did the crew survive?"

"Yes, thankfully all hands accounted for, but many's a time we thought we wouldn't."

Theodore pulled out his notebook and pencil. "Will you tell us what you went through?"

The lieutenant took a bracing sip of ale and nodded his head. "I suppose talking will help work it out in my mind, so I can write my report later." He noticed the items in Theodore's hands. "Is this going in your paper?"

"Yes, if you don't mind."

"I don't suppose so." He took another swig of ale and a deep breath. "Of course, we knew from the barometer it was going to be a gale, but we had no reckoning of how bad until midday. We thought we were done for several times before the end.

"By 1400 the current was passing our anchorage at over twelve knots – in the harbor. The *Morris* turned broadside in the tremendous wind, laboring heavily against her anchors. The mainmast was cut, not without some difficulty, to ease the strain. The pumps were constantly manned, and the crew was furiously bailing. We feared at any moment she would go down. By this time the harbor was inundated with debris from the town. A whole house roof floated past. Large timbers were turned end over end by the force of the wind, the likes of which I've never seen." Fortified by more ale, he continued. "We lost the starboard anchor. The port anchor began to drag. The compass flew around useless. There was so much water in the air we couldn't see. We had no idea which way we were headed. For fear of striking the reef and sinking, Captain Walden gave the order to cut the foremast. No sooner was that done and a wave rolled us over on her side. Everything loose on the deck was swept away along with the small house on the quarterdeck and one of the ship's boats. The leeward guns were heaved overboard with all haste and the ship righted. We drifted unknowing of which direction while still dragging the port anchor. It wasn't till after dark that she struck bottom again at the same time the anchor finally gave. She was battered against the shoals till the storm's end. At dawn, we found ourselves surrounded by wrecks of every description."

Henry said, "What a frightening ordeal you went through."

"Indeed! One I never wish to repeat."

Theodore asked a few more questions the lieutenant patiently answered before leaving him to his drink. And after a few more conversations with those around town getting their perspective of the storm, father and son walked away from the bight in silence, each lost in thought.

They returned to the hotel to wait for his mother and sister to finish for the night. Mr. Mallory arrived after a late afternoon consultation with the mayor and city council. He was more than willing to update Theodore.

"We have lost several dozen citizens and the count seems to keep growing. About twenty five have been reported as drowned, some were swept out to sea, or struck by debris, and there are those we found buried under their homes." He shook his head. "It's tragic the number of lives lost. Beyond that, food is scarce. Only a few boats are fit to sail. The mayor has contracted those to bring in as much fish and water as they can haul tomorrow. He is hoping a larger vessel can be sent to the Bahamas or the mainland, but as of now, there isn't one available." Stephen sighed deeply. "Without the arrival of such a boat I don't know what we'll do."

Theodore asked, "How many are homeless tonight?"

"More than half the town." He shook his head sadly. "It is unimaginable something like this could happen. Fortunately, the barracks are sound. The army has agreed to house the women and children in them. My mother has assigned all her rooms to families hit the hardest knowing it will take them the longest to rebuild."

"I spoke with Mr. Curry this morning. He is relieved his family has shelter, having lost his entire house to the sea."

"Where are you staying?"

"With Jonathon Keats. At least for now."

Betsy and Brianna came out of the house then. Mr. Mallory wished them a good evening.

Theodore looked them over, noting their fatigue.

Brianna proudly said, "We cleaned up all the bedrooms and half of the downstairs common rooms."

Betsy linked her arm with Theodore. "I am beyond tired but having helped restore order in this one corner of the island has given me hope and a measure of peace."

Theodore looked up to the roof. "I feel the same. Are you ready to go home?" He frowned at the poor choice of word. "I mean to the Keats."

Betsy smiled. "You were right to say 'home'. Our family is home, not the house."

"Hmm, you are a very wise woman, Mrs. Whitmore."

From years of habit, Betsy placed her hand in the crook of Theodore's elbow. They gave Henry an expectant look knowing where his heart lay.

Henry said, "I'll return later."

Betsy said, "Don't stay out too late."

"I won't. I promise."

Betsy turned to Theodore. "Do you mind if we go by our house first? I want to retrieve the food we scrounged from the kitchen."

For a moment, Henry watched his parents and Brianna as they walked away. He turned to make his way to the Marine Hospital eager to see Emily again. The sun was drifting towards the horizon bringing to a close the most horrific, heartbreaking day he had ever experienced.

To keep his emotions from drowning in all the destruction, he tried to keep his mind focused on the good. Besides the safety of loved ones, for which he was truly thankful, the street was now partially cleared and easier to navigate than this morning. The sound of hammers and saws still echoed in the air as men tried to repair their homes as best they could for the night. The island may be stripped of its foliage, but the softening of the evening sky was as beautiful as ever. And one day the flora would be abundant again.

It wasn't until he reached the front steps of the hospital that he became aware of his appearance. His borrowed clothes were stained with sweat and dirt from today's hard labor. His hair wasn't any better, but there was no help for it. He could only hope he didn't smell as bad as he looked. He started up the stairs and wasn't surprised when the door opened to reveal Emily. Her warm smile temporarily melted away his concerns. She brought a hand forward from behind her skirt and held it out to him revealing a small apple.

"I saved it for you. It's the last one. Mother shared our whole bushel, but I kept this one for you. I was worried you hadn't eaten all day." She noticed his scruffy chin. Of course he hadn't shaved in two days. She hadn't seen him like that since his arrival. His clothes were filthy, and he looked exhausted. Her heart went out to him.

Henry said, "I am grateful. The army provided rations earlier."

"They did for us too."

"What about supper?"

Emily sadly shook her head.

"Nothing?"

"No. And the water is running low again despite the addition of cocoanuts." She smiled. "I heard that was your idea."

He humbly ducked his head. "How has your day been?"

"Difficult. Do you mind if we sit out here for a bit?"

Henry nodded and waited for Emily to shift her skirts and to be seated on the top step before sitting down beside her. "You look pretty. I see you changed since this morning."

"Momma, Thorn and I went to the house this afternoon. We were able to freshen up a bit."

"How did you find the house?"

"Better than most others, I'm sure. We had a little flooding inside but nothing that can't be cleaned up. We hung the rugs out to dry, changed clothes, and came back here. So many have been coming here today with injuries that Momma didn't want to be gone too long."

He started to polish the apple against his shirt out of habit but caught himself in time. Ruefully looking down at the dirty article, he shook his head in wry amusement before biting into the crisp apple. The sweet flesh and tart skin burst in his mouth. He added it and Emily's loving concern to his list of things for which to be thankful.

Emily pressed her hands tightly together in her lap. Henry placed his free hand on them. She opened hers to clasp his. Her troubled gaze sought his. Did he somehow know she needed his touch? His reassurance? Her world, their world, had gone awry, and she momentarily felt too weak in spirit to deal with it. Her home was physically intact, but so much of life on this island was disrupted. She feared her security and comfort were forever gone. Two days ago, her biggest concern was how soon they could marry. Today, it was hardly a consideration. Too many were in need of food, water, and a dry place to lay their head. But the heaviest burden to bear was the unknown whereabouts of her father and brother. She couldn't help but overhear the talk of all the destroyed ships in the harbor. She felt empathy for the loss of life and vessels, but even more, it heightened hers and her mother's concerns for their family. Her mother hid it well, but Emily knew she was in need of her father's support during this trying time, and the worry of not knowing their fate was a constant companion. Henry squeezed her hand. The sympathy she saw in his eyes convinced her he was aware of her thoughts.

Abby glanced about the open ward in search of Emily. Suspecting she was taking a breath of fresh air, Abby walked to the front door. She smiled as she saw her daughter's red-gold hair gleaming in the fading sunlight. She sighed as she noticed Henry's honey-gold head leaned close to Emily's. Abby opened the door, not surprised when the two guiltily separated. That Henry dropped her daughter's hand did not go unnoticed. She wasn't against their attachment. It seemed inevitable from the day Betsy and Theodore married when the youngsters were caught playing-acting as bride and groom. She only wished they would use more discretion in displaying their feelings.

Henry awkwardly rose to his feet and bowed to Mrs. Eatonton. He was ashamed to have been caught touching Emily again.

Abby accepted his embarrassment as punishment enough this time. She pretended not to have noticed his indiscretion. "Hello Henry. How does your family fare?"

"Well enough compared to others."

"Your house, does it still stand?"

"No ma'am. I'm afraid not. In fact, father donated some of our roof to help repair Mrs. Mallory's hotel."

"That was most benevolent of him and not surprising. He has always been generous to this community. Where is your family staying?"

"We will continue with the Keats tonight."

Abby nodded. "It will take some time to rebuild. The Keats' house is much too small for so many. Tell your father, your family is welcome to reside with us until your house is rebuilt. Emily can share her room with the girls and you with my boys, leaving the old nursery for your parents and James." Knowing well Theodore Whitmore's pride, she added, "He can repay the kindness by helping to repair the roof."

Henry beamed with uncontrollable excitement. "Yes ma'am. I will tell him." He felt her desire for him to do so immediately, so he smiled and bid them good night, casting Emily a lingering look of farewell.

"Come, Emily. There is still much to be done before we can go home."

Abby bid Thorn and Nate to distribute the last bucket of drinking water while Emily assisted her in passing out rations of the food salvaged earlier from their family kitchen. Emily and Thorn understood their mother's charity in giving away their food to those in need, but still, they felt some resentment. What would they do when the food ran out as it was sure to by tomorrow?

* * *

Henry made his way back to the Keats' house in time to share a meager evening meal of porridge. Afterwards, Henry pulled his father aside to relay Mrs. Eatonton's offer.

Theodore watched Betsy settling the youngest children in for the night. Even without the Mallorys, room was still sparse in the house forcing the children to sleep on the floor in the main room so that he and Betsy could have one of the beds and Henry the sofa. It would not do for long term sleeping arrangements. He turned his attention back to Henry not unaware of his anxiety in awaiting an answer.

"I believe we have no choice but to accept her hospitality. First thing tomorrow we will work on repairing her roof using what is left from ours."

Henry had trouble hiding his smile. For the unforeseeable future he would be residing under the same roof as his beloved.

Chapter 21

All spun out
Once ocean's child now the reaper's claim
Pulled down into the cold Atlantic Drift

Tuesday, October 13th

Theodore awoke before first light to find Betsy watching him. "What is it love?" She looked down to the space between them. Theodore followed her gaze to find James nestled against her.

"He had another nightmare about the storm."

"I'm sure he'll get over it in time."

"I hope so."

Theodore continued the whispered conversation. "What else is on your mind?"

Betsy exhaled sharply on a suppressed smile. He knew her so well. "I was thinking about the house."

"Worrying is more like it."

"Yes, worrying."

"About?"

"How will we rebuild? If we should rebuild? There have been so many storms in the last few years. Should we consider moving to your estate in New York?" Betsy held her breath as she made the last suggestion, afraid Theodore would eagerly accept it.

Theodore stared into her eyes with earnest intent. "Do you want to leave?"

Quietly she answered. "No."

"Then we will stay."

"And how will we rebuild?"

"As you are always telling me, 'Have faith. The Lord will provide.'"

She bowed her head, contrite for having lost her faith, even momentarily.

* * *

Henry and Theodore set off after breakfast to begin harvesting material from their house to repair the Eatonton's. Upon reaching the fallen down house, they were greeted by a sight even more disheartening. Someone had taken the rest of the roof shingles, most of the roof deck boards and almost all the siding from the backside and the eastern wall revealing the wall studs and the interior wallboards. Taken without asking. The two men stared at the house filled with dismay.

Theodore shook his head. "Who could have done this?"

Henry asked, "What do we use now for the Eatonton's?"

Neither expected the other to answer.

As they stood there debating what to do the culprit returned. It was their neighbor from a few houses further down Whitehead Street who had also helped with repairing the Cocoanut Grove roof. Theodore was at a loss of what to say. While it was an act of theft, knowing the integrity of Mr. Goodman, he had to believe it was an unfortunate misunderstanding.

After gentlemanly greetings, Mr. Goodman said, "I want to thank you, Mr. Whitmore. Without the wood from your house we wouldn't have been able to repair ours. I have heard the other folks whose houses are too far gone to rebuild are selling their lumber at exorbitant prices. Certainly more than I have in my pocket. It was very generous of you to donate yours."

Theodore's silence made Mr. Goodman fidget nervously. "I hope I didn't misconstrue your meaning yesterday. You said you were donating the lumber to the community."

It was on the tip of Theodore's tongue to admit he had indeed misunderstood, but he couldn't bring himself to actually say the words knowing how deeply it would wound Mr. Goodman's sense of honor. "I'm glad it helped you. Have you need of more?"

Henry gasped. *What was his father doing?*

Theodore gave Henry a warning look to keep silent. If anyone was in need of charity, it was Mr. Goodman and to gainsay him now would hurt the humble man's pride.

"If you don't mind, I just need a little more of this wall to finish securing my home."

Theodore and Henry helped him harvest the boards and carry them to his house. The men shook hands and Theodore said, "I would appreciate it if you didn't tell others where the wood came from."

Mr. Goodman nodded. "If that's the way you want it."

Theodore knew Mr. Goodman was attributing a more altruistic reason for requesting his silence, but as it served the purpose, Theodore left him to believe it. He could only hope others hadn't had the same misunderstanding of yesterday's generosity or there would be nothing left of his house.

Once out of Mr. Goodman's hearing, Henry asked, "Why did you do that?"

"Because God wanted me to."

"God told you to give our house away? He actually spoke to you?"

"Not in words but in feelings. Have you never had the feeling you should do something for another person against your inclination?"

The corner of Henry's mouth lifted. He was here now because of a feeling his family needed him. "Yes."

"Besides, Mr. Goodman's honesty is above reproach. He wouldn't steal a crumb of bread, much less lumber. It was a misunderstanding. To bring it to his attention would have embarrassed him, and he would not have accepted the lumber. He has thirteen children to feed. His wife is caring for her ailing mother. Their house is small, and they likely have nowhere else to go, whereas we do, so his need is greater than ours."

Henry was amazed but not surprised by his father's generosity and concern for a neighbor. He still wasn't sure he could agree with giving away the lumber knowing it was in short supply, but he respected his father's decision. They would have to have faith there would be enough to repair the Eatonton's roof and pray the Lord would provide a means to rebuild their home.

Henry put aside the troubling thoughts to focus on the task at hand. He climbed the tilted wall of the single story addition on the side of the house that was the morning room to perch on the bare roof decking over it. From there, he tried to pull down a hanging piece of siding, but it was still held by a nail. He looked at his father in bewilderment. How had they not anticipated something so fundamental to their task?

Theodore came to the same realization. "We forgot to bring tools."

Henry dropped down to the ground. "How could we have not thought of something so obvious?"

"I don't know. I feel like I've not been able to think clearly since this ordeal started."

"I'll run get them."

Henry returned ten minutes later with two hammers and a crowbar.

They began piling up useable boards and the few remaining shingles to take over to the Eatonton's. As they uncovered personal items that could be saved, they put them aside to pick up later. Thorn soon arrived with a wheelbarrow to help.

At nine o'clock, Theodore left the boys to continue working while he went to the mayor's meeting. He returned an hour later to find Betsy and Brianna inside the house combing through the rubble of the first story for personal effects. Horrified by how easily they could get hurt on the unstable mass, his command was harsher than intended. "Betsy, get out of there this instant." He rushed forward to give her a helping hand.

Betsy stepped into an opening between the vertical frame boards. She handed Theodore a stack of papers from his desk which he passed to Henry. She allowed Theodore to grasp her by the waist and lift her to the safety of the ground without protest. The shifting boards had caused her some concern, but the desire to save anything of value had her ignoring the danger until she saw the fear in Theodore's eyes. When she was safely on the ground, Theodore turned to help Brianna.

"You two are not to go in there again. If the walls had given way you would have been crushed."

Betsy laid a hand on his arm to calm him. "We will not do so again. What did the mayor have to say?"

Henry and Brianna paused to listen.

It took Theodore a few more breaths to calm down enough to

answer her query. His heart still raced from finding her in imminent danger. "He is asking for volunteers to sail to Nassau or Charleston for food and water and monetary donations to purchase the goods. Captain Walden gave the salvaged stores from the *Morris* to Reverend Richardson to distribute to the needy."

"Well, that's something, I suppose. Though it isn't likely to last long."

"A few fisherman went out today. Hopefully, they will have some luck. Two turtles were found and given to the army cooks to make soup for those in need today. Now that some of the immediate crises are under control other pressing issues need to be addressed like burying the dead."

Betsy's indrawn breath was testimony to the raw emotions of the islanders for the friends, neighbors, and loved ones lost in the storm. Of the forty or so casualties, most were lost to the sea, but at least a dozen bodies waited to be buried.

"I volunteered Henry and me to inspect the cemetery in preparation for the funerals."

Betsy asked, "Is there anything I should help with?"

"Mayor Maloney did mention needing help serving the women and children taking shelter at the army barracks."

Betsy nodded. "Then Brianna and I shall go to their aid." Betsy cast a worried glance over the remains of their house.

Theodore reached out to lay his hand against her cheek. "The cemetery shouldn't take too long nor the roof repair at the Eatonton's. As soon as those tasks are complete, we'll spend the afternoon taking care of our needs."

"I couldn't tell you what it is, but I feel like something in that pile is important for us to find."

His thumb caressed her cheekbone. "I know. It was our home and there are lots of sentimental things in there. Whatever we find will help diminish the loss, but even if we find nothing, we carry the memories."

Betsy gravely nodded in agreement. "You had best be going if you are to keep your promise."

"Until later, love." Theodore reluctantly parted from Betsy.

Betsy, touched by his voiced endearment, watched him walk away.

Henry walked with his father down Whitehead Street towards the southern beach. The unending piles of debris lining the road were disheartening. There was so much of it, it could daunt even the most stalwart. How would they ever get their community back to its former glory? They passed the edge of town and soon came to a place permeated by the fetid odor of rotting death. Marked by the swarm of flies, they soon discovered the source to be a bloated animal, likely someone's dog. They hurriedly moved past.

Coming to the end of the road, the trees gave way to the open shore. It was an area Henry was well familiar with and yet it seemed foreign. He stood in this very spot weeks ago with Emily declaring his feelings for her. Then, it felt like a private green sanctuary for them. Now it was brown, tattered, and exposed.

Henry resolutely refused to look toward Whitehead Point. He didn't need the reminder of the missing lighthouse or his lost friend. At least he could take comfort in the fact he didn't die alone. His father paused to stare at the empty space in silence before following Henry to the left.

They wove their way down the beach strewn with broken coral, dead fish, and torn sponges. He wondered, not for the first time, how much damage the reef and sponge beds sustained. He wished with all his heart he could be out on a normal day of sponging instead of faced with the daunting demands of recovery. Henry glanced at his father's profile. His clenched jaw belied his calm. His father, too, was struggling with his emotions and their overwhelming needs.

They noticed odd protrusions as they approached the cemetery. Their task was to ascertain how much clean up would be needed before burials could be made so the mayor could pull together a group of volunteers and tools to undertake it. Henry was sure his father assumed the same as he did, that they would need to clean up surface debris and maybe fix or replace a few headstones. They were ill prepared for what they found.

The two men stood at the edge of what was once a peaceful resting place in shocked disbelief.

The fierce storm had struck another devastating blow to their community. Disinterred caskets were strewn in disarray about the ground. It appeared as if few graves were left intact. They slowly moved closer. It soon became evident bodies and caskets were missing. They both looked to the water expecting to see... something. The lapping surf mocked them.

Henry couldn't speak. Couldn't think. Couldn't act. His mind could not accept what his eyes were seeing. Just weeks ago, he stood in this very spot watching Emily place flowers on her sister's grave while he held flowers for his loved ones. Now those graves were no more. The questions ran torturously through his mind. What was it going to take to make it right again? How would they figure out which box belonged where? How many were lost forever?

His father suddenly spoke in the silence. His voice hoarse with emotion. "Come Henry."

"We're just going to leave it like this?"

"For now. We need help, and burial records, to fix this."

The return walk was somber. Henry realized, in retrospect, they should have expected what they found.

Upon reaching the settlement, Theodore told Henry to start work on the Eatonton's roof while he went to report to the mayor. Henry watched him walk away and for the first time ever, he saw his father's shoulders bow with the weight of his concerns. At least he could help with one of them.

Henry didn't have a lot of experience in building, but he hoped he had enough skill to repair the roof. He welcomed the challenge to get his mind off the horrible scene still lingering in his head.

Thorn opened the front door to greet him as he stepped on the porch. Henry wished it was Emily instead. He sorely needed to see her smiling face. The house was quiet as he entered. "Where is everyone?"

Thorn gave him a shrewd look. "You mean, where is Emily? She is at the hospital with my mother and brothers. It's just me, I'm afraid."

Henry wondered if he had been as sarcastic when he was twelve. Probably. "I'm here to start on the roof. We could use Nate's help. Will you run get him while I figure out how we're going to do this?"

"Are you sure I shouldn't bring back Emily too?"

Henry pierced him with his gaze in response. Thorn took off pleased with getting a reaction from him. Henry shook his head suddenly feeling older than his years. He hesitated before going further into the foyer. He had never been in the house alone. Always before the Eatonton's were present filling the space with noise and laughter. The silence, like so much else in the last few days, was disturbing. He passed by the dining room on his way to the stairs and noticed the ledgers spread out to dry. Even this house had damages to overcome. Recalling what Emily said about the flooding, he looked down at the floor and noticed the footprints on the soiled boards. Just like his family, they have been too busy helping others to take care of their own needs.

He climbed the stairs to the second floor and had to pass Emily's room to get to the attic. He paused in the doorway. Fortunately, her room was on the opposite side of the damaged roof. He glanced over the tidy room, his eyes coming to rest upon her scrapbook laying open in the center of the neatly made bed. Henry was thankful she was not suffering the losses his family was enduring. His sketchbook and pencils were somewhere beneath the caved in walls of his home; the drawn images likely ruined by flood waters long before the book was buried. He shook off his melancholy. The sketch book could be replaced. His family was safe. There were so many others not so fortunate. He turned from her room and climbed the stairs to the attic.

He studied the hole in the roof from underneath. It wasn't too large. About six feet by ten at the bottom edge of the roof. He guessed the wind had caught a loose deck board and ripped them away one by one until it changed direction. At least, the rafters were still in place. They should have enough lumber to replace the decking boards. He just wasn't sure there would be enough shingles. Henry climbed the ladder to the Captain's Walk. He lifted the hatch and climbed out to the decking. The cupola seemed secure and undamaged. He leaned over the railing to view the hole on the backside of the roof. He could climb over the railing to do the work saving the need for a ladder. They should probably use a rope to bring the lumber up. He could tie it to a corner post of the cupola. He glanced over the rest of the roof and found several places with missing shingles on the front and the back side. They definitely did not have enough to replace them all. He frowned. They would have if Mr. Goodman hadn't taken them, but what was done, was done. He would have to find another way or cover it with oilcloth or an old sailcloth. Maybe he could figure out how to fashion shingles.

Henry raised his eyes to the surrounding area. He felt like he hadn't had a moment to just breathe since before the storm began. He took a deep breath now, closing his eyes to shut out the sad truth of his world. He cleared his mind and breathed in the fresh salt air and for a moment he felt peace. But then the wind shifted and the beginning notes of decay ruined it. He opened his eyes.

Looking at the damages from above was even more heartbreaking. Instead of seeing only the part of the horror he was dealing with in the moment, he now had a sense of the whole. Nothing was untouched. No escape for the eye or the mind. The Eatonton house was the least damaged of all he could see. Several neighboring houses were collapsed like his. Some were shifted from their foundation. The rest all had major roof damage. The only area cleared of debris and having any semblance of normal was the center of the street. The immediate shock was fading. Now, he looked past the material damage to see the more devastating emotional damage. Men, women, and children wandered everywhere picking at the remnants of houses. A few were hard at work trying to clean up, but most seemed too overwhelmed yet to focus on any one task.

Thorn and Nate's return broke into his thoughts. He waved to the two boys and then hurried down to meet them.

An hour later, deck boards covered the hole, Henry was trying to decide how to prioritize the shingles when his father returned. He climbed up to the roof to inspect Henry's work.

"Good job, son."

"Thank you. Are we needed at the cemetery?"

"Not yet. The town council is gathering to determine a new location for the cemetery."

"A new location?"

"The old city cemetery and the military burials near the Marine Hospital were also near completely washed away. It was deemed prudent to move the cemetery to higher ground."

"For new burials or will all the graves be moved?"

"I believe the consensus is to eventually move them all. For now, we focus on finishing this task."

Henry said, "I was just trying to decide how best to use the shingles we have."

"I know where there is a large piece of oilcloth we can use to cover this patch, so let's use the shingles to replace the other randomly missing areas. Nate, could you bring me a hammer?"

Henry brushed an arm across his forehead as he surveyed their work from the shade of the cupola. It was mid-afternoon, and the roof repairs were nearly complete. A burnt sienna cloth now draped from the peak of the roof over the repaired hole contrasting with the weather-gray shingles. Only one more shingle was needed to finish replacing all the other missing ones. He was waiting for his father who was in the yard fashioning one out of a remnant of wood. In the distance, he saw his mother and Brianna returning from the barracks. He descended from his post and waited to greet them knowing they would have news to share.

Theodore took a final shaving from the piece of wood. He held up the shingle for inspection thinking he had done pretty well for his first attempt. It was not perfectly tapered but he was confident it would at least shed water. Henry appeared at his side, and he handed it to him.

"Mother's coming."

Theodore looked down the street. His heart joyfully lifted as it always did in Betsy's presence. None of the hardships they were currently facing mattered as long as he had his family. He hastily brushed the shavings from his shirt and eagerly went to meet his wife and eldest daughter.

Betsy smiled at her husband's approach. "Are you done with the roof repairs?"

"Nearly. Henry has one more shingle to install. How are the families at the barracks?"

"As good as can be expected for not having enough food or clean clothes. There are so many the younger children sleep in the spaces between the beds and the older ones in hammocks strung over them and down the center of the room. Most are still wearing the same clothes from the storm."

"So are you."

"Yes, but at least you and the children were able to change. If you're done here, can we look for our belongings now?" Theodore's hesitation answered her question. She tried to contain her annoyance. "What is it now?"

"The cemetery is going to be moved. We're waiting on the city council to decide where. As soon as they do, we will be needed again."

"Why must it be moved?"

Theodore hated having to tell her, but she would hear of it soon enough if he didn't. "The storm destroyed the old one."

"Destroyed?"

"The graves were disinterred."

Betsy paled. Her words faded to a whisper. "Madalyn...Aunt Agatha...?"

He nodded. They shared a silent moment of grief. Theodore cleared his throat. "We don't know for sure how many, but it looked to be a good number of the graves were disturbed."

Betsy shook her head as she fought a fresh wave of tears. "Our baby, ripped from the ground. What more must we endure?"

Theodore squeezed her hand in support. "We will find our way through this."

"I know we will, and we're not alone, but that also makes it worse. My heart aches for all our friends and neighbors suffering with us. It's so hard to help each other when we all have lost so much, and we all need help."

Knowing Betsy needed something positive to focus on, he said, "While we wait for word from the council, we can start on our house." His words had the desired effect. The smile returned to her face. "Wait here."

Betsy watched Theodore return to the Eatonton house and call out to Henry on the roof to join them when he was finished. She gave a concerned look for her son's precarious position two stories above the ground and moved to her husband's side. "I would rather wait for him to finish."

Five minutes later, Henry was safely back on the ground. The family silently walked to their crumbled house passing neighbors occupied with repairs or salvaging lumber and possessions. Reaching the toppled house, they stood for a moment assessing the situation. The upper story was now minus the roof and siding, exposing the interior wallboards. The front facade was tilted upwards. They would have to secure it before they could remove any more wall supports.

Theodore said, "The only way I see it is to work from the top down, but I'm worried about further collapse as we move about. This is very dangerous. Our lives are more important than what's in that house."

Betsy turned to him in distress. "Are you saying we should leave it?"

"No, dear. I'm saying we need to proceed cautiously. Henry, can you find some rope?"

"Yes." He ran around to the backyard to rummage under the fallen kitchen in the hopes a coil of rope he left there days before the storm had not washed away. A few minutes later with only a few minor scrapes from broken lumber, he returned to his father triumphant.

Theodore was relieved to see Henry carried a nice sized coil of rope. "Do you think you can tie that around the upstairs window?"

Henry smiled. His campfire lasso lessons from a former cowpuncher turned Texas Ranger were about to come in handy. The technique of throwing the rope would help him now. He undid a good length of rope from the coil and let it drape to the ground. He tied a hand sized coral rock at the end for weight. The upper window was completely broken. He decided to aim for it being closer to the ground rather than over the top of the wall and have to worry about the rafters being in the way. He made a few practice movements before tossing the coiled rope. It hit the upper window frame and thankfully slipped into the opening.

Henry scaled over the collapsed porch to walk up the tilted wall of the morning room to the roof deck. His left hand followed the side of the main house for balance. Beneath his feet the wood creaked and shifted causing him to slow down and take more care in his foot placement. He found a spot with reasonable footing and then took the hammer he had secured in a belt loop and used it to beat against and pry loose the interior wallboards of the second floor. When the opening was deemed large enough, he turned sideways to slip between the exposed framing.

Betsy couldn't hold back her concern. "Henry, be careful."

Henry gingerly stepped onto the tilted floor praying it would hold his weight. He breathed a sigh of relief to find it solid beneath his feet. He was in what used to be Aunt Agatha's room. He crossed the high side of the room to get past the furniture and into the hall where he expected to find the coiled rope. He took care not to slip on the shards of broken glass and slick leaves littering the floor.

Betsy held her breath as Henry disappeared from her sight. She released it with a rush of relief when the coiled rope came flying over the house.

Theodore caught the rope and secured it to the nearby trunk of a frondless palm. He gingerly followed Henry's path up the house with a hammer and prise bar.

Together they moved between the rooms taking in the chaos that was once their home. In each bedroom, the furniture was piled up on the downside wall. Their possessions were haphazardly strewn about; clothing, linens, shoes, hats, toys. In his room, Henry picked up a toy sailboat with a broken mast. Maybe he could fix it later for James. Both men were feeling the pain of loss while trying not to be overwhelmed by the daunting task before them.

Henry looked to his father. "Where do we start?"

Theodore ran a hand across his sweaty brow. "I'm not sure. It seems getting the furniture out of the way would make sense, but I don't know how to go about getting it out of the house."

"What if we made a larger opening in the back wall at the end of the hallway? We could use rope to lower the pieces directly to the ground."

Theodore nodded. "Hmm." He moved to the back wall.

Henry followed. "We would have to take out at least two, if not three studs, to create a large enough opening." His gaze panned the upper reaches of the room assessing the structure's integrity. "Hopefully, she won't fall in on us."

Theodore shook his head. "It's too risky. All the weight is pressing down on this wall. The morning room is in the way on the open side. I think we need to make an opening on the other side." He led Henry into the master bedroom on the back left corner of the house. It was tilted closest to the ground. He climbed over the bed to get to the window in the side wall. He tried to open the window but the twisted framing made it impossible. He used the prise bar to break the glass and then clear the shards from the window pane. Carefully he stuck his head out to see what was below. Nothing was in the way beneath them. "I think this will work."

They moved the furniture to one side and began prying the wallboards loose to expose the studs. They knocked out the rest of the window and began prying loose the window frame.

Betsy's muscles tensed and her breath froze at the sound of the breaking glass. She cried out as she ran around to the other side of the house, her voice high with fear. "Theodore! Henry! Are you alright?" She halted abruptly as the window frame fell to the ground a few yards in front of her. She was at once relieved and irritated to see both men grinning at her from inside the house. They began working to pry loose the interior lap boards as Brianna joined her.

Henry called down to his sister. "Do you think you could find more rope?"

"I'll do my best." Brianna took off running to the neighbor's house.

Betsy held her hand to her brow to shield her eyes from the afternoon sun as she watched them toss wood out of the window opening. There was nothing she could do to help. She was aware that some of the neighbors around them were having to dig through the piles of rubble their houses had become to find what little they could. They were fortunate the second story had not fully collapsed. Hopefully much would be saved from the bedrooms.

Once the lap boards were gone exposing the studs, they started at the top of the wall, beating against the siding until it fell to the ground, one board after the other. Reaching the bottom, they sat down on the bed to rest, both breathing hard and sweating. It was surreal to be sitting at an angle looking through open framing at the board strewn ground below.

Betsy cautiously stepped onto the pile of torn lumber and held out a canteen.

Henry leaped forward to lean out between the studs. Betsy tossed it up to him. He caught it easily and gave her a big grin. "You always know what we need."

She grinned back. "You're welcome."

While they took a break, Betsy began moving the torn boards, sorting them into keep and discard piles, a short distance from the house.

Theodore called out, "Be careful of the nails."

After their rest they knocked out the short studs above and below the window and the full studs on either side. As the last board fell to the ground, Theodore studied the opening. "I think that will do for now. Let's see what we can toss out while we wait for more rope."

The men disappeared from Betsy's view. She was dragging the last board away just as the mattress and bedding from her room was pushed through the opening to land with a soft thud. Betsy dragged the cumbersome piece in the opposite direction of the wood, propping it against the green and gray stripped trunk of a buccaneer palm. It was the start of the pile of personal items to be saved. Where they would be taken for safekeeping until they could rebuild, she had no idea. That was a problem for later. The other mattresses subsequently followed.

Brianna returned in the company of their neighbor, Mr. Ned Naylor, with a coil of rope slung over each shoulder and carrying block and tackle.

"How do, Mrs. Whitmore."

"Mr. Naylor, how are you keeping? Are Mrs. Naylor and the children faring well?"

"They are being taken care of at the army barracks. I was going through the house for some requested items when your young Brianna here came to ask for some rope. I thought you might could use some assistance."

Theodore overheard the last from his perch in the opening. "Hello there, Ned. I would be much obliged to have your help."

"Brianna told me what you were planning so I brought these." He held up the block and tackle.

"That was extremely thoughtful. I hadn't thought that far ahead."

During the next forty-five minutes they got the rope and tackle set up and all of the furniture out of the master bedroom and started on the girls' room. Henry and Theodore worked inside the house and Mr. Naylor helped on the ground to untie the pieces and move them out of the way.

Betsy ran her hand over her dresser, feeling grateful to be able to reclaim something from the storm. She was thankful not to have lost everything and even more thankful when the armoire was lowered with all the clothes inside. She would finally be able to get out of the awful dress she had been wearing for three days.

From behind Betsy came the mayor's voice. "Mr. Whitmore, can I speak with you?"

Theodore called out from his perch against the open framing. "Have you found a new site?"

"We have."

Theodore nodded. He turned and spoke to Henry and then made his way down to the ground to greet the mayor. "Are you ready to start work?"

"Yes. Major Dutton offered his men to assist with whatever was needed. I have them clearing the new site now in preparation."

"What do you need from me?"

"Nothing. The army will help with the dead." He nodded towards the house remains. "You have your family's needs to tend to."

"We have a place to stay and our basic needs met. Henry and I will help. Taking care of our loved ones is more important than the material belongings in the house."

"Very well then. We will bury the newly deceased first, but the carpenter won't have the coffins ready until tomorrow. For what is left of today, I am asking those who can spare the time from their needs to begin gathering and help identifying those to be moved from the old cemetery."

Theodore gave a nod. "Henry and I will be there shortly. We just need a little time to take care of some things here."

The mayor shook his hand and moved on in search of other volunteers.

Theodore turned to the group. "We are going to have to bring this to a close for the day." He shared a look of resigned frustration with Betsy. "We'll work on the furniture again tomorrow. For now, Henry and I made a pile of smaller items we need now. Betsy, do you remember where you last had the laundry basket?"

"I believe it was in the girl's room."

"Good. I was afraid you were going to say it was downstairs."

Henry disappeared inside. He returned to the opening a moment later with the basket in hand. Theodore said, "I'll be right up."

Mr. Naylor said, "Keep the rope as long as you need it. I'm going to take what I've found to my wife. I'll see you at the cemetery."

Theodore nodded. "Thank you for your help. If you need ours, you have only to ask."

Mr. Naylor shook his head. "Don't see the need. Our house isn't as difficult as yours."

"Still, if you do...."

"I'm much obliged for the offer. See you later."

Theodore shook his hand. "Until then."

As Mr. Naylor walked away, Theodore climbed back into the house. He and Henry filled the laundry basket and lowered it by rope to Betsy and Brianna. They unloaded it and returned it to be filled again with shoes, hats, hairbrushes, hand mirrors, Theodore's box of valuable keepsakes and money, two of James' favorite storybooks and blanket, the sailboat Henry was going to repair, plus one favored item belonging to each of the girls.

The dressers had all been lowered to the ground with the rope tied around them to hold the drawers intact so their clean clothes were already within reach.

The last item Theodore took to the ground himself to hand to Betsy. It was Aunt Agatha's carved jewelry box. Betsy held it to her chest as tears pooled in her eyes so very thankful she had returned the cameo to the box when she took it off the night before the storm.

Theodore took a handkerchief from his pocket to wipe the dust and sweat from his brow before kissing her cheek. "I hate to leave you, but Henry and I are needed at the cemetery."

"Go and take care of our loved ones. Brianna and I can use the Keats' hand cart to move what we can to the Eatonton's."

Theodore looked deeply in her eyes, once again amazed at the strength of his mate. From the very beginning she had to be strong with his long absences while following the Seminole War. She had to bury his aunt and their daughter alone during that trying time. Now, he would see to their reburial while she struggled to hold on to what little they had left. She was his partner in life. He was truly blessed with her. How he wished he could stay and satisfy her need to retrieve what was left of their belongings, but duty called again. With a ghost of a smile, he turned to leave.

Betsy sighed in disappointment tinged with the frustration of waiting another day to retrieve the rest of their belongings. She gave a longing look at the sad remains of her beloved home. She then resolutely turned to the items surrounding her on the ground. She sighed deeply, thankful for what she did have. "Brianna, let's get to work."

Chapter 22

Marine Hospital

Emily was tired, hungry, and dispirited. She didn't sleep well again last night despite being in her own bed. Every sound disturbed her, bringing to mind the tense hours of waiting out the storm in imminent fear of the roof collapsing. Her mother insisted she and her brothers return to the hospital with her bright and early this morning. Their breakfast was a half serving of oatmeal each. It was now midday and there was nothing to serve for lunch. But it was the underlying concern for her father and eldest brother's return which truly had her on edge. It was exacerbated by her mother's unspoken worry. Whenever she had a free moment, her mother could be found staring out the western windows hoping to see the masts of her father's ship.

The morning was spent helping tend to the patients and the islanders who came in with cuts, sprains and contusions from cleaning up without benefit of work gloves and moving about on precarious building materials. Emily hated the sight of blood and so the odious task of cleaning wounds further irritated her while the constant hammering of those working on the roof repairs was bringing on a headache.

Taking a break, Emily moved to one of the open front windows. Idly, she watched the army men attach a chain to one of the many timbers strewn about the street. When it was secure, they attached the other end to the camp horses and began the slow process of dragging the log back to camp. They had two teams and four horses working on it all morning. It was a good thing the animals survived. Emily couldn't imagine how they would have moved the timbers without them. Bored, she turned from the window and wandered over to sit with Meredith and Sadie to watch her brother, Nate, and their brother, Jeremy, playing marbles.

Suddenly Sadie turned to her sister and plaintively cried, "I want mama."

Jeremy paused to turn his stricken gaze to his sisters.

Meredith pulled her sister to her side. "Hush Sadie. Mama's gone to heaven." She turned haunted eyes to Emily for comfort.

Emily's own worry made her speak rashly. "At least you know what happened to your mother. I have no idea if my father and brother are still alive." Instantly, she regretted her words.

Tears welled in Meredith's eyes.

Abby happened to be passing by and overheard her daughter's caustic remark. She stopped, shocked by what she heard. "Emily Rose! I raised you better than to be so selfish and cruel. How could you say something so spiteful?"

Emily cast her eyes down in shame. "I am sorry mother. I am just so worried."

"It is not me you need to apologize to."

Emily turned to her companions. "I am sorry for what I said, and I am truly sorry for your loss."

Meredith murmured something. Jeremy turned away. Sadie, feeling the tension, buried her head in her sister's shoulder.

Too uncomfortable to stay, Emily got up and followed her mother.

Abby laid an arm across her daughter's shoulders. "I know you are worried about your father and brother. We must maintain hope for them, but more importantly, we must treat our friends and neighbor's with courtesy and respect, or we will not get through this."

Emily lashed out in distraught anger. "How can you go about so calmly when we don't even know if they are alive?"

Abby replied firmly. "By holding on to hope. We do not know they are dead either." She softened her tone. "And by doing what has to be done now. As long as I stay busy, it makes it easier to bear the not knowing. But do not think I don't care about your father or everyone else that is affected here. We are not alone, and we will get through it, but only if we are compassionate. You and I must take care of our family, but we must also help others less fortunate. Besides the McCreary children losing their mother, there is Mrs. Baxley who has to go on without her husband. Look at her over there. She is helping her neighbors despite her enormous grief. And I shudder to think of the horror Mrs. Mabrity will be facing upon her return. Already a widow, now she has lost half her family and the means of supporting herself until the lighthouse can be rebuilt." Abby pulled Emily to her. "Daughter, you cannot know how deep the loss of a child can cut you. I can only begin to imagine how Mrs. Mabrity will cope with the loss of seven."

As intended, her mother's words made her feel small and contrite. Others were certainly suffering more than her. She needed to focus on the good and not the bad. Her father would want her to act bravely.

* * *

Theodore and Henry arrived at the southern cemetery to find a dozen men gathered. The mood was somber to match the sanctity of the task at hand. They worked in pairs righting overturned caskets and moving them to a designated spot in preparation of being moved. Some were easily identified but most were plain boxes that would have to be opened to try and determine its occupant. A few coffins were found opened, some with the bodies missing, presumably washed away. One was found half displaced and carefully restored to its box. Henry was thankful, so far, he and his father had not found one of those.

Next, the partially unburied were dug out and added to the growing pile along with their headstone. Aunt Agatha was one of these. Henry and Theodore tended to her in silence. It was easier to face than the empty hole next to hers where Madalyn once resided. The small box containing Emily's sister was also missing. So far, their coffins had not been found. Henry's heart ached for his father who was stoically trying to ignore his grief-stricken pain.

They were working on Aunt Agatha's tombstone when a voice called out. "There's more of them in the trees." Henry saw hope flash in his father's eyes as he dropped his spade and rushed forward to help search. Henry followed.

The depth of the flood waters was evidenced by dried rushes lodged high in the trees. Some over seven feet. Henry found it hard to imagine that standing in this spot at the height of the storm, he would have been underwater. Men spread out among the trees finding coffins here and there in the lengthening shadows of evening.

Henry was walking with Mr. Naylor when they came across another coffin with a loose cover. Mr. Naylor pried it open to look inside. "This be Mr. Mabrity."

Henry said, "How do you know?"

"There's a wick trimmer in the pocket of his jacket."

"A wick trimmer?"

"Aye. Apparently, he was very particular about it. Mrs. Mabrity thought it was a good jest to bury him with it."

"Hmm. Amazing it wasn't lost in the storm."

"Yes, it is. I'm glad we found him. She has lost enough to this storm."

Miguel's laughing visage surfaced in Henry's thoughts. "Yes, she has."

Henry picked up the spade he left behind and wandered through the remaining headstones in search of Mr. Mabrity's marker. He found it without too much trouble. It was the third one he had to set right in order to read the engraving. He and Mr. Naylor carried the heavy stone to the casket.

Ignoring the swarms of mosquitoes and gnats, Henry went a little deeper into the woods. He covered his mouth and nose as he passed the rotting flesh of a loggerhead turtle left inland, beaten and battered by the storm. No sooner had he recovered from that horrific sight, his breath left him in a rush as he unexpectedly came face to face with a skeleton in a coverless coffin standing upright in the spindly embrace of a buttonwood stripped of leaves. The macabre scene sent a shiver down his spine. His stomach churned as he turned away. This latest horror was nearly Henry's undoing. He was sure what he just saw would forever haunt him.

Would the nightmare never end?

Sheriff Coslin was passing by. Henry called out to him for assistance. Together they pulled the coffin from the tree being careful not to dislodge the occupant. Neither of them wanted to pick up bones. They looked around for the cover, but didn't find it. Henry picked up the foot of the casket and then turned to hold it from behind so he wouldn't have to continue looking at the corpse as they moved it to join the growing pile of coffins.

As they placed their burden with the rest, they overheard one of the volunteers ask, "What about the military graveyard? Will those be moved as well?"

The mayor shook his head. "I'm afraid it has been completely washed away. Nothing remains of it."

Henry noticed his father returning with a dejected slump to his shoulders. Obviously, he hadn't found Madalyn's casket in the trees. They could only assume she had been washed out to sea. He hoped his mother wouldn't be too upset by the news. Silently, together they moved Madalyn's headstone from the graveyard and placed it alongside Aunt Agatha's so they would remain together in the new cemetery.

It was getting late. The mayor called an end to their activities for the day. He asked for volunteers to meet again tomorrow to continue work on identifying remains.

As they walked back, Henry's mind was numb from the trauma of the day, indeed the last few days. His father had to nudge him to turn towards the Keats' house instead of heading to theirs.

They came upon two men in a heated argument. Between them stood a disgruntled cow. Each man tugged on the frayed rope around its neck. Henry heard his father give an irritated sigh. He walked up to the cow and laid a hand on its forehead as he demanded from the men, "What is going on here?"

The both spoke over each other declaring the cow to be theirs.

"And what proof do you have?"

Henry walked around the rear of the Jersey cow looking for any markings on her brown hide. He looked to his father. "I don't see a brand."

Theodore gave each man a shrewd look. "Mr. Bush just because you found her on your lot doesn't make her yours, and Mr. Payne, I clearly remember your cow being a Holstein. I say she belongs to neither of you."

Mr. Bush snarled. "Finders, keepers."

Mr. Payne sneered. "You're trying to keep her for yourself, Mr. Whitmore."

Theodore had never been so thankful to see Sheriff Coslin approaching. "No sir. I am suggesting she be turned over to the sheriff. Henry would you bring him over, please."

Henry turned to find the man about twenty yards away. He loped over to him and explained the situation as they walked back to the cow. The sheriff circled around to the head of the cow. "Boys I have to agree with Mr. Whitmore. The cow doesn't belong to either one of you. The mayor has asked for donations to support all those in need. This cow will help feed the starving children if she's still giving milk."

Mr. Payne growled, "And if she's not?"

Sheriff Coslin held his gaze. "Then she will feed a lot of desperate people."

Mr. Bush said, "But I found her. I should get a share."

"I promise both of you, if the cow is to be slaughtered I will make sure you each get a portion."

Not happy, but resigned, they dropped their claim on the rope leaving the cow to the sheriff.

Sheriff Coslin shook hands with Theodore and Henry. "I'm glad not everyone is turning on each other. I hope we can get supplies soon. These situations are getting more frequent and more hostile as time goes by. Do you have any idea who this cow may belong to?"

Theodore shook his head. "No. There were several Jerseys on the island."

The sheriff led the cow away. Henry followed his father's angry strides only to have him suddenly stop.

"What is it?"

He shook his head. "I find I have no patience for men like that." His contemplative gaze turned towards town. "You go on without me. I need time to release this anger before going home. Besides, I need to see how bad the damage is inside the print shop."

Henry was astounded. "You haven't been to see it yet?"

"I have only had the chance to walk past it. The building still stands."

Henry understood. His father was putting so much effort into helping the town and seeing to his family's needs that he hadn't seen to his business. He made sure Henry had the opportunity to assess his interests, but he had not taken that opportunity for himself. "I'll go with you."

They followed the narrow footpath of cleared rubble leading down Front Street. Henry said, "How are we ever going to recover from this?"

"It is daunting. It would be easier to list the homes and buildings with little to no damage than the other way around."

They came to the door of the printing shop. It was slightly ajar. Theodore cautiously pushed it open. The setting sun cast a golden glow through the broken front window over the typeset desk but did little to light the dim interior. Theodore found the oil lamp and matches where he left them sitting on the bookcase behind the door. He lit the wick and held the lamp aloft to survey the muddle.

All the furniture in the front room was askew, pushed around by the flow of water. The printed draft of the next edition he left on the typeset desk was strewn about by the wind from the broken window. Some of the pages were plastered to the walls. The box of typeset was turned over on the floor. The small metal letters were hopelessly scattered in all directions. The high water mark on the wall was at shoulder height. Theodore didn't need to go further into the room to know his stores of ink and paper, kept within easy reach on the floor, were ruined. He could only hope the expensive printing press could be saved from the damaging salt water but having the time to clean it was days, if not weeks, away. His archives stacked in crates in the back were likely a complete loss. The destruction of his shop was every bit as bad as he imagined, and yet the confirmation was still a crushing blow.

There was no time to work on it today. He extinguished the lamp and set it back in its place on the bookshelf. The door must have kept the rushing water from disturbing it too.

Henry saw his father's broad shoulders slump. He laid a comforting hand on his back. Witnessing his father's strain, he was thankful God had sent him to help. "You are not alone. I will help you get the paper running again." He expected the usual response of 'hmm' to the emotional situation, and when it didn't come, he turned to study his father's profile. He saw his Adam's apple move several times and realized his father was working to contain powerful emotions. Many moments passed before he broke the silence.

"I am grateful beyond measure to have you here."

For the first time since boyhood, his father pulled him into his embrace.

No matter that they had lost everything, their family's love would endure.

* * *

Henry sat down at the Keats' dining table with his parents, their hosts, and Mrs. Keats' parents, Mr. and Mrs. Sanchez. The children had eaten earlier, leaving the adults to consume a meager fish stew after the younger ones had been put to bed. Talk around the table was somber, each sharing the woeful tales they witnessed during the day. Mrs. Keats had helped distribute food and water at the barracks and took in some wash and mending. She had many horrific stories to share of families separated and loved ones lost during their flight to higher ground, and the misery of those who spent the night clinging to bushes and trees, soaked and shivering, until dawn.

It was hard not to feel downtrodden with so much misery and despair surrounding them.

Captain Keats suddenly laid both hands on the table. "I know we usually only do this at Thanksgiving but I think today it is needed even more. We should all share what we are thankful for today." Seeing the acceptance of those around them, he shared his first. "Dear Lord, I am thankful to have a roof over my head when so many do not and thankful to have enough food and shelter to share with friends and family."

Mrs. Keats squeezed her husband's hand. "I am thankful for the safety of my family and those we care about."

Mr. Sanchez spoke for both he and his wife in broken English. "I thankful *mi familia*."

Betsy said, "I thank the Good Lord our family was kept together and safe and for good friends to give us food and shelter when we have none."

Theodore said, "I share the same gratitude as all of you, and I am thankful, although it seems bleak now, that we can and will rebuild our home and our community."

It was Henry's turn. "I am thankful for being here to help my family get through the storm and its aftermath." He was also thankful they would be moving to the Eatonton's after supper. Knowing he would soon see Emily perked up his spirits.

* * *

Henry waited by the open front door for his parents to finish saying goodbye to Captain and Mrs. Keats. James was holding his hand, and his sisters were sitting on the porch steps. None of them were as impatient as he to leave. Emily was waiting for him.

They arrived at the Eatonton house with nothing more than the clothes on their back and a few donations from the Keats. The cart load of items taken from the house were brought over earlier along with all their clothes. Mrs. Eatonton stood in the open front door welcoming them with a genuine smile. They entered the front room to find Emily, Thorn, Nate and Jacob waiting for them.

Emily was excited and a little nervous for Henry to be staying under the same roof. She hoped it meant they would see more of each other, at least in the evenings.

It was getting late and all were tired from the long and emotionally trying day. Sleeping arrangements were quickly worked out so that the younger siblings could be put to bed. Emily would share her room with Brianna, Agatha, and Emmaline. Henry would temporarily sleep in Christoff's bed until his return. James would sleep in the old nursery with his parents.

Henry watched his mother follow Mrs. Eatonton upstairs trailed by his younger sisters and Emily's brothers. His father followed behind carrying a sleeping James.

Theodore followed Betsy into the old nursery to put James to bed. Betsy stopped in the middle of the room surprised by what she saw before her. Somehow their mattress had been brought to the house and made up with clean sheets. She was expecting that she and Theodore would be sleeping on a made up pallet the same as James.

Abby said from the doorway, "It was Thorn and Nate's doing. They brought back all of the mattresses you pulled from the house after you returned to the Keats."

She was nearly reduced to tears by the kind gesture. "How very thoughtful of him. So the girls have theirs too?"

"Yes. The younger ones do. Brianna and Emily will share her bed."

Betsy could hear the low murmurs of the boys in their room. She told James to get settled on his pallet while she went to seek out her benefactors. At the threshold of the boys' room she knocked on the door. It took a moment for it to be opened by Thorn in his nightshirt. Nate and Jacob appeared behind him. "Boys, I wanted to personally thank you for bringing the mattresses. It was a wonderful thing to do for us."

"Aw shucks, Mrs. Whitmore. It wasn't nothing."

She smiled at his unintentional slip. "You're right. It *wasn't* nothing. It couldn't have been easy to do and it is very much appreciated by me and Mr. Whitmore. It was the best welcome you could give us. Thank you."

Thorn was embarrassed by her praise for something he considered to be only right. He mumbled, "You're welcome."

With everyone else upstairs, for a moment, Henry was blessedly alone with Emily. Shyly she smiled at him from across the room. He wanted, nay, needed to embrace her. He took a step towards her. Actually, he really wanted to kiss her. Emily read his thoughts and shook her head. He understood. He was a guest in this house and Mrs. Eatonton would not take kindly to his being too familiar with her daughter, no matter his intentions.

She looked tired. He laughed to himself. They were all tired.

Her mother called from upstairs. "Emily."

She gave him a sympathetic smile. "I should see what she wants."

He grasped her hand as she passed. She paused. It was a simple touch and yet it profoundly gave them connection and comfort. Henry turned to follow her. Together they climbed the stairs surreptitiously holding hands until they came in view of her mother. Mrs. Eatonton sent Emily to her room to help his sisters settle in for the night, and then she led Henry to his bed. She pulled a night shirt, pants, tunic, and socks from Christoff's chest of drawers to supplement Henry's. As she turned to him, she said, "I trust you will not take advantage of this situation with Emily."

Henry was hurt she had so little faith in him, but then he remembered the scene downstairs and reasoned she had every need to be concerned. He would have to guard against his desires. "Yes, ma'am."

She handed him the clothes with an intent look that said to Henry, *You had better behave.* On her way out of the room she picked up a pile of clothes for James that Jacob had outgrown.

Their parents returned downstairs. Henry could hear them in the parlor sharing the news of the day. He wasn't ready for bed. He was considering joining them when voices from down the hall pulled him from the room. He needed to see Emily. Looking at her would not break his trust with Mrs. Eatonton. He left his room and wandered to the other end of the hall to stand outside Emily's open door. Inside the girls were animatedly talking. He drank in the sight of Emily with her hair down and her face lit with a delighted smile. It was refreshing, especially after all they had endured the last three days. Had it only been three days? It felt like three weeks.

Emily caught his gaze. She uncrossed her legs and got up from the bed. She excused herself from his sisters to come to the door. Henry backed up into the hall forcing her to leave sight of the room to speak to him. He was surprised when she took his hand and pulled him into his parents' temporary room. The door was left open, but it gave them a modicum of privacy from their siblings.

She lifted her face to his with a soft smile. "How are you, Henry?"

He brushed his hand against the soft color staining her cheek. "Better now." He dropped his hand to take hold of hers, rubbing the spot where one day he would place a wedding band. "It was a gruesome day."

She nodded. "Yes, it was."

The intensity of her answer surprised him. "What did you do today?"

"I had to clean bloody lacerations and mop up after a retching patient." She shuddered in remembrance. "What did you do?"

"Searched for corpses." He remembered her missing sister's casket but decided now was not the time to tell her.

"Ugh. I'm not sure which is worse."

He smiled faintly. "Shall we call it even?"

She grinned. "A gentleman would say the lady won."

"Oh. And would you prefer a gentleman's response or honesty?"

Sensing the underlying seriousness of his question, she answered, "Between us, I would always prefer honesty."

He squeezed her hand. "I'm glad for it. And perhaps vomit does trump bones and you win."

She laughed. "It's too late now to play the gentleman."

Henry was charmed by her mirth. He raised her hand to kiss her ring finger. "This is going to be difficult."

"What is?"

"Living in the same house with you, so close, and yet unable to do anything more than speak to each other. It will be sweet torture."

Brianna called from the bedroom. "Emily?"

Emily stood on her toes to kiss his cheek. She then moved around him to return to her room leaving him feeling more bereft than before he sought her out. He sighed heavily. Yes, her proximity was going to be damned difficult. It was easier to keep his distance when there was actual distance between them.

Chapter 23

Wednesday, October 14th

Breakfast the next morning, though sparse, was a lively affair. They were gathered around the formal dining room table as it was the only space large enough for both families to eat together. The antics of Jacob and James kept the group quite entertained, temporarily suspending their worries and concerns for the day ahead. It was an enjoyable half hour, but at its close, the mantel of hardship was taken up once again.

Before leaving the table, the Whitmore children were assigned shared chores with the Eatonton siblings. Emily and Brianna had dish detail, Agatha and Nate oil lamps, while Jacob and Emmaline simply had to make their beds. Normally, they would be charged with refilling the water pitchers and emptying the basins, but as water was scarce this chore was on hold. There wasn't enough water to refill the pitchers. The basin water would have to be reused.

First to leave the house was Theodore, Henry, and Thorn. They carried with them shovels and picks for digging eternal resting places for those friends and neighbors who perished in the storm. The city council designated acreage at the northwest edge of high ground for the new city cemetery. Today, they would bury the newly deceased. Even though the mayor said the army would carry out the task, Theodore felt they should care for their own. After much debate amongst the council members, it was finally decided those to be moved from the old cemetery would wait till the more immediate needs of the living had been met.

Emily and Brianna cleared the dishes from the dining table to the makeshift kitchen. Emily felt more than saw Brianna's glances as they scrubbed and rinsed the dishes. Guilt made her wonder if Brianna was aware of her stolen moments with Henry.

Brianna finally worked up the courage to speak what was on her mind. "Are you in love with my brother?"

Emily turned to find Brianna's gaze open but intent. She answered as hopeful honesty. "Yes, I am. Do you mind?"

Brianna turned back to the dish she was drying. "I think he loves you."

She couldn't help smiling. "I think so too."

"Do you still plan to marry him?"

"Do you want me to?"

"I do."

Emily bumped shoulders with her in a kindred way. "Me too."

* * *

In the hall, Abby was donning her gloves, preparing to leave the house. She stopped Betsy as she passed by. "Do you mind watching the children? I need to pay my respects to Mrs. Baxley. She was at the hospital yesterday, but we didn't have a chance to speak privately. I am thinking of asking her to move in with us. The Youngs barely have enough room for their brood, much less a guest, and I believe she is reluctant to return to her house alone. We can easily make room for her here. Why, we can move Max's office into the library or parlor." Saying his name brought her simmering fears to the surface. She tried to tamp them down, but still her voice broke. "I am sure he would approve."

Betsy was quick to embrace her friend. She knew how awful it was to live with the uncertainty of a husband's fate. It may have been many years since she last felt such fear, but seeing Abby suffer was a stark reminder.

Abby pulled away before tears overcame her. She donned her bonnet and with a nod to Betsy left the house. She walked the short distance to the Young's residence amidst the growing piles of debris cleared from the street and yards. The humid heat of the last few days accelerated the foul-smelling decay. It made the walk unpleasant. If it wasn't burned soon, the odor was going to make their lives even more miserable.

Mrs. Young welcomed Abby into her two room home with its sparse furnishings made even more austere by the loss of rugs and padded furniture; victims of the flooding. The water had risen three feet high inside the house as evidenced by the discernable line marring the plank walls. Despite their cleaning efforts, the house had a musty smell. It made Abby once again thankful Max insisted their house be built off the ground to accommodate flooding.

"I wish I could offer you tea, but I'm afraid it was lost in the storm. Would you care for some water?"

Knowing the Young's likely had little water to spare, Abby politely declined. Mrs. Baxley entered the room carrying the youngest Young prodigy on her hip. "Hello, Mrs. Eatonton. I thought I heard your voice. How are you faring?"

"We are managing well, all things considered."

"Have you received any word of Captain Max?"

Abby had to look away from her sympathetic gaze. "No." She stepped forward to touch Mrs. Baxley's shoulder. "I am so sorry for your loss and for not speaking to you sooner."

"Nonsense. You have been busy doing more than your share to help others."

"As have you. Mr. Baxley will be missed." They shared a poignant look before Abby took a breath to add, "I have also come to ask for your help."

"My help?"

"Yes. I have taken in the Whitmore's, but with my work at the hospital and the Whitmore's helping the community, we need more help keeping up the house and watching the youngest. I was hoping, since we are already on familiar terms, you would be willing to do so in exchange for room and board. That is, of course, if Mrs. Young can spare you."

Mrs. Baxley's gaze moved to Mrs. Young who came forward to take her child and said, "It's your choice. You are welcome to stay, of course. I will leave you and Mrs. Eatonton to talk." Mrs. Young left the house by way of the back door where her elder children could be heard playing in the yard.

Abby patiently waited for Mrs. Baxley to speak.

"You truly need me? I won't take your charity."

"It's not charity. The older children are needed elsewhere, so we, Betsy and I, need someone to look after the younger children, and there is no one I would rather have than you."

"Alright, I accept your offer. When would you like for me to start?"

"As soon as you can."

"Let me say goodbye to the Young's, and I'll be ready to walk back with you."

Abby smiled with heartfelt sincerity. "Thank you, Mrs. Baxley."

* * *

Gathered by the kitchen, Emily helped Agatha and Nate with their chore of cleaning all the oil lamps, refilling those in need, and trimming the wicks, while she waited for her mother to return from her errand. She was dreading another day at the Marine Hospital and wishing she could do something different. Maybe, her mother would let her stay home today and help Brianna look after the younger children.

When all the lamps were taken care of, they were returned to the house. Agatha and Nate then hurried to join Jacob and Emmaline's game of Scotch-hoppers in the yard. Emily wandered to the front porch and took up a seat next to Brianna who was reading a novel. They were soon joined by Betsy carrying an irritable James. They were both tired from a restless night of James's nightmares; another lingering effect in the aftermath of the hurricane. She took the rocking chair hoping to soothe him into a nap. The sticky heat was not helping.

Abby and Mrs. Baxley heard the children before they saw them. The surprising sounds of laughter and squeals of delight brought healing reassurance to Abby's heart. She watched their carefree play, finding joy amidst the ruins. The adults could take a lesson from them.

The children suddenly broke from their game, racing to greet Mrs. Baxley who dropped her bag of meager belongings to open her arms to them with a huge smile. The noisy greeting brought Thorn outside to investigate. He greeted Mrs. Baxley with more reserve than the others, feeling too old to be so demonstrative. As he was taught, he took charge of her bag and the one his mother carried, leading the group back to the house.

Emily rose with the others on the porch to welcome Mrs. Baxley. The children went back to their play and Betsy to her rocking. Inside, Emily, Thorn, Brianna and Abby moved aside the furniture in the office to make room for a temporary improvised bed of piled quilts and Mrs. Baxley's belongings.

* * *

New City Cemetery

As two soldiers came over to help, Henry took a break from digging into the hard limestone. He leaned on the shovel, wiping the sweat from his brow. The morning temperature was rising faster than the sun. He took a sip of water from his canteen while he surveyed their work. Ten graves were finished. The one he was working on was nearly done. Next to him, his father and Thorn were working on the last one. They should have needed more. Too many of those lost to the storm had not been found. The last count he heard was more than thirty were believed to be lost to a watery grave or yet to be discovered beneath the rubble.

Mayor Maloney approached. Henry couldn't help but notice the weary and drawn look about him. His father stopped work to speak with the mayor. Immediately a soldier took his place beside Thorn to finish digging the grave.

Mayor Maloney shook his father's hand. "Thank you for doing this, Mr. Whitmore."

Theodore nodded.

He turned to Henry with his hand outstretched. "And you, Mr. Whitmore." It was the first time the mayor addressed him as a man. The last time he spoke directly to Walter Maloney was before he fled the island. The novelty lasted but a moment to be quickly replaced by the gravity of the situation. And as he listened, he witnessed his father, the journalist, at work.

Mayor Maloney said, "We'll hold the memorial service here at eleven and see the bodies interred. With everyone so busy doing recovery work, it seemed best to hold one service for all of them. I've sent others to spread the word."

Theodore said, "Seems sensible under the circumstances. How are the food donations coming along?"

"Meager, I'm afraid. The soldiers who went collecting reported back with few goods. They said most people claimed they had none to spare. One man held them off at gun point from collecting the fallen cocoanuts in his yard even though he had more than he needed."

Henry said, "It's hard to share when there is so little and no idea when availability will return."

The mayor nodded in agreement. "It has been suggested I declare martial law so that the food can be confiscated."

Theodore said with more than a little concern, "Are you considering it?"

"Let's say I am trying to avoid it for now, but if things continue as they have been, I won't have much choice."

Theodore said, "Maybe sending out volunteers instead of soldiers would produce better results. It would be harder to deny a neighbor in need."

"I believe you're right. I'll ask for volunteers today. But that's not the only cause for martial law. Sheriff Coslin has had to recruit deputies to control the drunken lawlessness and looting that started yesterday. He's already arrested so many we have nowhere to hold them. The jail is full. The city council decided this morning to forbid alcohol sales and institute a curfew. Sheriff Coslin is putting up the notices as we speak."

Theodore said, "Are you ready for the protests and complaints that will follow?"

The mayor shrugged and shook his head. "As much as we can be. If these problems continue, I may be forced to declare martial law."

Henry said, "After witnessing two grown men fight like toddlers over a cow yesterday, I can see the need for it."

"I hope it doesn't come to that. For now, I am assessing what we have and hoping to find a ship soon that can be sent for supplies. At least, we have fish and cocoanuts."

Theodore said, "Has word been sent out of our situation?"

"Yes, and another is to be sent on a courier ship leaving for Charleston this afternoon."

"Will you be sending Congress a plea for help?"

"Already drafted and delivered to the captain. I assume you will want to send out something?"

"Yes. I will. I'll work on it after the funerals. Can this courier bring back supplies?"

"Unfortunately not. They must carry out their assigned ports to deliver important correspondences for the military and government. But we are not without our resources. John Bartlum has put his family concerns aside to work on repairing one of the storm damaged vessels. Unfortunately, even the least damaged is going to take some time to repair. We must pray for outside help to arrive soon. By the way, we learned Cuba was struck on Saturday. Havana is devastated. We will find no resources from there. The courier captain said the storm continued north from here up the Florida coast, striking Tampa and then seems to have turned inland."

Henry said, "Hopefully it weakened by then."

Thorn joined them having finished with his work.

Theodore scrutinized the mayor. "All of this is taking a toll on you."

"It is. I can't seem to do enough. The minister is concerned about rebuilding the church, the doctors have a list of needs for the hospital, Mr. Howe has concerns for his salt works, Mr. Wall for his cigar workers, the captains for their ships and lost cargos, Mr. Mallory with the resumption of the harbor business and replacing the lighthouse, and I am a man with only so many answers." He shook his head in despair. "I'm sorry. I don't mean to burden you with my problems."

"Sometimes it helps just to share them with another."

The mayor smiled. "It does lighten the burden a little." He took a deep breath and straightened his shoulders. When he spoke again, he sounded more like his usual self. "Gentlemen, I have much to attend to before the funerals. The procession will begin at the court house and proceed down Eaton Street to here, it being the clearest path. I'll see you then. Good-day."

Henry and Thorn turned to Theodore for direction.

Theodore said, "It looks as if we are finished here. We should return home and let the ladies know of the plans."

They returned to the Eatonton house to find Abby and Mrs. Baxley had gone to prepare Mr. Baxley's body for burial. The others occupied themselves with various pursuits while somberly waiting for the appointed time. Theodore was writing an article and request for help to send to his New York publishing friend on the afternoon courier ship. Betsy was mending clothes. Brianna was tending James and Jacob. The other children were playing outside, leaving Henry and Emily a rare chance to talk privately while watching over them from the porch. The younger boys worked hard all morning to clear the yard of debris. It was piled high on one side leaving them ample area for a game of stickball.

Henry reached across the expanse between their chairs to take her hand. Emily turned her gaze to him. He was surprised by the depths of her anger and despair.

"What is it Em?"

Her jaw clenched for a moment and her gaze fanned out over the ruined houses surrounding them. "Why did this have to happen? I don't see how things could ever be the same again. How are we to go on from here?"

"By rebuilding as we can."

"And watch it happen again with the next storm."

Henry sat up straight and turned to face her. "Emily, what are you saying?"

She paused. The words once said would change everything. She meant them, but wondered if she could truly live with them. "I am thinking of leaving the island."

His heart plummeted. "Leaving? Where would you go? What about us?"

Emily looked at Henry in surprise. "Of course not without you."

Henry took a relieved breath. She still wanted to marry him. At the same time, he despaired. He didn't want to live elsewhere, but he would do anything to make her happy. He did his best to keep his tone neutral. "Where do you think we should go?"

"Your family has an estate up north. We could go there to live where there are no hurricanes to destroy our home."

"True there are no hurricanes, but you would be trading them for blizzards."

Emily smiled weakly. "I would like to see snow. I never have, you know. I've always lived here. I haven't traveled any further than my uncle's plantation in Montgomery." She turned a cajoling smile on Henry. "Could we move away?"

He would do anything to please her, even sacrifice his own happiness, but it was a hard commitment for him to make. "Is that truly your wish?"

She was disappointed in his less than enthusiastic response. "Yes."

"Can you give me some time to consider it?"

"Of course."

They turned back to watching their siblings play. Neither spoke again. Emily keenly felt Henry's withdrawal. It made her regret her rash declaration.

* * *

At the stroke of eleven on the mayors pocket watch, the procession of twelve caskets and mourners was begun. It was led by Reverend Richardson and the visiting Catholic priest from Havana trapped on the island due to the storm. The mayor and other city dignitaries brought up the rear. No music played and voices were muted at the start. Along the route, neighbors paused in their labors to pay homage. Many of them joined the procession and someone started singing Amazing Grace and soon all joined in.

Reaching the grave sites, the mourners gathered around to listen to the mayor gave a short speech, but Henry could not recall a word of it. He was realizing how easily it could have been one of their family being buried today or worse, missing. He was thinking of those families like Emily's maid, Lydia, who did not have a body to bury. He looked to his father and was so deeply thankful his injury during the storm had not been his demise and that James had not drowned.

The priest and reverend took turns reading from the Bible and praying. The priest's Latin words had an uncomfortable, hypnotic cadence. Henry felt relief when Reverend Richardson took over speaking the familiar, "Ashes to ashes and dust to dust...." Finally, the caskets were lowered into the ground and covered one by one accompanied by the now expressive mourning of loved ones.

Mrs. Eatonton held Mrs. Baxley tight to her side as Mr. Baxley's casket was covered.

Henry's thoughts turned to Miguel and the others lost. They felt dismissed and forgotten even though the mayor promised memorial services would be held for the missing victims later after the crisis had calmed down and all were accounted for.

Afterwards, the reverend announced a prayer vigil would be held in the new cemetery at dusk for all their needs. The mourners began to move away, although many hung around in groups to talk of their trials and experiences since the storm began.

The Whitmores, Eatontons, and Mrs. Baxley returned home for dinner. Abby insisted the last of the ham in the larder be served with peas and rice. Understandably, Mrs. Baxley was too distraught to eat. She retreated to her room. They respected her need for solitude by speaking softly and keeping their distance. Betsy put a plate aside for her to eat later.

After the meal, Abby planned to return to the hospital. "Emily are you ready to leave?"

Emily approached her mother with trepidation. "I was wondering if I could help Mr. and Mrs. Whitmore today instead of helping at the hospital."

"I know you dislike working at the hospital. I suppose the situation is at a point now I can forego your help. Emily, I am proud of you for not complaining and for doing what must be done despite your feelings. I am sure the Whitmores could use your help." She added in a hushed whisper, "Mind, you behave yourself with Henry."

Emily smiled in relief. "Yes, ma'am."

Abby kissed her forehead and left the house.

Theodore came down the stairs with his letter in hand for Bob Jenkins of the *New York Weekly*. He asked Emily, "You're not going with your mother?"

"No. I offered to help you and Mrs. Whitmore."

Theodore was touched. "We appreciate it. Do you know where Henry is at the moment?"

Henry came around the corner from the dining room. "I'm here father."

Theodore handed him the letter. "Can you find the mayor and make sure this gets on the ship headed for Charleston?"

Henry accepted the folded papers sealed with wax. "Yes, sir."

"Meet us at the house after."

Henry gave his father a nod. He covertly winked at Emily, pleased to see an embarrassed blush flood her cheeks. He left the house with a jaunt in his step.

Finding the mayor proved difficult. Fortunately, he ran across Captain Dutton carrying his own letter for the Charleston courier. Henry fell instep beside him. "Do you think the army will rebuild the fort?"

"I'm not sure. The storm was a huge setback to our progress." He lifted the hand with the letter. "I've detailed the events and all the losses in this letter. I'll have to wait and see what they say. If a repeat occurrence concerns them, they may choose to build in another location."

"You mean somewhere else around the island?"

"No, I mean somewhere else entirely."

"I hope not."

"Until I hear different, we will salvage what we can in preparation of starting again. How is your family faring?"

"Better than most, I suppose. Our house is a complete loss. We are currently taking it apart to try and save what belongings we can and of course, the lumber. My father's print shop is in shambles, and I'll have to start over with my little sponge operation." He thought of Emily's request earlier to leave the island. Despite his losses, he didn't want to leave. Could he do it for her?

"A strapping lad such as yourself is probably needed elsewhere. I can take your letter as well as mine."

"As a matter of fact, I am. Thank you, Captain Dutton." Henry handed over the letter and turned to hurry back towards his fallen home. Everywhere men were busy cleaning up the street, businesses, homes and yards, repairing what they could, and getting ready to rebuild what they couldn't. Every hour, it seemed, the debris piled along the roadside grew higher and smellier. As ugly as it was, it was progress, and progress felt good.

Chapter 24

Emily trailed behind Mr. and Mrs. Whitmore as they walked the short distance from her house to their tumbled one. Brianna, Agatha, Thorn and Nate walked with her. Thorn was pushing the empty cart. She listened as Henry's parents discussed possible plans for rebuilding their house. She noticed that like her parents, his parents also shared ideas with each other. Mr. Whitmore openly listened to Mrs. Whitmore, but where her parents seemed to compromise, or at least her mother had equal say, Mr. Whitmore had the final say, always. Would Henry expect the same from her? If he did, could she concede to him, always? She worried her lower lip, concerned that she could not.

As they came to their house, Theodore noticed the neighbor industriously cleaning his cistern. Why had it not occurred to him sooner? They were working on the wrong priority. He stopped walking and turned to Betsy. "We need to go back. The cisterns have to be cleaned and ready to receive fresh rainwater, especially the Eatonton's, although whatever ours can receive of rain will help too."

Henry's approach delayed Betsy's response.

"That didn't take you long."

Henry was surprised and pleased to see Emily. Suddenly the task ahead did not seem so bleak. "I was intercepted by Captain Dutton. He was running the same errand and offered to take your letters too knowing I would be needed."

Betsy said, "How kind of him." She turned to Theodore. "As for our priority, I still firmly believe we need to work on the house first. I cannot rest easy until we have all our possessions that can be rescued. There is something important in there."

Theodore shook his head. "What could be more important than water? We have your jewelry chest and our clothes. The rest can wait."

"I don't know what it is. Perhaps, the money in your office?"

Theodore sighed. "It can be retrieved later."

Henry looked to his father. "Maybe not. Remember what the mayor said this morning about looting?"

Theodore looked at the clear blue sky showing no chance of rain. "All right, we'll work on the house first, but we can be prepared for work on the cisterns. Thorn?"

Thorn stepped forward. "Yes, sir?"

"I want you and Nate to go to Mr. Patterson's store. If he's there, get some lime. Tell him to put it on my account. Take the lime back to your house, leave it by the cistern, and then come back here to help."

Thorn said, "Yes, sir, but if I may say so, I know how to clean the cistern. Nate and I could get ours done."

"You know how to get the salt water out and scrub it with slacked lime?"

Thorn's shoulders stiffened with pride. "Yes, sir."

Theodore clapped him on the shoulder. "Then by all means see that it is done."

Eager to prove himself, Thorn stiffly said, "Yes, sir." And then sounding more his age, he eagerly said to his brother, "Come on Nate."

The boys took off at a run. The adults smiled at their exuberance and Betsy was relieved the house would not be again postponed. Theodore and Henry turned to survey the house. The rope holding the front wall was still firmly tied to the tree.

Betsy asked, "Teddy, did you move the lumber we removed yesterday?"

"No."

Both his and Henry's gaze swiveled to the missing pile of exterior boards.

Betsy walked around to the other side of the house to find the interior wood was also missing and worse. "My dresser's gone." Betsy's distress flared into anger. "Who would do such a thing? Haven't we lost enough?" Apparently the mayor's curfew had not helped the thieving. Theodore reached out to comfort her, but Betsy waved him away. She refused to dwell on their losses. Today was about moving forward. "We need to get to work."

Theodore saw the jut of her determined chin and let her be. He turned to check the knot securing the rope from the house to the tree before following after Henry.

Henry climbed up the fallen house. Inside he wandered around the slanted rooms now empty of most of their possessions. It didn't take long for Henry and Theodore to remove the rest of the furniture and belongings, sending them down to the ground to Betsy and the girls. Now all that remained were the walls and floor. Yesterday, working on the house was like scenes from a nightmare. Today, it was just sad.

Henry and Theodore returned to the ground to take a break.

Henry gestured towards the broken window of the addition. "We could go through the window to get directly into the morning room and into the house."

Theodore grimaced. "It would be the most expedient, but I am still concerned about a collapse."

"We have been climbing about. The floor seems stable."

"True, but we don't know what is holding it up. It is obviously not the walls. If there is a collapse, I would rather we were on top than crushed beneath."

Henry reluctantly conceded his point.

Theodore said, "We should take down the upper interior walls first, and then the outer walls, leaving the front one for last since it is secured. When they are gone, we can open up the floor to assess the lower house."

"Sounds reasonable."

Once again, Henry and Theodore climbed into the second story. They made quick work of removing the interior lath and plaster. White dust clung to their skin soon marred by trails of sweat. The heat of the afternoon sun was unrelenting. The mosquitoes were even worse.

And then the wind shifted carrying with it the tendrils of smoke and a horrendous malodor to overpower the rotting vegetation they had grown used to. The ladies all halted in their tasks to cover their noses.

Emily pulled her scented handkerchief from her pocket. "What is that?"

War images flooded Theodore's mind, brought to bear by the loathingly familiar scent. "Burning hair."

Brianna raised her stricken face to her father. "Hair?"

Betsy looked to her husband in confusion. "We buried all the bodies earlier. Why are they burning them?"

Henry swallowed hard. He too had memories related to the stench. "Animals. They are burning the dead animals."

"Oh." Betsy and Brianna echoed each other.

Work was resumed and all breathed a sigh of relief when the wind turned, once again blowing the smoke away from them.

Next, they dismantled the interior framing, tossing the boards out the window and wall openings. The ladies arranged the boards into neat piles. All the while, Brianna couldn't help thinking she was aiding the thieves instead of her family.

Slipping on the dusty upper floor soon became a problem. Agatha was sent to find a broom.

All that was left of the second story was the exterior walls and floor. Henry and Theodore made quick work of removing the back wall. It soon crashed to the ground. They began working on the longer side walls taking them down in sections leaving the front wall for last. As the pieces fell away, the front wall of the second story was left, held in place by the rope tied from the window to the tree. They pried up the bottom board working from the edges inward.

Theodore called out, "Watch out, Betsy. We've almost got it loose. Can you pull on the rope so that it falls clear away?"

Betsy and Brianna moved just in front of the tree trunk to grasp the rope and braced themselves. Ignoring the rough fibers digging into their skin, they pulled hard.

Theodore and Henry waited until the tension increased before prying the rest of the sole plate loose. "It's almost free. When you feel it give way, pull hard to bring it down towards you and away from us." Theodore turned to Henry. "Be aware, the bottom of the wall could kick back towards us. Be ready to move."

There was a give and then Betsy and Brianna quickly stepped backwards pulling on the rope as the wall tumbled towards them. It landed on top of the crumpled front porch with a resounding crash.

When the dust settled, they could see Theodore and Henry already at work pulling up the floor boards.

The house now looked oddly squat, reduced to one story, half tilted and collapsed in on itself. Betsy didn't expect to recover much from the parlor or dining room at the rear of the house.

Henry pushed aside another board pried up from the floor of his former bedroom. He peered into the dimly lit cavern below. It was the study where they spent the night before the storm. Once they had a good four feet of opening, Henry's impatience got the better of him. Despite his father's protests, he lowered himself between the exposed floor joists and gingerly dropped to the floor below.

Betsy's muscles tensed and her breath froze at the sound of splintering boards followed by a surprised cry heralding from behind the walls. She cried out, her voice high with fear.

Emily moved to Mrs. Whitmore's side and took her hand in shared concern.

It was an agonizing moment before Theodore responded. "We're fine. Henry fell through a weak spot in the flooring. His leg is scratched and his pants are hopelessly torn but otherwise he's fine."

Emily released the breath she hadn't realized she was holding.

After the unexpected fall, Henry tested his weight with each step before trusting the floor. Not that he could move far. The downwardly sloping and twisted second floor limited his movement forward. He turned to the window behind him and ripped down the curtains of the front window allowing more light to penetrate into the ragged room and splay across the far wall. It appeared as if the bookcases along the interior wall were supporting a good amount of the collapsed weight. He was afraid to move too far towards the back of the house until they could shore up the supports.

Musty air threatened to smother him even with the open ceiling and broken windows. He was headed for his father's desk and the cash kept in the back of the middle side drawer. The lighter furniture was piled against the lower end of the room, clustered in front of the bookcases. He had to push aside end tables and chairs to reach the desk. The plain wooden box was easy enough to find once he worked the swollen wooden drawer open. Although it had a lock, Henry had never known his father to use it, so he didn't bother looking for the key.

He glanced around at the disheveled disarray of his father's once tidy office looking for anything else of immediate importance. His gaze landed on the bookshelf. He forged his way through the shambles and reached into the recesses of the highest shelf to retrieve the flintlock and revolver. He would have continued searching if not for the marshal's voice drifting through the window calling out a greeting to his parents. A glance at the ceiling confirmed exiting the way he entered would be difficult. He met his father's gaze and gave a nod towards the side window. His father gave a nod of agreement and disappeared from his sight. He could hear his footsteps cross the floor above to make his way down to the ground.

Henry approached the warped side window. He placed his palm against the frame and tried to shake it, testing its solidity. He then retrieved a large brass candlestick and used it to clear the remaining jagged glass from the lower window frame. Small fragments remained, so he worked one of the throw rugs loose from the furniture pile and laid it over the window frame. By now his father was waiting on the ground. He tossed down the money box so he would have both hands free to maneuver his body out of the window. He let go of the frame to drop several feet to the ground below.

His mother and Emily were quick to approach, anxiously checking his injuries. They soon deemed the scrapes on his leg as non-threatening but in need of immediate care. It was easy for Henry to capitulate when somehow Emily managed to arrange for the two of them to return to her house alone. At least, alone for the walk. Mrs. Baxley and their younger siblings would act as chaperone once they reached the house.

Emily was unusually quiet as they walked beneath a smoky haze. Controlled fires were burning across the island as the islanders attempted to get rid of the debris.

Henry reached for Emily's hand. "Is something bothering you Em?"

She swatted at a mosquito hovering in front of her face before turning her doleful gaze to Henry's. "I feel so sad for your family and ashamed of myself. I have been wallowing in my misery, but I see now I have only suffered discomforts in helping others while you and your family and so many others have lost everything. I have no right to complain."

"I haven't heard you complain. In fact, I have proudly watched you do things you abhor to help others. You have made sacrifices, and you have every right to your feelings. You are hurting too. I know how worried you are for your father and brother."

"Still, it gives me no right to act as I did yesterday. I was horrid to someone and I should have had more patience."

Henry stopped. The tug on her hand halted her stride and turned her towards him. "None of us can be expected to behave perfectly under these circumstances. Forgive yourself and move forward. I am sure you apologized to whomever it was you hurt."

Emily bowed her head. "I did."

Henry lifted her chin. "Then forgive yourself and put it behind you. Your heart is good, Emily. It's one of the reasons I love you." He gently kissed her forehead.

The shimmering tears in her eyes were instantly forgotten with the onrush of heat in her cheeks. She pulled away and glanced around, anxious they might have been seen. "You mustn't do such things."

Henry dropped her hand. "You are right. Sometimes, I can't help myself."

"You must try harder."

He gave her a cheeky grin. "Yes, ma'am."

She frowned at his mocking tone.

Henry threw up his hands. "I'm sorry. Of course, you are right."

They soon reached the outdoor kitchen where Henry obediently perched on a tall stool while Emily set about cleaning the scratches on his leg under the watchful gaze of Mrs. Baxley who was making hardtack with the last of the flour at Abby's request. They would share it with the starving families at tonight's prayer meeting.

Emily took a deep breath to calm her racing heart as she applied a wet cloth to Henry's leg. The scratches were not deep. In fact, they had already stopped bleeding. She was merely cleaning away the dirt and would wrap it in a bandage to keep it clean. Henry winced at her first tentative touch. She pulled away and quickly looked to his face to gauge the severity of his pain. The twinkle in his eye made her swat his knee. How dare he tease her! She set back to her work unaware she was biting her lip.

Henry was all too aware of her white teeth manipulating her bottom lip.

"Hold still. I'm almost done."

Henry's eye caught Mrs. Baxley's smirk. He tried harder to sit still and keep his eyes on the far wall. The gentle sweeping touch of her fingers as she wrapped the bandage around his calf required all his forbearance. He breathed a deep sigh of relief when she declared the job done and stepped back. He hopped off the stool and ruefully looked down at his leg. "I think I will go change these pants."

"I'll wait for you here."

Henry returned to her wearing clean pants. The two of them had not stepped far from the house when they were met by the others returning for supper before the evening service. Thorn pushed a loaded cart and the others all carried as many of the items as they could from yesterday's salvage not wanting to lose any more to looters. They deposited the items on the front porch and Thorn wheeled the cart around to the back returning to the front with two empty buckets.

Theodore said to Henry, "A ship has returned with water. They are rationing one bucketful per family. Would you go with Thorn to collect ours please?"

"Yes, sir." Henry cast Emily a warm look before leaving, pleased with her answering blush she tried to hide by turning to follow Brianna into the house. Nate followed Henry and Thorn into town.

Betsy's gaze travelled over their meager possessions now filling up one corner of the porch. "I don't know where we are going to put everything. There isn't room in the house."

Theodore rubbed his hand across the middle of her back. "I was thinking of using the lumber from the house to build a temporary shed to store our furniture. It won't be anything fancy, just enough to keep it protected from the sun and rain."

Betsy looked up at him with a smile. "It will be enough for now."

The boys soon returned with buckets full of water having arrived early for the distribution. They deposited them on the kitchen table. Mrs. Baxley watched over the children as they washed their hands for supper making sure a minimal of water was used for rinsing and it was saved later for bathing.

Theodore checked the cistern before washing up for supper. He put a hand on Thorn and Nate's shoulders. "You boys did an excellent job cleaning the cistern and the yard. Are you willing to clean our cistern tomorrow?"

Thorn solemnly answered, "Yes, sir." Nate echoed him with resignation.

They sat down to a meal of pan seared fish and little else. Betsy's eyes turned to Abby. "Let us pray for the safety of all those still missing."

Abby's heart caught. Her worry for Max and Christoff was never far from her thoughts but taking a moment to bring them into focus was painful. Worry surged forward in her breast nearly stifling her. Seeing the same pain in Emily's gaze, she squeezed her daughter's hand. Across the table, Thorn's shoulder's stiffened under the burden of his encumbrance. They all chose to believe Max and Christoff were alive but as the days passed with no word it grew harder to keep the doubts at bay.

Theodore said the blessing for the food, adding Betsy's request for the missing.

After prayers, Mrs. Baxley shook her head. "It is ridiculous what the fishermen are charging for their catch. Only the richest families can afford it. The others are having to resort to catching their own supper on top of trying to rebuild their lives. This snapper was five times the cost of last week."

Theodore's brow furrowed. "The laws of supply and demand would raise the price as there are fewer fishermen with boats able to supply the need, but that kind of increase does seem to be taking advantage of the situation."

Henry looked to his father. "Can the mayor do something about it?"

"I am sure he is trying to. If these things continue, he may be forced to declare martial law."

Emily frowned. "It's sad that we can't all work together to help each other."

Theodore nodded. "Under trying times such as these, it is natural instinct to be concerned for taking care of your own first. It is hard to be generous when there is so little."

Betsy's face was downcast. "I must admit my first thoughts were selfish when it came to the lumber from our house."

Henry frowned. "Mine too."

Emily dipped her head in shame. "I have felt the same about Momma giving away our food."

Betsy lifted her eyes to Theodore. "I am sure we will all do our best to be kind to others."

Abby spoke to them all. "I can give away what I have least of by remembering I cannot out give God. He will always provide more than I can give."

Theodore said, "Amen."

The meal was consumed in tired silence and afterwards they trudged across the island to the cemetery.

Mrs. Baxley broke away from the rest of the family to kneel beside her husband's grave. Abby sent Thorn after her to help her rise when she was done.

Reverend Richardson soon arrived and gathered them close to hold hands and pray. He then preached a lesson of endurance. "We should make ourselves like the palm trees. The strong ones may bend to the ground in the heavy wind, but they will once again stand up straight and be stronger for the trial. The weak ones will break or remain bent over unable to recover. We must strive to be strong under our burdens and remember to be kind and helpful to our neighbors. Let us pray."

The gathered bowed their heads to receive his prayer for their endeavors. It was followed by an announcement from the mayor listing some of the more urgent needs of the community along with reiterating the posted curfew and alcohol ban.

When the service ended, much as after church services, they broke into smaller groups to visit. Talk, however, centered on three subjects: their storm experience, comparisons of their current situation, and plans for the future. Most spoke of rebuilding better than before, but some planned to leave on the first available transport much to the disappointment of their friends and neighbors. Lydia's family was among those planning to leave. Emily was saddened by the news.

As the light began to dwindle, the islanders made their way home.

Henry and Emily trailed behind the others. He reached for her hand, needing the reassurance of more than just her presence. Emily pulled hers away with a concerned glance over her shoulder to see who may be watching. Her misty gray gaze turned to him. "We mustn't be so familiar."

"My apologies. I forget myself when I am with you."

Her mouth quirked. "You are forgiven." Her face turned serious. "I have been thinking of our conversation."

"Which one?"

"Moving to New York."

"Have you changed your mind?"

The hint of eagerness in his voice bothered her. "No. If anything, I am more determined. This place will never be the same."

"Emily, I know it is hard to see it now, but the island will return to normal. It will take time is all. If that is your only reason for leaving…"

She shook her head. "No, that is not the only reason. How could you think me to be so shallow?" She stormed off ahead of him.

Her childish actions were a sudden reminder; she was only seventeen. He trailed behind. He needed to find a way to talk privately with her to sort out her true desires. Did she really want to leave the island, or was she running from the ruins of her former life? There were too many in the house to find any place to have a moment alone.

Emily stormed up the stairs of the house and flopped face down across the counterpane of the bed she now shared with Brianna. What was wrong with her? She felt fretful, anxious and defensive for no reason. Henry asked a simple question, but she felt compelled to run, unable to provide an answer for what she was feeling. It was more than the devastation all around her. It was an urgent, undefined and unreasonable need for someplace new and different.

Her mother's presence in the room was soon felt with the dip of the mattress as she sat down at Emily's side. Her hand smoothed the hair from her crown to the back of her head.

"What is bothering you, dearest?"

Tears pricked Emily's eyes in reaction to her soothing tone. She impatiently wiped them away and turned her head to her mother. She felt trapped, unable to tell her everything but in desperate need to share something of her feelings. Her mother was visibly upset when longtime friends and neighbors announced they were leaving the island. Emily knew it would hurt her even more to know what she was contemplating with Henry. Besides, she and Henry agreed not to say anything until her father returned. She hated holding the secret from her mother.

"You know I was not always a wife and mother. Once, I was young like you. Headstrong and reckless and wanting more from life than what was in front of me. Mind you, there was nothing wrong with my life. In fact, I knew there were many who were envious. I had more freedom being a merchant's daughter than the noble debutantes. Being motherless and rich, I had less restrictions. In essence, I had all a young lady should want, including the attentions of a rather dashing lord. But I wanted more. I think you understand the feeling."

Emily was speechless. Her mother was describing her girlhood, but their feelings were the same. "I do."

"You are restless. Do you still want to marry Henry?"

"Yes. I love him with all my heart."

"Then it is this place."

Mutely, Emily nodded.

Abby couldn't bring herself to question her further. She knew the answers would be unsettling and worry over Max and Christoff was already weighing her down. She kissed Emily's forehead. "Don't do anything rash. I promise we will talk more once your father is home."

Abby drifted down the stairs lost in her thoughts. She encountered Henry at the bottom and an idea occurred to her. "Henry, did you not say your boat was spared and is still usable?"

"Yes, ma'am."

"I want you to do something for me."

"Of course."

"Emily is in need of a distraction. Could you take her sailing tomorrow or the next day?"

Henry's momentary excitement fled. "I'm afraid my boat only holds two. Maybe..."

"I understand. I will allow it this one time if you stay close to shore and promise to keep your hands to yourself."

Henry tried to hide the surprise of her unorthodox request. "I promise."

"Emily is feeling restless. Let her believe it is your idea. Maybe doing something a little risqué will satisfy her for now."

She walked away leaving Henry feeling bewildered and elated. He was suddenly looking forward to tomorrow.

Chapter 25

Thursday, October 15th

The bright light of morning shone across the polished dining room table to highlight a platter with stacks of pancakes and sliced ham, sitting next to a steaming bowl of fluffy scrambled eggs. The light poured through a glass bottle of maple syrup to touch the table with its amber glow on the other side. It was her family's favorite breakfast on special occasions. Her mouth watered as she waited for the blessing to end. As plates were heaped high with the succulent offering, around the table, her family talked with their usual enthusiasm. Her mother's cheeks glowed with vitality and her smile was bright. Emily followed its direction to her father whose eyes shone with the love he still strongly felt for his wife. Beside him Christoff, looking older and wiser, eagerly shared new stories of adventure with his younger brothers.

Emily's eyes opened.

She stretched and yawned still feeling the happiness surrounding her in her dream. It was shattered by reality as her hand came in contact with Brianna sleeping beside her. She sat up in bed confirming Agatha and Emmaline were on the floor and outside her window the once beautiful emerald green fronds of a royal palm were torn, ragged, and a dry brown. Her world was in reverse. Instead of waking from a nightmare to her idyllic home, she was waking from a dream to the devastating nightmare her world had become.

Her friends and neighbors were homeless, food was scarce, water was almost gone, the rotting stench of decay was becoming a constant and increasingly strident companion, and her father and brother were still missing. Tears pricked her eyes. She feared nothing would ever be as it was again.

Emmaline stirred in her sleep. Emily left her bed to brush a soothing hand over the little girl's head, hoping to soothe her nightmare. It was likely a lingering effect of yesterday when she found Agatha tormenting Emmaline and James, telling them the monster broke their house and knocked down all the trees they liked to play under. Emily could reason with Emmaline in the light of day, but she had to take James to his mother to get him to quit crying. Emily continued stroking the red-gold hair. She was pleased when a few moments later, the six year old was once again sleeping peacefully. It was still too early for the little ones to be awake. Dawn was just making its first appearance in the sky.

Emily dressed in a printed calico skirt and white shirtwaist. She tiptoed to the bedroom door, into the hall, and down the stairs. She opened the front door and from long practice slipped between the dual shuttered doors without a sound only to squeal in startled surprise as Henry's face materialized before her in the darkness of the porch. They both froze in breathless silence waiting to hear if any of the sleeping occupants within were disturbed. When no sound came to their ears, Henry gestured for her to proceed him to the end of the porch away from Mrs. Baxley's window.

Emily whispered, "What are you doing out here?"

"The same as you, I imagine."

"Then I am disturbing you. I should leave."

"You disturb me alright, but not in the way you mean."

Emily's heart raced at the compelling look in his eye. He reached out for her hand to draw her near. Her gaze dropped to his lips as they descended towards hers. Her mother's admonishments surfaced in her mind. She lifted her hand to push him away, but the warm feel of his rapid rising and falling chest kept her from doing so. She wanted this as much as he did. She understood now how girls could get in trouble. She closed her eyes as his lips touched hers, gentle at first, expecting her retreat, and then with increasing ardor as she returned the caress.

She felt bereft when he suddenly pulled away.

"Ah, Emily. Whatever are we going to do?"

She gazed at him in bewilderment.

"I lose all sense of reason when I'm near you."

"Then I should leave you." She turned from him.

"No." It came out a little more forceful than intended.

Emily froze.

"What I mean is, I want you to stay, but perhaps we should keep some space between us."

"How much space?"

"An arm's length at least."

She wanted to be able to touch him, but she supposed he was right. She moved back a step since he could not, standing as he was at the corner railing. They both turned to look towards the street.

Henry quietly said, "I'm sorry if I offended you yesterday."

Emily turned to him. "You didn't. I was being defensive. I'm sorry I walked away. It was immature of me."

"Why do you want to leave the island?"

"I want to see more, experience more of the world." She softly smiled. "With you."

"We could do that and still live here."

"You mean travel?"

"Yes."

"It's a lofty idea, but your mother, my mother, they never leave here. It seems to me like the everyday demands of life keep it from happening."

"So to avoid their same fate you want to live somewhere else."

"At least until I grow weary of it."

He laughed. "And how long do you suppose that will take?"

"I have no idea having never been anywhere else."

"How do you propose I make a living?"

She frowned. "I don't know. I'm sure you could find something."

He smiled. "I appreciate your faith in me."

"How could I not have faith in you? You have taken care of yourself ever since you left here."

His smile turned rueful. "That is not entirely true. I found out my father was enlisting the help of my uncles and his friends to keep watch over me."

"Maybe so, but they never had to actually help you, did they?"

He chuffed and grinned. "Not that I'm aware of."

"If you are opposed to New York, we could go to England. I would like to see where my mother is from."

"England?"

"Or maybe Ireland or Scotland. I love the way they speak."

He gave her a speculative look. "And do my wants not matter?"

Emily's face fell. She was being selfish again. She hadn't even considered his desires. "They do."

Henry stepped to her and took up both her hands. "I have just returned home and rediscovered my love of this island. I want to settle here."

Her heart sank. Her gaze fell to his hands to keep him from seeing her distress, but she couldn't keep the petulance from her voice. "So you don't want to leave."

"Let me finish." He waited for her eyes to meet his. "I want you to experience more of this world than this island and your uncle's plantation. I am suggesting we take a wedding holiday in New York and then we return here to build our life together. I don't mind visiting the city and the snow, but sweetheart, I don't want to live there."

"What of the other places?"

"Ocean voyages are expensive. I don't have that kind of money. At least not yet. One day I will. And when we have the money, I will take you everywhere your heart desires. You have but to say the word."

"You promise?"

"I promise, and I seal it with a kiss." He leaned in to kiss her, pulling back before passion could take hold again. The sweetness of her lips was hard to resist.

Emily smiled. Perhaps she could have all she desired.

Henry retreated to the corner railing. Kissing made him want things he couldn't have, at least not yet. And her vixen smile made it darn difficult not to kiss her again. He took a deep, calming breath and grasped for a mundane topic while he composed himself. "What are your plans for today?"

Emily watched the brightening sky behind him reveal the dark misshapen shapes of the once proud houses. It was a harsh reminder of their current situation. "I was thinking I would suggest to Momma that I could be of more help to the families at the barracks than at the hospital. Maybe I could watch over the children so the women could take care of chores or help their husbands. What about you?"

"Unless I am needed elsewhere, I expect I will be helping Father with the house and cistern."

Her gaze strayed again to the sky behind him. The morning gray was brushed with pink tinged clouds bringing to mind the seashell story her mother often told them as children of how the angels poked holes in the sky to watch over them, and the falling bits of sky became seashells. That was why the sky and shells often shared the same colors. She told it as a reminder that though apart, they were under the same sky and watched over by the angels. Emily needed to believe her father and brother were being watched over. She wished they would come home.

"I'm sure they're fine."

Emily turned a questioning gaze to Henry.

"You were thinking of your father and brother, were you not?"

"I was."

"Your father is the best sailor around. Remember when we were kids, he sailed home after a big hurricane with his ship mangled, the mast gone, a small cannon for an anchor, and he still managed to salvage a ship to boot."

Emily gave him a ghost of a smile. "I remember. Momma was beside herself then waiting for his return, and she grows more anxious as each day passes." Her gaze turned intense. "Last time it took him four days to return. Today is the fourth day. What if this time..."

"Shh. You have to hold on to hope." He reached out for her hands holding them downwards between them. "We will pray he returns today."

Emily bowed her head, closed her eyes, and listened to Henry's dear voice praying for her father and brother and their safe return. She lifted her heart to the Lord echoing Henry's plea.

They raised their heads from prayer to hear the sounds of their families stirring inside.

"We should go in." Henry opened the door for Emily to proceed him inside.

Twenty minutes later they were all gathered around the table as Mrs. Baxley placed a steaming bowl of oatmeal next to the last jar of honey. They each had a mere quarter cup of water as this morning's ration. They bowed their heads as Theodore led them in prayer.

"Lord we offer thanks for all the blessings you have bestowed upon those gathered at this table. Please help us to better follow Your Son's example as we work through this trying time. Lord, please watch over our loved ones still missing and guide them safely home. In Your name, we pray for the needs of all the islanders."

"Amen," was echoed around the table.

Abby dished out each meager portion of oatmeal.

As Betsy took a bowl from Abby to pass down the table she said, "I was thinking the boys could spend the morning fishing for conch. I could make a modified version of my conch chowder with the ingredients we have, perhaps enough for our dinner and to share with the patients at the Marine Hospital."

Abby nodded. "It would be appreciated. They have hardly had anything to eat."

Henry looked skeptical. "I'm not sure how many conch can be found. The grassy beds we usually find them in were torn apart by the storm. They will likely be difficult to locate."

Thorn spoke up. "Difficult but certainly not impossible. I'm sure we can find them."

Nate nearly rose out of his chair in excitement. "I want to help."

Brianna eagerly added, "I can help too."

Betsy turned to her eldest. "Brianna, I'm sorry, but I need your help with washing clothes." She hated seeing the crestfallen look on her daughter's face but couldn't help the wash of pride in her as she put her feelings aside and gracefully accepted the task at hand.

When the meal was finished, Henry, Thorn, and Nate eagerly left on their fishing expedition. Brianna and Agatha helped clear the table while Mrs. Baxley set about boiling salt water to wash the dishes and the clothes.

Emily followed Abby to the foyer. "Momma."

Abby turned to Emily as she donned her bonnet. "What is it dear?"

"Would you mind if I volunteered to help at the barracks instead of the hospital? When I was there with Mrs. Wall it seemed as if the mothers might need help watching the children."

Abby ran a gloved hand down the side of Emily's face. "I know how much you dislike the hospital. Might I suggest you spend the morning helping Mrs. Whitmore with the laundry and making chowder and go to the barracks after dinner?"

Emily eagerly nodded her agreement, relieved to be released from the hospital. "Yes, ma'am."

Abby finished adjusting her glove. She kissed Emily on the forehead. "I am proud of you for wanting to help others and not just doing as I ask."

Emily relished her mother's praise as she watched her slip out the front door. Emily turned in time to follow Brianna up the stairs to gather the dirty clothes, returning with two large, overflowing baskets. Agatha had charge of Jacob and James until the wash water was ready and then Mrs. Baxley would take over minding the boys.

In the dining room, Betsy and Theodore were momentarily alone still sitting next to each other at the table.

Betsy asked, "What are your plans for today?"

"I think I will take a walk into town first."

She smiled having expected his answer. Even though he couldn't print his paper, he still needed to know what was going on around town. "When will you start cleaning up your office?"

"I don't know. I feel as if the house needs to be finished first. Besides, I can't print anything until I can get a shipment of paper." Theodore took up her hand to soothingly rub his thumb across her knuckles. "I know you are disappointed to be pulled away from the house again."

"I am, but the needs of many outweigh those of the few. After speaking with Esperanza yesterday, I felt I had to do something to ease the suffering. Making chowder is the least I can do for others."

"Your generous heart is one of the things I love most about you."

She bowed her head and shook it. "You are far more giving than I. I would not have offered our lumber."

"Yes, you would. Maybe not as quickly, but you would not hold onto a stack of lumber for us to rebuild someday knowing a family's house could be made secure today with the offering."

"You're right, I couldn't. You do know me well."

"Hmm."

Betsy laid her head against his shoulder. "I hope we can finish work on the house before the rain comes. On the other hand, we need rain more than we need our belongings."

Theodore said, "Our needs are so many they fight against each other."

"They do indeed. I wonder how long it will take to get back to some sense of normality."

James came running into the room, having escaped from his sister's watchful eye. He crawled into his father's lap from under the table. His antics lightened the somber mood of the room. Theodore scooted his chair back to allow room for his little boy to bounce on his lap under the indulgent smiles of his parents. They were grateful for the small carefree moment.

* * *

Emily dumped the last bucket of dirty salt water, glad that the laundry was finally done. She straightened from her task stretching the kink out of her back from bending over the wash buckets for so long. Even with five of them working on it – herself, Mrs. Whitmore, and Henry's three sisters – it took all morning. Fresh water was so scarce there was none to spare for the laundry. Everything, including their underwear, had to be washed and rinsed in salt water. Agatha and Emmaline were hanging the clothes on the line. The material felt fine now, but once dried, it was going to be stiff and itchy adding further discomfort to their miserable situation. She looked up at the cloudless sky as she waved away an annoying mosquito and sent another prayer heavenward for rain.

She returned the empty buckets to the kitchen where Mrs. Whitmore was gathering ingredients for the chowder. "What can I do to help?"

Betsy handed her the carrots and potatoes. "Would you mind dicing these?"

"Not at all." Emily accepted them noticing the empty bin behind her from which they came.

Betsy grimaced. "I know. I'm afraid that's the last of the root vegetables. You're mother said we should share them and have faith the Lord will provide for us."

"That sounds like her, and it's something you would do. I'm not sure my faith is strong enough. I see that empty bin and worry about what we will eat tomorrow."

"Do you believe Jesus multiplied the bread and fish to feed the crowd?"

"I do."

"But you don't believe he would take care of us?"

"I suppose I have doubts because I don't feel worthy."

"Do you think all of those people he fed were worthy, that there were not those among them undeserving?"

"I suppose in a crowd there would have to have been some who didn't deserve it."

"Jesus often chose the unworthy for his lessons, did he not?"

Emily nodded. "He did."

"He only required their faith."

"So I must have faith."

"Yes. Even if it is only the size of a mustard seed."

Emily smiled wryly. "I have at least that much faith." Her expression sobered. "I will strive to grow it."

Emily turned her gaze towards the doorway having heard the boys approaching. Henry caught sight of her and held aloft a conch, wildly grinning, conveying the success of their morning fishing. He, Thorn and Nate brought in six buckets full of conch.

Betsy smiled. "Well done. Those should make a hearty chowder." She handed two empty buckets to Nate. "I need you to run these over to the Keats and ask them for water. Mrs. Keats promised they could spare enough for the chowder."

"Yes, ma'am." Nate took off at a run, eager to do her bidding.

Betsy turned to Emily. "See. The Lord provides. They left thinking they would have a hard time finding any and they brought back plenty."

Emily smiled. "Not a mustard seed anymore."

Henry took up a position at the table across from Emily. He picked a conch out of the bucket and took up the knife and hammer laying nearby to begin preparing the meat. Thorn stood next to him ready to take on the next step in the process once Henry pulled the animal from its shell. Betsy gave them both a grateful smile before resuming her task of chopping the dried herbs. By the time Nate returned with the water, all but the conch was ready to go into two pots hanging over the stoked fire. To the vegetables, herbs, and water, Betsy added canned tomatoes and finally the conch. It was a watered down version of her usual recipe, but it would help nourish many.

Theodore, returning from town, called out from the yard, "I'm back."

Anxious to hear the news, Betsy left Brianna in charge of stirring the simmering pots while she, Henry and Emily went to meet him in the yard.

Henry noted the grim look about his father's mouth about the same time menacing tendrils of acrid smoke drifted into the yard.

Emily lifted her apron to her cover her nose and mouth. "Not again."

Henry held back the bile rising in his throat.

Theodore said, "The mayor directed the army to burn all the dead animals. There was a cow this side of Geiger's yard."

The wind shifted, momentarily bringing relief from the burning cow. It carried with it the now familiar sourness of marine life rotting on the beaches and decaying vegetation.

"The sheriff has his hands full. As expected, the grog shop owners are protesting the mayor's ban on alcohol, and he is having trouble controlling the looting despite the curfew."

Betsy said, "He had to have expected their reaction."

Theodore said, "Expecting and being prepared for it are two different things. I'm not sure he can lay claim to the latter. He is being hounded by hungry citizens too. There is so little food left on the island. On a lighter note, Mr. Tift has reopened his dry goods and Mr. Patterson is nearly ready to reopen."

Henry and Emily turned happy smiles to each other.

Betsy said, "That is good news. Now all we need is supply ships to restock the shelves."

Theodore said, "They will come."

Betsy said, "Has there been any word of the *Mystic*."

Somberly Theodore shook his head.

A short while later Abby returned home for dinner and to help Betsy carry the conch chowder to the hospital afterwards. As they rose from the table after finishing their repast, Henry offered to escort Emily to the barracks.

They followed the same path Emily took with Mrs. Wall just two days ago. It felt more like a week to Emily. It was a miserable walk through rank rushes, shimmering heat, blazing sun, and mosquitoes. Gone was the island's mantel of green. Everywhere she looked was a depressing brown. It filled her with an overwhelming desire to escape.

Emily's unusual quiet concerned Henry. "Penny for your thoughts." It was a moment before she turned her attention to him. It was obvious she heard his voice but not his words. "What is troubling you?" He offered his hand to help her over a fallen tree.

"Don't you wish you could get away from this?"

"Away from what?"

"I want to be somewhere where everything isn't torn apart; where there's enough food and water; where I don't risk stepping on someone when getting in and out of bed."

Henry stopped and turned to her. "Emily, this is all temporary. Every day there is progress made in rebuilding. It will rain again and fill the cisterns. Food will arrive soon. You just have to hold on a little longer. Things will be better."

"That hurricane took everything."

Anger surged within him. She hadn't lost her house like he and so many others had. She wasn't going to have to struggle to rebuild her livelihood like he and his father and so many others were going to have to do. Why was she so angry? "You have not lost everything, Emily." His voice trailed away. "Not like others have."

"Oh, Henry. That's what I mean. Of course you and so many others have lost more than I have. And what is the point of rebuilding if another hurricane is going to come along and take it all away again? It seems so hopeless."

"Is that the real reason you want to live elsewhere?"

"I suppose."

"You'll just be running to other problems. Everyplace has its trials. You're just worn down right now." He gave her a mischievous smile. "Come with me." He grabbed her hand and turned them away from the barracks.

She laughed, infected by his excitement. "Where are we going?"

"For a sail."

"Sailing? What about helping your father? I'm supposed to be helping the families."

Henry continued to pull her along following the northern shore. "You need a new perspective on things." In his excitement, he set a hurried pace until they reached the edge of town where he slowed to a more dignified brisk walk side by side.

Emily's spirits dropped a little more as they passed the ruins of the Episcopal Church. They sank even further as they crossed the empty lots where Mr. Curry's house once stood on their right and the old pirate shack on their left, both washed out to sea. A shiver ran down her back as she gazed out over the water where storm stranded ships still lingered, forlorn and abandoned. They rounded the bend in the coast and came to where Henry's storage shed once stood.

While Henry checked on the sponges he left drying two days ago, Emily studied the changes wrought by the storm. The nearby footbridge on

Simonton used for crossing the pond's tidal egress was gone, but it mattered not. The stream that fed the tidal pond was filled with sand swept inland by the storm. The captive water behind the town was now stagnant. Emily's nose wrinkled as the breeze brought a whiff of the briny backwater filled with rotting botany. Emily wondered how long it would take for her once beautifully garbed island to recover. The awful browning left by the passing storm hurt to behold. It was as if a piece of her soul was taken too and in need of healing growth.

The clang of the blacksmith's hammer drew her attention. Where once the roof of his open shed protected him, he now labored under the blazing sun. The covering was yet another casualty of the storm. The remains of it lay in a nearby pile he appeared to be using to feed his forge. At least his house was still standing, albeit missing its roof as well. In the distance, Emily could discern the busy sounds of the shop owners and tradesmen hard at work rebuilding their businesses along the wharf.

"Emily."

She turned to find Henry waiting to assist her into the boat at the water's edge. She didn't spare a thought for impropriety as she eagerly walked towards him anxious to enjoy the smooth glide of the boat as it cut through the sparkling water under the mid-October sky. Away from shore with Henry's sure strokes sending the boat headlong through the salty breeze, Emily finally found some relief to the oppressive heat that lingered over the island since the storm's passing. She turned her face to the wind, closed her eyes, and let the cooling sensation ease her worried mind. When she opened them again, her gaze fell to the water and the blurry images of coral and fish passing beneath them. Neither seemed as abundant as before.

She turned in her seat to face Henry. "Thank you." He gave her a questioning look. "You were right. Coming out here is a peaceful rest from everything." Her eyes drifted to the shoreline surprised to discover they were far away. "Didn't you promise my mother to keep close to shore?"

"You overheard us?"

"Yes."

"No wonder you didn't offer any protest." Henry stopped rowing and allowed the boat to drift. The wind died down leaving the water's surface as smooth as glass. He rested on the oars crossed over his knees.

"I doubt I would have made a protest regardless. I am always eager to spend time with you."

Henry regarded her open smile. "I hope you wouldn't sail off with just anyone."

"Of course not. Only my betrothed."

"I am relieved to hear that."

Emily looked around them. "The water is so still."

"It makes it easy to see the bottom." He leaned a little to the left to study the corals. Torn elkhorn, staghorn, and fan corals lay strewn across the bottom but fortunately the deeper coral did not suffer as drastically. Schools of fish swam by giving further encouragement of life continuing on after the storm.

Emily leaned on her elbows as she peered over the port bow. The colorful fish captured her attention first, but she soon took notice of the damage wrought by the storm. She sat up and turned her distressed gaze to Henry. "Even here we cannot get away from the destruction. What about the sponges Henry? Are there still sponges for you to fish?"

He shrugged. "I haven't seen many yet, but there are other places they were more prevalent. I pray they still are."

"We should look while we are out here."

Her blue gaze met his with earnest appeal. Knowing she would not release the idea he slipped the paddles into the water and deftly turned the boat around to sail across the north side of the island. They were silent as they passed by the numerous abandoned ships, victims of the storm surge as it first pushed them northward before dragging them back south to be caught and held fast by the shoals. Henry's mouth was grim as he approached the sponge beds.

"You're afraid of what you might find."

Henry's eyes snapped to Emily. He was surprised she read his thoughts so easily. "If the sponges are gone and the fort isn't rebuilt, I don't know what I'll do for work."

"I am sure there are plenty of opportunities to find work in a big city."

He forcefully pulled on the oars. They popped out of the water. He impatiently swung them forward and dug deep into the water. Tension tightened in his shoulders, and his mouth was grimly set. "You are speaking of New York."

Hearing his tone, Emily's good humor evaporated.

Henry pierced her with his gaze, but he tried to keep his tone neutral. "It doesn't matter to you that I have said I don't want to live there again?"

"It doesn't seem to matter to you that I don't want to live here anymore."

"I thought we settled this the other day. We would live here and travel as we can."

"You settled it. I suppose I have yet to resign myself to your decision." For the first time she felt the bonds of being a woman. To marry Henry meant submitting to his will. If he wanted to stay she would have no choice. But to not marry him would hurt just as much, and she would still be stuck on this island.

Having reached the largest sponge bed, Henry lifted the paddles from the water, but his grip remained tight upon the handles as he tried to contain an angry retort to her declaration. Why must she be disagreeable? He counted to ten as his mother taught him. It didn't help. Leaving this island again after rediscovering his love for it was unthinkable. He would not do it.

He looked up to meet her gaze intent upon telling her so, but her distress stopped him.

"Henry, I don't want to fight with you." She didn't want to give up her dream of leaving the island, but Henry was more important to her happiness. Having him angry with her was not something she knew how to handle.

"I don't want to fight either." The sadness in her eyes struck deep in his heart. Above all else he wanted her to be happy. "If it means so much to you, I'll give more consideration to leaving." Henry was pleased to see her face light up with joy. He was pleased to be the cause of her radiant smile. Dragging his eyes from Emily's, he glanced over the boat rim hoping to find treasure beneath the undulating water. The broken and torn corals were not encouraging. They skimmed over the water and where normally he would have found several sponges, he found none. Leaving may be a foregone conclusion if he could not provide for them. He lifted sad eyes to his beloved.

"No sponges?"

Henry gave a slight shake to his head.

"I'm sorry."

"I brought you out here to lift your spirits. It seems I have failed."

"Maybe we should try deeper water."

Henry glanced at the sun's position. "Perhaps another day. We should get back. There's too much to be done for us to be gone so long." He smiled. "Besides, your nose is turning pink."

Emily self-consciously raised a hand to her face.

Henry set to work on the paddles, easily bringing them in to shore at the army camp. He got out, pulled the boat up on shore, and offered Emily a hand. He walked her to the barracks and saw her settled to watch over the children for the afternoon. He promised to come back to walk her home for supper.

As Henry walked back to his little boat, he tried to resign himself to having to leave the island to find work. His heart protested, but he was afraid, in the end, he wouldn't have a choice. He pushed the boat into the water and jumped aboard. He set to rowing, frustration adding power to his strokes.

He had to work to support a wife and to provide a place to live. In New York, they had the choice of his father's house or Aunt Agatha's. But how could he stand living in the city? He spent the last four years on the frontier under the open sky, and these last few months gave him a new appreciation for Key West and the open waters surrounding it. The confines of the city would be tortuous to his soul. What kind of work could he do? He wasn't a businessman. He supposed with his experience with the rangers, he could find work as a lawman.

He soon returned to his starting point. He tied up his boat and trudged through town with a heavy heart.

Chapter 26

Henry arrived at the fallen house to find his family steadily piling their belongings on the borrowed cart. Brianna paused to swat a mosquito and was first to notice him. "Hello, Henry."

Betsy turned from the cart and wiped a sleeve across her brow. She smiled at Henry. "Did you have a good sail with Emily?"

Not wanting to share his disturbing thoughts with his family, he simply nodded, then he frowned. Had everyone overheard Mrs. Eatonton's request? He turned towards the house to see his father handing more items to his sisters through a downstairs window. He looked in need of a break. Henry grabbed a canteen and climbed inside the window his mother and sister used the other day. He handed the water to his father. "Let me take over for a while."

Theodore pulled a sweat dampened handkerchief from his pocket and wiped his face. He gratefully accepted the water realizing how tired he truly was in the first moment he was still since eating lunch several hours ago. "Don't move the bookcase."

"I know. It's holding up the rest of the floor above."

"We are thinking of foregoing the rest of the furniture. Everything that has gotten wet will soon be too moldy to keep."

Henry noticed the desk drawers were open but not much had been taken from them. "What about your papers?" He picked up a few pages lying on top of the desk and discovered they had gotten so wet they were stuck together.

"There's nothing in there that really matters. The estate solicitor has a set of all the legal documents for our New York holdings. I've taken anything else of importance. I've been retrieving all that can be saved from the front rooms."

"Have you looked in the back? I think we can get through the doorway in the parlor."

"Now that you're here, we can try."

Betsy's voice came from the window. "You two be careful. There is nothing in this house worth either of you getting hurt."

Theodore grinned. "So says the woman who has been insisting for days there is something valuable in need of saving."

Betsy frowned. "I know and I still feel that way, but whatever it is, is not worth either of you getting hurt."

Henry reached through the window to squeeze her hand. "We will be careful, mother."

The two men cautiously searched the back rooms. They handed out the knick-knacks and belongings that could be saved, which included most of the hand-painted china in the dining room. Only the pieces kept on top of the china cabinet were lost to the collapsed ceiling. The last room to be searched was the parlor. The back corner of the house had collapsed leaving the ceiling in this room slanting downward to a mere few feet from the floor. Henry crawled through the twisted doorway leading from the hall into the parlor.

The room reeked of mold. His lungs tightened in revolt. Other than the books in his father's office, the upholstered furniture in this room absorbed the most water accounting for the higher mold content. Mrs. Eatonton's repeated stories of mold sickness had him pulling a handkerchief from his pocket to hold over his nose. He wished he had his bandana instead. His father handed over his handkerchief and by tying the two together he could secure them to his face to leave his hands free.

From his forced crouched position, he turned to take the lantern from his father. Shining it into the depths revealed the overturned tea table in the center of the room. The painted glass oil lamp once placed prominently in its center lay shattered across the floor. He swung the light towards the low side of the room to find the settee and wing backed chairs now crushed into a space the height of the coffee table. He crawled towards them careful not to place his hands or knees on broken glass. Judging from the dirty residue on the tables, the water had risen higher than their surface. He didn't find much to save on this side of the room other than a brass candlestick and a box of tapers. He grabbed the sewing basket by his mother's chair in the hopes something could be saved from it, perhaps at least the needles. He left the lantern in the center of the room far from the spilled lamp and crawled back out with his finds, passing them on to his father. Seeing his eyes light up, Henry grew hopeful.

When Henry handed him Betsy's knitting basket, Theodore thought he had found the elusive important item they were to save for he knew how she valued her tortoiseshell knitting needles. He was disappointed when Betsy lightly smiled and added them to the cart without comment. Returning to Henry, he shook his head.

Feeling let down, Henry turned around to retrieve the lamp and see what else he could find. His mother didn't hold value in too many possessions. She liked beautiful things, but she treasured her family. The jewelry box from her room was already saved which held her more sentimental items. He was at a loss as to what important item they had yet to find. He held the lamp aloft to the opposing wall, passing the light over the gaming table and chairs, the liqueur cabinet, his father's rocking chair, and a wrought iron floor candelabra. He moved to the cabinet to search the drawers. He saw many small items so he pulled the drawers out and stacked them to take to his father. He then grabbed the candelabra and the matching one from the adjacent corner.

Next, he moved to inspect his mother's secretary bookcase. He could fully stand in front of it. Lifting the lantern high showed the ceiling well above the piece sparing it from damage. It would be worth saving but

Henry wasn't sure how they could get it out of the room. He opened the desk lid and perused the contents but found nothing of great value except the inkwell and two bundles of old letters—one from her family in Pennsylvania and the other from his father while he was away during the Seminole war.

He cast the lantern light back towards the doorway and gasped as it passed over the sideboard.

His sketches!

He rushed to them, anxiously brushing the fallen plaster and dust from the leather cover of the portfolio. The height and raised sides of the sideboard spared it from most of the water. He lovingly rubbed his hand across the cover before lifting it to his chest. His eyes closed in a silent prayer of thanksgiving. When he opened them, he beheld a sight even more satisfying. The family Bible lay beneath his portfolio. He was sure this was the item his mother longed for with its record of family births and deaths. He gathered it up along with his cloth roll of charcoals and pencils. He eagerly swapped these items for the empty wooden crate his father held out for gathering other smaller items.

"This must be what mother is looking for."

Theodore ran his hand over the elaborately engraved leather cover. "I believe you're right."

"Some of the furniture can be saved if we can figure out a way to get it out of this room."

Theodore said, "It will be difficult. We may have to..."

A shout from the street drew their attention. "Ship ashore."

Henry's eyes met his father's and in them he saw the same building hope he had that help had finally arrived. They hurried to the window as Betsy called out to them. She smiled broadly when she caught sight of the Bible. "You found it."

Theodore handed it over to her. "Is that the important item?" He climbed out of the window. Henry followed.

Betsy clutched the Good Book to her chest as her eyes fell to the other items he carried. "Yes, this and Henry's drawings. The rest is of no consequence."

The bright sunshine was a shock to Henry's eyes after being in the cave-like room. He pulled the handkerchiefs from his face and took several gulps of fresh air to clear his lungs of the moldy aftermath. His mother approached clutching the Bible to her chest. He leaned down for her to bestow a kiss on his cheek.

"Thank you."

Henry smiled, relieved to have found the important item at last and glad he was able to make his mother happy. In the midst of their hardships, even the smallest of good was cause to rejoice. "Did we hear right? There's a ship ashore?"

Brianna nodded. "Yes. Several people have hurried by already."

Theodore asked Betsy, "Can you and the girls watch over our belongings while Henry and I go to the wharf to find out what kind of ship has arrived? If there is food, it would not be wise to delay."

Betsy waved them away. "Yes, yes. We will be fine. Hurry back if you can."

Theodore felt torn between leaving them in the hopes of gaining food and water and staying because he hated to leave them alone with the burden of securing their belongings. "Send Brianna to bring back the boys to help you get the cart home."

Betsy gave him a stern look. "We can manage. You need to go."

Henry and Theodore approached the angry crowd surrounding the custom collector, Stephen Mallory. It was soon evident word had gotten around there was food on the ship. Mr. Mallory pushed his way to the wharf where he took the step up onto the weathered boards, turned, and held his hands up to the gathering. The shipping manifest fluttered in the clutches of his right hand. An uneasy hush fell over the bevy.

"I realize we are all struggling to find enough to eat, but there is nothing on this ship to be distributed. These goods belong to Mr. Patterson."

Around them the noises escalated from groans to expletives to loud arguments. The crowd surged forward.

Sheriff Coslin stepped up beside Mr. Mallory. "I will have order in these streets. There is nothing here for you. Go home." He raised his voice to be heard. "And don't rush over to Mr. Patterson's. He needs time to stock his shelves. You can make your purchases tomorrow."

Grumblings from the crowd rose to accusations thrown at the two men of authority.

"What are we supposed to do for food?"

"What about those of us who have lost all our money?"

"How do we feed our families?"

"When will there be more food and water?"

When those answers weren't forthcoming, the angry mob turned on each other. A man standing in front of Henry raised his fist at his neighbor standing nearby.

"My family's needs are greater than yours. You have more than we do. I've seen you hoarding cocoanuts from your yard when you had plenty to share."

"Those are my cocoanuts. I have every right to collect them."

Henry and his father moved at the same time to step between the two men.

Theodore held each man's gaze in turn. His voice was firm and compelling. "Gentlemen. We are all suffering. Let's not take our frustrations out on each other."

Henry was amazed how his father was able to diffuse the men. With that situation under control, Henry followed his Ranger instincts and made his way to stand beside the sheriff in a show of support. His father followed and calm followed in his wake. The people of the town respected his father. He took up a position on the other side of the wharf next to Mr. Mallory. Mayor Maloney soon arrived. Mr. Mallory stepped back allowing the mayor to step up and address the crowd.

"Quiet everyone. Quiet." He waited for obedience. "I know you are suffering. We all are to some degree or another. I have sent word out far and away appealing for aid. More ships should arrive soon. Please have patience. Mr. Patterson has assured me he will open his store at the usual time in the morning to sell what he has. In the interest of all, I have asked him to limit how much each person may purchase. Anyone who disputes him should bring your complaint to me. Any misconduct in his store will result in forfeiture of any purchase. I hope you understand.

"As some of you are aware, the army has a detail helping to clean cisterns starting on the north side of town. They will work them in order from north to south. If you are in need of assistance in cleaning your cistern please be patient and wait for them to get to you.

"On another note, I am asking every able-bodied male to provide their help tomorrow in moving the disinterred from the old cemetery on the southern beach to the new cemetery. We will be starting at ten in the morning. Come as soon as you are able. There will be an army detail to dig the new graves. Those who arrive early with family members to be moved will have first choice of location."

When the mayor paused, a voice in the crowd rose up. "Mayor Maloney, what does the council plan to do about the stagnant water in the tidal pond?"

Mayor Maloney said, "Mr. O'Hara, the topic has come up, but I'm afraid a decision has not been made what with all the other pressing matters we are dealing with."

Another voice in the crowd asked, "How many fishing vessels are working?"

Stephen Mallory stepped forward to answer. "We have three sailing now and hope to have two more repaired by weeks' end. People, have patience just a little bit longer. Our regular supply ships are due in and relief aid should soon follow."

The mayor continued answering questions even after the crowd began to disperse. Most people were seeking reassurance their needs had been heard and something was being done. After witnessing the near violence today, Henry had his concerns for tomorrow's crowd at Mr. Patterson's store. Apparently, the sheriff did too. He approached Henry. "I can see your thoughts are similar to mine."

"How so?"

"You think there may be trouble tomorrow."

Henry nodded.

"With your military background, I could use your help. Would you be interested in swearing in as a temporary deputy?"

Henry was surprised by the request. The idea of being involved in law enforcement on the island had never crossed his mind. "Wouldn't someone older hold more authority?"

"Not necessarily. The secret is to command authority. Besides, your family's situation is stable. They can spare you. Most of the other men are too busy meeting basic needs for their families to be spared."

'What do you need me to do?"

"Meet me at Patterson's store at sunrise. I will swear you in then. Do you have a gun?"

"Yes, sir."

"Good. Bring it. I sincerely pray we won't come to need them but desperate men can be volatile."

Henry nodded. In his time with the Rangers, he had seen men do unimaginable things, bringing them to the attention of the Rangers and even more so to avoid being caught or attempting to escape once captured. There was every likelihood of trouble tomorrow with so many hungry and not enough food to go around and those without money to pay. He sincerely hoped tomorrow would not come to violence.

The sheriff was being called away so the two men shook hands and parted ways as Henry's father approached having left him to speak with the mayor. Henry answered the question in Theodore's gaze. "Sheriff Coslin asked me to be a deputy."

"Hmm."

Henry frowned. *What did that sound mean?* "Do you approve?"

Theodore had turned to head back to the house but turned back to face his son. He placed a reassuring hand upon his son's shoulder. "I do. You are a good choice for the position. Now, let's go. We still have much work to get done."

Henry's shoulders rose with pride. His father's praise affected him deeply. They walked side by side back to the house in companionable silence to find the rest of the family and the cart were gone. They climbed into the house, returning to the slanted parlor.

"It's too late to worry with the furniture. Fill up the crate with what you can, and we'll head home. We still need to build a shed."

"Yes sir." Henry took up the crate and pulled more items from the china cabinet and as much as he could take from the secretary, being careful to secure the inkwell so it wouldn't turn over. The letter bundles were placed on top. His father was waiting at the opening to take the crate from him. Henry retrieved the lantern and regretfully left the room.

Outside the house, Henry glanced at the sun's position in the western sky. They had only a few hours of daylight left. While his father carried the crate and lantern, Henry retrieved more of the salvaged lumber to take back to the house for the shed.

The next few hours were spent quickly constructing a rough storage building. With the help of the Eatonton boys, the frame rapidly came together. The roof height was eight feet in the front sloping down to six feet in the rear. Dusk was fast approaching so as soon as the roof was covered, Henry left the others working on the siding as he took up the lantern, lit it from a taper in the kitchen, and left them to escort Emily home for dinner.

It was a very tired Henry who cut across the island to the army base in the gathering darkness. Emily eagerly met him at the door of the barracks. He waited till they were outside the fortifications to ask her, "How was your day?"

Emily's voice overlapped his with the same question. They laughed which helped relieve the tensions of the day. Emily said, "You first."

"I found my sketch book."

"Oh, Henry, that's wonderful news. And it wasn't harmed?"

"Miraculously it was just out of reach of the water. I also found the family Bible underneath, which made my mother happy. It was the one important item she was anxious to find."

"I am glad to hear your family has more of your treasured belongings restored."

"I have one more bit of news. Sheriff Coslin asked me to swear in as a deputy tomorrow."

Pride, fear, and concern flew through her mind before she could find the words to respond. "I suppose it is an honor for you to be asked."

"It is."

"Did you accept?"

"I did. He is going to need help to manage the crowds at Mr. Patterson's store tomorrow."

"Is he expecting violence?"

"We hope to prevent any with a show of strength. People are hungry, and while Mr. Patterson received a shipment of dry goods today, it is not enough for everyone."

Emily didn't like to think of Henry putting himself in harm's way, but she knew he wouldn't change his mind now after accepting Sheriff Coslin's offer. Henry's pride would not allow it. All she could do was pray no harm would come to him.

Henry grew concerned at Emily's lingering silence. He helped her over a now familiar downed tree in their path. "How was your day?"

"Keeping watch over dozens of children is tiring enough. Trying to keep them occupied as well is even worse. After playing all the games we could think of, we took to inventing new ones. It would have been nice to at least have a ball or some hoops."

Childhood memories broadened Henry's smile.

"What are you grinning about?"

"You."

Emily's face fell. Surely he wasn't laughing at her.

"You know what I love about you?"

She shook her head, but her spirits lightened. Whatever he was thinking must be good. One didn't laugh at a person they loved.

"Your daring, determined, fearlessly stubborn spirit."

"Whatever do you mean?"

"Your determination to keep the children occupied today reminded me of your determination to follow me as a child."

"I recall you inventing some pretty dangerous games trying to get me to stay home."

Henry chortled. "But you never did."

"I should have when you and your friends started taking chances swimming on the deep side of the reef with the big sharks or playing underwater tag around the fire coral."

"You were good at that game. We never could catch you. Do you remember that day Franklin and I were daring each other to climb the gumbo-limbo tree? Neither of us were willing, and then you burst out of the bushes saying you could do it. You started up the tree before we could stop you, and you were so determined you didn't stop till you were sitting on the highest branch looking down at us gloating. When you came down your dress was a mess."

Emily was smiling more because of Henry's humor than for the recollection. "It took me a week to get all the sticky sap off my knees. The dress and shoes were ruined. Momma was furious with me."

"It's that same determination that has you able to help your mother at the hospital even though you hate it."

The admiration in his voice warmed her spirit. That he understood how difficult it was for her to work in the hospital made her feel appreciated. Softly she said, "Do you know what I love most about you?" The lantern light barely reached his face, so she couldn't see his features, but she felt him waiting for her to answer her own question. "I love that you love me. After so many years of yearning for a return of your affection, the fact that you do so now is precious."

They had reached the front porch. Henry pulled Emily to a halt next to the bare stems of the rose bush. "I'm sorry you had to wait so long, but I suppose the timing is for the best. You were too young before I left. Our affection could not be shared equally as it is now, for now you love as a woman not as an infatuated girl."

"I was never simply infatuated with you."

The front door opened bringing an abrupt end to the conversation. Light from inside spilled around Thorn. "Oh there you are. Momma asked me to look for you."

Emily gave her brother a saucy look. "Well here we are."

"Good. Supper's on the table."

Emily found herself ushered into the house between Henry and

Thorn. Her brother spoke over his shoulder. "I went out crabbing for our supper, wound up spearing a redfish."

Henry said, "Thank goodness. I'm starving."

Emily said, "It smells heavenly."

Talk around the dinner table was mostly sharing news of the day.

Abby said, "Three new cases of mold sickness came in today and one possible case of typhoid fever."

Theodore's gaze sharpened on her. "That sounds serious."

"It is. The last thing we need is an epidemic."

Betsy asked, "How can it be avoided?"

"Clean water would be most helpful."

Theodore said, "The ships are due back tomorrow with water from the upper keys."

Henry said, "That is if water can be found." He received reproachful looks from both his parents. They did not believe in voicing doubts, preferring instead to maintain a positive outlook, especially for the younger children.

Abby broke the tension by engaging her daughter. "Emily, how was your day at the barracks? Was it better than helping at the hospital?"

"For the most part, yes. It was more tiring. I did my best to keep the children entertained."

Betsy said, "Children are exhausting, especially in multiples."

Emily said, "Mrs. Keats was there. She and her mother spent most of the day helping the ladies wash and mend clothes."

Betsy asked, "Did they finish or will more help be needed tomorrow?"

"I believe they finished."

Henry asked, "Do you plan to return tomorrow?"

Emily's response was less than enthusiastic. "I suppose so."

Theodore said, "How are the families faring?"

"They were doing well I suppose, all things considered, but tempers were occasionally frayed with the lack of food and water and tight living space."

Betsy nodded. "It's to be expected."

Abby let the silence stretch out for a moment before asking, "Theodore, did you by chance hear of a wrecker making port? I heard rumors of it at the hospital."

"I did. It arrived shortly before the supply ship, dropped off salvages from a brig stranded near Bahia Honda and one of its passengers, a Commander Sloat. The captain said there were a lot of wrecks up that way but none were the *Mystic*."

Abby dropped her eyes to her plate to hide her worry.

Emily reached out to lay a hand on her mother's arm, giving it a gentle squeeze.

The others around the table pretended not to notice.

When they were done eating, Theodore said to Betsy, "I'll be back in a little while."

"Where are you going?"

"To interview Commodore Sloat."

Henry earnestly asked, "May I join you?"

"Hmm."

Assuming his father was agreeable and not willing to give him a chance to gainsay otherwise, Henry walked to the foyer and donned his hat. His father followed suit. They stepped out into the night on their way to the boardinghouse. The darkness enveloped them.

Henry suddenly remembered why they had not been out after dark since before the storm. "What about curfew? I hope you have permission."

"As the new deputy sheriff, I would imagine you can garner us an exception if we are stopped."

"I am not officially sworn in. What was your plan if I hadn't come along?"

"Not to get caught."

"Good plan."

Fortunately, they reached the boardinghouse without confrontation. They found their quarry ensconced in a comfortable armchair in the parlor, smoking a pipe, and conversing with Mr. Mallory. The two rose from their chairs to greet his father warmly, as if he was expected.

Theodore placed a hand on Henry's shoulder. "And this, sir, is my son, Henry."

Henry eagerly shook the proffered hand. "It's a pleasure to meet you sir. Are you the same Commodore Sloat who in July, at Monterrey, claimed California for the United States?"

"Aye."

"I feel as though I am in the presence of a legend." When his enthusiastic admiration was met with uncomfortable silence, Henry ducked his head to hide his embarrassment.

Mr. Mallory covered the moment by indicating two side chairs for Henry and his father to pull towards them. Henry sat near Mr. Mallory while his father faced Commodore Sloat. Several other boardinghouse residents occupied other corners of the room engaged in their own conversations or amusements. Soft light from the various oil lamps and the mellow aroma of cigar smoke gave the room a feeling of cozy companionship.

Theodore said, "Commodore, I would like to thank you for taking time to share the story of your ordeal."

"Mr. Mallory here was just telling me of how the cyclone pressed upon the island all of Sunday and the suffering you have endured since."

"Indeed we have, though I gather facing such wind and waves is of even more peril upon the sea."

"I wouldn't know if it's more or less not having experienced one on land."

When he seemed ready to say no more, Theodore prompted him. "How came you to be in the storm?"

"I was in Havana in need of transport to Washington. The USS Perry arrived, and I was able to come to an agreement with Lieutenant Blake to take me as far as Charleston. We set sail early Saturday from Havana before the storm's intensity was known. By evening we were caught in the beginnings of the gale. All canvas was sheathed when it became apparent the storm was building to a raging tempest. As you can imagine, all aboard where quite concerned for our precarious position between the rocky Cuban coast and the perilous reefs of the Florida Straits and with the Bahamas to the east. The captain decided to head west when a burst of heavy wind tossed us on our beam end. From that point on there was little we could do to control the ship." The commodore paused to puff on his pipe and take a sip of his whiskey.

Theodore asked, "How did the crew behave?"

"Admirable to the end and stoic in the face of certain death, of which we believed ourselves to face from Saturday evening to the last hours of Sunday. Now where was I? Oh yes, on our beam end. The ship was slow in righting. The spars were in the water. Lieutenant Blake had the men ready to cut away the mast when she finally began to right. We all breathed a sigh of relief, but it was short lived. The wind and water built to heights never witnessed before. The waves were mountainous and the wind screamed through the lines. We couldn't lie to or we would be turned over. The only choice was to keep the ship turned to run before the storm. It scudded us along at an alarming rate back from whence we'd come. We were in constant fear of being engulfed by the towering waves or dashed upon the coast. We could only pray the wind would soon change direction as we held to the lines for dear life. Such was the way we spent the night.

"The sky turned an unholy red with the dawn. Not surprising, the sailors spoke of demons and hell. Then the ship became sluggish. The bow anchor was cut away and the heavy guns threw over, but it did little to help."

A hush had descended upon the room, made noticeable as the commander paused in his tale for refreshment. Henry cast a surreptitious glance about them confirming they now had a rapt audience.

"When the wind finally did haul around, just like Mr. Mallory said occurred here, it came with even greater force not thought possible. We took slight comfort in knowing we were no longer in imminent danger of being cast upon the Cuban rocks, although we could only guess at our position.

"The noise of the storm made it impossible to be heard. Any communication was done by hand signals. All hands were on deck silently awaiting our fate, not even given the comfort of speaking with each other. Thus was how we spent all of Sunday. Despite our tenacious hold on the lines, at times we were thrown violently about the deck. Not a man was left unbruised.

"We soon began to fear being struck upon the reef. Darkness fell, and still we floundered in the wind and waves. Near midnight, we felt our fate was upon us as we were tossed now in white water. We were soon struck with a tremendous sea crashing upon us. She struck again and an ominous cracking was heard. Again and again the brig was dashed upon the reef until the rudder was torn away and the seams began to open. Lieutenant Blake ordered the masts cut away. Finally, a huge wave lifted her over the reef into relatively speaking calmer water, but the wind pushed us hard upon the shore before the tempest subsided. Miraculously all souls were accounted for. We were most fortunate in where we landed as many vessels around us did not survive the reefs. Our arms were stiff from holding on for dear life. And still our peril was not over yet. We had no water and could not be sure of rescue.

"Monday morning it was decided an officer would be sent ashore to find an encampment, but it was later deemed unnecessary. A Spaniard was rescued by our boat. He was the sole survivor of twenty crewmen in a wreck about a half mile from ours. Two wreckers arrived on Tuesday reporting the whole channel was filled with wreckage of vessels and cargo. We had been fortunate in passing through a narrow opening in the reefs. Anywhere else and all would have been lost."

Mr. Mallory said, "As would have been your fate if you had not left Havana when you did. Word from there is more than a hundred vessels were lost. Only a dozen are fit to sail."

"So I have heard."

Theodore turned to Mr. Mallory. "Speaking of vessels, has the northwest lightship been found?"

"Not yet. Did you hear that Sand Key is gone too?"

"No, I haven't."

"Not just the lightship but the whole key disappeared under the water. The saddest part is Captain Appleby had five visitors with him, including his daughter, son-in-law, and three-year-old grandson. That six lives were lost during what should have been a happy visit seems especially tragic.

Mr. Mallory grimaced. "Tragedy and trouble. That's the lighthouse business these days. I just found out the schooner carrying the new lenses for the Garden Key lighthouse sank in the storm. So not only do I have to request three new lighthouses for our area, but the expensive Fresnel lenses for Garden Key will have to be reordered. I doubt all my requests will be filled. I honestly don't know what to do if I have to choose between the lights. They are all equally important. At least the Cape Florida light is finally being rebuilt after ten years of darkness thanks to those darn Seminoles."

Normally their champion, Theodore let his remark slide. The Seminole attack on the lighthouse was especially vicious, burning one man and leaving the other for dead. It may have been ten years ago, but he still vividly remembered listening to a badly burned and shot John Thompson tell the tale of his survival.

Talk dwindled to the latest news of the war efforts against Mexico and the yearlong battles to secure the Texas and California territories. Henry's interest peaked when Commodore Sloat mentioned Colonel Taylor's high praise for Jack Hays and his Texas Rangers.

Mr. Mallory said, "Young Mr. Whitmore is himself a former member of the Texas Rangers."

Henry sat up a little straighter when Commodore Sloat looked his way with a new found respect. He answered the seaman's questions, eagerly confirming the unusual loyalty given to Jack Hays by his men.

As the hour grew late, the men parted ways. Henry and Theodore walked home in somber silence. The commodore's story of so many wrecks along the reef increased their worry for Max and Christoff. But that was not all that was bothering Henry's father.

Theodore broke the silence. "Do you wish you were still with the rangers?"

Henry shook his head. "I don't miss being a ranger, but I wish I could be there to help them fight. A contradiction, I know. Why do you ask?"

"The pride in your voice when you spoke of it."

"I am proud to have served beside those great men, but have no fear, I do not regret having come home."

* * *

Brianna walked into the girl's room to find the bed piled high with clothes and Emily sitting on the floor sorting her stockings. "What are you doing?" She ran her hand over the blue printed muslin of a day dress. It was nicer than her best dress.

Emily answered without looking up from her task. "Donating my clothes. The families at the barracks are in dire need of clothing. Besides, I should have done this a long time ago. I didn't realize how many dresses I've outgrown. And we need more room for yours and your sisters' clothing."

Brianna noted there was more than Emily's clothes on the bed. She had already gone through her brothers' too. It gave her an idea. She turned to the dresser brought in from their house which she shared with her sisters. Emmaline had outgrown some of her clothes. She pulled them from the bottom drawer and added them to the piles on the bed. She didn't bother going thru hers or Agatha's clothes as they would be passed down to Emmaline.

Mrs. Eatonton happened to walk by and see her. Her eyes widened at the sight. She walked into the room as Emily rose from the floor to add stockings to the growing pile. "What is all this?"

Emily jubilantly replied, "A well needed donation."

"For the families at the barracks that lost their homes."

Emily nodded.

Abby smiled. "That is very thoughtful girls."

Brianna said, "It was all Emily's idea."

Abby said, "I see you've already been through the boys' clothes. I believe we can spare a few towels as well. I'll see what I can add from our closet."

By the time Henry and Theodore returned, the dining table was covered with piles of neatly folded clothing including contributions from Betsy and Mrs. Baxley, who had the boys retrieve all of her husband's clothing from her former home. The ladies were in the process of packing it in baskets and crates to be delivered to the barracks. As they finished their task, the men relayed what they had heard from the Commodore.

Abby shook her head. "I wish we had more to share with Cuba."

"I wouldn't worry too much. I will be sending a request on their behalf to Bob Jenkins. I'm sure with circulation of the newspaper much in the way of donations will find its way to Cuba."

Emily stifled a yawn. It was getting late.

Mrs. Baxley spoke to Emily and Brianna. "You girls should head up to bed. I'll see this is finished."

They bid good night to everyone and headed upstairs. Emily paused before disappearing from sight to catch Henry's eye. He winked at her and mouthed, 'I love you,' warming her heart. She mouthed it back to him and continued on her way.

In her room, Brianna held the candlestick aloft casting a golden glow over the single dress left on the bed. The younger girls were asleep so Emily whispered, "I caught you admiring it and thought you should have it. I'm sure your mother can alter it for you."

Brianna handed her the candle. She reverently lifted the dress to her torso and twirled.

Emily smothered a laugh.

Brianna abruptly stopped to give her a hug. "Thank you."

"You're welcome. I would have given you several if they weren't needed elsewhere."

"This is enough. It's more than enough. Thank you." She carefully hung the dress in the closet on the empty side Emily designated for her and her sisters.

The exhausted girls climbed into bed to get their rest to meet the morrow and its demands.

Downstairs, Henry wasn't ready to sleep. He was too eager to draw. A simmering excitement to do so had been under his skin ever since he found his sketch book. He opened it to the first blank page. He made a rough charcoal sketch of the disinterred cemetery. It was the scene haunting him the most. He then did one of their house. One after the other as fast as he could finish them he drew the scenes in his head.

His father picked up the first one. "This is good son." He separated the pile to see the rest of them. "Would you be interested in selling them to the paper? I could send them to Bob Jenkins."

"I suppose."

"I think they would be very useful in helping people understand the true devastation."

Chapter 27

Friday, October 16th

Henry quietly crept from the bedroom careful not to disturb the three sleeping boys. It was well over an hour before dawn but anxiety for the day made any further sleep impossible. Downstairs, he picked up his haversack hanging on a peg by the door. He checked again that he had his revolver, powder, shots, and percussion caps, even though he had carefully packed the contents last night before going to bed. He removed the revolver from the bag and slipped it into the holster attached to his belt before slipping out the front door with nary a sound.

Emily watched from her open window as Henry walked down the street with the waning light of the setting moon upon his back. Today may find her beloved facing the wrath of an angry mob. She sent a prayer heavenward no one would be hurt. She didn't like the idea of him being a deputy and the dangers it may bring, but she supposed it was safer than his time as a Texas Ranger facing certain conflict with Indians and Mexicans. She stood there long after he was gone from her sight worrying her bottom lip.

* * *

Henry had been waiting outside Patterson's store for a half hour when Sheriff Coslin arrived. He was surprised, although pleased, to see Henry. "Good morning, Deputy Whitmore."

Henry gave him a lopsided grin. "That's putting the cart before the horse seeing as how you haven't sworn me in yet."

"True. How about we get that part done right now?"

Henry straightened from leaning against the wooden store front to face the sheriff with shoulders square and chin firm. The sheriff produced a pocket Bible and administered the oath of office. He then pulled a tin star from the breast pocket of his vest and handed it to Henry. It was simply made and embossed with the words; Deputy Sheriff Key West. Henry pinned it to his chest. He felt more than a little pride to be wearing it while at the same time he felt the weight of the responsibility settle upon his shoulders.

Sheriff Coslin said, "I see you have your gun. Now, I hope it goes without saying the last thing we want to do is to have to use bullets. Is it loaded?"

"Not yet. I was waiting on a little light to do so."

The sheriff held up his lantern.

Wryly Henry said, "Thanks." He set to work loading four of the chambers leaving the fifth empty to safely rest the hammer. He caught Sheriff Coslin's nod of approval out of the corner of his eye.

Mr. Patterson arrived with the first hint of light in the eastern sky. He greeted them as he unlocked the door. "I have never dreaded opening this store like I do today."

Sheriff Coslin said, "It will be fine. We'll keep order."

Mr. Patterson gave him a strange look. "I'm sure you will, but who is there to help me take care of all the customers sure to be lined up. Why I bet the whole town comes at once to buy me out. And in that madness, I'm supposed to ration how much a person really needs too? Impossible, I say!"

Henry asked, "Have you not considered hiring help?"

"I was stocking shelves until late last night. There has been no time."

"Emily, I mean Miss Eatonton, is good with numbers. She could help you tally receipts and take payments."

"That would be a help but there is so much I would have to show her and no time left."

"I bet I could have her here inside thirty minutes."

Sheriff Coslin looked at the brightening sky. "I would need you back in even less time." As if to prove his point, two men appeared from around the bend in Front Street.

"Would it undignify my position if I ran?"

"I think it is crucial that you do run, and fast. Hurry back Henry. I shall need your help to maintain order."

Henry took off before Sheriff Coslin had finished speaking. He reached the house out of breath to be greeted by Mrs. Baxley in the hall.

"Slow down boy, you'll give yourself apoplexy."

Henry didn't pause to answer. He took the stairs two and three at a time. He knocked softly on the girls' door hoping Emily would be the one to answer. He heard rustling and footsteps and then the door opened a crack to reveal one eye of his beloved.

"You are needed."

"Where?"

"At Patterson's store. Can you be dressed and hasten there on your own?"

"Of course, I can. What kind of silly question is that?"

"I must get back right away."

Theodore appeared in the doorway behind Henry. "Son, what is the meaning of this?"

"I came to get Emily's help at Patterson's store. The situation is expected to be more than he can manage alone. I'm sorry I can't explain further. I must get back." He didn't wait for either to respond but dashed down the stairs, out the door, and was back having been gone a mere fifteen minutes.

The sheriff's line was now ten men long and the store was not expected to open for another hour and a quarter. So far it was a simple process to have everyone queue up in the order they appeared. The rapidity in which they were appearing gave merit to Mr. Patterson's fear that the whole town would be upon his doorstep.

Fifteen minutes later, Emily arrived accompanied by Henry's father. She was promptly ushered inside, with little more than a nod in his direction, to receive instructions from Mr. Patterson. Theodore greeted the sheriff and those he passed as he took his place in line.

The sun steadily rose and the line steadily grew longer. Henry didn't think there could be enough food for all even severely rationed. Some of these people were going to be turned away empty handed. And that was when his new job would really begin. Sheriff Coslin was positioned by the door and Henry was walking the line seeing that order was maintained. For now, everyone seemed to be neighborly, quietly conversing.

At eight o'clock Mr. Patterson opened the door and gave a nod to Sheriff Coslin before retreating back inside. The sheriff positioned himself in front of the opening and announced to the crowd only three people would be allowed to go in at a time. The people shuffled with impatience and a few grumblings were heard, but the mandate was accepted. The first three people went in and five minutes later two came out with meager rations and dour looks. Seeing those in line grow more impatient, Henry walked the line faster, trying to remain calm and not place his hand on his holster which might instigate aggression.

The third person exited the store vocalizing everyone's fear. "There isn't much to be had. Flour is being rationed one cup per household. He doesn't have enough for everyone."

The line began to fall apart. Henry stepped forward. "Keep to your place. Anyone falling out of line forfeits."

An older sailor Henry had only seen in passing angrily answered, "What are you going to do about it?"

Henry steadily met his gaze refusing to back down. "I am going to keep the peace."

The man stepped back in line, but his gaze didn't falter. Henry expected when the real trouble started, it was going to be with this man.

The pace of people going in and out of the store picked up. So too did the angry energy grow outside as the day grew warm and tempers grew short. Within two hours, Mr. Patterson announced he was sold out. He added that more shipments would be arriving soon, but his words were lost in the angry shouts of those still in line. Henry glanced down the line in search of the angry sailor from earlier. He saw him with fist raised headed towards the door. While Henry debated what to do, he was startled by the explosion of Sheriff Coslin's shot fired in the air. A hush fell over the crowd and in it the sheriff spoke.

"People, go home! There is nothing more to be had here until another ship comes in."

His words were met with rancor but most reluctantly turned away. About a dozen men banned together. One shouted, "My family is starving. I will not turn away empty handed." Another added, "We will see for ourselves what is in the store."

Sheriff Coslin stood his ground and Henry quickly joined him. Mr. Patterson appeared in the doorway behind them. "I assure you gentlemen there is nothing left to be had."

Theodore came to stand perpendicular to the group. He had made it inside. He pocketed a small pouch from his purchase and then lifted the bag high. "Whoever needs this the most, may take it."

A tense moment passed before the men turned away unwilling to take food from a neighbor's hand.

With a sigh of relief, Sheriff Coslin said, "I expect next time will be worse."

Henry grimaced. "Hopefully next time there will be enough food to go around."

Emily appeared from behind Mr. Patterson. "We can only pray."

Mayor Maloney approached with a cheerful disposition. "Is the food gone already?"

Mr. Patterson said, "Yes, sir."

Theodore said, "I am going to escort Emily home and then return to help with the burials as planned."

The mayor nodded. "Thank you Mr. Whitmore. You can always be counted on." He then noticed a flash of silver. "What's this? Young Mr. Whitmore has been made a deputy. Congratulations, sir." The mayor held his hand out to Henry.

"Thank you, Mayor."

"Will you be helping as well?"

"Yes, sir."

"Good. I will meet you at the old cemetery." The mayor left them with purposeful strides.

Emily turned to Mr. Patterson. "Thank you for thinking of me to help. It was a pleasure to put my learning to purposeful use."

"It is I who should be thanking you. I could never have managed on my own." He pulled a coin from his vest pocket and handed it to her. "Your wage."

"Thank you sir, but I require no payment."

"Of course you do." He held the coin out with thumb and forefinger until Emily held out her palm to accept it. "And we both should thank young Henry. It was his suggestion."

Emily bestowed a dazzling smile upon Henry. Its effect was such he heard not a word of Mr. Patterson's gratitude. His attention was restored with a blush at the robust laughter from the men surrounding him. An even darker hue stained Emily's cheeks.

Theodore lifted his gaze to the sky. "Miss Emily, perhaps I should be getting you home. It looks as if we might get rain at any moment."

Her gaze followed his. "It would be a blessed relief."

Sheriff Coslin said, "Deputy Whitmore, I think you and I should head towards the harbor. I see the masts of a large ship coming into port. If it carries food and water it will need guarding."

Henry and Emily reluctantly parted.

Theodore said, "Henry, if it does rain, I'll be at the paper."

Henry nodded and turned away.

On their return walk, Theodore stopped at the home of a widower with several young children. When she answered the door he handed her the goods he bought from Mr. Patterson. Inspired by his generosity, Emily pressed her earnings into the grateful lady's hand. When she saw what it was, she looked at Emily in wonder. "You are an answered prayer. This is exactly the amount I needed to have enough funds to purchase passage to return to my family."

A chill swept over Emily. "Then I am grateful to be the bearer of God's answered prayer. Although, I will be sorry to see you and your family leave."

"I hate to leave, but it is too difficult to provide for my children on my own."

Rain drops began to fall.

Theodore doffed his hat. "We wish you safe travels madam."

He and Emily hurried home in the increasing wind and rain.

They entered the house in a flurry of laughter. They were thankful for being wet as the rain meant water would fill the cisterns and provide drinking water thanks to Thorn and Nate's hard work.

Mrs. Baxley greeted them in the foyer. Theodore pulled the small pouch from his pocket and handed it to her. She opened the drawstring and smiled. Emily looked on in bewilderment as Mrs. Baxley rubbed the bag between her hands, lifted it to her nose, and inhaled deeply. Then Emily caught a whiff of fragrant goodness. English tea.

"I'll go brew us a pot right now. It will surely lift our spirits."

"But it's raining."

Mrs. Baxley smiled. "What's a little rainstorm after what we've been through?" She tucked the pouch in her pocket, threw a shawl over her head, and made a dash out of the door for the kitchen.

* * *

Theodore watched a short while later as his wife lifted her head from the shirt she was mending to sniff the air. Her eyes met his shining with wonder. "Is that tea, I smell?"

Mrs. Baxley entered the room carrying a tray with a tall silver pot, three cups and saucers. The usual cream and sugar set was absent having nothing to fill them. "Indeed it is."

Theodore rose to take the tray so Mrs. Baxley could remove her rain soaked shawl. He placed the tray on a nearby table. Mrs. Baxley poured the fragrant brew and then with a broad smile handed a cup to Betsy.

Betsy lifted the painted bone china cup to her nose and inhaled deeply, closing her eyes to better savor the aroma. Her home may be gone, food scarce, neighbors displaced, and her family was living on the charity of friends, but the comfort of tea gave her a momentary sense of peace.

It abruptly ended with a sobbing Emmaline running into the room to bury her face in her mother's lap. Betsy placed her cup on the side table to comfort her daughter. "There, there dear. There's no monster outside." The other children soon followed. A sudden clap of heavy thunder made them all jump, children and adult alike, despite the warning flash of lightening. Apparently, a storm would never be just a storm again.

* * *

Henry pulled his collar tighter trying to keep the rain from running down his neck. He and the sheriff were watching over the water barrels until the city council and mayor could decide how best to distribute it. He wished he had his hooded slicker. His mind drifted from his discomfort to worry over the patched roofs. He hoped all the salvaged sail cloth providing temporary cover in place of missing shingles was holding well. Even the waterproof oilcloth like the one they used on the Eatonton home may prove inadequate against the rain.

Sheriff Coslin leaned towards him to be heard over the rain. "There would be irony in protecting water barrels during a rain storm if so many cisterns weren't still unclean."

Henry chuckled. He liked the sheriff and his sense of humor. He was also enjoying this unexpected job. He wondered how long it could last. Once their island life returned to normal would his services still be needed? Then he remembered Emily's wishes. It wouldn't matter if he could keep the job. Emily wanted to leave the island. Henry was willing to travel, but he was secretly hoping in doing so Emily would discover more quickly than he had that Key West was home.

Mr. Mallory approached under the cover of a black umbrella. His gaze was fixed out in the harbor. Henry turned to see a row boat with three men coming in to shore from an anchored merchant ship.

The sheriff turned to him with a grin. "Ah young Henry, it appears we will have more to guard than mere water."

"Do you know what that ship carries?"

The sheriff said, "Not specifically, but it is bound to be food and goods, both of which are desperately needed."

Mr. Mallory reached them and in a few moments more the row boat was pulled ashore. A hurried consultation under the stormy sky ensued. Mr.

Mallory accepted the manifest from the first mate as he inquired, "Who is your cargo consigned to?"

"The town of Key West, sir. We have brought aid in answer to your message of distress."

All three islanders looked to the sailor in surprise.

Henry said, "It's too soon for Commodore Sloat to have reached Charleston."

Mr. Mallory glanced down at the paper.

The first mate said, "The cargo is from Fort Lauderdale and New Smyrna."

Mr. Mallory smiled. "You must have received word from the messenger sent out Monday by the mayor."

"I wouldn't know, sir."

"Well come, come. Let's get you out of the rain while I consult with the mayor on where to unload your ship."

One man stayed with the row boat while the other crewman trailed behind the first mate and custom collector.

Henry looked to the sheriff with a smile and a nod out to the harbor. "What do you reckon's on that ship?"

"I hope there's flour to make bread."

"Maybe a pig to slaughter."

"Vegetables would be nice."

Henry's mouth began watering thinking of having something other than fish.

* * *

As the rain began to let up, Theodore left the house with the intention of finally starting the cleanup process in his printing office. He hurried through the rain, passing many yards with all the kitchen pots, buckets and even bath tubs set out to collect water. He soon arrived at his office.

He had to push hard on the door as it now sat a little crooked on the hinges. He stood in the entry listening to the pitter patter of rain on the roof while his eyes drifted over the mangled mess of his once orderly front room. His nose wrinkled at the stale mustiness in the air. He grabbed the ladder back chair from his typeset table and used it to prop open the door. The fresh rain drenched breeze swirled inward from the door and the broken front window.

He looked around debating where to start. His eyes alighted on the bookcase. He took off his hat and laid it on his desk. His foot hit the overturned typeset tray on the floor and so it was Reverend Richards found him on his knees picking up tiny cast metal sorts strewn across the wooden planks.

The reverend stepped across the threshold. He called out to the dark room, his eyes not yet adjusted to the dim interior. "Mr. Whitmore?"

"Down here Reverend."

"Ah, Mr. Whitmore, good afternoon."

Theodore laid the half-filled tray on the desk, rose to his feet, dusted his hand on his trousers and held it out to his visitor. "Good afternoon, Reverend."

"Seeing all that you have before you, I hate to make this request, but I feel I must with the Sabbath fast approaching."

Theodore spoke with a reluctant sigh. "What is it you need Reverend?"

"Maybe I could offer you a trade. It won't be entirely fair but something. I could help clean up here in exchange for your help once the rain stops. I am in need of volunteers to help build a temporary church."

"Of course, I'll help. You don't need to help me in return."

"Nevertheless, I will. Just give me some direction." He shrugged out of his coat and hat and rolled up his sleeves.

"Very well, you could finish picking up the sorts."

"Sorts?"

"The metal letters that belong in that tray."

"Oh, of course."

The reverend set to work and Theodore turned his attention to the bookcase, first lighting the lamp and setting it upon the desk to make the reverend's hunt easier. He pushed the bookcase back into place against the wall and then began picking up other items from the floor and returning them to their proper place.

"Did you notice these have begun to rust?"

"Yes."

"Can you clean them?"

"I don't know." It was a problem for another day. Today he would be happy to put his office to rights.

When the reverend could find no more sorts, Theodore handed him a broom to sweep the floor while he went into the back room with another lamp to inspect the damage to the printing press. Much to his dismay, all the metal parts of his press were coated in red oxide. He was going to have to figure out how to take it apart, clean each piece of metal and reassemble it. The mere idea of what it would entail was daunting. And just like the type, he had no idea how to go about getting rid of the rust. He was anxious to put out a newspaper, but now it would take more than just the arrival of fresh paper to make that happen. He turned his attention to the easier tasks of righting those items dislodged by the storm. He soon had the room in order making him feel somewhat better. Reverend Richard appeared in the doorway, broom in hand. "I believe the rain has stopped."

The two men left his shop and soon met with other volunteers at the wreck of the stone church. They took what they could of the available lumber and stone and set about building a small structure in place of the original church that had washed away. Progress was soon interrupted when word spread of the arrival of ships bearing food and water. The men raced to take their place in line at the custom house. The rain had brought a temporary cooling relief, but in its aftermath, they were left with sweltering heat and swarms of hungry mosquitoes.

Women were gathered nearby talking excitedly, giddy knowing relief from hunger was at hand. Children ran about in joyful abandon. It was a celebratory atmosphere despite the insects, as everyone was thankful to receive aid from the outside world. They no longer felt so alone in their struggle to survive. Mrs. Baxley was one of several women who volunteered to make food for the hospital, and so Theodore was sent home with extra rations, including a crate of noisy chickens.

* * *

That evening was a celebratory dinner at the Eatonton house of roasted chicken, fresh bread, and canned green beans. Similar meals were being had all around the island thanks to the generosity of their northern neighbors. There was much to be thankful for. After the meal, Emily helped Mrs. Baxley make bread and stew for the hospital, which Thorn and Nate helped Theodore to deliver.

* * *

Saturday morning, Emily, carrying a heavy basket of food, joined her mother at the bottom of the porch steps. She was staring at the blackened branches of the rose bushes.

Abby raised her sad eyes to Emily's. "I suppose I should cut them down, but I just can't bear to do it." She struggled to hold back her tears.

It was the first tears Emily had seen her mother shed over their ordeal. She quickly recovered herself.

"Enough of that. There's no sense mourning over roses."

Her mother took up half the basket's burden and they started off for the hospital to help serve breakfast to the patients. The basket they carried between them held an abundance of scrambled eggs, biscuits, and bacon thanks to Mrs. Baxley.

Emily turned to wave to Henry who was also leaving the house. He and his father were headed in the opposite direction to help Reverend Richards. He blew her a kiss. She giggled, both thrilled and abashed by his gesture.

* * *

While Theodore was occupied with finishing the church, Betsy took the older children to see what more could be salvaged from their house. She hesitated at the window as concern grew for the structure's integrity. Had yesterday's rain changed its stability?

Assuming her hesitancy for fear, Thorn brushed past her and entered the house before she could call him back. Nate followed on his heels. Brianna moved forward to follow them, but Betsy pulled her back. Thorn soon returned.

"There's nothing left to save. Everything is covered in mold."

Betsy had a hard time accepting his decree. She lifted her skirts and climbed inside. It was more disturbing than she expected to be in the familiar surroundings of her beloved home but with everything askew. The ceiling was lower and angled, walls were leaning, and the air was heavy with the musty odor of mold. She pulled the handkerchief from her sleeve and held it to her nose. Thorn was right. Everywhere she looked things were dotted with black; the wood and fabric of the furniture, the walls, the paintings, everything. It was heartbreaking. Getting the furniture into the sun would stop the growth, but there was no way they could get it out the window without making a larger opening, which without Theodore and Henry was out of the question. The paintings were beyond help at this point so no sense even trying to retrieve them. Besides, none of them were of any real value. She turned around and followed Nate back outside.

She held back her tears as she followed the boys back to the Eatonton house.

* * *

By mid-afternoon the reverend's makeshift church was completed. It would do for services and Sunday school until the more permanent structure could be rebuilt.

Reverend Richard gathered the men to him. "Thank you for the gift of your labor. I wish I could say it was all that was needed, but the mayor has asked me to ask for your help with one more task; to help rebury our disinterred loved ones from the southern cemetery."

* * *

It would take several days to move the over sixty bodies found. The mayor had to coerce enough men to help by refusing to distribute food to families whose men did not do his fair share to help the community.

Not all of the disinterred were found. Some, like Mrs. Mallory, were to grieve all over again as the graves of her husband, Charles, and eldest son, John, were obliterated by the storm. As bodies were laid to rest again, those who remembered them could not help but share their history.

"This here is Captain James Johnson. He died in 1829. He was a mariner from Virginia and a member of the Dade County Masons. He was first to be buried in the southern cemetery and his will be the oldest headstone in this one."

"Do you recall the Sawyer brothers from Connecticut? Both mariners. James was thirty-two when he died in 1829. I don't remember the exact cause. Likely yellow jack. His brother John died just a few years ago. He was but forty-one."

"Here's old Pardon Greene. He was one of our original founding fathers you know. He left the island for a while and came back with big plans for profiting on the salt. He and William Whitehead were chums. He died shortly after his return."

"David Pinkham's was a tragic death. He was shot in a duel and then lingered for days before finally passing away."

"Poor Mrs. Mabrity. When she comes back it will be to find her husband's body moved and nothing to bury of her other lost loved ones."

* * *

"Emily!"

Emily heard the unusual frustration and urgency in her mother's voice. She picked up her skirts and rushed to her side to find her holding pressure on a lacerated hand. Bloody water in a nearby white porcelain basin turned her stomach. She fought the rising nausea. "What do you need me to do?"

"We are out of bandages again. Could you go find a clean towel or something to make do?"

"Yes, ma'am." Emily hurried to the cupboard where the linens were kept. All the towels were gone as well, having been used already in various tasks. The hired laundress for the hospital was laid up with an injury from the storm, not that it mattered since they had no fresh water to spare for laundry. Emily grabbed a pillowcase and hurried back to her mother's side where she picked up scissors from her mother's surgical basket and cut the bed linen into strips. Her mother's nod of approval banished her anxiety over the wisdom of her find. She helped wrap the hand, eager to turn away as soon as it was tied it off.

When they arrived this morning to serve the breakfast made by Mrs. Baxley, they found the ward was filled with the ragged sound of coughing. Many of their neighbors were seeking relief for mold sickness, the result of living in houses that had been flooded and not properly dried out. The meager hospital staff was overwhelmed with all the new patients. Emily sighed deeply, knowing it would be late in the day before she returned home. Despite her abhorrence for the sight of blood, she, like her mother, could not walk away and leave Doc Weedon, Nurse Millie, and Nurse Mary to struggle alone.

Hours had passed since their arrival. Yesterday's sudden rain had brought temporary rejoicing around the island and a rush to put out every possible receptacle to capture the fresh water, but miserable heat and mosquitoes burst in its wake and continued to flourish today. The sultry afternoon air was stifling. Emily brushed her arm across her forehead to soak up the moisture dotting her brow before bending to place the back of her hand against the brow of the patient. This one was a young boy brought in with a fever and breathing issues. She administered willow tea and resoaked the cloth with tepid water to place upon his forehead. It was all she could do for him. She tried to stretch her back as she moved to the next patient's bed.

She wondered how tired Henry must feel laboring in this heat to build a temporary church and rebury the dead from the old graveyard. It had to be grueling work, not just because of the sun and pests. She was proud of the way he was stepping up to help their community.

A sailor was sitting up in the next bed. He grinned at her, revealing several missing teeth. Despite that, he had an infectious smile. He was suffering from a fractured leg, but he was the lucky one. The rest of his shipmates drowned. Their boat collided with the reef, stoving a hole in the bottom. The receding flood waters released the boat from her coral anchor only to sink in deeper water. The sailor was fortunate to find flotsam to sustain him through the rest of the storm. He was picked up the next morning by a wrecker returning to the island with a broken mast.

After hearing his tale, Emily fled to the storage room under pretense so she could have a private moment to release her tears. The sailor's story was a vivid reminder of the peril her father and brother faced and maybe even their fate. Her mother insisted on having faith that all was well, but it was hard to do so in the face of so much tragedy. Why should their family not have their share? So far they had lost little in the hurricane. Henry's family lost their house while theirs still stood. Most other houses still standing were severely damaged but theirs had been minor and soon repaired thanks to Henry and Mr. Whitmore. Many others had lost loved ones, maybe they had too and just didn't know it yet. That was the worst of it. The not knowing if they lived or had died, perhaps were injured and desperately trying to return home, or lost at sea.

She had no sooner recovered her spirits when she noticed a father comforting his sick daughter. The longing for her father overwhelmed her. She turned away again choked with her emotions to be enveloped in her mother's comforting embrace. She buried her head in her neck to hide her tears, feeling ashamed to display such emotion. When she was sure she wouldn't burst out in sobs, she lifted her head to see her mother's concerned gaze.

Abby whispered, "I know. I feel it too. You have helped enough for today. Go home and get some rest and try not to worry so. They will be fine. God has told me so."

Emily started. Her eyes widened on her mother's serene face desperately wanting to believe her words. Many of the wreckers had returned in the last few days but none had news of the *Mystic*. Granted, those wreckers were from the upper keys and her father had sailed west towards the Dry Tortugas, so they would not have crossed paths. Still, news often traveled fast between ships. Surely they would receive word soon one way or another.

Abby patted Emily's hand in comfort. "All will be well. You will see. Now before you go, send Jacob in with one of the water buckets, and then take him home with you please."

Emily gave her a closed smile nod. Her mother ran a hand down the side of her head and then left to heed a call from across the room. Emily's gaze followed her progress. She was thankful for and proud of her mother. She sent a prayer heavenward for being blessed with her.

* * *

Emily paced the parlor floor. She was feeling cooped up and useless after her busy morning at the hospital. Actually, it was the first time since the storm she didn't have something to do. Betsy and her daughters were seated around the room mending clothes to distribute among the storm victims. Emily was incompetent at best when it came to sewing. She offered to help Mrs. Baxley with supper and was turned down, so now she paced. She turned on her heel at the south wall and huffed with exasperation. What could she do with herself? She could go to the barracks to help the families she supposed, but her mother would not approve of her crossing the island without an escort. They only reasonable thing that came to mind was something she hadn't done since before the storm.

She cast her gaze to Brianna with her head bent over a torn shirt and sighed. Only one other option presented itself. "Jacob, we're going for a walk." She knew better than to ask him if he wanted to go as he would refuse while he was happily playing with his toys and James, and he could be stubborn for a six year old. He grumbled, but he rose to his feet.

Meanwhile, Brianna and Agatha both looked up from their work with wistful looks that did not go unnoticed by their mother.

Betsy smiled at her daughters. "You may go if you take Emmaline with you." She turned her gaze to Emily. "I assume the girls would make better companions for you."

Emily smiled broadly with relief. "Yes, ma'am."

Betsy dropped her gaze to Jacob. "And you, young man, may return to your play."

Jacob wasted no time returning to his wooden sailboat and make believe adventures on the high seas inspired by his father's tales.

The four girls skipped down the front steps, enjoying the respite from chores and hurricane recovery. Following Emily's lead they made their way down the backside of town towards the Watlington's house. Emily would rather have walked into town to the Geiger's, but their house was not livable and she didn't know where they were staying. Besides, with all the fires burning to clear the debris, Front Street was clouded over with smoke. As it was, they held handkerchiefs to their faces until they were further inland.

The happy sound of many children could be heard long before they were seen gathered in the Watlington's backyard playing games. When they grew close enough they spied not only the Watlington girls but also the Geiger girls and the Keats children.

Emily called out a cheery greeting when she spied Louisa and Sarah Geiger standing by the back porch watching over the younger children. Her friends hurried to meet her in the yard. They gushed as if it had been years instead of merely a week since they last saw each other. Brianna, Agatha and Emmaline eagerly joined their respective age groups.

Louisa grasped Emily's hand. "My mother sent us girls from the house. We came here on account of the heavy smoke in town. We would have come to your house, but I was sure you would be with your mother at the hospital, so we came here."

"I was earlier."

"Well, I'm glad you aren't now. I'm so happy to see you."

Sarah said, "We saw your beau working on the new cemetery as we passed."

Emily wasn't sure how to respond to that gambit.

Louisa said, "Sister don't tease."

"Why not?"

"Because it isn't nice or polite."

And just like their adult counterparts, they soon found themselves sharing their storm story.

Emily sobered. "I saw your house. Where have you been? I didn't see you at the barracks with the other displaced families."

"No we aren't at the barracks. Judge Marvin took us in. Father kept going down to the shore all morning long watching the storm. We were so afraid he would get hit with everything flying around. He always came back soaked to the skin. As soon as he saw the water level rising on the beach, he had us gather up food, water, and clothes and moved us to Judge Marvin's house. They had us all go into the center room downstairs. Sarah and I had the younger ones huddled between us. By the end of the storm I could hardly walk from sitting still for so long."

"And you've been there ever since?"

"Yes. Though mother is insisting father take us to her family in the Bahamas until he can have the house rebuilt. Oh, it is going to be grand with two rooms for us girls to use instead of one."

"That sounds wonderful. The house I mean. I will miss you while you are gone."

"It's not settled yet but mother usually does get her way. What about you?"

"Momma made us go with her to the hospital before the storm got really bad. At its worst, when the flood waters came, I thought the building was going to fall down. I was so scared. But it held. We didn't go home until late Monday."

Sarah asked, "And your house was still standing?"

"Yes. There was a hole in the roof, but Henry fixed it. The Whitmore's lost their house. They are staying with us."

Louisa gave her a sly look. "Henry is living in your house. Do tell! Have you had a secret tryst?"

Emily blushed.

"You have!"

'Well, not as you imply. It is after all a house full of people, but we did manage to have a private conversation one morning."

"And was there a kiss?"

Sarah belligerently interrupted. "You're teasing her."

It gave Emily the space she needed not to answer Louisa's pointed question.

Louisa gave her sister an annoyed look before picking up the conversation. "I'll bet your father is keeping an eye on him, not to mention your brothers."

Emily hung her head to hide her distress. "Poppa and Christoff have not returned yet."

"Oh Emily. I am so sorry. I didn't know. I am sure they are fine."

"Momma is sure too, but I'm not. He is sailing the *Mystic* for Captain Keats. No one has heard from them since the storm. A lot of the wrecking ships have returned heavily damaged."

Also being a salvage captain's daughter, Louisa well understood Emily's distress. "Have faith. Your father's one of the best captains on the island."

Emily took a deep breath. "Did you hear about Miguel?"

Louisa's face tightened.

Sarah said, "We did."

Emily reached out for Louisa's hand and gave it a gentle squeeze. "I'm sorry." She intuitively realized now, Louisa's good humor was a cover for her sorrow. Emily wished she hadn't brought it up. Not knowing what else to say, she redirected the conversation. "I heard many of the ladies at the barracks talking about leaving either for good or, like your family, just until reasonable housing can be assured. Have you heard of any other families leaving?"

"You have been about more than I have. Mother has kept me close until today when she declared she needed a break from us girls. I only know the Watlington's intend to stay. Mrs. Watlington is so close to her time, she is too miserable to travel, and besides, the baby could come any day now."

"I know. Momma has been keeping an eye on her."

"Speaking of which, there she is." Sarah nodded towards Mrs. Eatonton making her way to the house.

Her mother's arrival brought an end to the visit, for it was promptly followed by Mrs. Keats calling her children home. Louisa decided it was time to lead her sisters back to her mother. As soon as she had seen to Mrs. Watlington, Abby led Emily and the Whitmore girls through the late afternoon shadows to the house. They arrived just before Henry, Theodore, Thorn and Nate returned from their work at the graveyard. Supper was soon served.

Emily noted the dark shadows under Henry's eyes and attributed it to his hard day's work. Little did she know it was near midnight before he could pull himself away from his drawings the previous night.

After the meal, the household adjourned to the parlor in quiet pursuits.

Emily tried to focus on a book she was reading, but her eyes kept drifting to Henry's. Her blush deepened every time she caught his intense gaze focused on her instead of his sketch book. He continued doing so purposefully. The flirting game ended abruptly with a withering look from Abby directed at each of them.

An overnight thunderstorm brought much needed rain, adding more water to the cisterns. It also sent Emmaline fleeing to her parent's bed for comfort only to find she had to share their attention with her little brother, James. Both were frightened the monster had returned.

Chapter 28

Sunday morning was clear and bright having been washed clean by the overnight storm. Families made their way to Reverend Richard's makeshift church to celebrate the Lord, to be thankful for all they had, and to find solace for all they had lost. The day marked one week since the hurricane changed their lives forever.

Emily hid a yawn behind her gloved hand. She had been up since sunrise having awoke early with a troubled mind. Captain Keats stopped by yesterday to tell them he hadn't received any word of the *Mystic*. As news trickled in of more and more wrecking vessels returning damaged or not at all, Emily's fears grew. Her mother was trying to keep the news from her brothers, but they were aware. The presence of the Whitmore's and Mrs. Baxley kept them from broaching the subject over meals. In between, they were all too busy with the arduous task of meeting basic needs in the storm's aftermath. This morning she woke from a restless sleep, her mind keenly worried for her father and brother.

Henry walked next to Emily, following in the wake of their parents. He sensed her somber mood. His desire to touch her, to comfort her, was a nearly tangible need. He slept in the next room. He sat across from her at meals. They passed in the halls and could do no more than share smiles and polite conversation. It was very frustrating. If they were engaged he could hold her hand, even in public. They would be engaged if her father were home to ask. The younger children suddenly raced around them to join the Geiger children. Henry cast a glance over his shoulder and seeing the road empty he reached out to clasp Emily's white gloved hand. She turned her head with a surprised look that turned worried. She cast a glance over her shoulder and then gave him a soft smile as she squeezed his hand. It felt good to share something intimate with her, even if was only for a moment.

Emily reveled in the feeling of her hand nestled within Henry's stronger one, and in the fact, he was willing to risk censure to touch her as if he needed her touch. It pleased her to be needed by him. They shared another smile. She anxiously looked to their parents to make sure they weren't being observed. Anxiety turned into concern. Her mother was looking out to sea. Her face was creased in concern despite her declaration of faith in their return. Emily squeezed Henry's hand before releasing it to move to her mother's side. She slid her arm across her shoulder. Her mother turned to look at her with a sad smile and slipped her arm around Emily's waist.

"I forgot how hard it was to wait for him not knowing when he will return."

They leaned on each other, emotionally and physically, the last few yards to the church.

* * *

Reverend Richard tried to greet everyone as they arrived for Sunday service, but he was soon overwhelmed. The gathering increased as the minutes passed to surprisingly include most of the town. Reverend Richard was pleased having made an extra effort to invite the Episcopal parish to join them since they were still awaiting a replacement pastor. It was apparent the makeshift church could not accommodate all, not even by half. He had the young men bring the benches outside. He would preach his sermon in the bright sunshine. There wasn't enough seating for all; only a few hastily constructed benches that were given to the elderly and infirm.

He began the service with Amazing Grace followed by a prayer of thanksgiving for God's mercy during and after the hurricane.

He opened the Bible to the marked passage and waited for the congregation to quiet. So far he had not been able to find his beloved English Standard Bible in the wreckage of his church. It was a gift from his parents when he entered the seminary. He feared it was lost forever. For some reason it was the little things that hurt the most. Today, he was using a loaned King James Bible. He smiled feeling God's hand at work in even something as small as the version of scripture. The wording of his chosen passage was well suited for this Bible, which used the word charity. He hoped to encourage his parishioners to be charitable and help each other in this time of great need.

He read the scripture with a resounding voice to carry over the crowd.

I Corinthians 13
Though I speak with the tongues of men and of angels, and have not charity, I am become as sounding brass, or a tinkling cymbal. And though I have the gift of prophecy, and understand all mysteries, and all knowledge; and though I have all faith, so that I could remove mountains, and have not charity, I am nothing. And though I bestow all my goods to feed the poor, and though I give my body to be burned, and have not charity, it profiteth me nothing.

Charity suffereth long, and is kind; charity envieth not; charity vaunteth not itself, is not puffed up, Doth not behave itself unseemly, seeketh not her own, is not easily provoked, thinketh no evil; Rejoiceth not in iniquity, but rejoiceth in the truth; Beareth all things, believeth all things, hopeth all things, endureth all things. (He emphasized the last)

Charity never faileth: but whether there be prophecies, they shall fail; whether there be tongues, they shall cease; whether there be knowledge, it shall vanish away. For we know in part, and we prophesy in part. But when that which is perfect is come, then that which is in part shall be done away. When I was a child, I spake as a child, I understood as a child, I thought as a child: but when I became a man, I put away childish things. For now we see through a glass, darkly; but then face to face: now I know in part; but then shall I know even as also I am known. And now abideth faith, hope, charity, these three; but the greatest of these is charity.

He followed with a homily more direct to their situation and short, knowing many parishioners would be uncomfortable standing too long in the warm sun.

"Look not at what all we lost last Sunday but rather focus around you on all that we as a community have accomplished this week and be thankful. With generosity of time and resources we have fed and clothed each other, repaired or provided shelter, cleared the streets, burned the debris, buried the dead, and taken care of each other. Let us continue in this manner of brotherhood as we move forward rebuilding our businesses and community. Be kind and generous to your neighbor. Let us pray to the lord for his blessings with thankful and rejoicing hearts."

* * *

The community spent longer than usual greeting each other after services in the shadow of the nearby warehouses.

Theodore leaned to Betsy. "Is that Mrs. Mabrity over there?"

Henry's head snapped up to look where his father indicated. "It is her." He followed his parents and Mrs. Eatonton to greet her.

They reached the matron in time to hear her share her news of the last week.

"...arrived yesterday. It took some time to find passage home. Tampa was hit as well."

A listener asked, "Was it as bad as here?"

"No, but it was bad enough. It started Sunday evening and by midnight the weather glass had fallen so far as we knew we were in for a big storm. The full gale didn't hit us until Monday morning when it had to be blowing a force eight or better. It was strange though; there wasn't more rain. Fort Brooke had damages but not nearly like here. I had a feeling it had struck Key West based on the wind's direction, but I never expected it to..." Overwhelming emotions kept her from finishing her thought.

Those closest to her laid comforting hands on her shoulders and arms though only for a moment as the lady's fierce pride pushed down her grief. When the others had moved on Henry's family stepped forward. His mother reached out to grasp Mrs. Mabrity's hand with both of hers. "We are so sorry for your losses." Her gaze swung from Mrs. Mabrity to include her daughter, Mrs. Wall.

Mrs. Mabrity lifted her chin. Her gaze was steady. "Thank you."

Abby said, "If there is anything we can do for you, please don't hesitate to ask."

Mrs. Wall said, "Thank you, Mrs. Eatonton."

Wanting to lighten the mood, Betsy changed the subject. "How did you find Nicholosa and your grandchildren?"

"Hale and whole. The twins are adorable but such a handful, especially now as they are learning to walk. It's a good thing Nicholosa has the older children to help watch over them."

Betsy said, "Indeed. I couldn't imagine having two at once."

Abby said, "Nor I."

With more friends waiting to greet Mrs. Mabrity they moved on to speak with the Keats standing nearby. Henry surreptitiously watched Emily across the yard visiting with her friends.

Emily sought out Louisa and Sarah Geiger after service. Having spent time together yesterday, they had shared their storm stories and so today spoke of lighter topics.

Louisa gave a nod indicating someone behind Emily. "He looks quite dashing today."

"Who?" Emily cast a glance over her shoulder and knew immediately to whom she was referring. 'So he does." She tamped down the spurt of jealously that Louisa would notice Henry's looks, well aware she did so simply to taunt her.

Louisa said, "You didn't answer yesterday. Has he kissed you?"

"That is none of your business Louisa Geiger, especially on a Sunday. Have you no shame?"

"Meaning you haven't."

Emily opened her mouth to say otherwise but promptly closed it. She would not let Louisa goad her into sharing such intimate details.

Sarah well knew her sister would continue until she harassed the truth out of Emily. She sympathized with her, so she offered another direction for Louisa's attention. "I'm glad Reverend Richard's sermon was short. These borrowed shoes are pinching my feet something awful."

Louisa said, "Don't let mother hear you complain. We are to be grateful to have something to wear at all."

Emily said, "I would loan you a pair of mine, but I just donated all my extra shoes to the families at the barracks."

Sarah said, "Just as well. I think my foot is larger than yours too." She watched a girl headed their way. There was something oddly familiar and out of place. Her gaze held on Gretchen as she spoke to Emily. "Isn't that your dress?"

Emily turned her head to see a smug looking brunette headed their way. "It's one of the dresses I donated."

Gretchen inserted herself between Emily and Sarah. "Have you heard? Havana lays in ruins. Nearly all the ships are lost and they say most of our wrecking fleet is damaged." She turned to Emily with a sickly sweet sympathetic smile. "What about your father Emily? Have you heard from him?"

Louisa's brows lowered ominously. "Hush Gretchen."

Gretchen ignored the warning. "Every day we hear of more ships limping into port. I just wanted to know if she has heard from her father since he is obviously not here."

Emily knew Gretchen was trying to get a reaction but perversely enough it was Louisa who sparked her temper. "You don't have to protect me." She turned to Gretchen. "Yes, I am aware of all the ships lost, of all the lives lost. I realize chances are my father and brother are lost too, but I will not believe it until there is proof. They are alive and they will come home. My mother is sure of it, and so am I."

Louisa rushed to embrace her. "No one is saying they won't come home." She turned to glare at Gretchen. "You should be ashamed of yourself. A proper friend would think of her feelings before speaking such things."

"I was only asking out of friendly concern."

Sarah glared at her in disbelief.

Emily spoke to no one in particular. "I am sure they are only delayed in helping others. There must be hundreds of ships stranded by the storm in need of a good wrecker like my father."

Gretchen said, "For your sake, I hope so." She moved away before any reply could be made.

Sarah mumbled, "Wretched girl."

Emily couldn't help but grin, enjoying Sarah's vehemence on her behalf.

* * *

The Eatonton and Whitmores returned home to enjoy the luxury of a meager Sunday dinner having foregone the midday meal all week due to lack of food. Afterwards, they gathered in the parlor. Finding it hard to sit idle when there was so much work to be done, Theodore picked up the Bible and began reading to the family. They all found it a difficult Sabbath to keep.

At bedtime, the girls in their white nightgowns and bare feet kneeled beside Emily's bed as they had done all week to silently say their prayers. Emily prayed for the safe return of her father and brother and her usual intentions. She opened her eyes and looked over her room companions. She couldn't say she liked sharing her room, but she was getting used to it. Agatha and Emmaline opened their eyes. They smiled at her and quietly said, "Goodnight." They crawled into their bedding in one corner of the room. A few moments later Brianna opened her eyes. Emily stood up, blew out the oil lamp, and she and Brianna climbed into their shared bed.

Brianna turned on her side to face her. "I prayed your father would return tomorrow."

Emily's throat unexpectedly tightened. It took her a moment to reply. "Thank you."

Brianna settled in on her back, and they both studied the ceiling waiting on sleep to come.

* * *

Henry reported to the sheriff first thing Monday morning only to find he wasn't needed unless a ship of supplies arrived to be guarded. At a loss of what to do, he went to his father's printing shop knowing he could probably use help. He found his father kneeling at the metal base of the printing press using sandstone to brush away the rust caused by the flooding. He looked up upon hearing Henry's approach.

Henry said, "Is the sandstone working?" That morning over breakfast they had discussed ideas for how to remove the rust.

"It's tedious, but it appears to be working. I'll polish the metal with oil when I'm done. Hopefully that will be enough to prevent any further rusting."

"It seems I'm not needed for deputy work. Would you like some help?"

Theodore gave him an assessing look. "What about your sponging? Have you had a chance to look at the beds?"

"No. The little bit I saw when I took Emily out was discouraging."

"I think you should go have a closer look."

"What about the rest of the house?"

"It's not going anywhere. We can finish it up this afternoon."

"But shouldn't I help someone else in need then?"

"You've spent the better part of six days helping everyone else. Take this morning to look after your own affairs."

He felt guilty for it, but he followed his father's advice. Henry trudged to the northern beach. He passed a grocer sweeping the sidewalk and a merchant stocking the bins in front of his store. Neither seemed in need of charity, so he felt better about taking his boat out.

He tugged his boat into the water and climbed in. Almost immediately his spirits lifted to be out on the water again. Knowing the southern side, and especially the reefs, took the brunt of the storm, he headed to the north side, further than he went with Emily, to what the spongers called the bay. It was part of the larger Bay of Florida where so many of the ships were stranded after the storm. It was of no surprise he found several were still stranded, including the Revenue Cutter *Morris*.

Henry tried to follow the mangrove paths Mr. Tate had shown him but the sandbars in the shallow water had been rearranged by the winds and surge of the hurricane. It shouldn't have surprised him. After all, if Sand Key could disappear entirely, why wouldn't these smaller spits of land not be moved about? He would have to find a new path. He rowed several nautical miles northward where he found a promising location.

For a while he was alone and encouraged to see some beds still intact. It took some time, but he found a few sponges of good size. As he pulled the fourth sponge into the boat, he was joined by two more boats of older spongers.

"Ahoy, young Henry. I see you found a honey hole."

He would hardly call four a honey hole. At least not before the hurricane. Now it very well may be one. "Have you not found any?"

"A couple the other day. All the beds towards the Gulf are chewed up."

The eldest of the group said, "Ain't seen nothing like this in all my days. Not enough left to support more than one of us."

His boat mate said, "What do we do now, George?"

"Find other work or other sponge beds until these recover. You can always fall back on wrecking and turtling."

Henry said, "How long will it take for the sponges to grow back?"

George said, "I don't know. Years. Maybe never."

The man in the other boat said, "No home and no work. I'm thinking of heading north."

Henry looked at the sponges in the bottom of his boat. He was going to have to find other work too or forego any immediate plans of marrying Emily. Weakly he said to the others, "Hopefully in a year or two there will be enough sponges to support all of us again."

George said, "We'll just have to make do until then."

* * *

Theodore left the shop to meet Henry as planned to finish salvaging lumber and furniture from the house. He was pleased to run into Mayor Maloney and Stephen Mallory on the way. "How do, gentlemen?"

"Good afternoon, Mr. Whitmore. What is the news today?"

"I was hoping you would tell me. I'm afraid I've been at work in the shop this morning instead of listening around town."

"The mayor and I were just discussing the need for a temporary light structure at Whitehead Point. We've already had several wrecks occur from ships watching for the expected lighthouses."

"I suppose there's no question of it being funded."

"I don't expect so. The north pass lightship was found."

Theodore said, "That is good news. Where was she?"

Mayor Maloney said, "She dragged anchor some sixty miles into the Gulf."

Mr. Mallory said, "I expect to have her back on duty in a few days. Not having to replace her should help with securing funds for the others. I have requested funds for a permanent lighthouse on Key West. I expect it will be funded with all expediency, but even so, a stone structure will take time. We need a temporary one now. I was on my way to see Captain

Dutton for his suggestions."

Theodore said, "Sounds like a reasonable place to start since he is with the Corp of Engineers."

Mr. Mallory said, "If you'll excuse me, gentlemen, as I am anxious to speak with him."

The mayor waved him away. "Of course."

Theodore turned to the mayor. "And do you still have concerns for maintaining our status as a port of entry?"

"It does seem less likely to be an issue than the crisis it felt to be a few days ago. With Mr. Browne and Mr. Tift racing each other, their wharves will soon be complete. There is no reason we can't resume our maritime business the same as before the hurricane."

"That is good news."

By day's end the crew of the *Morris,* under guidance of Lieutenant Pease, started work on erecting a sixty foot staff with a large black ball on top near the sight of the lost lighthouse. It would serve as a marker until a temporary light could be erected and later a permanent structure.

* * *

Henry was surprised to reach the house before his father. He stepped inside to retrieve the tools his father had dropped off that morning before heading to the print shop. Back outside with a hammer and crowbar in his hands, he considered where to start. Their plan was to remove any and all salvageable building materials and any furniture that could be retrieved. Whatever remained would be burned to clear the land for rebuilding. They hoped to be finished by day's end. Henry sighed deeply looking over all that was yet to be done. He was fairly certain it was more work than they anticipated.

His father arrived not long after Henry started removing the upper floor boards. Not surprising, he went to work without speaking, just a simple nod in greeting. It was over an hour later when they paused to drink water that he asked Henry, "How was your morning?"

"Rather disappointing."

"I gathered as much when I found you here ahead of me. I was hoping you would still have been out sponging."

"I found four. I met up with some old-timers. They confirmed the beds are destroyed all around the island. They are speculating it is just as bad all the way up Florida's western coast."

"Will they regrow?"

"I'm sure they will eventually, and when they do, I'll be ready."

"What about in the meantime?"

He sighed. "That is as yet, undecided."

Key West Harbor

Max laid his hand on Christoff's shoulder after ordering the anchor dropped. They were home. Almost home. They still had to row ashore. Anxiety plagued both father and son.

They were salvaging a wreck near Loggerhead Key in the Dry Tortugas when they were struck by gale force winds that pushed their cargo heavy schooner onto the reef. Their attempts to free the *Mystic* were hindered by the winds until the retreating storm surge lifted them off again but not without damage. They were barely able to make it to the inner harbor of Garden Key before the hull flooded even with the men constantly working the pumps. They unloaded the ship and were forced to keel haul it in order to affect repairs. Thanks to the generous aide of the lighthouse keeper and the crew from the ship they were salvaging the task was completed faster than if his crew were on their own. Still it took several days.

Before they were done a passing ship stopped by with news of the devastation at Key West. The captain had no specifics. He could only tell them almost every building was damaged, many were completely destroyed, and the death toll was unknown.

The two day sail home was excruciatingly long and fraught with worry. Was their house still standing? Who were the victims of the storm? Was their family safe? They did their best not to contemplate the worst, but the thoughts could not be silenced.

Over and over, Max prayed to God his family was unharmed.

As they sailed into the harbor, the changes to the wharf and the missing lighthouse were the first confirmations all was not as they left it. Even though they had imagined the worst, it did not prepare them for what they faced.

While his crew lowered the row boat over the side Max walked to the port rail as if in a daze. His heart constricted painfully while his hand clutched the balustrade in a white knuckle grip. The island looked as if a giant hand swiped across it leaving a swath of nothingness in its wake, although bits here and there escaped. Buildings were crushed. Trees were gone. The once lush, green island looked scorched as if a fire had raged across it. How did anyone survive? He was supposed to be the one in danger, not his wife and children. Where was his family? What horrors would he find ashore?

Eventually, his focus changed from the buildings to the movement of people. Men were at work everywhere cleaning up and rebuilding. It gave him a flutter of hope he desperately held close. Christoff came up beside him. His worried eyes lifted to his father's sharing their deep concern. Max opened his mouth to offer a platitude but none would come. Instead, he squeezed Christoff's upper arm feeling the strength in his bicep from long hours working the ship's lines.

Christoff said, "We'll soon have answers."

Max's throat tightened. He gave his son a nod of agreement. His gaze was drawn back to the brutalized island. What if they were gone? His breath hitched. He couldn't stop the thought nor could he answer it.

"Boats ready, Captain."

Max and Christoff hurriedly climbed over the side and down the rope to drop into the rowboat followed by his first mate and another crewman. The four of them rowed swiftly to shore. Anxiety gave strength to their strokes, moving them speedily across the water, though for Max it was still too slow.

They landed on the coral shore next to Mr. Tift's damaged dock. Max and Christoff stepped out of the boat leaving the other two to secure it. They were met by Stephen Mallory.

"Welcome back Captain Max. Do you have cargo...?"

Max abruptly interrupted him, desperation clear in his harsh words. "My family?"

Compassion swamped Stephen's demeanor. "They're all fine."

Max's relief was so great his legs went weak and his chest collapsed. His hands dropped to his knees to support his torso. He drew in a ragged breath. "Thank you, Lord."

Stephen's hand came to rest on his shoulder. Max straightened.

"Your house is one of the few still standing."

Max's relief was so great, he could not speak. He patted Stephen twice on the shoulder and bolted off towards home. Nothing could stand in the way of the urge to see his wife and children and verify their safety with his own eyes. Christoff easily kept pace with him. Greetings of those they passed were answered with a wave of the hand as they ran past. Peripherally, he noted the strange sight of sailcloth stretched upon gaping roofs, their loose ends fluttering in the breeze, but his focus was on reaching home.

Max landed on the front porch having taken the steps in two strides. He opened the front door and flew into the foyer nearly colliding with Mrs. Baxley. As it was, he unbalanced her sending an armful of laundry fluttering in the space between them.

Her voice was arrested in the beginnings of a sharp reprimand as soon as she realized it was not one of the boys. "Captain Max!" She reached out to shockingly embrace him. "Missus will be so relieved your home." She turned to call up the stairs. "Jacob, come downstairs. Your father's home." She turned back to him with a broad grin. "It's so good to have you home safe."

Max hurried to speak while he had the chance. "Where's Abigail?"

"Oh, she is at the hospital, of course."

"The hospital?"

Jacob and James appeared at the top of the stairs.

Seeing the renewed concern on Max's face, Mrs. Baxley quickly added, "She's working. With all the injuries and sickness and doctors and nurses taking care of their own, she's been helping out night and day it seems like. We barely see her home."

"What about Emily and the boys?"

"I suspect the boys are somewhere around town with Henry. Emily is with Abby."

Max was barely restraining his impatience to get to his wife. He climbed the few steps needed to sweep Jacob into his arms. As expected, the six year old squirmed in Max's tight embrace while the suddenness of Max's movements frightened four year old James. He didn't question the boy's presence in his house, assuming Mrs. Baxley was watching him for the Whitmores. Max set his youngest down at the bottom of the steps. To Mrs. Baxley and Christoff he said, "I'll be back." He left the house as rapidly as he entered it.

Max ran the distance from the house to the hospital, skirting past piles of burning debris and neatly stacked lumber salvaged from the fallen house behind his; clear indications of the work being done since the storm. He didn't slow his pace until he reached the steps leading up to the hospital entrance. He took a few deep breaths to slow his breathing while he noted the timber and board bracing supporting the cracked bricks on the front corner.

He climbed the steps, entered the cool interior, and moved through the front entry to the doorway of the hospital ward. He heard her voice before he saw her. His already fast heartbeat quickened. He stepped into the ward and stopped. Swamped by emotions, he didn't want to move among the patients' beds. His gaze sought her out.

His beloved. His Abigail. His Princess Rose. His life.

She was safe.

He was overwhelmed and close to tears. It was always him facing danger. Never her. The feeling of relief to know she was safe, to see her safe, drained him of strength. He now appreciated what he had put her through all these years. No wonder she didn't want him wrecking.

She was bent over, tending a patient. One of her auburn tresses dangled by her rosy cheek having escaped the bun at her nape. She was more beautiful to him now than the first day he saw her, and even then, he thought he had never seen a more beautiful woman. A new urgency filled his mind and body just as potent and strong as his need to see her.

Abby straightened from her task of bandaging another cut. It was the third one this morning. She wiped her hands on her apron and lifted her torso trying to ease the ache in her back from bending over. An unknown force drew her attention across the room. Nurse Millie was speaking with a soldier. As she moved away, Abby gasped and her heart wrenched.

Max!

Her beloved was home.

His intense gaze pierced her from across the room, spanning the distance between them to touch her soul. Relief and joy exploded within her in a bursting crescendo erasing all her worries and doubts. They both took steps towards each other before Abby rushed across the room to be caught up in his tight embrace not unlike their first encounter so many years ago. The security of his arms never felt so good.

She held on a second longer than he did. She opened her eyes, dropped down from her toes, and took a slight step back reflexively smoothing the front of her smock. She expectantly looked around him. "Where's Christoff?" Curiosity rapidly turned into panic. "Is he alright? Is he hurt? Is he..."

Max pulled her head into his chest to soothe her distress. "Shh. He is fine. I left him at the house."

Emily wiped away the tear drifting down her check. Her heart was bursting with joy and a broad smile stretched across her face. Her father was home! He was safe. Watching her parents reunite she had some understanding of the depths of their emotions having felt something similar when Henry came to her the morning after the storm. A glance around the ward showed she was not the only one affected by the profound reunion.

"Can you leave?" Max wanted to take his wife home to answer all of her questions.

Abby cast her eyes over the patients assessing their status before landing on Mary and Millie standing together observing her. They both motioned for her to leave. She turned back to Max. Her hand was still clasped in his from their last embrace both reluctant to let go of each other. "I can."

"Good. Emily too?"

"Yes. Of course."

Max warmly looked to his daughter. "Let's go home."

Emily eagerly retrieved their bonnets and followed her parents into the foyer where they donned their head covering. Once down the front steps they each took one of Max's arms and headed home while Abby filled Max in on all that had occurred since the storm first began.

Henry and the boys returned home in time for supper. Thorn and Nate held their exuberance in check when they discovered their father and brother had returned, offering sedate handshakes even as their faces couldn't contain their grins.

Supper was a joyful homecoming celebration. They talked carried long into the evening as they shared their experiences in the time apart.

* * *

Two days later, they celebrated James' fourth birthday with conch fritters and a sugared cake. Mrs. Baxley refused to say how she managed to get her hands on the ingredients for the confection.

Chapter 29

In the days, weeks and even months that followed, they learned of the hurricane's far reaching destruction. On October 5th, a barque encountered the beginnings of the storm off the coast of Venezuela. It rapidly grew as it crossed the warm Caribbean Sea, passing south of Jamaica and sending a swell of sea water to wreak havoc with the island's southern coast. It then crossed the Cayman Islands, completely drowning Grand Cayman under an estimated fifteen feet of water. On the 10th, it struck Cuba with a devastating blow.

News from Havana, some ninety miles south of Key West, was just as calamitous as their own, if not more so. Suffering the same direct hit from the hurricane, much of the western side of Cuba was destroyed. It was reported all but a dozen of the over one hundred ships in Havana harbor were sunk or wrecked. Stories were told of waves so high they reached the lanterns of the Moro Castle lighthouse. Buildings fell, people died, bodies were left floating in the harbor. The residents of Key West understood their pain.

The following day it struck Key West. All but eight buildings were damaged or destroyed. Nearly fifty lives were lost: some buried under houses, drowned, carried out to sea in the surge, struck by debris in the hurricane, or lost at sea. Every vessel anchored in the harbor was lost or harmed. Only one of the fleet of twenty-one wrecking vessels weathered the hurricane unscathed. The lighthouses were gone. The landscape was forever altered. The people were forever emotionally scarred.

After leaving Key West, the cyclone rushed up the western peninsula of Florida turning inland north of Tampa. At Fort Brooke, as with Key West, the rainfall was not significant as compared to other hurricanes, but the winds were substantial, reported at force eight. North of the hurricane, the Florida panhandle was indirectly affected. Ochlocknee Bay reported an unprecedented receding of water leaving a massive number of fish dying on the exposed flats in the bay.

The monstrous gale then crossed the peninsula. Its leading edge reached Jacksonville by Sunday evening while its tail end was still tormenting Key West. By Monday afternoon, Jacksonville's wharves and Bay Street were flooded six feet above the high water mark. Then the winds shifted southeast, headed out to sea, pulling all the wharves with it. In its wake, it left the sawmill destroyed along with several other buildings along the river.

Savannah's oldest residents claimed it to be the worst hurricane since 1824. In Charleston, the hurricane reached its height Monday evening with a wind force of six, accompanied by rain. The winds began to wane for them Tuesday morning. Residents claimed it was the worst storm in a dozen years even though the damage was not as bad as they feared, suffering much the same destruction as Savannah. Further up the South Carolina coast, Georgetown had a tide two feet above normal but no significant damage, while inland, Columbia had torrential rain amounting to four and half inches and heavy winds resulting in crop damage.

The waning hurricane continued to be felt up the eastern coast on Tuesday. Wilmington, North Carolina also reported a two foot surge and minimal damage. Norfolk, Virginia had heavy rain and wind with no major damage. Washington D.C. reported the Potomac River reached its highest level in twenty years. At Baltimore, it flooded the wharves and most of Pratt Street at the harbor. At New Castle, Delaware, the lowlands along the Delaware River flooded higher than they had in seventy years and the wind toppled the steeple of the Episcopal Church.

Southern New Jersey saw many downed trees and buildings. The salt marshes flooded and livestock drowned. Philadelphia, too, felt the tremendous gale with flooded wharves along the Delaware River from storm surge and over an inch of rain in the course of seven hours. An old friend of Key West, William Whitehead, recorded the significant wind and rain of the "disastrous gale" as it hit his home in Newark, New Jersey. The heavy wind driven surge caused the upper New York Bay to wash away a hundred yards of The Battery. Trees were uprooted throughout the city.

From there the storm veered out to sea to its death.

* * *

It was nearing the end of the second week after the storm. Some houses had been repaired while others were in need of materials. Sail cloth still covered many roofs. The debris piled up along the edge of the streets was gone, but there was still much detritus to be burned. They were working on it sections at a time to keep the smoke to a minimum.

The rapid cleanup of the city could be directly attributed to the mayor's requirement that donated rations must be earned by contributed labor. Fortunately, food and water were arriving in abundance this week from Tallahassee, Mobile, and New Orleans thanks to the mayor's requests for aid. The town's urgent needs were being met, and it was duly appreciated by all. The army's help was indispensable in providing much needed shelter for the displaced families and men to aid in the recovery efforts. It was because of their assistance the islanders could now turn their focus towards rebuilding.

* * *

In the early hours of Friday morning, the 24th of October, an urgent knock sounded at the Eatonton's front door. Mrs. Baxley easily woke from her slumber at the disturbance. She donned her slippers and dressing gown and hurried to answer the summons. It only took a glance at Hannah

Watlington's tight features to know what was needed. She held her hand out sideways towards the frightened girl. "Come in child. I'll go wake Mrs. Eatonton."

Hannah could only nod in response.

Mrs. Baxley returned in a few moments. "She'll be down directly. Come. Let me make you some tea." She placed her arm along the thin shoulders and ushered the girl out to the kitchen where she stoked the banked fire and moved the kettle to the burner to heat. "Try not to worry so. Your mother will be fine."

Emily opened her eyes to find her mother leaning over her fully dressed.

"I need you to get dressed and come with me."

"What is it, mother?"

"Mrs. Watlington's time is here. I will need your help."

As Emily sat up her mother left the room in a rush of twirling skirts. The meaning of her words sank into Emily's groggy mind. Her mother wanted her to help deliver a baby. She was both horrified and excited by the prospect. Emily dressed with expedience. She found her mother in the kitchen with Hannah and Mrs. Baxley. She accepted the mug of sweetened tea Mrs. Baxley pressed in her hand. She managed a few sips before her mother finished supplying her medical basket and was ready to leave.

They entered the brightly lit house to find Hannah's two younger sisters in the main room, concern creasing their brows. Captain Watlington was gone wrecking. Mrs. Watlington moaned from her upstairs room. Hannah took the girls in hand leading them out to the kitchen to set water to boil per Abby's direction. Emily followed her mother upstairs where she promptly sent young Sarah from the room to help her sisters. Emily took up Sarah's task of wiping Mrs. Watlington's head with a damp cloth while her mother examined her.

Abby smiled at her patient. "Not long to go now."

Emily was in awe as she cleaned the newborn babe. It was her first time witnessing a birth. Now that she was so close to being married herself, the prospect of giving birth both excited and frightened her. She swaddled the tiny infant and handed her over to Mrs. Watlington. "What are you naming her?"

Mrs. Watlington eagerly accepted her fifth daughter. "Mary Amanda."

Abby finished tucking in the clean sheet around her patient. "That is a pretty name."

As Abby and Emily walked home in the chilly morning air, Emily asked, "Why did you want me to go?"

Abby's mouth thinned in a sad smile. "Since you are set on leaving the island, I thought you should have some sense of what child birth is all about since I would not be with you."

Emily's heart dropped. "How did you know I want to leave?"

"The porch is not as private as you might think."

Being overheard dismayed her, but she realized too, she hadn't given any consideration to the consequences of leaving her family behind, especially her mother.

Abby twined her free arm in Emily's. "I had no idea what to expect when I was carrying you. Mrs. Mallory told me very little, not wanting to cause undo concern, I suppose. I gained a better understanding when she taught me how to be a midwife." Her voice grew wistful. "I always imagined being with you when it was your time."

Emily couldn't imagine going through it without her. It was something to consider in leaving.

* * *

It was late afternoon when Henry approached the courthouse to deliver a message. He climbed the steps and paused before entering to look north up Whitehead Street from whence he came. Despite the progress they had made over the last two weeks, it was still a sad sight. Only the Eatonton house was intact. The others were in various states of disrepair or missing altogether like his family's home, the remains of which were burned away yesterday. As distressing as the buildings were, it was the damage to the trees that hurt most. So many were gone, their void was felt as a visual affront. Those that were left were stripped of green and often the trunks were blackened by wind and salt damage. He feared the loss of trees would be felt long after the rebuilding was complete. Fortunately, the courthouse, jail, and the few homes beyond it had fared better than most.

He entered the cool interior and passed by the open courtroom headed for Judge Marvin's office. It was now also functioning as the temporary headquarters for the custom house. Mr. Mallory and Judge Marvin were sharing the space until the custom house could be rebuilt. Henry approached the open door to find Mr. Mallory deep in conversation with Mr. Duncan Cameron, the Scots builder. It sounded like they were discussing details for the new lighthouse. Mr. Mallory happened to look up as he was turning away.

"Hello there, Deputy Whitmore."

Henry turned back. "Good afternoon, gentlemen."

Mr. Cameron said, "Evening, young Henry."

Henry smiled inwardly. He wondered how old he would have to be before everyone used his surname.

Mr. Mallory said, "Did you need me for something?"

"I wanted to let you know the donations have all been unloaded from the ship and locked away in the jail per the mayor's instructions. I'm headed home for the night unless you need me for anything else."

"I don't believe so. Have a good evening, Deputy Whitmore."

Mr. Cameron gave him a cocky grin. "Evening, young Whitmore."

Henry's lip twitched at the Scot's teasing. Somehow he must have betrayed his feelings in the greeting. He nodded to them. "Gentlemen."

Henry returned home to find Emily waiting for him on the front porch. He said, "You look tired."

Emily laughed demurely. "It was an early morning."

"I know. I missed you at breakfast. How is Mrs. Watlington?"

"She and her new daughter are both well."

"Another girl. I wonder what Captain Watlington will think."

"Probably the same thing he thought with all of them."

"Which is?"

"I wouldn't know. You'll have to ask him." Her eyes narrowed on him. "What would you think?"

"Maybe the next one will be a boy."

"Ha. Easy for a man to say. He doesn't have to do all the work."

Henry bit his lip rather than comment. The subject was highly improper, especially for a front porch conversation. "Is supper ready?"

"I believe so." She drew a breath. "Henry?"

"Yes?'

"Will you speak with him tonight? Poppa has been home for days now."

"I am waiting for the right time."

"When is the right time?"

"I'll know it when it happens."

"Do you think we should wait? Is that why you haven't asked?"

"Wait for what? For everything to get back to normal? That could take a year or more. We may have to wait that long to be married, but I can't wait that long to declare my intentions." He reached out to grasp her hand. "I want to be able to hold your hand whenever I like."

"Then you must ask before he leaves again."

They heard Mrs. Baxley calling the family to the table. Henry lifted her hand to press a lingering kiss on her knuckles. "I promise I will soon."

Fatigue made Emily quiet, but the others around the table made up for it. Henry told of bountiful donations of food and clothing that arrived today. Her father told of Mr. Fontane and Mr. Patterson's plans to bring back dismantled houses from the Bahamas to rebuild on their lots. Mr. Whitmore shared news of the rebuilding efforts around town.

She lifted her napkin to her mouth to try and hide her yawn.

After the meal they adjourned to the parlor with the exception of

Henry and his father. Emily wondered if maybe Henry was seeking his council. A few moments later, a commotion was heard in the foyer.

Theodore appeared in the doorway. "Betsy, you'll want to see this." His tone was intriguing.

Curiosity had them all following Betsy from the room. Two large barrels sat in the open space.

Henry said, "These arrived today. A bit earlier than usual." He smiled at his sisters' squeals of delight as they rushed forward. They were well familiar with the annual early Christmas gift from their northern relatives. They danced around the barrels anxious to see inside. James and Jacob joined them, enjoying the merriment.

Theodore pried the lid off first one and then the other. He found the usual letter for Betsy lying on top. He passed it to her. She read her mother's neat script while the others investigated the contents. The first barrel was half filled with sacks of sugar and flour and topped with linens and clothing.

Betsy said, "They read of the storm in the paper and sent all they could spare in anticipation of our needs."

Abby squeezed Betsy's shoulder. "You have a very thoughtful and generous family."

Betsy turned to her with tears in her eyes. "I do, don't I."

The second barrel contained root vegetables, preserved meat, seeds and nuts, coffee, tea and plenty of canned fruits and vegetables. The clothes and linens were set aside to take to the displaced families in the barracks. Betsy and Mrs. Baxley were deciding how best to stretch the food to not only feed their family but many others when Henry reminded them plenty of provisions had been donated for the town.

They soon returned to the parlor where Theodore sat down with his mail. Betsy retrieved the writing desk to begin a thank you letter to her family. Abby resumed reading her magazine, Max was reading a book, and the children returned to their play.

Henry was working up the courage to address Captain Max when he noticed his father's frown. One of his letters must contain bad news. "What is it, father?"

"It's quite shocking." All eyes turned towards Theodore. "It seems the same storm that blew down our house here took down the ancient oak tree beside our Manhattan home nearly hitting the house. As it was the heavy branches caused some damage to the roof and brickwork that will have to be repaired."

Betsy laid her hand on his arm. "And what of the tenets?"

"They are fine."

"That is a relief, at least."

Max said, "Did he say when it happened?"

Theodore scanned the letter. "Tuesday, the thirteenth. That was just two days after striking here."

"Incredible."

"Yes, indeed."

As the family further discussed the storm and its aftermath, Henry's thoughts turned towards how best to speak with Captain Max. Maybe he should wait. Really, he had no way to support a wife right now. What right did he have to ask for her? But then he heard Captain Max say he was considering offering his ship to take Mr. Fontane and Mr. Patterson to the Bahamas. If he did so, he would be leaving in a day or two.

Emily noticed Henry had turned pensive. He must be anxious. It was after all a very important question. In truth, she was too. She knew her father would accept Henry as her betrothed. She only worried that he might make them wait longer to become engaged. Did her father know how much she wanted this? What if he thought her indifferent? Maybe she needed to speak to him first to assure him of her feelings for Henry. Just as she was considering crossing the room to ask to speak with her father, Henry did so. She bit her bottom lip anxiously watching her sire's reaction.

Something in Henry's purposefully stride across the room caught Max's attention. His chest tightened when he realized Henry was focused on him. His glance cut across the room to find Emily's eyes wide and beseeching. He wasn't ready for this. Henry was almost upon him. He felt Abby grasp his hand and give it a squeeze. He turned to look at her. Her eyes were filled with peace and acceptance telling him without words that she gave her blessing. He lifted his gaze to Henry's. The lad was beyond nervous. He supposed that was a good sign.

Henry glanced at his father for support before turning his attention back to Captain Max. His father's gaze was steady but unreadable. Henry didn't have time to question it. He was committed now. "Captain Max, if you don't mind could we speak in private?" Without a word or gesture, Captain Max rose from the settee and led the way to his study expecting Henry to follow.

Henry crossed the threshold as Captain Max turned to face him.

"Shut the door, please."

Henry swallowed hard. His tone did not sound promising. Was the captain going to turn him down? Maybe he should wait to ask, but then what reason could he give for this meeting.

The silence stretched between them. Henry cleared his throat to speak and nearly lost his nerve again. He took a deep breath to brace his courage. "Sir, with your blessing I would like to formally ask for Emily's hand in marriage."

"And what has changed from our last conversation? It seems to me you have even less now than you did then."

"I would beg to differ, sir. I now have the means to start my sponging business, and I am employed as a deputy sheriff."

"The job is temporary and it is my understanding the sponge beds have been destroyed by the hurricane."

Henry blanched. Captain Max was well informed. "The sponges will grow back sir. They only need time. And we don't intend to marry right away."

"I am afraid it is not enough. Not yet. For now, I cannot give my consent for more than courtship."

Henry's shoulders slumped. Max said nothing more. He led the way from the room back to the parlor where he encountered the expectant faces of his wife and daughter. It tore at his heart to see Emily's hopeful joy fall to deep disappointment. He hated being the cause of her unhappiness. She quickly hid her feelings behind a bland expression and excused herself from the room. Blessedly, Betsy and her daughters were unaware of the situation. Henry followed Emily from the room. Max trailed behind, but he needn't have worried. Emily climbed the stairs to her room, and Henry left the house with only a shared glance between them.

Abby joined him in the doorway laying a gentle hand on his arm. "What reason did you give?"

"He doesn't have the means to support her."

"They could wait to be married."

Max turned to her in surprise. "You think I should allow them to be engaged even though he may never earn enough."

"He is not poor. He inherited his aunt's house in New York, and he has a trust fund from his mother's side."

"I wasn't aware of that."

"No. I don't suppose you would be. Does it change your mind?"

"It gives me something to consider." He forgot the Whitmores had ties up north. "I don't want Emily to move to New York."

Abby gave him a sad smile. "Nor do I, but it is not about what we want. It is what is best for Emily."

Max's gaze sharpened on her. "You don't think she would...."

"Run away with him? It is possible. She is more like me than I would care to admit, and if my father refused to allow me to marry the man I love, I would certainly consider elopement." She watched her husband's face blanch. "As for Henry, he has left before. Although, I do not believe he would do so again, at least not in disgrace. Who is to say, he would not move to New York to expedite a wedding."

"What do I do now?"

She rubbed his arm. "Nothing. I think we should wait and see what Henry does. If he asks again..."

Max's tone was resigned. "I should give him my blessing."

Abby nodded. "I will go speak with Emily."

* * *

It was the first time in two weeks Emily had the room to herself. She was grateful. The tears were falling before she made it to the sanctity of her bedroom and once there she couldn't control her sobs. Her heart felt ripped to pieces by her father's denial. Why would he do such a thing? She lay down on the bed curled around her pillow clutched tightly to her chest. She barely heard the soft knock on her closed door. When it registered, she hurriedly sat up and brushed away her tears hoping to hide her distress.

The door was slightly opened. Her mother peered inside. "May I come in?"

The sympathy on her mother's face brought on a fresh bought of tears. Her mother closed the door and hurried to sit beside her with open arms. Emily welcomed her motherly embrace.

Abby whispered as she rocked her distraught daughter, "Shh, dear. It is not as bad as it seems."

When the worst of her crying was past, her mother handed Emily a handkerchief to dry her face.

Emily hiccupped. "How can it not be?"

Abby brushed a stray lock from Emily's forehead. "Your father did not forbid the marriage only the timing. Henry may still court you."

"He may court me, but he can't marry me. What is the point?"

"One day you will marry when the timing is right."

"And when is that going to be?"

"I cannot answer that, but I have a question for you. What if marrying him now meant moving to New York?"

Emily brightened. "I would embrace it. Indeed, it is what I desire." Her face fell. "But Henry does not. He said he wants nothing to do with a northern winter."

Abby filled in what she left unsaid. "And you have never seen the snow."

"I want to try living somewhere other than this tiny island. I want to see more of the world. I want to visit the places I have read about. At least some of them."

"Dearest, before any of that can be considered, what about Henry? Are you absolutely sure he is the one? Are you sure of your woman's heart and not that it is simply carrying the crush of your childhood?" She held up her hand when Emily started to speak. "Say nothing now. I want you to seriously consider what it means to love and what it means to be a wife. A wife should defer to her husband's wishes. You must learn to do so if you are to be married."

"But you don't defer to father."

"Not always, but I do more often than not and always on the big decisions like where to live."

"But that doesn't seem fair."

"Life is not fair. You know this, Emily. What you may not realize is marriage, too, is not fair. It is never an even give and take. A wife's duty is to care for her husband, raise their children, and maintain a happy home. She is to submit to her husband in doing so. That is not to say she should allow him to run roughshod over her, but it takes a special man to give a strong woman equal say in their marriage. I pray Henry is that man for you."

Abby rose from the bed to retrieve Emily's Bible from her dressing table. She caressed the cover with a smile. It was once hers, brought with her on the passage from England. She gave it to Emily years ago. She opened it to 1 Corinthians 13 and handed it to Emily. "Study on this passage and how it relates to you now as you yearn to be a wife. Reverend Richard read from the King James version last Sunday, but I think you will find help in many ways from this English Standard version." She leaned over and kissed Emily's forehead. She left the room praying she helped her daughter.

Max stepped into the hall from their bedroom upon hearing her leave Emily's room. She walked towards him and followed him into the room.

"How is she?"

Abby was endeared by his loving concern for their daughter. "As expected, heartbroken, but she holds no ill will towards you." Abby stepped into his embrace. "She yearns to leave the island."

"No."

Abby ignored his denial. "I think she believes she wants to live in New York. I daresay one winter will convince her otherwise if the realities of city life do not convince her first. But you know, I can understand her wanting to see more of the world. I suppose we should have taken our children abroad at least once in their lives."

Max leaned back to see into the depths of her gray eyes. "Is that your way of saying you want to take a voyage?"

Abby responded with a soft, breathy laugh. "No. I am content here. Although, now that the subject has come up, it would be nice to visit Elizabeth and Tria."

"*The Abigail Rose* is sailing for England in a few weeks. It would be easy enough to sail on to Southampton after making her delivery in Liverpool." He watched her eyes turn luminesce as the idea took root.

"Surely, you do not want children running about your ship. It is a foolish idea."

"Not foolish at all. Perhaps even needed. There are too many in this house."

"Surely you do not mind the Whitmores staying with us."

"Not at all. I am only saying we all could probably stand a little space."

"What about earlier? You said you were considering taking Mr. Fontane and Mr. Patterson to the Bahamas."

"Didn't you say Jonathon was getting around very well now? He can take them in the *Mystic*. It would be nice to have the undivided attention of my family for a few months."

"Are we really considering a family voyage to England?"

Max chortled. "Woman, I am already well into planning it. On my word, you will be packing your trunks in a couple of weeks."

"And what of Emily? She will not want to leave Henry."

Max kissed the worry lines on her forehead. "We will cross that bridge when we get to it." He wasn't ready to admit it aloud, but he had a feeling he would see his daughter wed and on her way north before they sailed for England.

* * *

Emily laid the Bible aside. She rose from the bed and crossed to the window. Night had fallen over the island. The moon was rising in the clear sky. A cool breeze stirred the mosquito netting hung on the window and the tendrils of her hair. The girls would be coming in soon for bed, but she had a few more moments alone to contemplate all her mother had said and what she had read.

'Love is patient.'

She was going to have to work on that one. Deferring to Henry? She would have to work on that too. He had experiences elsewhere. If he chose to come back and would rather live in Key West than anywhere else, wasn't that saying something about the island? Was she a fool to want to leave it? Could she really leave her family? And her mother brought up a good point earlier. She wanted her mother by her side as she made the journey into motherhood.

Henry promised they could travel. He wanted her to see more of the world. She was coming to realize the hope that they could do so would have to be enough. For Henry and for her family, she would be satisfied with her island home.

And one day, it would once again be an emerald paradise.

* * *

A week had passed since Henry's disastrous meeting with Captain Max. He was uncomfortable being in his company even though Captain Max was treating him as if the conversation never took place. They were at an impasse.

Fortunately, the island was moving forward. Wood and building materials arrived early in the week donated by their northern neighbors. As he patrolled the streets in his duty as deputy he noticed the gradual decrease in sail cloth covered roofs and increase in fresh slates and shingles. Siding was also repaired. Emily told him the number of families in the barracks was steadily decreasing as homes became livable again. Mrs. Eatonton wasn't needed as much at the hospital as sickness and injuries had also steadily declined. It was all good news for the island, though they still had problems. Sadly, a few more families decided to leave for good, but overall the community was steadily recovering and life was getting back to normal.

Normal, except for food staples. Shortages were still common and the mayor's decisions on rationing the donations were a source of contention between the mayor and the citizens. Some thievery was still taking place, so he and the sheriff were taking turns walking a patrol to keep it in check. Henry volunteered for the night shift. He left the house after supper to relieve the sheriff and patrolled until dawn when he was relieved. He didn't mind as it limited his time in Captain Max's company and helped check his wayward desire to spend time alone with Emily. Especially since she and her family would be leaving soon for their trip to England.

"There you are Mr. Whitmore. I have been looking for you for days."

Henry enthusiastically greeted the man walking towards him. "Good evening, Captain Dutton. How have you been?"

"Well. And yourself?"

"I am well. My deputy duties are keeping me busy."

"I see that."

"And you, sir?"

"I have been very busy indeed corresponding with Washington and the Corp of Engineers. I received orders to continue work on the fort. We are to resume building as soon as materials can be supplied. I have mailed off my requisitions. It was quite a lengthy order. Now I am recruiting men to fill the ranks. I was hoping I could count on you to come back to work."

"How soon?"

"It could be a few weeks to a few months. It will depend on how soon my requisitions are filled. Getting enough bricks for the project has always be an issue."

When Henry continued to hesitate Captain Dutton said, "I will double your pay and decrease your labor. You will mainly be overseeing the workers."

Henry would be a fool to turn down his offer. "You can count on me, sir, at least for a year. I still have hopes of being a sponge fisher, but the beds need time to recover."

"Fair enough. We can renegotiate when the time comes."

They robustly shook hands. "Thank you, sir."

"No. Thank you, Mr. Whitmore. I am glad to have you. If you were to decide to reenlist, I could easily get you commissioned as a lieutenant."

"That is very generous, sir, but I don't think so. I have had enough of army life."

"It's not for everyone. Have a good evening."

"You too, Captain Dutton." Henry watched him walk away as a grin spread across his face. He had solid income for the foreseeable future. His savings was steadily growing with his deputy pay and would rapidly increase once work got started on the fort. It was what he needed to change Captain Max's mind. Now all he had to do was find a good time to ask again. It would make him feel better about her leaving if she did so as his betrothed.

Chapter 30

Henry was still feeling euphoric as he strolled through the crisp morning air on his way home after his shift. Captain Max would have to give him his blessing now that he had a solid job in hand. Granted they probably wouldn't be married until the family returned from their holiday, but he could endure it knowing upon their return she would be his to have and to hold until death do they part.

However, he didn't plan to speak with Captain Max first. He needed to talk to Emily. Moving away from the island was no longer an option. He had to know if she would still have him if they remained tied to the island. His heart raced. This was the most important conversation of his life. The chance that she wouldn't accept staying settled heavily upon him.

He entered the house as it was beginning to bustle with activity. He found his father and Captain Max breaking their fast in the dining room. Mrs. Baxley bustled in from the kitchen to set a bowl of steaming porridge at his place at the table. Henry took his seat just as his father hurriedly stood up.

Henry said, "Leaving so soon?"

"Yes. My shipment of ink and paper arrived yesterday. I just need to make one more proof, and I can start printing the paper today."

"Congratulations."

"Thank you son. It feels really good to get back to doing regular work again." He turned and was gone.

Henry glanced at Captain Max. He was reading a correspondence. Henry focused on his breakfast instead. Upstairs, he could hear the rest of the family moving around beginning their day. Soon Emily's brothers were hurrying down the stairs. Captain Max looked up to offer them a warm greeting. Emily and his sisters soon followed. There was a lot of excited chatter this morning as most of them would be returning to school. The school master convinced the army to allow him use of one of the large tents on the far side of the parade grounds for the purpose of a makeshift school. Henry doubted much learning would take place today. It was going to be hard to hold the youngsters to a routine after being separated for so long.

Emily appeared wearing a blue gingham skirt with matching belt and a starched white linen shirtwaist. Sturdy scuffed kid boots peaked from beneath her hem. His heart hitched and then jealousy bit him. She would be spending the day assisting the schoolmaster.

"Good morning, Henry."

"Good morning, Emily."

"I trust your evening was uneventful."

He held her gaze. "You could say that."

"Oh." Her questioning look told him she knew he left something unsaid. She seated herself in her usual place. Casually, she asked, "Would you care to walk me to the school this morning?"

"I would enjoy it." Captain Max's glances between the two of them did not escape Henry's notice, but he said nothing.

They were soon joined by the rest of the household. The ladies talked of all that needed to be done for the trip. The younger siblings chatted excitedly about their return to school.

When the meal was finished, Henry and Emily followed their brothers and sisters out the door. They had to cross the island to the barracks, but in the weeks since the hurricane the path had become well worn. The pair dropped a little further behind while still keeping their siblings in sight. It was the first moment they had been alone since her parents announced the trip to England.

Emily knew Henry had something to tell her, but she couldn't determine if it was good news or bad. The trip to England lay between them. They both were dreading the separation. Could that be what was on his mind? But then again, it seemed like something new had occurred. Her father didn't appear to be wise to it. His behavior this morning was normal. She could barely restrain her curiosity long enough to get out of the house and away from all who might overhear them. She couldn't wait any longer. She turned to him and whispered, "What is it, Henry? Did something happen this morning?"

"Yes." Telling her was more difficult than he expected. "I have some news. Good news, I hope."

Emily's brow furrowed. "If it's good news, why then the reticence?"

He sighed. "I am not sure you will see it as good news." He wished they could stop walking. He wanted to face her when he told her so he wouldn't miss any feelings that might cross her face. He should have waited for another time.

Emily suddenly stopped and put her hands on her hips. "Henry Whitmore, for heaven's sakes would you stop hem-hawing and just come out with it. It can't be anything that bad."

Henry stopped when she did and stood facing her, an arm's length between them. "I think I can get your father to agree to let us marry."

She squealed and launched herself in his arms. "That's wonderful!" She leaned back. "How?"

Henry set her from him. A glance ahead confirmed the other's had heard and took notice. He put her arm in his as he turned to continue walking. "Captain Dutton sought me out this morning. He offered twice my pay to continue working for the Corps of Engineers on the fort. It means I will have enough income to provide for a wife."

Emily stared at the ground. "I see. When would you start?"

"He said a couple of weeks or months, as soon as enough bricks have arrived to resume building the fort's foundation."

She lifted her gaze to his. They both stopped walking and turned to each other. Her smile had a tinge of sadness. "Then it's settled. We will live here."

"You're willing to do that?"

Her smile brightened. "To be with you, of course, I am. My mother, and God, I suppose, helped me understand; the people you love are more important than the place. I will be happy anywhere with you. My home will always be where ever you are."

Henry kissed her. His heart was so full of love it was the only response he could manage to her sweet declaration. It was an abrupt kiss. He broke away, but the bond between them pulled him back to kiss her more fully. He became lost in her.

A noise finally penetrated his awareness. They broke apart to discover seven pairs of eyes watching them in various states of fascination and disapproval. Christoff, Thorn, Nate, Jacob, Brianna, Agatha and Emmaline were fanned out on the path in front of them. Emily's face turned crimson with embarrassment.

Emmaline said, "You can't do that unless you're married."

Emily swallowed visibly. "You're right, Emmaline."

Brianna pulled her sisters away. Thorn, Nate and Jacob followed but Emily's eldest brother lingered.

Christoff held Henry's gaze. Henry gave him a nod of understanding. Christoff turned to continue walking. Henry and Emily fell in step behind him.

The space between them and Christoff didn't increase until they were almost at the parade grounds.

Henry smiled at Emily. His heart was so much lighter than when they left the house. He wanted to do something to please her. They slowed a little more. He whispered, "We can honeymoon in New York if that is what you truly wish." Her answering smile was brilliant enough to rival the stars. "It won't be winter by the time you return from England, but summers aren't too bad, at least not compared to here."

"What if I refuse to go to England?"

"Why would you want to do that? You wanted to travel. I can't give you that trip, and I can't go now. I promised to work at the fort."

Emily smiled. "I would rather marry you now than see England or any other country for that matter."

Henry gave her hand a quick squeeze in loving gratitude before they were forced to separate for the day.

* * *

Henry walked home in a blissful stupor. He couldn't believe Emily was so charitable in giving up her dreams of travel to be his wife. Now all he had to do was convince her father. He entered the house to find Mrs. Baxley dusting trunks in the foyer. Mrs. Eatonton was headed upstairs with a load of freshly laundered clothing.

Mrs. Baxley straightened to greet him with a swipe of her sleeve across her forehead. "Your mother and James are in the parlor."

"Thank you." Instead, Henry went to the study where he found Captain Max sitting at his desk writing in his journal. "Could I speak with you a moment, sir?"

Captain Max looked up, but his pen hovered over the page. "Certainly, give me a moment to finish my thought, and you may have my attention." He went back to his writing, and a few scrawled sentences later, he blotted the ink and put aside his writing. He lifted his gaze to Henry. "I had a feeling you would be coming to see me this morning." He rose from his desk and walked to the door, closing it, and then returned to his seat. "You have news to share."

Henry recognized it was a statement, not a question. For a brief moment, he wondered just how much the captain was privy to or maybe even had a hand in bringing about. "I do. Captain Dutton has engaged my services for the foreseeable future. It seems Congress still deems the fort necessary and worth funding."

"That is good news, for both you and the community."

"Yes, it is." He took a deep breath. "And with it, I have met our stipulation."

"Yes, you have."

Henry was disappointed when he didn't say more. He waited another moment, but still, Captain Max kept his silence. "Will you give your blessing?" The answer was so long in coming, Henry began to fear the worst. He was ready to bolt from the room to avoid the fatal words.

"You have my blessing."

Henry's sigh of relief was audible. "So, we may announce our betrothal before you leave on your trip?"

"Yes. But aren't you forgetting something?"

"What is that sir?"

"Don't you need to ask Emily first?"

Henry swallowed. Of course! Her father didn't know they had already spoken, at least unofficially. "You're right. I plan to as soon as she returns this afternoon."

Max stood and walked around the desk to approach Henry. "Then you should probably get some sleep before then. It sounds like we may be celebrating tonight."

Henry shook the proffered hand of his future father-in-law. This day was so long in coming it felt surreal to him. "Thank you, sir."

Max put his hand on Henry's shoulder and escorted him out of the study. Henry climbed the stairs in a daze headed to his room. He wasn't sure he would be able to sleep. Bewilderment, excitement, and wonder were coursing through his veins. He pulled the shade on the window, undressed and climbed into bed. It took a while, but he finally fell into a light slumber.

* * *

Afternoon shadows stretched across the wall when Henry rose from his slumber and lifted the shade six hours later. The house was bustling with the busy adults but lacked the cacophony of its younger inhabitants. Henry ignored the rumblings of his stomach as he descended the stairs. He was in a hurry to intercept Emily on her return from school. His mind was racing through ideas of where to ask her and what words to say. Nothing seemed right to him. He started thinking of all the private conversations they managed to have since his return. The most meaningful ones were when they were sailing. He took off at a run.

A few moments later he intercepted the group's return. He barely acknowledged the others. He grasped Emily's hand and turned her back the way she came. "Come with me." She smiled and complied with amazing ease.

Christoff moved in front of them, blocking their path.

Henry brushed past him with a grin. "I have your father's permission." He didn't really. Not in fact, but Henry figured he did in spirit. Besides, he doubted Christoff would question his father and it would be too late to stop them even if he did. Henry's pace was hurried, but Emily kept up. "Where are we going?"

"You'll see."

And she did. It became obvious when they veered away from the army encampment. She was more than eager to join Henry for a sail. Minutes later he was helping her into the boat. Emily wished she had a wide brim hat or a parasol. The brim of her straw bonnet was too high on her head to provide much in the way of protection.

Henry simply rowed straight out from shore. Every time his gaze met Emily's she was watching him with a secretive smile hovering on her lips. They both recognized the significance of this trip. He kept rowing until the land was too distant to distinguish details. Only a person with a good telescope would be able to see them. He pulled the oars into the boat.

"Well, Henry Whitmore, is this how it is to be then?"

"I thought it appropriate."

"Appropriate for us maybe but improper in the extreme." She cast a coy look about them. "You have me completely alone and defenseless."

"I wouldn't say defenseless, but it matters not. You have no need to defend yourself from my attentions."

"I should dare hope not." She giggled.

He heard the hint of nervousness in her laughter. It lashed a tingling pain across his chest as the importance of the moment came to bear. This moment was the beginning of their future. There was no turning back now. He moved forward to kneel before her, careful not to rock the boat.

"Emily, my love."

She inhaled and the breath stilled in her chest. This was it. She focused on his cerulean irises edged in ultramarine but soon was lost in the deeper depths of his soul. There she found her love returned in full measure.

Henry struggled to remember what he meant to say next. In Emily's eyes, he saw a future filled with love. He saw happiness and children. He wanted to grasp it with both hands. Blindly, he reached for her hands, unable and unwilling to break eye contact with her. "Will you have me for your husband?"

Too impatient to wait for him to say more, Emily exhaled in a rush and leaned forward to breathily whisper "yes" just before their lips met in the sweetest kiss he had ever given or received from her. She pulled back mere inches to see his face. Tears of joy pooled in her eyes. He raised his hands to her face and met her lips again and again.

Emily reluctantly pulled away from him. They had to stop before they went any further. "We must return. They will wonder where we are, and I am sure my father did not give permission for this."

Henry swallowed hard as he rocked back on his heels. "No, he did not." He licked his lips savoring the feel and taste of her lips.

Emily swooped forward to kiss him again but quickly pulled back. "We won't be allowed alone together again until we're properly wed."

It was Henry's turn to steal a kiss. And then a few more, until they were both breathing hard. Shakily he returned to his seat. "I think it best we get back to shore."

"I agree." As he rowed she lifted a hand to her mouth. Her fingers lightly brushed over her kiss swollen lips. The skin above them was sensitized from the fine blond whiskers of his mustache. She watched the expanse and contract of his arm muscles as he rowed and recalled the feel of them beneath her hands as she pushed away. He had strength of body and spirit. He would be a good protector and a good provider. And if his kisses were anything to go by, a good lover. She felt the blush creep across her skin at the risqué turn of her thoughts. What did she know? All she knew of husbandly love was they would share the same bed. She had no older sister to tell her more and her mother had been reticent to explain.

* * *

A half hour later they paused outside the parlor door. Within, both their families were gathered before the evening meal talking and laughing. Emily was nervous. How were they going to react to the news of their engagement?

Henry slipped his hand in hers and gave it a reassuring squeeze. He didn't let go as they entered the room. Silence descended as all eyes turned to them. Emily unconsciously moved closer to Henry. He said, "We have an announcement to make."

Brianna jumped up from her seat. "You're engaged!" She laughed as their jaws dropped. "I'm sorry it was plain as day on your faces."

Abby and Betsy moved forward, followed by Max and Theodore, to offer their congratulations. The newly engaged couple accepted the hugs and handshakes with aplomb.

Abby took Emily's arm. "Now we must plan the wedding. When will it be? I suppose it must be after our trip."

Emily looked from her mother to her father with pleading eyes. "About the trip..."

Abby patted her daughter's arm. "Of course, Henry can come too. But then we will have to have the ceremony before hand. It wouldn't do for you to travel unmarried, even in our company."

Max gave his wife a reproachful look. "I don't believe that is what Emily meant."

Abby turned a questioning look to her daughter.

Emily said, "Henry can't be gone that long, and I want to see the snow in New York."

Betsy asked, "What does New York have to do with anything?" Her face fell as an explanation occurred to her. "Oh Henry, you haven't taken a position in New York. You've only just returned."

"No Momma. I will be working here, on the fort project. What Emily means is that she wants us to be married in time to have a winter honeymoon in New York. With the trip to England, it would mean being married before her family sets sail." He met Mrs. Eatonton's gaze. "With their approval of course. We could always wait a year."

Emily inhaled sharply. "Surely not."

Abby and Betsy shared a conspiratorial look. Abby turned to Max. "They should be married before we leave. It would be good for the community too. We need the excitement of a wedding."

Betsy chimed in. "It is the continuation of life's events that pull us together, move us forward, and keep us going. It is the hope of tomorrow that will move us past the trials of today. As a community we need new beginnings such as birth and marriage to renew our spirits. So you see, this wedding is important for everyone. As for Henry and Emily, I have full faith in their love and commitment to each other. It has been there from the moment they met."

Abby smiled fondly. "Remember catching them playing at getting married the day you and Theodore wed?"

Betsy and Theodore nodded.

Max groaned. "Vividly."

Emily couldn't recall it.

Abby saw her daughter's frown. "You were about four at the time."

Emily looked to Henry.

"I remember."

Emily said, "Of course you do. You would have been eight."

Max said, "I don't think I can postpone our sailing. There are commitments to meet in Liverpool."

Abby said, "I am not suggesting we should postpone. They can be married before we leave."

Theodore looked concerned. "In less than two weeks?" He turned his gaze to his son. "Are you sure?"

Emily looked to Henry. Together they said to the room, "We are."

Betsy said, "We can manage the ceremony in two weeks. What about posting banns? Do we forego those?"

Theodore said, "I have plenty of material to print a special edition of the paper. We can get in at least one announcement before the actual ceremony."

They all looked to Max waiting for his final approval. "Very well."

Abby said, "This Saturday simply won't do. It's All Hallows Eve."

"Wednesday is usually a good day. But surely we need more than a few days to prepare. What about the following Wednesday? Surely we can manage the wedding and still be ready to sail on Friday."

Henry and Emily anxiously watched the adults. They weren't about to disagree and risk having the wedding set for after the return from England.

"I believe that would be November fourth."

Abby and Betsy looked to their children for approval.

Henry and Emily looked at each other and then turned back to the group at large.

Emily said, "The fourth will be fine." She would be a married woman in nine days' time.

Chapter 31

Emily awoke with a giddy excitement in her breast.

It was her wedding day.

She sat up in bed and stretched her arms to the ceiling. Today was the beginning of her married life.

Brianna stirred in the bed beside her. She looked at Agatha and Emmaline asleep on the floor. Sharing the room with them, they had become like sisters to her. After today, she would forever be tied to them as a sister-in-law. The realization brought additional joy.

She swung her long legs over the side of the bed and rose to begin her morning ablutions.

Nervous butterflies were already taking flight in her midsection.

The days had flown in a furious flurry of preparations. Her mother and Mrs. Whitmore said the town needed something to celebrate. As the days passed, more and more of their neighbors latched on to their celebration, swelling the wedding reception to huge numbers. Their simple gathering would now encompass almost everyone on the island. At least they were all bringing food to share. Her brothers worked hard for days to catch enough conch and lobsters to feed everyone. The islanders would eat better today than they had in weeks.

She answered the soft knock on her door, letting her mother slip into the room. She roused the sleeping sisters, rushing them to get dressed and head downstairs to help prepare for the day, leaving mother and daughter alone.

The green dress from her birthday ball was hanging on the door having been pressed. There was no time or material to make a new dress. The loss of Esperanza's shop was keenly felt in the matter. Esperanza offered the loan of her wedding dress, but alas, Emily was too well endowed to make it fit, so they settled for the best dress she owned.

Lydia soon arrived to work on her hair. The timing was fortunate, as Lydia's family was leaving the island tomorrow. Today was the last day she would act as her ladies maid. It was bittersweet. Emily sat patiently in her chemise and corset as Lydia braided small sections of hair and then worked them into the gathered twist at the back of her head. The effect was alluring and far more elegant than her normal style. Next, her mother and Lydia helped her into her crinolines and then lowered the gown over her head.

Abby spoke softly. "I have something for you."

Emily watched her mother open a blue velvet bag she hadn't seen her bring in. What she pulled out made Emily gasp in delight. It was a jewel encrusted tiara. She handed it to Lydia who worked it into her coiffure. Emily was stunned by the dramatic effect it made in her appearance. Her mother gave Lydia a nod of approval, and she left the room.

Abby moved to stand beside her daughter as they faced the mirror. "You are the fourth woman in our line to wear this on her wedding day. It was a royal gift given to your great, great grandfather who gave it to his bride."

Emily gingerly brushed a finger over the jewels. The connection to her past made her speechless. "You wore this on your wedding day?"

"I did and as it happens I loaned it to Betsy on her day. We have all had happy marriages. So shall you."

Emily grew silent. Her thoughts had moved hours ahead from now. "Mother, may I ask you something?"

"Certainly."

It took her several starts before she could finally say what was on her mind. "What... what will happen tonight? What should I know?"

Abby had to look away. Part of her wanted to tell Emily what to expect, but these subjects were so deeply rooted as being taboo, she couldn't bring herself to utter the words. Funny how she could be so bold in so many other aspects of her life, but it failed her when it came to discussing coitus. Perhaps it was because she never had a mother to tell her. Finally, she said what other mothers told their daughters. "Your husband will teach you the ways of love."

"What if he doesn't know?"

"Men usually do know. They have experience."

"I'm not sure that Henry has experience."

Abby was shocked. "Have you discussed it?"

"No! Of course not. I am only gathering as much from what he has told me of his past."

"If not, then I am sure his father will have explained it to him."

"Mr. Whitmore doesn't seem like a very communicative man when it comes to personal matters."

Abby had to agree with her, but she would say no more. "Emily, enough. I promise you, it will work itself out. You have nothing to fear."

"Fear? Why would there be anything to fear?"

"There is not."

Emily stared at her mother, unsure what to believe.

"Well, there is nothing to fear." Once started she couldn't seem to stop. "It is a natural act. It is meant to be by God's design. But.... There will be a little pain. And blood. Only the first time. Then it will be good. If.... Oh heavens, I have said enough already. Just know it is necessary to have a baby."

"That much I did know." Emily didn't think she had ever seen her mother blush before. She wished now she had never asked. Her mother's cryptic words only served to heighten her nervousness.

"We should get downstairs. We're going to be late."

Her father was there to greet them at the base of the steps. "Emily Rose, you make a beautiful bride."

338

"Thank you."

Theodore, Henry and all their siblings left a half hour ago. They were to meet them at the church.

Betsy hurried in wearing her best navy dress. She stopped when she saw Emily. "Oh my dear..." She became too emotional to finish her sentence.

Mrs. Baxley had no such trouble. "My little sprite is all grown up. Have you got your something old?"

Emily grinned as she touched the tiara. "Yes, I do."

"Something new?"

Nothing came to mind. "I suppose you could consider this gown new. I only wore it once before."

Mrs. Baxley said, "I suppose it will have to do at this late moment."

Abby searched the faces around the room. "Surely we can come up with something new for the child. We can't ruin her day."

Max scoffed. "It will not ruin the day. It is a silly old wives tale and nothing more. The dress will suffice."

Mrs. Baxley said, "How about something borrowed?"

The ladies looked at each other at a loss. Betsy's hand went to her throat. "You may borrow Aunt Agatha's cameo. It seems very appropriate that you do." She reached up to untie the ribbon.

Emily touched the engraved ivory rose while her mother tied the keepsake around her neck. "Thank you, Mrs. Whitmore. I know Henry will appreciate having the reminder of her today."

Mrs. Baxley said, "Something blue?"

Emily lifted her handkerchief with embroidered blue forget-me-nots. "A wedding gift from Brianna."

Max held his hand out to her. "I believe the last line is a six-pence for your shoe." He placed the coin in her upturned palm and closed her fingers upon it. Mrs. Baxley nodded approvingly.

Abby said, "You are as prepared a bride as you can be. We should head to the church. You do not want to keep your bridegroom waiting."

Max stood on the middle porch step handing each lady down, one at a time. Mrs. Baxley was first, followed by Emily. Max let go of Emily's hand and turned to take Abby's. His wife gasped. He barely caught her hand as she hurried down the steps pausing on the last one to peer over the railing.

Filled with wonder, she turned her bright gaze up to Max. "I can hardly believe it."

He and the others followed her gaze to the rose bush. There, miraculously bursting forth from a salt charred stem, was a bright green shoot with a single rosebud just beginning to open.

Max said, "Wait a moment." He turned back into the house. The ladies shared their amazement over the perfect bloom. Max returned a moment later. He approached the bush with a knife in hand. He gave Abby a questioning look and receiving her nod of approval, he cut the stem and trimmed away the thorns. He presented it to his daughter. "A rose for my Emily Rose. I believe it will serve nicely as your something new."

Mrs. Baxley beamed. "Indeed it does."

Emily basked in the approving smiles surrounding her. She lifted the blush colored rosebud to inhale its sweetness. Its silky petal brushed her upper lip. Now she was truly ready to be married.

It was decided with so many wanting to attend, the service should be held in the ruins of the new church. In the days prior, the fallen roof and siding was removed and the stone foundation was swept clean of debris. Pews that could be saved were cleaned and repaired. Stumps and boards made up for the ones that couldn't be. The marble alter was cleaned and buffed to a shine and adorned with candles for the occasion. Unfortunately, in the open air the flames would not stay lit. There were no flowers to be found - not anywhere - so what few nice palm fronds that could be found were cut and placed in a large vase in front of the alter.

Emily floated on her father's arm to meet her groom. Afterwards, she could remember nothing of the walk to the church. The vision of so many people gathered around and inside the stone ruins brought her to the present. She returned the smile of so many friends and neighbors who parted way leaving a path for her and her family to the front opening of the church. Her gaze travelled the isle to where Henry stood so gallantly waiting for her. He looked handsome in a dark suit she gathered he must have borrowed from his father. She knew he felt uncomfortable wearing the snowy cravat tied beneath his chin, but no one would know to look at him. It gave her the feeling of a special connection to her beloved to know something others did not.

He didn't smile when he saw her, but she noticed his deep inhalation. She affected him and knowing so stroked her feminine vanity.

Reverend Richard stepped forward bringing her attention to him. Her father leaned down to whisper as they hovered in the doorway. "Are you ready sweetheart?"

She turned a radiant smile on him that nearly stopped his heart. "I am."

Max could only think, *But I am not.*

Slowly they walked forward to the soft melody Captain Keats played on his guitar.

Henry felt like he could hardly catch his breath, and it had nothing to do with his uncomfortable cravat. Emily practically glowed with radiance. He had never seen anyone look so beautiful.

This morning, while he was getting ready, he spent some time dwelling on the past several months; from the moment he first felt God's calling and how it lead to the horrific tragedy of the hurricane, and now to this moment of pure beauty. He felt close to his Maker today. He felt the fulfillment of his calling, and yet a continual pull to follow the path God was leading him on, which included joining his life with Emily's.

Reverend Richard absently rubbed at the layer of brine clinging to the ruined leather cover of his Bible as he waited for the bride to reach the alter. Beside him, the young groom fidgeted impatiently. His gaze drifted over the sea of faces before him, gathered today in the shadow of the remains of their horrific tragedy to celebrate a joyous occasion. He was proud to have been a part of it, to see all that this community was able to accomplish together, and the strength they showed in bearing each other up through a most difficult time. It was times like this he knew he was where he belonged.

He opened his Bible, found just yesterday under layers of rubbish. He opened the once bright gold-edged pages to the place he sought. His favored verse of love: 1 Corinthians 13:4.

He began the ceremony in the time honored tradition.

"Who gives this bride?"

Captain Max solemnly replied, "Her mother and I do."

The father kissed the bride, handed her off to his soon to be son-in-law, and took his place beside his wife. Reverend Richard read the passage.

Love is patient and kind; love does not envy or boast; it is not arrogant or rude. It does not insist on its own way; it is not irritable or resentful; it does not rejoice at wrongdoing, but rejoices with the truth. Love bears all things, believes all things, hopes all things, endures all things.

Love never ends. As for prophecies, they will pass away; as for tongues, they will cease; as for knowledge, it will pass away. For we know in part and we prophesy in part, but when the perfect comes, the partial will pass away. When I was a child, I spoke like a child, I thought like a child, I reasoned like a child. When I became a man, I gave up childish ways. For now we see in a mirror dimly, but then face to face. Now I know in part; then I shall know fully, even as I have been fully known.

So now faith, hope, and love abide, these three; but the greatest of these is love.

Henry and Emily exchanged their vows feeling the power of God's love surround them from the sky above, the caress of the breeze, and most of all, emanating from the people watching them promise to love and cherish each other all the days of their lives.

It wasn't until he looked up from slipping Aunt Agatha's wedding band on Emily's finger that Henry noticed the cameo at her throat. His eyes had hardly left hers before now except when he was paying attention to the preacher. He wondered what Aunt Agatha would have to say about this day.

Her tart tongue would have something to contribute, but Henry was sure she would approve of Emily.

"You may kiss the bride."

Henry leaned down to Emily's upturned face and placed a gentle kiss upon her lips.

His wife.

Together they turned to face everyone hand in hand. Henry noticed both his mother and Emily's were dabbing their eyes.

Applause broke out as the reverend introduced them. "I present Mr. and Mrs. Henry James Whitmore. What God has joined together, let no man put asunder."

Henry led Emily down the aisle. It was hard to continue forward with so many reaching out to congratulate them. Emily clung to his arm; the rose held tightly in her hand. Its drifting scent teased him, knowing he would later smell it upon her skin.

Under the minimal shade of a designated palm tree, they received their guests, smiling until their cheeks hurt, and murmuring countless thank yous for the well wishes.

The abundant food and drink made for a merry party lasting well into the evening with plenty of dancing, especially for Emily. She took a turn with almost every man. Henry finally took pity on her and whisked her away from the crowd so she could take a moment to rest her feet and eat something.

Emily accepted the bite of cinnamon bread Henry fed her. The dwindling light meant her wedding night was near. The warm look in Henry's eyes sent a batch of butterflies winging forth making it hard for her to swallow. Henry's smoldering gazes excited her but also added to her distress. She wished now her mother had kept silent. What little she had said only made her nervous anticipation worse. All too soon for Emily, the wedding cake was served, and the party guests began to drift away.

Henry noticed Emily's fluttering movements and trouble holding his gaze. She was nervous. He had to admit, he was too. Tonight was a first for both of them, in so many ways. His mouth went dry and his body tight the more he thought of what was to come. He wondered if it would be impolite for them to leave now. Earlier, Captain Max came to him to say they would have the *Mystic* all to themselves. Henry was overwhelmed with gratitude. If they had to spend their wedding night at Emily's house it was for sure their marriage would not be consummated until they reached New York.

Abby watched as Henry and Emily passed out of sight of the torches. Her baby girl was married. She didn't feel old enough or wise enough to have a married daughter. Next thing she knew, she was going to be a grandmother. The thought didn't sting like she expected it to. In fact, it made her smile.

Max came to her side and offered his arm. "I have made arrangements for others to see to the party's end and clean up. Would you like to go home now?"

The musicians began playing a waltz. She gave him a smile and without a word they both recalled the night when Max surprised her with a special dance, having made Betsy secretly give him lessons. Once again, Max and Abby floated in each other's arms until the last note faded. They slowly walked home under the moonlight. Betsy and Theodore trailed behind with all the children.

Mrs. Baxley greeted them at the door having retired from the party earlier. Abby noticed the eerie silence as she entered the house. She turned a questioning look to Max, not really expecting him to have an answer.

"I imagine they are aboard the *Mystic* by now." Max inwardly flinched, still suffering from an odd mixture of protectiveness for his daughter and sympathy for Henry. Hours ago sympathy won out when he offered the refuge to Henry. Now it was protectiveness making him uncomfortable. He wanted nothing more than to retrieve his little girl from the brink of womanhood. He wasn't ready yet.

Betsy followed Theodore into their bedroom. She watched him gently lay a sleeping James on his pallet. He was such a good father to their children. He came to her and wrapped his arms around her waist. She lifted a hand to his temple brushing the hair back from the faded red scar at his temple. She had come so close to losing him again. If not for Henry... She smiled. The little boy who came to visit her shop and brought so much joy back into her life was now a married man. She said a prayer for Henry and Emily to have a happy life together.

Theodore leaned down to kiss her and all thought fled as they celebrated their love.

* * *

Hours later, Emily lay cradled in Henry's loving arms. Her earlier concerns completely forgotten as Henry proved himself knowledgeable, tender, and understanding. The gentle swells of water rocked her father's ship, luring her into contented sleep.

"Em?"

"Hmm?"

"Do you have any regrets?"

She turned her head and kissed him. "No. How could I when this is what I waited for my entire life? Do you have regrets?"

"No, except maybe to wish it had happened sooner."

"I love you, Henry Whitmore."

"I love you, Emily Whitmore."

"Thank you for coming home to me."

Henry smiled broadly. "It was the best decision I ever made."

Chapter 32

Henry turned and reached out his hand to help his wife transition from the gang plank to the fresh lumber of the new dock. Together they faced the shore they left behind three months ago when they sailed to New York.

He and Emily had a wonderful honeymoon. He took her to see Niagara Falls before the first snowfall on the Canadian side, so she could official say she had visited another country. They spent many an evening enjoying their solitude in Aunt Agatha's old house. Emily declared the house to be charming albeit a bit drafty. Once the snow started, they enjoyed sledding, and he taught her the finer arts of building snowman, creating snow angels, and how to make the best snowballs. He forgot how much fun snow could be. The best part was slipping out of their wet clothes and warming up again in front of a roaring fire.

But none of it could compare to the enduring love he felt for the island. He hoped Emily wouldn't be too disappointed to be back in Key West.

As if on cue, Emily gave a deep sigh. "There is no place like home."

Henry turned to find happiness glowing in her upturned face. "I'm glad you agree." He held out his arm. "Shall we, Mrs. Whitmore?"

She curled her hand around his strong bicep. "We shall, Mr. Whitmore."

Henry's family was there to greet them by the time they reached the end of the dock.

Betsy hugged Emily tightly. "Welcome home, daughter."

"Thank you, Mother Whitmore. It's good to be here."

"You look radiant." Betsy's eyes were drawn to her necklace. "I see you are wearing Henry's pearl."

Emily raised a hand to caress the smooth pink teardrop dangling from a fine gold chain. "He surprised me with it the day before we left New York."

Betsy barely heard her words. Her mind had wondered back to a little boy eagerly perched upon a stool in her tiny kitchen, ready to learn all there was to know about harvesting conch meat.

Eagerly Brianna, Agatha, and Emmaline escorted the reunited family to the Eatonton house by taking them the long way around the land-locked tide pond, past the church they were married in a few short months ago that now boasted walls with framed window openings and rafters, to enthusiastically show them the progress being made on the new Whitmore house. At Betsy's insistence, Theodore purchased a lot on higher ground not far from the Keats.

Theodore led Henry inside the newly built grand Victorian house and across the Dade County pine floor to proudly show Henry the mortise and tenon joints that would keep this house standing in the next big storm.

Throughout the town, the butter hue of new lumber made it easy to see all the progress made in the last few months. Most of the damaged homes seemed to be repaired. Only one or two sail cloth covered roofs remained. Several new homes were under way with framing rising above the cleared ground. The ring of hammers filled the air in every direction.

Behind the dry goods store long awaited piles of timber, boards, slates, siding, and windows waited for purchase. Henry noted these changes just as he noticed the newly unfurled fronds atop the surviving palms, the budding leaves filling in on the vines and bushes, and new blades of grass reaching towards the sky. The island was steadily putting forth a new mantle of green.

Before supper, Henry and Theodore headed towards Whitehead Point to see the progress Mr. Cameron and his crew had made in building the new lighthouse.

They walked in silent companionship for a few blocks before Theodore said, "I am glad to have you home again. I missed you."

"I missed you too, Poppa."

Theodore gave him a keen look and grinned. "No you didn't."

Henry laughed. "Well maybe not until now." He did miss the months of not seeing or speaking to his family. He could get on without them, but he really didn't want to.

"Do you like being married?"

Henry grinned "More than I dreamed possible." They walked a few more yards in silence. "I checked on your tenants and the tree repairs as you requested. All is well. The damage really was minimal, and the tree has been completely removed."

"Hmm."

His 'response' made Henry grin again. The broken trees they were passing sobered him again. "Have there been any other changes here?"

"Progress has been slow. It took a while to get materials, and we struggle sometimes to help each other, getting caught up in our own needs. Oh, something odd did happen. You know how the lighthouse and Sand Key completely disappeared?"

"Yes."

"Sand Key resurfaced last month about fifty feet west of its original location."

"Well that's extraordinary. Are they going to replace the lighthouse?"

"They already have. A lightship named *Honey* arrived a few weeks ago from New York of all places. She dropped off a dismantled cottage here for use as the keeper's house and is now anchored on Sand Key." Theodore pointed to a clearing on Henry's right. "And there's the cottage."

Henry saw the prebuilt walls laying in a pile with slates for a roof neatly stacked next to it. Surrounding it was a large recently cleared lot. He looked further down the path. "Seems to be quite a distance still to the beach. Why is it here?"

"The lighthouse is going to be built here. Inland. It is the edge of the ridge closest to the original site."

"But this is hundreds of feet from the water."

"About eight hundred actually. It was deemed that high, solid ground would be a better choice. This spot is fifteen feet above sea level and as you can see with all the trees downed by the hurricane, it will have a clear sight distance."

"Why haven't they started building?"

"Mr. Mallory has submitted his budget, but he is still waiting to receive funds."

Henry sighed. "When I saw Captain Dutton earlier, he said he is waiting for funds too."

They continued on to the coast and circled around the island back to Front Street, passing the empty sight of the old lighthouse, the fort and army camp awaiting work to begin, the repaired Marine Hospital, and on to Front Street and into town where the salvage warehouses and wharfs were fully repaired. They ended up at Mr. Fontaine's grocery to share drinks. They talked of the recent months and marriage. They reminisced of Aunt Agatha and of days gone by. Most importantly, Henry discovered he was truly at peace with their past. The anger still haunting him when he first came back was gone. Now he enjoyed spending time with his father.

* * *

Emily was temporarily unpacking their trunks in her parents' room. She and Henry were to make use of it until her parents returned or the Whitmore's finished their house. Whichever came first. While Henry was exploring the island with his father, Brianna eagerly questioned Emily from her perch on the bed.

"What was New York like?"

Emily turned to face her, contemplating how to answer as she shook the wrinkles from a dress before hanging it in the wardrobe. "Where we first got off the ship, it was crowded with buildings like it is here by the warehouses, except they are all so much bigger, towering into the sky, and there's hundreds and hundreds of them. The air above them was filled with smoke from the chimneys and the streets were filthy. I was ready to turn around and come back home." She retrieved another dress from the trunk. "You know Henry's house is on an island. A very large island. I don't believe I saw the whole of it while I was there. As we got out of the business ward and closer to his home there was more space, and I felt more at ease. The house, Brianna! You would not believe the size of his aunt's house. And as large as hers is, his father's is even bigger. Although, I couldn't explore it as it is occupied with tenants. We only saw the public rooms when we visited to assess the damage from the fallen tree. His aunt's house is as lavish as the Eatonton's only the décor is more ornate, and older. Everything is much older. I would swear a good many of the pieces date back to the Revolution."

"Never mind the house. What did you do? Did Henry take you anywhere special?"

Emily smiled broadly. "He did. We no sooner arrived and he packed us up again. He took me to Canada."

"Canada! You were in another country?"

"I hardly saw enough of it to mention."

"But now you can say you have been to another country."

Emily giggled. She could indeed. "We saw Niagara Falls. Brianna, you wouldn't believe how big it is. Massive amounts of water endlessly falling over the edge like pouring water from a giant's glass that never gets empty. I wasn't even close, yet the spray soaked the front of my cloak as if I had been in a rainstorm. I was so mesmerized, I didn't even notice it until we were on our way back to the hotel."

"You stayed in a hotel too?"

"We did. It was so fancy with carpeting and wallpaper and gilded mirrors. The staff was all dressed in black and white. There was even an elevator and a man in hotel uniform to operate it."

"Ooh. You are so lucky."

"We had dinner in the dining room. The food was French. The people were too, or most of them anyway, but they spoke English, albeit with a heavy accent. It was quite charming."

"What did you have to eat?"

"Braised chicken with wine and mushrooms. It was divine. They called it *poulet au vin blanc*." She laughed. "I assure you it tasted much better than my mangled pronunciation of it."

"Oh, it sounds so romantic."

Emily paused to consider it. "Yes, I suppose it was."

"Did you see snow?"

"I did. Lots of it. It snowed often while we were there. Each time was a little different. The first time the sky became white and heavy. When it started the flakes were huge and falling fast. The ground and trees were soon covered in white, and then it turned into a thick blanket. The world seemed so quiet. Sometimes the snow felt cold and wet, sometimes it was dry. My favorite was when the flakes fell softly, slowly drifting down to the ground." She giggled at a memory. "We caught falling snowflakes on our tongues."

"What did it taste like?"

"Nothing. They are pure clean frozen water droplets with no taste. But you know what?"

Brianna shook her head.

"I think I actually missed the taste of our water. It's different than up there. You have no idea how glad I am to be home."

Emily told her of all the other fun they had playing in the snow. "The only downside was I was forever cold. I just could not get warm. I have to agree with Henry. I do not want to live there. I am very happy here."

Brianna jumped up to hug her. "I am glad. I missed you something terrible."

"I missed you too."

"What else did you do?"

"One night, Henry took me to Niblo's Garden to see a musical. We had such a grand time that night. I never wanted it to end. I never imagined such a production existed. The orchestra had to have been more than twenty people. The music filled the theater. Oh, and the costumes. You wouldn't believe how lavish they were. I wished we could have seen a Shakespeare play too but that was not practical."

Brianna nodded in understanding.

Emily shook out another dress. "We spent a lot of time walking around the city. We saw so many places I've only read about like Bowling Green, Wall Street, and Castle Clinton. We visited museums and listened to street musicians. Of course we had to stop by the *New York Weekly* office where his father used to work. Mr. Jenkins, the owner, insisted on treating us to dinner at Astor House."

"Did you get to meet Mr. John Astor?"

"No. You know what I found interesting about Manhattan?"

It was Brianna's turn to shake her head.

"The similarities. There is a diverse culture in their city as well as ours, and just like here, there's a lot of building taking place. We saw the new Custom House. Would you believe they built it out of marble? That's how it survived last year's fire when so many buildings around it didn't. Of course, Henry had to spend a few minutes every day watching the workers rebuilding Trinity Church. It made him anxious to get back. He really is excited about helping to get the fort started again."

* * *

It didn't take long to fall back into the routine of island life. The months passed quickly. April was upon them when the Whitmore house was finally complete and just in time too. The Eatonton's were expected home soon. Neighbors helped move all the furniture and belongings and set up new beds in the new house. Mrs. Baxley was put in charge of organizing the kitchen. Mrs. Keats provided supper for the hungry workers.

Afterwards, Henry and Emily returned to the now very quiet Eatonton home. For the time being, they would only be sharing it with Mrs. Baxley. The following day they moved their belongings to Emily's room in preparation for the return of her family.

A week later Henry was with Captain Dutton standing upon fresh cut lumber forming the decking between the shore and the fort. They were reviewing the day's progress in repairing the breakwater wall when a familiar ship sailed into the harbor.

Henry turned to the captain. "Would you mind if I took the rest of the day?" He nodded towards the majestic *Abigail Rose*. It seems my wife's family has finally returned from England."

"Not at all. Please, give Captain and Mrs. Eatonton my warmest regards."

"I will, sir. Thank you"

Henry took off at a run to the house. He burst into the parlor expecting to find Emily and Mrs. Baxley. He was brought up short by the additional presence of his mother, Mrs. Keats, Mrs. Watlington and her daughter, and several other ladies taking tea.

Emily stood in alarm. "Is something wrong?"

He strode towards her and reached for her hand. "No. Something is right. Your parents have returned."

She squealed in delight and followed him to the door, momentarily forgetting herself. Just before entering the hall she turned back to the room. "Ladies, please excuse me for leaving you. I hope you understand." Their murmured assurances followed her from the room.

It was all Emily could do not to run through town. The distance to the wharf never seemed so long.

Henry could tell she was restraining herself. "Don't worry. We will probably get there before the ship has docked."

"I can't help it. Before they left for England, I was never away from my family, not even for a night. After nearly five months, I am anxious to see them again."

They arrived at the wharf amidst a gathering of friends and were joined by Henry's family. The *Abigail Rose* soon docked and the gangplank was positioned. Henry led Emily to the front of the crowd and then out on the wharf so she could be first to greet her family. The others politely waited on shore. Emily lifted her gaze to the foredeck and saw her parents waiting at the railing ready to disembark. They eagerly waved to their daughter.

Both mother and daughter were visually impatient for their reunion.

Max helped Abby navigate the narrow gangway. As soon as her feet touched the dock, she hurried towards Emily with open arms. "Oh, my sweet darling. It is so good to be with you again. I missed you so." They held the embrace for some moments as Captain Max, Christoff, Thorn, Nate and Jacob robustly shook hands with Henry. When Abby finally let go, Max stepped forward to embrace Emily as well.

As a family, they walked to the shore to greet the rest of the gathering. It took twenty minutes for Max and Abby to make their way through the throng of grateful well-wishers welcoming them home. Before leaving them, Max held up a hand to gain their attention. "We have brought back a gift for the island. More than a hundred palm and pine trees from the Bahamas fill the cargo hold. We hope everyone will take at least one to plant in your own yard to help fill the void of all the trees we lost in the storm."

Cheers went up in reply.

It took several days for the family to share all they had experienced while apart. The trip to England was sedate in comparison to Henry and Emily's time in New York. They stayed in the family home in Midanbury. Abby spent most of her time visiting with her friends, Elizabeth and Victoria. Max found himself coerced into fox hunts with Lord Avery Kendall and his old nemesis, Lord Jason Malwbry, now the Duke of Rothebury. Having never ridden before, Max begged off the second day because he was too sore to continue riding. If he thought he would get to rest, he underestimated his hosts, for they were quick to arrange a grouse hunt instead. The Eatonton boys were happy roaming the woods and fishing in the river with the sons of Duke Malwbry and Lord Kendall.

It was late the first night of the Eatonton's return to Key West. The family reluctantly rose to adjourn to their bedchambers. Henry cast Emily a questioning look as he helped her to rise from her chair. She gave him a nod of agreement before turning to her parents. She was thankful her brothers had left the room. She wasn't ready to share her news with them just yet.

Abby saw the look in her daughter's eyes. She grew excited but held back her delight for confirmation. "Are you with child?"

A smile bloomed across Emily's face. "Yes."

Abby wondered how she had missed the signs all day. They were quite obvious to her now. She hugged her daughter. "I am so happy for you. You'll be a wonderful mother."

Max held his hand out to Henry. "Congratulations."

Epilogue

It was a brisk October morning as Henry escorted Emily up Eaton Street on their way to Sunday services. Every yard along the street boasted flourishing young trees. Ahead of them the spire of the newly finished Methodist Church stood strong against the azure sky. The toll of the bells rang out in the clear morning air. As they neared, Reverend Richard's could be seen in the yard proudly welcoming his parishioners with his new wife at his side.

Their pastor had every reason to be proud. He not only went forth in the southern states to raise the money needed to buy material for the church, he did so in a few short months. Then, heeding a premonition and against better council, he insured the ship that set forth from Charleston in July carrying those materials. It wrecked and all was lost. Reverend Richard was able to have the mill duplicate the order and with all expediency had the church built from the stone foundation. This time including chimed bells in the belfry mostly donated by citizens. Now he could enjoy the fruits of his labor having most of the town attending his Methodist church while the newly appointed Episcopal minister, Reverend Adams, still remained abroad fundraising.

Henry wondered if his and Emily's families would return to the Episcopal Church once it was rebuilt or remain with the Methodist, having given Reverend Richard so much support.

If only such quick work could be done with the lighthouse. The temporary light was still in use. Mr. Mallory was awaiting the arrival of funds to start. He had Mr. Cameron's assurances it would be built with all expediency as soon as materials could be purchased.

At least their new home would be finished soon. It was on a lot close to Jackson Square situated between their two families. It was a simple two bedroom Bahamian cottage, but he was sure it would prove safe and comfortable for his soon to be growing family.

Emily squeezed his arm to gain his attention. "Do you know what tomorrow is?"

Henry's eyes widened as the day's date resonated with significance. "It will be a year tomorrow."

"We have accomplished so much this year in rebuilding. Look how the fresh whitewash of the church gleams in the sunlight. But, there is still so much to do to get back to where we were before the hurricane."

"No. We will end up better than where we were before; stronger and even more resilient because we have an enduring love for this island and this town."

Emily looked deep into the eyes that held hers. "No. It is because we have an enduring love for each other."

January 15, 1848

As dusk approached, Henry and Emily joined the islanders gathered in front of the new lighthouse. Emily carried her three and half month old daughter, Ella Rose, in a sling Betsy made for her. They were stopped often by curious friends wanting to see the baby. Her sweet cherub face was getting more attention than Mayor Maloney who was giving the expected speech publicly thanking Mr. Cameron for his hard work. While the mayor was speaking, Barbara Mabrity climbed the steps of the forty-six foot tower to light the thirteen Argand lamps for the first time.

Delays may have prolonged the funding of the new lighthouse, but Mr. Cameron was true to his word, completing the project faster than anyone believed possible. He built the lighthouse in just forty-eight days including the keeper's cottage. The solid four foot wide brick walls of the foundation were firmly set into the island's limestone rather than built atop. It was also located on a rise of high ground far from shore. Even if the sea came inland again, this structure would stand the test of time.

Emily leaned towards Henry. "It's a wonder Mrs. Mabrity still wants to be the light keeper after losing so much of her family, especially to do so without Miguel."

Henry swallowed hard as Miguel's face appeared in his mind. He missed his friend. He could well imagine how much harder it must be for Mrs. Mabrity. "She has always had an affinity for the light. I'm sure it helps her to feel useful, but she told me she does it to honor her husband's memory."

He placed his hand over Emily's in the crock of his arm. He felt the wedding band beneath her glove. It brought forth a wave of protectiveness. He would do anything to make her happy and keep her safe. Even endure winters in New York. He was very thankful she came to agree with him, there was no place they would rather live than their island home.

A cheer went up as one by one the reflected lantern light beamed forth circling the island. Mrs. Mabrity appeared on the gallery silhouetted in the bright light.

Emily looked deeply into her husband's eyes. "I pray our love is as true as hers."

Henry leaned down to kiss her cheek. "I promise you, mine is."

The End

Moisture gathers above dry grass catching a Sahara wind
Puffy cumulus rising high, ominous thunderheads to become
Shifting winds, a westward spin
Ocean's devilish child is born

Become a **Key Friend**

You can sign up to receive email updates on upcoming books, contests and promotions.

Visit www.susanblackmonauthor.com for more details

Check out the 'Behind the Scenes' page for more details, photos, history, resource lists, character lists of who is real and who's not, and many other behind the scenes extras.

See my Pinterest boards for images of people, places, and things that have inspired the writing of each book.
www.pinterest.com/susanblackmonauthor

I hope you enjoyed reading *Enduring Love*

Please consider posting an honest review on

Amazon and/or Goodreads

Your recommendation is the highest compliment.

Read on to catch a sneak peek of

Once Upon an Island Christmas

The next installment of the Key West series

Author's Notes

The hurricane was real.

The Great Havana Hurricane as it came to be called was real and if not in fact a category five in today's classifications, it would have been darn close to one as it moved from Havana to Key West. Any barometric readings taken at Key West were lost to history. There were three reported low readings from Havana. The lowest pressure reading was recorded as 27.06 inches but was later disputed by a renowned hurricane historian. Even so, the officially accepted lowest reading of 27.70 inches (938 millibars) recorded aboard the Steamship Thames in Havana Harbor held the record as the lowest recorded reading for 78 years, until the 1924 Cuba hurricane.

The details portrayed of the devastation and losses were taken from firsthand accounts of the hurricane. However, the post hurricane cleanup and the actions of the mayor and others are products of my imagination. The only detail given of post storm activity is a quote from Colonel Walter Maloney: "They did not stop to shed tears over their misfortunes. The sun rose the morning after the storm to behold active limbs and stout hearts clearing the ground of the debris, and the waning moon of the next night shone upon the bright hammer of the mechanic as he drove firmly home the nails in the reconstruction of their homes and business houses."

Where were you, Barbara Mabrity?

If you have read my other books you are aware my main characters are fictional, but they interact with those who lived in that time. I also like to weave my stories around the facts, but sometimes the facts are hard to find. Barbara Mabrity has fascinated me from the start. She is one of those women who endures, and the 1846 Havana Hurricane was one of the biggest trials in life. A genealogy site showed she lost three of her six children plus a daughter and son-in-law and one or two grandchildren in the fall of the lighthouse. The problem is I could find no mention of her whereabouts. If she did survive the fall of the lighthouse, I would think it to have been miraculous enough to be glorified in history.

For the sake of a dramatic story and my romanticism of this remarkable lady, I first thought to write a story of survival choosing to believe she was in the midst of the disaster overseeing her duties as light keeper when they mattered most - in the midst of the worst tropical cyclone the settlement has ever seen. But with my strong desire through this series to relay the truth as accurately as I can with limited and sometimes conflicting knowledge, I ended up ditching this idea when I realized three firsthand accounts specifically state no one survived.

So where was Barbara during the storm?

I find it hard to believe a lady so dedicated to her profession for twenty years would abandon her post without due cause especially when three of her four children living on the island had sought shelter there. What could have pulled her away? Perhaps one of her elder daughters needed her more, and so she left the lighthouse in her son, Miguel's, care. Maybe she was with one of them due to her health. Being sick or visiting family elsewhere was common enough to not have been noteworthy in island history. Since Barbara is never mentioned in the firsthand accounts, it seemed to make sense to me that she was not on the island during the hurricane. Two daughters lived elsewhere and in looking at their genealogy I noticed the one year old twin grandchildren giving plausible reason for Barbara to be in Tampa with her daughter, Nicholosa. So, while the Mabrity family and their resulting fate is real, everything I have written about them is purely fictional created from my own imagination of what might have happened.

Another literary license was taken in creating a love interest between Louisa Geiger and Miguel Mabrity. Purely, my imagination, but who knows? Maybe there was one. I thought about creating another character in place of Louisa for this purpose, but when it came down to it, I didn't have the heart to cut Louisa out.

And I ended up taking literary license with the Marine Hospital. I learned from the Key West library historian, Tom Hambright, after writing the first draft, that there was a letter written by a soldier who told of the hospital being evacuated before the storm. Unable to move due to his injuries, he was left behind. He didn't say where the other patients evacuated to, but he went on to describe his solitary escape when the building threatened to collapse. I haven't been able to get my hands on the letter. If I could, I may have changed Abby's story line to match history. Not having it, after much debate, I decided to leave my story as is since it is about Abby and Emily's fictional story and not the soldier's real one.

Things they didn't know.

The average 19th century person wasn't aware of germs or disease causing bacteria and they didn't have the means to disinfect as we do today. Bleach was discovered by this point in time, but its usefulness was only just being realized overseas. Sunlight and lime were their main defense against mold, mildew, and disease. As pioneers and as islanders with limited means when it came to rebuilding they must reuse what we would trash. Supplies were limited, had to be brought in by ship, and often were costly.

And now, turn the page for a sneak peek at

ONCE UPON AN ISLAND CHRISTMAS

Once Upon an Island Christmas

Tuesday, November 21st, 1859

      Patrick Johnson impatiently watched from the starboard rail as the ship sailed past a partially built fort into the busy harbor of Key West. He was anxious to get ashore. More to the point, he was anxious to get off the rocking pile of lumber he had been confined to for more than a week other than a brief stop in Charleston. He may be fine in a rowboat on a quiet mountain lake, but he knew now without a doubt he was not, nor would he ever be, a seaman. He needed firm ground, and they couldn't reach it soon enough.

      Finally, the lines were cast ashore and tied off. As soon as the gangway was in place, Patrick hurriedly made his way off the ship and down the wooden planks to thankfully stand, once again, on solid ground. The last week had been the longest of his life sailing from Portsmouth, Virginia to Key West, Florida. Despite good weather, his stomach rolled the entire journey. He hoped his apprenticeship with his uncle worked out. He didn't think he could face a return voyage anytime soon.

      Curiously he still felt the swaying deck under his feet. He looked down to be sure he was indeed standing upon solid ground. He frowned. How long was this sensation going to last?

      He took a deep breath of balmy salt air to steady his nerves while he took in the large unpainted wooden warehouses before him. At the next dock over, a large amount of barrels and boxes were hauled on carts from the docked ship to the cavernous interior of O'Hara's warehouse. The other passengers from his ship were now passing him by headed in purposeful directions.

      Patrick pulled his uncle's letter from his pocket and read his instructions once again.

> Make your way from the wharf past the warehouses to Front Street. Turn left and then turn right just past the burned out lots onto Simonton Street. Follow it until you come to the shop on your right.

      Easy enough, he thought. He folded the letter and slid it back into his jacket pocket. He followed another passenger down an alley between the buildings to a wide, dirt road worn smooth by decades of use. He stopped to take in his new surroundings. Across from him was the burned lots his uncle mentioned in his letter. Uncle Preston didn't say when it happened. It was not recent as the lots were for the most part cleaned up and some rebuilding was under way, nor was it long ago judging by the lack of vegetation and charred bits that remained.

Simonton Street was not far off to his left. He could see it from where he stood. He was instructed to go straight to his uncle, but Patrick hesitated. He hardly knew Uncle Preston, but he knew enough about his father's brother to know once he set foot in his forge, he would be put to work and have little time to himself. Before him was a new world to explore. He wanted a taste of it before he was put to the grindstone, or in his case, the anvil.

To his right the road followed the coastline and led in the direction of the lighthouse and half-built fort he saw from the ship. His uncle and work could wait a little while. Curiosity irresistibly lured him. Without another thought he shifted his carpetbag to his other hand and set off at a jaunty pace. Two ladies approached. Side by side, their hoop skirts were so wide they took up all the space on the wide boardwalk. Patrick stepped into the street and lifted his cap as he passed. They were snuggly wrapped in their shawls. It made him smile. He was ready to cast off his coat for it felt quite warm to him. It was the beginning of winter when he left home with a dusting of snow on the ground, bare trees, and a frigid wind whipping across the mountain ridge upon which sat his family home.

This place could not be more different.

So flat! And green. And warm. And crowded.

There were more people on this street than he saw in church on Sundays back home. The closest town of Covington consisted of only a few buildings and most of them were thanks to the railroad depot and not the population which was miniscule. Here there must be a thousand people and they were quite diverse. Already he had heard Spanish, Irish, Scottish, and many other accents he couldn't identify from both the works at the wharves and the men and women he passed on the street. The deeper into the city he went, the more he was convinced it was a vibrant cultured city despite the unpainted clapboard buildings.

On his journey to the coast, he passed through Richmond and Portsmouth both of which were larger cities than Key West, but to his disappointment, he didn't get a chance to see either other than a few glimpses through the passing train window and from the rail of the ship leaving the harbor. He was determined before going to his uncle's to see something more of this town than what he gleaned as the ship sailed into the harbor.

On his left there were a few new buildings to replace those burned down and several under construction. The ring of hammers and voices of the workers were carried far on the breeze. To his right, he passed a grocer, a boarding house, a custom house, ship chandlers, warehouses, and a cigar shop. He deeply inhaled the pungent aroma. It brought comforting reminders of winter evenings spent with his family by the fire while his father smoked his pipe and told stories. It was the first hint of home-sickness he felt but it was quickly banished as he ogled all the goods for sale through the window of the mercantile. He would have to make a point to return one day to browse inside.

Across the way was the Gem as denoted by the painted sign above the open door. Ruckus laughter spilled from within. Curiosity lured him to the entrance. The rows of glass bottles filled with various shades of clear and amber liquids behind a long bar gave clue to the nature of the establishment. His father would tan his hide to know he was considering entering the premise of a grog shop. The uncouth and rowdy nature of the patrons and the early hour of the day discouraged him from crossing the threshold.

Patrick forced himself to move on coming to another cross street. The street sign read Duval. This one was bustling with activity drawing him to follow it. He was awed again by what he found. Some of the architect was simplistic and practical, but many had elaborate artistic trimmings. Each building housed something different. A curio shop, a milliners, a cobbler – he hardly paid attention to where he was walking for reading the signs and peering in the windows. Across the street was a photographers with an advertisement board next to the door displaying various samples of photographs. He was tempted to take a closer look until the rich aroma of coffee drew him forward to the coffee shop. He had a few coins left from his journey. Perhaps he could indulge just once and pretend he was a man of leisure like the men across the street lounging in front of the huge three story hotel. They were well dressed men with fancy top hats and homburgs, neatly trimmed beards and sideburns, nice suits, and elaborate cravats. It made him all too aware of his simple farm clothes and worn out visor cap. He resumed walking as he continued to watch the men conversing, wondering how he could change his fate to one day join their ranks.

Umph!

Patrick's head whipped forward to find he had bumped into a young lady. "Pardon me, miss." He reached out for her arm to steady her, unprepared for the affect just touching her would have upon him. It was as instantaneous as lightening and no less surprising. She lifted her head to reveal the beautiful face that from his height was until then hidden beneath the brim of her bonnet.

Her gaze dropped to the hand on her arm. "You can release me now. I am quite recovered."

It was not said unkindly, but Patrick heard the betrayed impatience in her voice. He removed his hand. She moved on past him. He turned to watch her hurried progression down the street, while he waited for his heart to resume its normal rhythm. Her skirts swished with the rapidity of her gait. She may not have noticed him, but he certainly noticed her. He couldn't help but notice her. The moment she lifted her face to his, he was taken. He was drawn to her as he was to no other, and it stunned him. Her eyes didn't quite meet his, but if they had, he was sure she would have felt it too.

They were destined for each other.

And he didn't even know her name.

Compelled by need, he followed her. As he tried to close the distance between them, he considered how he, a stranger, could ask for her name. It was against all propriety. His pace faltered. What if she belonged to another? He cast the idea aside sure he would not feel this way if she was already taken. He caught up with her just as she entered a dressmaker's shop. He couldn't follow her inside. That would be the height of rudeness, and she could be in there for hours. He didn't have that kind of time to wait. His uncle was expecting him. There was no choice for it. He would have to wait for another opportunity. Surely their paths would cross again. It was an island, after all, and a small one at that.

She had led him back to Front Street. He considered continuing his exploration, but his enthusiasm to do so was gone. He turned in the direction from whence he came and soon reached his uncle's blacksmith shop. His uncle's workshop was a lean-to built on the side of a two story building and open on three sides. A brick fireplace took up most of the space on the far side. It was different than one found in a house. There was a lower hearth filled with ashes and above it an open work area where his uncle had a coal fire burning hot beneath a vent to the chimney.

His Uncle Preston had his back to the flames, swinging a hammer against heated metal lain across a large anvil strapped to a heavy tree stump. All around the work space were many tools of the trade and the various orders he was working on. His uncle turned back to the fire using tongs to hold the piece of metal in the flames. Patrick waited until he turned back to the anvil and was facing him to approach. He stepped from the bright sunlight to the shade of the roof, but the expected coolness was not offered, mitigated as it was by the intense fire.

Uncle Preston gave him an assessing look and said between hammer blows, "Your ship arrived an hour ago."

He didn't say it, but Patrick heard the unspoken question. *Where have you been?* Patrick didn't feel inclined to answer. "Hello Uncle Preston. Pa sends his regards."

The rhythmic pounding of the hammer continued. "Just call me Uncle. Never did much care for my moniker. Always sounded too pretentious to me. Folks around here call me Smithy."

Patrick had no idea what the hunk of metal was supposed to become, but his uncle pounded on it with apparent precision shaping the red hot metal as he saw fit. Patrick wiped away the sweat on his brow and felt it begin to soak the back of his shirt. His uncle turned the piece of metal and hit it some more before returning it to the fire. He spoke over his shoulder. "Set your bag down and come give me a hand with the bellows."

He did as he was bid setting his bag on a bench on the left side. He discarded his coat laying it over the bag. A door leading into the building stood open. Patrick glanced inside to see all kinds of unshaped wood and metal stores and a display of finished pieces. In the corner was a simple desk where his uncle transacted business. Patrick rolled up his sleeves to his elbows as he returned to the fire. He picked up the bellows and gave them a squeeze over the fire garnering his uncle's immediate ire.

"Don't you know nothing? Won't do no good blowin' air that way."

Uncle Preston took the bellows from him and returned them to the place where they were laying but what Patrick now noticed is the end was inserted in a hole in the bricks. He gave the bellows a pump and then stepped back for Patrick to take over. The fire flared as he squeezed once than again.

"That'll do for the moment but don't go nowhere," said Uncle Preston as he turned the metal.

Patrick's gaze wandered over the plethora of tools. There was a waist high wooden rack of varying tongs, another one of hammers, and yet another full of tools he had never seen before. A nearby table held what looked like chisels along with more shapes he couldn't identify.

"Hand me the splitter."

When Patrick gave him a blank look, his uncle impatiently pointed to the tool he wanted. He hammered it against the hot metal to make a hole in the piece he was working. He then moved the metal to the brick edge near the fire and turned back to Patrick, taking off his gloves. "You hungry?"

"Yes, sir."

Preston grabbed the dipper from a bucket of water and drank deeply. He then gave a nod to the stairs behind the lean-to Patrick had yet to notice. Taking up his belongings from the bench, Patrick followed his uncle up the stairs to his living quarters.

Inside his uncle pointed to the front corner of the room. "You'll sleep on the cot. We eat twice a day. I expect you to help cook and clean besides learning to forge. I don't allow drink or cards while living under my roof. Got any problems with that?"

"No, sir." Patrick dropped his bag and coat on the cot and then helped his uncle serve the simple meal of salt meat, bread, cheese, and what he learned were sapodillas. He thought it had a slight similarity to a pear he once tried. Spying a whole basket full of them, it was probably a good thing he liked it.

After cleaning up their meal, they returned to the forge.

His uncle stopped in the center of the room. "Might as well see what you got for brawn and brains today."

Before Patrick could wonder what he meant, his uncle began rapidly showing and naming all the tools. Patrick tried to remember as many as he could, but he got lost with the hammers beyond which was the ball-peen and the cross-peen. The different pliers were a hopeless jumble in his mind and then they moved on to the drifts, slitters, punches, chisels and more. He thought this apprenticeship would be easy. He was having misgivings.

Uncle Preston turned to his nephew and took no pity on his confusion. "At the end of each day you are expected to bank the fire, sweep the floor..."

Patrick mumbled under his breath, "You mean the dirt."

"Don't sass me boy."

Patrick cringed. His uncle had keen hearing. "Yes, sir."

"You will empty the ash from the hearth into the bin by the door and leave it outside for Sandy Cornish. He comes by at odd times to pick it up for his crops in exchange for fruit. You are also to make sure all the tools are put away. We work six days a week. Sunday's we go to St. Paul's Episcopal Church. You have free time after dark and after church. We'll discuss wages at week's end." He turned to face Patrick. "Understood?"

"Yes, sir."

"Now let's test your brawn, shall we?" His uncle stoked the coal fire and then handed him the tongs with a billet of steel and proceeded to direct him in heating it to the proper color and taking it to the anvil to wield the hammer in shaping it. Patrick soon learned the advantage of the open structure allowing the breeze to offer some cooling relief to the hot and strenuous work.

* * *

And so the rest of the week continued just as Patrick expected. He was put straight to work upon arrival with no time for exploring. His uncle was a hard taskmaster but fair. He was gruff, not given to any soft emotion or sentimentality, but he was also hard working and honest. Patrick easily gave him his respect if not his affection. Each day his uncle gave him more of the heavy hammering to do while he did the lighter more detailed work. Each night Patrick fell into an exhausted sleep.

Every moment in between, he thought of *her*, his destiny with no name. How was he ever going to find her again?

ABOUT THE AUTHOR

Susan Blackmon has enjoyed reading historical novels all her life. With a talent for writing it was only natural for her to try her hand at creating one of her own. All that was missing was inspiration. An unexpected cruise ship detour to Key West and a few history tours later, Max and Abby's story began.

When Susan isn't writing, she enjoys being with her family, hiking waterfalls, reading, scrapbooking, and escaping to the coast every chance she gets.

Visit www.susanblackmonauthor.com to learn more about her books or to find your favorite way to connect via social media